BROTHERS
AND
SINNERS

Books by Rodman Philbrick

Slow Dancer
Brothers and Sinners

J.D. Hawkins Mystery Series
Shadow Kills
Ice for the Eskimo
Paint it Black
Walk On the Water

T.D. Stash Mystery Series
The Neon Flamingo
The Crystal Blue Persuasion
Tough Enough

BROTHERS
AND
SINNERS

Rodman Philbrick

SPEAKING VOLUMES, LLC

NAPLES, FLORIDA

2012

BROTHERS AND SINNERS

ISBN 978-1-61232-835-5

To the remarkable generation
who came of age in WWII, for their
courage and generosity—and,
as always, for Lynn.

ACKNOWLEDGMENTS

The author wishes to thank the following: the gracious staff of the Boston Public Library; Alex Neilson for sharing his recollections of the polio epidemics; and all those Rye Beach raconteurs who never noticed that one of the kids was listening—and taking notes.

Just felt the world go by!
Just girt me for the onset of Eternity
When breath blew back,
And on the other side
I heard recede the disappointed tide!

—Emily Dickinson, poet

When a man comes back from the dead,
it can be a great disappointment.

—Sugar McKane, ward boss

Prologue

Float Job

The boy knew by the weight of the rope that something was wrong. Had known from dawn break, really, when the *Irene* was found adrift in the harbor, her fuel tank run dry. His brother Roy, older by six years, would never willingly abandon the boat, or neglect the string of lobster pots that was their livelihood.

Roy nowhere to be found, the boat adrift, the pots untended—there was only one explanation, and yet still the boy hoped that his big brother might stumble home reeking of drink and high-tone perfume, and explain his absence with a telling grin.

The boy gripped the rope with both hands and yanked hard.

Something came free down there, in the muck of Boston Harbor. The boy put his back into it, pulling hand over hand as he fought against the tidal current. Slimed and soaking and icy cold, the rope cut into his ungloved hands. Up with the rope came the harbor stink, the pong of brine, and the pungent exhaust of the idling boat engine.

Not a cloud in the sky and the sun high overhead on this April day, making the water a luminous, translucent green. He could see the tight line to the pot rope vibrate with tension, and the shape of something large rising, and still he kept pulling.

One hand over the other, his teeth set hard as he worked. Heave and pull and keep a firm grim on the line or the tide would have it.

The boy thought he was strong and tough and hard to the world, but when the thing finally came free of the clinging water and bumped softly against the side of the boat, a wild cry broke from his throat.

"No!" he cried. "Don't let it be him!"

Tangled in the rope was the body of a man, or what had been a man before the crabs got to work. There were so many. Small green crabs the size of two-bit coins, hundreds of wet-slick crabs scuttling from the ragged cuffs of the clothing, from the open mouth of his brother Roy.

All the boy could think of, as he made his brother's body fast to the cleats, was that the crabs had eaten his eyes and made him blind.

The detective paused to light a fresh cigarette, squinting through the smoke as the Harbor Patrol cops covered the body with a tarpaulin. The East Boston fishing wharf was an ancient thing, and reeked of decay—as yet the deceased was not contributing to the stench, but it was a warm day and the corruption of the flesh began at the moment of death.

"Radio the medical examiner's office," the detective said to one of the patrolmen. "Tell them it's a float job."

When the cigarette had been inhaled down to the stub, the detective flicked it away into the oily water and made his way gingerly down a creaky ladder to where the lobster boat *Irene* was tied alongside the pilings.

The boy was sitting on the stern, hands folded tightly, as if in prayer. He seemed to be staring with unfocused eyes at the tangle of ropes on the floor of the cockpit. The detective was familiar with that reaction, the numbness that often follows the discovery of death.

"Detective Moakley," he said, blocking the boy's view of the ropes. "I'm with the homicide unit. It's our duty to investigate all violent deaths, accidental or otherwise."

The boy looked up. "Weren't no accident," he said.

"You recovered the deceased?"

The boy nodded.

"I understand he's your brother, is that correct?"

The boy nodded again—he was back to looking at his hands. The detective moved closer, touched the boy on the shoulder. "We've got to do this, son," he said. "Help me out. Tell me your brother's name, his address."

"Royal Drake. We live with my mother, over to Monmouth Street."

The detective wrote down the information. "Now tell me what happened," he said.

The boy took a deep, shuddering breath, and then looked him in the eye. "Ma got a call early this morning. It was the Coast Guard, saying they'd found the *Irene* adrift and nobody aboard. Fuel tank was empty, it appears she run out of gas. Roy wasn't nowhere to be found."

"Go on," said the detective, taking notes.

"Ma's out looking for Roy, see, she believes he's still coming home, and it was up to me to tend the traps. Which is what I did. That's how I come to find him, all knotted up in that rope."

The detective turned, glanced at the rope and the buoy attached to it.

"Weren't no accident," the boy said. "Roy was always real careful, he'd never let himself get yanked over by the weight of a trap. No, sir, he sure wouldn't."

The detective did not react. The sea was dangerous. It was not such a rare thing for a fisherman working alone to be drowned, but he did not want to argue with the boy. What he wanted was enough facts to make his report coherent.

"What do you think happened?" he asked.

The boy looked at him with unblinking eyes. It was not a friendly look. "Sugar McKane wanted him dead," he said. "That's what happened."

The detective stared at the boy, shaking his head. "You know what you're saying, kid?"

"Sure I do," the boy said. "I know who you are, too."

The detective waited.

"You cops," the boys said. "You're all a bunch of crooked Irish bastids who work for him."

The detective closed his notebook, tucked it away in his pocket. The official interview was over, that much was clear. "You better go find your mother," he said, "tell her the bad news."

The boy stood up. The anger came off him like a stink. "Are you gonna arrest him? Are you gonna send Sugar to the chair like he deserves?"

"That's crazy talk, kid."

The detective heaved himself out of the boat and started up the ladder.

''That proves it!'' the boy shouted at his back. ''You're all working for Sugar McKane. That means he'll get away with murder!''

Up in the sunlight the detective lighted another cigarette and waited for the medical examiner. Float jobs were the worst, he decided. They made people crazy.

PART ONE

Boston, 1949

One

The Pleasures of Deceit

The little man who ran the Parker House elevator was giving him the squint.

"Don't tell me," the little man said, holding up a white-gloved forefinger. "Something in blue. No, wait, a suit."

Jack Fitzroy adjusted the brim of his new hat, a straw boater, and told himself there was nothing to worry about here, not from the help.

"Some kinda cop," the elevator man said, sizing him up. "Used to be in here all the time, busting up that card game in suite five-five-two. You ain't a cop now, though."

"How can you tell?" Jack said.

The little man shrugged—just a wild guess, the shrug said—but his eyes drifted to Jack's left foot.

"I work for a law firm now," said Jack, adjusting his stance. "This is business."

"Oh," the little man said.

The elevator had always been damned slow, Jack remembered. Used to come up the stairs at a run, knowing you could beat the car. Just flying, your heart beating light, your blood sparking with youth and adrenaline. Wild times, that first year with the special squad.

"Funny thing about that card game," the little man said. "They never got the message, those boys. Kept right at it, the very same suite. Funny thing."

"Very funny," Jack said.

The doors opened. As he walked into the seventh-floor foyer, he could feel the elevator operator eyeballing his bad leg. Let him think what he liked. It could have been an old football injury, or a line-of-duty wound. You couldn't tell a virus, not just from the way a man limped.

* * *

Miriam answered the door in her new spring hat and coat. She turned slowly on the extended toes of her beige pumps, just a flash of slim, sun-tanned legs showing before the hem settled. He could feel that familiar Miriam edginess in the air, the smoky rawness she had brought into the room.

"No stockings," said Jack, throwing his hat on the bed. "You're a wicked woman."

"Wicked," said Miriam, revealing her white, white teeth.

She opened the coat and Jack couldn't help it, he stared. Aware of the hardening pulse in his throat, the vise-like pressure at his temples. *Son of a bitch.*

"Do you like it?" Miriam said. Using that husky, honey-thick voice that made him shiver a little deep inside.

Jack nodded. He bent over to untie his cordovans, still looking, and then decided he'd better sit down. Wouldn't do to fall flat on his face in front of Miriam. Looking up at *that.*

"It's a little gift," Miriam said, "from me to you."

He could feel the heat in his cheeks. How many years had it been since he'd blushed? And never, ever in this hotel.

"Cat got your tongue?" she said.

Jack slipped off his shoes. New nylon socks and already he could feel the sweat making them sticky. Ninety degrees in the middle of June, it was unnatural. He was getting used to unnatural, though; even the weather was different, new. "Did you do that yourself?" he said, the word sticky in his throat.

"Just me, myself, and my trusty mirror," Miriam said, turning her left knee out a little as she held the coat open. Giving him a better shot. That coy, bold way she had. "I was going to put a ribbon on it," she said. "But then I thought: no, this is perfect. With a ribbon it might look cheap."

"I've never seen anything like it," he said, fumbling at his shirt buttons.

This was the absolute truth. In all of his thirty years, Jack Fitzroy had never before seen a woman's pubic hair shaved in the shape of a heart.

* * *

Afterward he lay there on top of the covers and tried to pretend that his damaged leg didn't ache like hell. A pulse of pain tied to his heartbeat. The clarity of *afterward*: it was as if he could look into his own mind, see his thoughts as a kind of hidden architecture, a whole city of images and feelings he'd never known existed. Were there other cities in there, locations he'd not yet discovered? Secret places in his own head, what a strange and wonderful idea. Jack filled his lungs with the bedroom scent of her, held his breath.

The thrum of pain became a deep ache. He exhaled, felt the ache diminish slightly. A trick. You had to fool the pain.

Miriam sat on the pillow with her knees up and smoked a cigarette and said, "You know what I did? I checked in as Mrs. Fitzroy, no first name."

"That's crazy," he said. "Why take a chance like that?"

The cigarette crackled as she inhaled. Her voice was throaty, amused. "Everything we do is risky, darling. Besides, it could be you and Doris checking in for an afternoon of married passion. Getting away from the kids."

He shook his head. Doris agreeing to sex in a hotel room, in the afternoon. What an insane idea *that* was. "I can't stay long," he said. He turned, placed his hand on the inside of her thigh. Amazing heat there. Put Miriam in a dark room, you could probably see her glow, use her legs to read by.

"Let me guess," she said, hugging the pillow. "You've got a meeting with my husband."

Jack didn't bother nodding. Miriam knew that part already.

"He thinks I'm cheating," she said.

"You said he always thinks that."

"Yeah, but now he really thinks it. This morning he put the hat and coat on the Bonwit Teller account. When he spends money on me, that's the giveaway."

"Wonderful," he said.

"You never know with Michael, he might feel the need to hire a detective. I hope he hires you."

"Jesus Christ," Jack said.

"Wouldn't that be fun?"

He watched intently as her lips formed a red *O*, the white ring of smoke stabbed by the pinkness of her tongue. Red lips, pink tongue, black hair, green eyes. Miriam was a wonderful woman for colors. The color of infidelity, he decided, that was black. The texture of sin was silk and skin. These were just a few of the new things he'd learned in the last couple of months, lessons with Miriam.

The most surprising thing he'd learned: he was a good liar. No, a great liar. Morning, noon, and night he was lying now, and he never made a mistake, crossed himself up. Came to lying, he had a natural, God-given talent— all those years and he'd never suspected how exciting it could be, lying his head off.

"Don't worry about Mike," he said.

"Do I look worried?"

"You look . . ."

She came sliding down over the pillow and the nervous idea of *Mike* never had a chance to get started inside his head.

"The correct word is *ready*," she said. "I look ready."

Jack smiled. Last year at this time he'd been a square guy, a straight shooter, even did church most Sundays because he had liked pleasing Doris, it seemed an important example for the boys. Now he was a liar and a cheat and a polio cripple, and he'd returned from near death knowing this was it, this was all you got, there was nothing on the other side but fuzzy pain, endless dark. The things he knew now, Miriam had always known: she was the ward boss's beautiful daughter, and with Sugar McKane for a father the pleasures of deceit came in the blood. "Jack?"

He kissed her, right on the heart.

Two

What Danced in the Moonlight

There were monsters hiding in the vestry. Gargoyles carved into plaster trim, into the dark wooden doors. The old woman saw this and prayed, her fingers pressing hard against the rosary beads. Now and then, as the urge struck her, she lifted the tiny cross and touched it to her lips.

When the priest came back into the vestry, she froze with the beads in her gnarled fingers, as still as a small bird on a thin wire.

"Annie O'Hare, it's you again," said the priest.

"I've lost me faith, Father," the old woman said.

The priest, a small, florid man with a large, burdensome parish to look after, sighed wearily. It was hot, his patience had limits. "We've been through this before, do you remember?"

"Yes, Father, I remember. But I'm dead scared I've lost me faith for sure this time."

The priest settled onto a padded bench. Both hands gripped the baggy black knees of his trousers, as if he were leery of what those hands might do, left to themselves. "Do you believe in God, Annie?"

"I do, Father."

"And do you believe in Jesus Christ, His only son?"

The old woman nodded, her dark eyes filling.

"Do you believe in the Holy Ghost? The virgin birth? The testimony of the Apostles?"

The old woman stared at the floor, nodding. "I do, Father, yes, I do."

The priest took a deep breath, which he slowly expelled, a way to keep hold of his temper. His face reddened. "Then you can't have lost your faith, you feeble-minded old woman! You can't misplace faith like you misplace your master's grocery list."

"I haven't misplaced no list, Father. Never misplaced no list for Mr. Sugar McKane, you go on and ask him."

The priest snorted. "Christ give me patience," he muttered. Then: "Try to understand, Annie. You haven't lost your faith. You're a good Catholic. I can't help what's really troubling you unless you've a mind to tell me."

The old woman clenched her hands together and said, "The gargoyles, Father. The monsters."

"Here we go with the gargoyles again. Haven't I told you they're only a common decoration? Haven't I been to the McKane residence myself and admired the fancy woodwork?"

"Yes, Father."

"Then what do you mean by going on about the gargoyles? It's only carvings, Annie. What does that have to do with whatever silly thought has got into your head?"

Silence.

"Would you like to pray with me, Annie?"

A nod. The priest recited the Hail Mary, a race to the finish, Amen. He stood up abruptly. "Wait here."

The old woman waited. The fear was like a clot of ice in her womb. The priest did not believe her, that much was clear, and that meant she was in danger. What to do? Annie decided there was nothing she could do. She would put her faith in God, let Him decide.

When the priest returned, he had two men with him. Two large men wearing somber black suits, both with clear gray eyes and skin as pale as lace. Brothers, obvious at a glance.

"I believe you know these gentlemen," said the priest.

The old woman did not move. Her fingers went white where she gripped the beads.

"They've offered to help," the priest said. "They've a place for you to live. Work for you to do."

The old woman shook her head. "Can't go back," she said.

One of the brothers spoke. His voice was gentle and soothing, coming from so large a man. "Not there," he said. "This is a new situation. A very nice family. Name of Sheehan."

"It'll be lovely," said the priest, placing his hand on her shoulder. "They say you'll have your own room over the garage. A private bath."

The old woman was trembling visibly. "Father, I'm afraid."

The priest looked at the two men, shook his head. Clearly the old woman was daft and couldn't help herself.

"Father," the old woman said. "These men." She raised her gnarled, trembling hand and pointed. "The two Costello brothers, they work for him who employed me. That devil Sugar McKane."

The priest sighed, exasperated. "I know who they work for, Annie. That's why I called them, of course, expecting no less than a generous helping hand, as we've always had in the past. Now, what I want you to do, Annie, is I want you to get up out of that chair and go with these two fine gentlemen. They've found you a lovely situation."

The old woman motioned with her hand for him to come closer. He did so, though not willingly. "Monsters," she whispered. "Dancing in the moonlight. I saw them, Father. Him with his devil daughter, as naked as the day she was born."

The two large men made a chair of their arms and carried her out of the vestry. Gently, as they might have transported a coffin.

Three

The Fear of God

It was a brisk five-minute walk from the hotel to Park Square, or should have been. Twice Jack Fitzroy stepped into the gutter and raised his shaking hand for a cab, then thought better of it. It was absolutely essential that he strengthen the leg, ignore the concerto of pain being conducted by the damaged sciatic nerve. He knew it was the sciatic nerve because he'd asked the doctors, it helped to give a name to the pain.

Goddamn sciatic acting up again, yes, that sounded almost reasonable. Someday he would be an old duffer forecasting by the faint tremors of that same little villain, *twinge in the old sciatic, rain tomorrow.*

"Hey, Jack! What's so funny? I seen you laughing there."

Laughing? Had he been laughing? Jack squinted into the afternoon sun, recognized Bennie Bonzi, the newsdealer, there in his tin-roofed stand on the corner of Tremont Street. A fixture, old Bones, sold dirty French postcards in sealed envelopes. Had two kinds, the real thing for his trusted clients and slightly soiled Eiffel Towers for out-of-town suckers. Knew every cop in every rank and made all of them pay for their papers—and the postcards, too. The old-time cops called him Nickel Bones and begrudged him that nickel, but he had a great eye for faces, could put a suspect together with a grainy newsprint photo, tell you what he'd been wearing as he lammed by with his collar up sometime last week.

" 'Lo, Bennie. Long time no," he said after taking a deep breath.

"What? I seen you just yesterday, Jack. You drunk or something?"

Jack waved, walked on. An interlude with Miriam did that, drained his short-term memory, made him feel blank and baby-new in the world. The old sciatic—already he was thinking of it almost fondly—had muted to a dull ache by the time he arrived, thirty minutes late, at the office of Michael D. Fitzroy. The "ATTORNEY-AT-LAW" had been removed from the foyer listing, replaced by "FITZROY LEGAL SERVICES" shortly after the disbarment proceedings. Upstairs it still said "ATTORNEY" on the door, and Mike liked to say it didn't matter whether or not they let him into court, he still had the law degree.

"Is himself still here?" said Jack, taking his boater off to Rosemary Phelan, who managed the office, riding herd over the switchboard girl and the typists, part-time positions usually filled by students from Emerson College, kids who roomed with the Phelans on Beacon Street.

"Putting around in his office," Rosemary said. "You got a call from Doris. Fish, she said."

"Anything else?"

"Just fish."

Jack went through the door and found his brother, Michael, hunched over a golf ball.

"Watch this," said Mike. He stroked the putter. The ball rolled crisply over the carpet and into a Bakelite device marked with a tiny green flag. The machine spat out the ball, and Mike deftly corraled it with the blade of his putter. "Gilchrist's," he said. "In the basement, one of those discount tables. A buck fifty, huh? They had a whole shipment slightly damaged. I picked up one for you, little brother. Always thinkin'."

"I quit golf, Mike, remember?"

"Don't be ridiculous. We're playing weekends this summer with Sugar, you and me, so shape up."

"Maybe next year."

Big brother gave him a look, slow and amused over the top of his horn-rimmed glasses. Only two years older, already Mike was getting a little thin on top, carried his weight just a bit lower. In another ten years he'd be a dead ringer for the old man, fat and bald, although better dressed. "They have some nice spring hats over at Bonwit's, you're interested."

"I've got a new hat," Jack said. He sat down at his brother's desk, eased his left leg, felt the prickly numbness that always followed an interval of pain. There was a silver-framed photograph of Miriam on the desk: Mrs.

Michael Fitzroy in a pleated white skirt, holding a tennis racket and smiling like she wanted to screw every tennis pro in New England. Didn't matter, Jack told himself, and anyhow it was an old picture, from before.

"I meant you could buy a new hat for Doris," Mike said, grinning. "You'd look pretty funny in a Bonwit Teller bonnet."

"I'll tell her."

"Pick it out yourself. Give the little lady a surprise. Believe me, it works wonders."

"So," Jack said. "The shopping is good, huh?"

Mike put the putter away and went serious. "How about we grab a beer?"

"I thought we had an important meeting here."

Mike winked at the intercom. Rosemary Phelan was a notorious eavesdropper. "I've a sudden thirst," he said in a mock brogue that was a pretty fair approximation of Sugar McKane's mock brogue.

They walked to Jake Wirth's, a block away, and drank from frosted mugs of Kreuger ale. They still had the same old German waiters reeking of sauerkraut from the steamy kitchen, Jack noticed. Two wars had come and gone and nothing had changed here, except that the beer was colder, they'd finally put in refrigeration. Couple of times, on MP patrol in one little German town or another, Jack had noticed some old German gentleman who reminded him of a waiter in this place, like maybe the old guy had a brother in the States who stank of Jake Wirth sauerkraut and knew how to bow stiff from the waist. A coincidence so unlikely that he'd never bothered asking, although his German had been pretty good at the time.

"What we need to do," Mike said, wiping foam from his upper lip, "we need to discuss the future."

Jack shrugged. He was amenable to that.

"I had in mind we call it Fitzroy Security."

"You mentioned that," Jack said. "Months ago."

"I'm mentioning it again."

"I can't buy in, Mike. Not on what you pay me."

Mike sat up straight, folded his hands around the beer mug. "I never said 'buy in.' And I'm paying what you asked. What you said. Equal to you detective salary, I believe."

Jack nodded. Why was he punishing Mike? Right—for

buying Miriam the hat and thinking it mattered. "No complaints," Jack said. "I just meant it wouldn't be a fair deal. You carry the office, churn up all that business from shys who suck up to Sugar. I'm just a guy who serves paper. How could we be partners?"

Mike rolled his eyes. He'd always been an eyeroller, even as a kid. "Don't bullshit me, Jack, okay? You've been recovering. We thought we'd lost you back there, you came down with that polio thing. Guys your age are in iron lungs, watching the world through mirrors. Now that you're back all the way, we'll do things differently."

"I was just a dumb cop, Mike. You were always the brains."

Mike made a face. "Knock it off. You were a fine detective, a real investigator, smarter than any of those Southie micks, get on the cops because it's all they can do. I'm the dumbbell here, this new direction we're taking. All I know is attorneys who need investigations, paper served, whatever. You know the streets, the cops, all the angles."

"Some of the angles."

"More than some. You did good with the Granville case. Timmy Healy got his client a great settlement because of the depositions you put together. You, not me. Same with the Hannaford embezzlement. They had three of our guys on it and ten more from Pinkerton, and who figured it out, located the duplicate set of books? You did."

"So I'm a genius."

Mike shook his head. That big brother look of faint displeasure when the kid tried to sass him. Mike drained the Krueger, ordered another round. Now Jack had two mugs in front of him.

"You know your problem?" Mike said. "You're still pissed they won't let you back on the cops so you can make four grand a year for the rest of your life."

Jack traced an *M* into the frost of the new mug. "You're right, Mike. I liked being a detective. I figured, play my cards right, don't rock the boat too much, someday I'd make lieutenant."

"So?" Mike leaned forward, eager, the same boy who'd showed his little brother how to put cherry bombs in their model airplanes, blow them to satisfying smithereens. "Now you're a private detective, potential of making a hell of a lot more money. You want to be in charge? You'll *be* in charge. I don't see why the big difference, from your point of view."

"You don't?"

"No, I don't. So tell me about it," Mike said. "What's really bugging you. Let's discuss this thing, get on with it."

Jack shrugged. There was nothing to discuss, really. Things had changed. First they'd changed with the virus and later they'd changed with Miriam, something Mike couldn't know, couldn't even imagine.

"You think I haven't noticed," Mike said, "but you've had your head up your ass the last couple months. What is it, a delayed reaction? You're still alive after this big dramatic disease, you're maybe a little disappointed?"

"Talk about bullshit," Jack said. "This is bullshit. What'd you do, talk to some shrink about me?"

Michael had that look he got when he had a secret. Sometimes as a kid Jack had wanted to punch him, punch the secret right out of him. It never happened, though. Take a swing at Michael Fitzroy, you landed flat on your ass. Neighborhood bully or little brother, you went down hard.

"Not a shrink," Mike said. "Sugar."

"You discussed me with Sugar McKane? Jesus."

"He knows people, Jack. That's Sugar's expertise. If Freud was an Irish pol, he'd be Sugar McKane, lace curtains and all."

"Come on."

"I mean it. The man has a certain wisdom."

"So you went to your father-in-law about me? Hey, Sugar, please psychoanalyze my little brother?"

Mike grinned over the mug. "Hell no, I didn't. Never occur to me. We were discussing a certain situation, it came up. Your name. That's when Sugar says, 'Has Jack got used to it yet, being alive?' I didn't know what the hell he was talking about, I had to write it down." Mike reached into his suit jacket, extracted a green steno notebook. He was famous for writing things down, always had a notebook nearby. He flipped open the steno book and read: " 'A man comes back from the dead, it can be a great disappointment. A period of readjustment is necessary. When a man thinks he's dying, life is very clear, very precise, each moment has an inner significance. And when a miracle happens and he recovers, things can get out of focus.' "

"Jesus."

"The wisdom of Sugar McKane," Mike said, closing the book. "Ring any bells in there?"

Jack was stunned. "What," he said, "did Sugar almost die sometime?"

"Not to my knowledge," said Mike, lifting his mug, "but he sure as hell has put the fear of death in many a man, so I guess he took the trouble to notice. Which reminds me—he wants to see you."

"What?"

"He needs someone to look into a personal matter. And what the hell, Jack, you're the best."

Four

Sugar's Mausoleum

His brother called the place Sugar's Mausoleum, but that
wasn't quite right. While it was true that it had been built
at the turn of the century as a funeral home, and fitted
out with all the dribs and drabs of sentimental ornamen-
tation then in vogue, no funeral had ever been held on
the premises, not even that of the original owner, who
had died before the last gilded cornice was in place. Sugar
had acquired the house in the Thirties through some connection in the funeral business—something about a second mortgage foreclosed unexpectedly, a ploy typical of
the wily businessman—and he had disposed of the dour
original furnishings, repapered the walls in cheerful pas-
tels and hung them with the crisp, realistic landscapes he
called "snapshots of America"—views of midwestern
farm country, the great prairie, the Grand Tetons—all the
places Sugar had never been and had no intention of visiting. Now that his wife had passed away and his elder
daughter had married, the great house had an emptiness
that made Jack Fitzroy feel out of breath, and he could
not believe that Miriam came from this place, or, for that
matter, from this man.

"Jack, my boy," said Sugar at the top of his lungs,
striding into the mahogany dimness of the central foyer,
"this is indeed a pleasure. A very great pleasure indeed."

"Good afternoon, sir."

Jack had arrived at exactly the appointed hour, scarcely
thirty minutes after leaving his brother contemplating a
third beer at Jake Wirth's saloon. Tardiness being one
of the many vices the old ward boss did not tolerate.
Arrive a minute late and you would get a minute lecture.
Ten minutes late meant a ten-minute lecture, and so
on, with Sugar consulting his watch as he held forth, a

one-man filibuster eyeing the sweep of the second hand. Punishing you with his skill. The lecture wasn't the worst part of it. Imposingly tall and large-headed, Sugar enlarged himself when speaking, he grew huge with language. For years the chief speech maker and fund-raiser of the city's Democratic machine, Sugar McKane seemed to loom as large as a dirigible under the stage lights, holding forth on the Family, the Working Class, the Example of the Irish Immigrant, the True Meaning of Patriotism, any of a dozen or so lectures he had perfected over the decades on rally platforms, in boiler rooms, in school auditoriums, church basements, in parlors, from truck beds, wherever there were people who would let him speak. Always speaking on behalf of the party and its candidates, because Sugar himself never ran for elective office but was content to occupy various positions of power, some unnamed, within the party structure itself. The source of that power, however augmented by shady financial machinations and his uncanny ability to raise campaign funds for the anointed candidates, was his mastery of rhetoric, the "sweet voice" that boomed forth, for the most part unamplified by anything but the force of his personality.

The Great Gas, Mike called it, Celtic Helium. Jack had a cruder word, he called it bullshit, although never to Sugar's face, and never to Miriam, who would not tolerate criticism of the old man.

"The garden, Jack," Sugar said, turning on his heel. "We'll converse among the rose bushes."

The McKane house was on a hill in Hyde Park, and behind the house the grounds sloped away, contained by a high brick wall. Within those ivy-infested walls Sugar kept a garden, more varieties of roses than Jack had ever seen in one place, and raised cutting beds that, a little later in the season, would fill vases in every room in the big house, including the bathrooms—for some reason the idea of fresh flowers in a bathroom seemed a shocking waste of beauty to Jack, whose own dank privy in Jamaica Plain could boast, at best, an Air Wick behind the bowl.

"You know what I make here?" Sugar had rolled up his sleeves, was hefting a pitchfork with arms that seemed unnaturally youthful and muscular for a man who would soon be celebrating his sixtieth birthday.

"You make dirt."

Jack knew the routine, or had heard it from Mike. Seeing as how Sugar was going informal, he took off his jacket, sat on a nearby bench, and watched the great man playing in his garden. Was that thick, swept-back hair really still as black as the inside of a hat, or was Sugar tinting it now? That's what Jack wondered as he sat there: did Sugar McKane's vanity extend to hair dyes?

"Not dirt. Soil," Sugar was saying. "I take garbage and I make good, rich soil. It makes its own heat, did you know that? The transformation from waste to wonder." He displayed the pitchfork tines clotted with rot-dark earth and egg shells. "You can grow anything in this stuff. You could plant toenails here, grow a row of little men, that's how good and rich this soil is."

"I'd like to see that," Jack said. "A row of little men up to their hips in muck—sounds like a ward boss meeting. Hey, can I smoke out here?"

When Sugar frowned, the black tufts of his eyebrows furrowed together and the hawkish blade of his nose became even more prominent. He himself indulged in neither tobacco nor alcohol, just two more of the many weaknesses he disdained. "If you feel the need," he said. "Shall I have coffee brought out?"

"I'm fine, Sugar. Mike said you wanted to see me on a private matter."

"So we'll get right to business? Not even time to smell the roses, Jack?"

"I noticed the roses aren't blooming yet, Sugar. What I'm smelling at the moment is that compost. Pretty ripe stuff."

"An honest smell." He jammed the pitchfork into the earth, dusted off his large hands. Big head, big ears, big hands, big feet—he was large in all the extremities. "I happened to notice your limp is considerably improved."

"You mean it's a better class of limp?"

Jack couldn't help it. He got near Sugar and he wanted to mouth off, remind the old man that it was his greed that had gotten Mike disbarred from the practice of law. Sugar forging a signature on a back-dated deed, and when the fiddle was exposed, persuading his son-in-law to take the fall. Mike himself refused to discuss the incident now, or made light of it—all that mattered was Sugar McKane making good on his part of the deal, financing the expansion of Fitzroy Security. But Jack found the betrayal hard to forget, impossible to forgive.

"That limp has made you human," Sugar was saying. Standing ramrod straight, thumbs hooked in his suspenders, that wonderful public posture of his, taking center stage wherever he happened to be in the world. "You were too good to be true, Jack, and that is the point I was making in reference to your limp. A handsome boy who could run a fast mile, who did well in school, who broke the girls' hearts. A perfect young man who went off to war and came back a hero—a Bronze Star, no less, for having the courage to use your brains and save the lives of others—what was it, a whole regiment you rescued on that motorcycle of yours?"

"Just a platoon," Jack said. "They might have been okay without me."

Sugar grinned, showing all of his enormous teeth—the color reminded Jack of old piano keys. "And so this fine and self-effacing young hero returned in triumph to the streets of the city where he had been, ever so briefly, a rookie patrolman," he said, shaping the scene with his hands, his voice rolling full and rich, "and he was granted his only request and made, just like that, a detective on a fine police force, a man among men, with his life unfurling like a grand map, all the trails marked, the monuments noted. The chart of a perfect life. Isn't that how it was, Jack, before the sickness made you human?"

"Nice speech," said Jack, talking around the Pall Mall in his mouth.

"Mike tells me you swim every day to strengthen the leg."

"Not every day. Couple of times a week, at the Y," he said, thinking: *I wish Mike wouldn't talk about me to this guy.* It made his skin crawl just to think of his name on Sugar's lips. Why that should be, why such a strong repulsion for a man who had never harmed him. Jack could not have explained, not even to himself. He'd felt that way long before he started sleeping with Miriam, so it wasn't because of her—although, he had to admit it, he'd always wanted Miriam, right from the start. Mike walking into that beachfront juke joint with his hand on her white-gowned waist and saying: *Look what I found, the most beautiful girl in the world.*

"You were saying," Sugar prompted.

"Was I?"

"Never mind," Sugar said. "What you should do, Jack, if you can't get to the pool every day, is pedal a stationary bicycle. They say it does wonders. Also, and this is very important, you must never scrub your vegetables."

"What?"

"Scrubbing the vegetables removes the vitamins. Have Dottie wash them lightly, but never scrub. And eat them uncooked, or cooked very lightly. Boiling, that kills the goodness."

Jack smiled to himself. "I'll tell her that, Sugar. No scrubbing, no cooking. She'll appreciate your interest, I'm sure."

"And the bicycle, very important."

"Maybe Robby will let me borrow his Schwinn."

"Go ahead, make your jokes," Sugar said, tilting his big jaw skyward. "Many's the sickness that has been healed by laughter. But that's not really your way, is it, Jack? You're not a laugher. You're a very serious fellow."

Jack got to his feet, picked up his jacket. "Are we talking about me here, Sugar? Because all I am, I'm a guy doing a job for his brother, who is doing a favor for his father-in-law, as I understand it."

"Not a favor," Sugar said sharply, jerking his chin down, frowning, thumbing the suspenders.

"Right. A job, not a favor. Sometimes I get the two things confused, you'll excuse me."

"I will, yes," Sugar said, amused. "You've a tongue on you, Jack, and I know that well enough. Maybe it'll come in useful in this little task I have for you."

"Which is?"

"Inside," he rumbled, jerking his big thumb at the house, "out of the light of day."

Jack waited until Sugar turned, then flicked his cigarette into the rose bushes.

They went in through the basement, into an area Jack

supposed must have been originally intended to house
the mortuary: a large, cool, windowless room with
plaster-daubed stone walls, the foundations of the building above. There was a drainage trough around the edges,
cut into the gray slate floor. Sugar had installed overhead
lights and two full-sized pool tables, one with leather
pockets, the other without, for the formal game of cush-
ion billiards, at which Sugar excelled—or anyhow no one
dared beat him at it.

"We could have a go," Sugar suggested when he saw
Jack eyeing the billiard table. Jack shook his head—he'd
never played the game and besides, facing Sugar with a
stick in his hands, that wasn't a good idea, not at the
moment.

"I promised Dottie I'd pick up fish," he said. "It's
getting late, we always have supper together on Friday."

"The dutiful husband," Sugar said. He cupped his
hand around a billiard ball, made it carom off the rail.

"What's that supposed to mean?"

"It means I approve. Cleave to the family, Jack. That's
the best policy, a man in your position."

"For chrissake, Sugar, what's on your mind?"

McKane frowned and Jack remembered that cursing,
like booze and cigarettes and gambling and tardiness,
was not tolerated in this place. Sugar's Rules to Live by,
one of his original stump lectures, always a big hit at the
Knights of Columbus, with the boozing priests leading
the applause, or the lace-curtain Clover Club, all those
long-nosed society ladies. What was true on the stump
was just as true in his own home. There might be a dozen
ward bosses down here on a certain night, shooting at
billiard balls to please Sugar, having to step outside for
a quick smoke, a sip from the hip flask. Jack had never
been invited to such a meeting, he was an outsider, but
as Mike described it the scene was unnaturally quiet—
without Jesus as punctuation, he said, the boys can't
hardly form a sentence. Stake out the high moral ground,
put the other man off his stride, make him acknowledge
his weakness, that was a typical McKane strategy,
whether in business or politics or the wide gray area in
between.

The billiard balls clicked together, *snick-snick*, and for
some reason Jack was reminded of the cocking of a gun.

"I have made an enemy," Sugar said. "A certain low-bred person is saying unpleasant things about me."

"What kind of things?"

"Slanderous things." Sugar reached into a pocket, withdrew a folded envelope. "This was sent to the editor of the *Herald*."

"And he forwarded it to you?"

Sugar shrugged. "They wouldn't print such a thing, of course."

Jack read the letter. He had to squint because the handwriting was so crabbed.

> *Sugar McKane, the McKane who secretly owns the Costello Brothers Funeral Homes, the McKane who loans money like a Jew, this McKane is a liar and a thief and a murderer who raped his own daughter and killed an innocent man. There is proof if you know where to look, but the cops won't look because they're all a corrupt bunch of Irish bastards. Write the true story of Sugar McKane, that murdering thieving raping bastard, and your newspaper is guaranteed to win the Noble Prize.*

The letter was unsigned.

"I think he means the Pulitzer," Jack said. "They don't give the Nobel to newspapers."

Sugar reached out, took possession of the letter. "This young man is insane. He went to the police, who naturally ignored him, and lately he's been sending letters like this to all the newspapers."

"And you want me to find out who he is."

Sugar raised one bushy eyebrow, stared. "I know who he is. No problem there. Young scamp from East Boston, goes by the name William Drake."

"Then have him arrested. Or you could get a court order. A man like you, this must have happened before.

"Never." The rigidity went out of his posture and he slumped, leaning a hip against the weight of the billiard table. Behind him a green-shaded light swung slightly, as if reacting to air currents Jack couldn't otherwise detect.

"Oh, there have been one or two fellows who objected to me," Sugar said, "or to the men I've helped along the way, but never a terrible hatred like this. It makes me sick to read this filth. To know that others are reading it.''

''Newspapers get junk like this all the time.''

''You saw what it said in here?'' Sugar demanded, shaking the letter.

Jack nodded. Sugar came close, making Jack aware of the bayberry scent he used as aftershave, the baking soda dentifrice on his breath, the sick anger in his gut.

''Now I'll tell you what I told your brother,'' he said. ''I didn't steal from this man, but he thinks I did. And no one ever died on my say-so, although that's what he believes. He's wrong about those two things, Jack, but I can see how the idea of it got put in his head. It's the other thing, that's the terrible lie.''

''The part about raping your daughter.''

Sugar's big wet eyes hooded.

''But surely Miriam will—''

''Not Miriam,'' said Sugar, resting two large hands on Jack's shoulders, squeezing gently. ''My other daughter. My mental daughter who can't speak to defend herself. My poor, poor Deirdre.''

Five

Forgetfulness Therapy

Strangely enough, the mesh on the windows did not obscure the view. Not if she hooked her fingers in the grille and pulled herself close. Close up, the window itself was a blur, she could focus on the light reflected in the reservoir. Glittering light on the water. The lovely trees that swayed like little green fingers all around the edges of water so deep it went all the way down to an ocean under the earth, or so she imagined. By shifting her eyes slightly she could see beyond the Brookline Reservoir to the rolling felt of the golf course. There were patterns in the fairways there, in the thick green trees, if only she could find them.

"Miss McKane?"

She did not turn from the window until a hand touched her shoulder. Touched her through the thin cotton of the hospital gown.

"How are you feeling today, Deirdre? Can you tell me?"

Ah, yes. The plump little man with the sad eyes and the white hair parted right down the middle so that his skull showed underneath. He was nice, this man. Sometimes he held her hand and his voice was as pleasant and lulling as a voice on the radio.

"Do you remember me? I'm Dr. Parkay. This is the Parkay Clinic."

"Dr. Park-ay," she said, trying out the words. Her tongue was strange and heavy in her mouth.

"What did you have for breakfast this morning, can you recall?"

She turned away, looked through the mesh. Now the trees around the reservoir were in silhouette. No longer lush green but shadow black.

"I'm not surprised that you don't remember breakfast,

Deirdre. We don't expect you to, after the treatment. Forgetfulness is part of the therapy.''

She nodded dreamily. ''So beautiful,'' she said, working her fingers into the mesh.

The doctor did not attempt to turn her away from the window. He made notes on his clipboard, writing so quickly that tiny specks of black ink flew from his fountain pen. When he was finished writing, he said, ''Deirdre? Tomorrow another doctor is coming to see you. He's a famous surgeon, coming all the way from Philadelphia.''

She spoke, clinging to the mesh.

''What?'' he said.

''City of love,'' she said, and smiled at each word.

The doctor frowned, puzzled. ''Oh, yes,'' he said. ''Philadelphia is the city of brotherly love, quite right. Dr. Walter Freeman—he's the famous man from Philadelphia. Dr. Freeman is very interested in your case—he thinks that if certain corrective measures are taken, you'll be able to return home. Wouldn't that be nice?''

''Love, love, love,'' she said, touching her heavy tongue to the coolness of the mesh grille.

''Dr. Freeman has developed a special technique,'' he said. ''We're confident that he can relieve your . . . symptoms.''

Gently but firmly Dr. Parkay unpeeled her fingers from the mesh and guided her back to her bed.

''The nurse will be bringing in your supper in a few minutes,'' he said. ''I want you to eat everything on the plate because tomorrow you won't be having breakfast. Do you understand, Deirdre?''

She smiled and lifted the hem of her gown. She had it all the way up over her waist before he could stop her. Tugging the gown firmly down to her ankles, he said, ''No, Deirdre. No.''

She waited until her hands were clear and then swiftly, violently wrenched the gown up around her waist. She moved her hips, wriggled on the bed.

''We don't want to use the restraints on you again, Deirdre. But if you insist on this behavior, that's just what we'll do. Now cover yourself. Please?''

She turned her face to the wall.

''Please?''

The doctor sighed, tugged the gown back down. This time she left it there.

''You'll feel much better by this time tomorrow,'' he said. ''I promise.''

Six

Crossing the Line

Late as it was, the carts were still out on the Atlantic Avenue wharf. Jack Fitzroy, fighting the stiff wheel of the big eight-year-old sedan he still thought of as Mike's Packard, parked as near as he could before getting out and testing his leg on the cobblestones.

Maybe it was the two beers he'd had with Mike, or speaking his mind to Sugar, but he felt pretty good. It was all a question of balance and confidence, making sure you didn't slip on the fish guts or whatever. He'd always liked the smell of this wharf, raunchy as it was. Salt and blood and haddock going off in the summer heat. The diesel stink of the draggers down from Gloucester, rafted up tight, most on the verge of sinking they leaked so bad, always a couple of kids in the bilge, working the donkey pumps, you could hear the squeak of the wet leather if you listened. Noisy gulls up there on the warehouse eaves, keeping their distance. They knew better than to get too close to the fish carts, lose a beak to those big filet knives.

"Hey, stripah! Stripah heah!"

The striped bass were running, great big things that tail-flopped from the push carts. Robby, his seven-year-old, would get a kick out of that, a fish as tall as he was, but Jack walked on. Doris was very particular about the Friday fish, had to be cod or haddock, always baked and stuffed with that breadcrumb thing she did, learned it from her mother. Baked it good and dead. Boiled potatoes on the side, soft gray peas, bread and margarine. The margarine was left over from rationing—Doris thought it was a nice little touch to keep, that abstinence from butter. Put out the sad little stick of oleo, lard white because she didn't think it was right to mix in the coloring, for Jesus' sake.

Hey, Jack admonished himself, enough. The woman tries. She doesn't shave her privates or shudder in silk, but she tries. She believes in things. What do you believe in?

Not fish, he decided, I don't believe in fish today. And so he came in the door of their Jamaica Plain second-floor walk-up with a paper sack of live lobsters and upended them right on the linoleum, watch the little buggers skitter around backward on their clenching tails.

"What's this?" Doris said.

Robby was running to get his little brother, David, show him the sea monsters on the kitchen floor.

"Just for a change," said Jack. He put his jacket on the peg, washed his hands in the sink, couldn't help noticing the chipped enamel, not like that fine Parker House porcelain.

Doris with her arms folded, but she was interested, he could see the look in her eye. "Can we do this?" she said, clucking her tongue.

"I don't see any meat here," Jack said. "A lobster is a fish, right? Comes from the sea."

"But they say 'lobster meat.' "

"Dottie, you go down to Pier Four on a Friday night, the monseigneurs are all in there eating swordfish, baked lobster, whatever. Dripping in butter, too."

Doris got out her broom, began herding the lobsters back into the paper bag. "Well, that's all right then."

Without turning from the sink he said, "Mike raised me twenty a week."

A moment of silence from Doris. He heard the rustle of claws fighting the paper bag. Then: "I suppose you mentioned the overtime?"

With the towel in his hands Jack turned and kissed her on the cheek. No response, no response at all. He was getting the dead fish whether he bought it or not. "We're going partners, honey. I'm on salary. No overtime on salary."

She had that stubborn stiffness as she reached a pot down from the top shelf. "You were on salary on the cops, and you always got your overtime."

"I'm not on the cops now, Dottie."

He said it in a way he had that ended any further discussion. Robby and little David, recognizing the tone, went out to play quietly in the living room. Jack could heard David whispering, "Wobstah? Wobstah?" as they huddled over toy fire trucks on the floor.

Doris got the water on the stove, smoothed out her apron. "Well, that's good news about the twenty, Jack. It really is. I guess we can take the boys to Revere Beach tomorrow, like you've been promising."

He saw that she was leaving an opening, wanted to get the evening back on the rails, and he took it. "We'll do that, sure. See, what it is, Mike wants to double the operatives," he said, "make them all full-time. He thinks he can shake out enough legwork to keep six men busy at least through the summer. And maybe double that in a few months."

"He's always been as good as his word, Jack."

Jack nodded. Before their marriage Doris had been a little put off by brother Mike, although she never said so. You could tell the way she eyed the big cars he drove, her habit of glancing away whenever he happened to mention his famous father-in-law, that Doris thought Michael Fitzroy was putting on the dog, a sin worse than murder in her family. You only had to meet her grim-lipped old man (a B&M fireman who, Jack was convinced, kept dabbing on a little coal dust long after the railroad had converted to diesel) to know that. Never trust a man who talked openly about earning money, about wanting to make something of himself, that was a clan rule with the Dorchester McLaughlins. Then in those eighteen months when Jack was overseas, brother Mike, good as his word, had made sure there were groceries on her table, saw she was driven where needed in his then new Packard, did whatever was necessary to make life tolerable for a woman with an infant son who insisted on living apart from her family so as not to hear her husband bad-mouthed for not being there, never mind he was riding MP motorcycles within pistol shot of the front lines. Jack had come home to find that Doris still didn't like Mike much, but she trusted him now, more than ever since Jack's illness and recovery.

"Michael has a head on his shoulders," she said, putting margarine into a saucepan.

"Yes, and wouldn't he look funny without one?" said Jack with a grin, snapping his napkin.

They ate a nice meal together, four at the table. The potatoes had already been peeled, Doris had only to slice and brown them in crackling Crisco, with the boys crying "French fry, french fry," David maybe a little unclear on what exactly a french fry was, but he seemed to catch a whiff of his older brother's excitement. After tugging at the legs and claws and attempting to push meat out of the tail, neither boy ate more than a taste of the lobster itself. Doris let them have bread and jam—a great adventure on Friday night—and said lightly, "I suppose you planned it this way?" as she transferred the uneaten lobsters to the adult plates.

There was an underlying intimacy in that simple statement. He'd forgotten what it was to see her glow a little, and he was not surprised when she suggested, with a look he hadn't seen in quite some time, that they bathe the boys and pack them off to bed early. Time to ourselves, she called it.

"Hell with the bath," he said. "They'll hold until morning."

He'd been wondering the last few weeks how this would go, doing it with Dottie. He discovered it was easy, nothing to it. Didn't even have to close his eyes and think of Miriam. Anyhow, it was Doris who always closed her eyes, although even that part was different this time. What a surprise to find her watching as he lowered himself between the warm limpness of her outspread legs; what a greater surprise to discover that she was—and this was very rare with Doris—truly aroused. Wanting to kiss him with her tongue—what did she taste there, deep in his mouth, besides the salty margarine? The tang of his lies? Or was it deeper, could she taste Miriam's deceit?

It made him feel oddly powerful, to endure these thoughts and yet remain vital. Odd because a year ago he had no idea he was capable of such duplicity, or rather of not suffering from such duplicity. He had believed in inner retribution, the erosion of guilt, if not the soul-shriveling punishment promised by the church. Given the level of his betrayal, Jack now believed himself capable of anything. It was almost exciting, waiting to see what he would find himself doing next. Would he, this new man who had emerged from his old self, would he come to a place he could not go? Was there a line he would not cross?

Not, he decided, if Miriam was on the other side of that line. But still—he was thrusting now, pushing himself deep inside this other woman, his wife who loved him, or thought she did, and taking pleasure, too, real, excruciating pleasure—crossing a line was not a thing you decided, as he had discovered, it simply happened, and there you were.

"Ahh," said Jack, collapsing. "Jesus, that was good." Raising himself up on one elbow, he shook his fist at the ceiling and said, "You hear me, Jesus?"

"Jack!" Doris said, but she was giggling, and her hands were slick and hot on his shoulders, urging him closer.

Seven

Serving Notice

The glassy water lifted with the tide, nudging the boat
against the creosoted pilings. There were lobster pots
stacked in ragged rows on the pier and along the transom
of the boat. The bait boxes were already stowed on deck;
redolent redfish, ripe and eye-watering in the sun. Inside
the cockpit a hatch cover had been thrown open and
a thin, bare-chested boy in stained overalls crouched
over the engine and concentrated on taking apart a carburetor, his expression as intent as if he were defusing a
bomb. Drop one tiny piece in the bilge and he'd be all
day trying to retrieve it, fishing under that six-cylinder
Ford, all the sea-slimed objects that had settled there.
What he'd have to do, if he dropped a piece, row himself
back to the East Boston docks, find a rebuild kit somewhere, row himself out again. Minimum of four hours
lost, assuming he found the right kit, assuming he could
fight the tide in that heavy flat-bottomed skiff.

His right hand worked the screwdriver counter-
clockwise, backing out the bronze machine bolts. He positioned his left hand under the carburetor, catching the
reservoir as it dropped away, and managed to push the
loosened bolts into the pan. So far, so good. Now the pin
from the throttle linkage. Yes, in there with the bolts.
The problem, once he had the lower half of the carb off,
was obvious: he could see where the cork float had gotten
twisted around, stuck in the down position, flooding gas
into the manifold. Lucky he hadn't blown himself up, all
those fumes wafting from the bilge when he opened the
hatch cover. He untwisted the brass hinge on the float
and reassembled the carburetor, tightened the machine
bolts down so that he could see the gasket squeezing out
around the rim. Good as new.

He had the big Ford idling and was sliding the last of

the traps into the cockpit, using a short gaff for leverage, when the Harbor Patrol launch *Argus* came out of the sun, put itself adrift ten yards off the pier. On board was a uniformed cop with his fat butt splayed on the fantail, another cop at the helm. The Harbor Patrol flag limp in the stillness of the air.

The fat cop had a navigation chart out, spread over his knees. "Hey, you," he said, "is this Drake Island?" The cop at the helm squinted and said, "That's him, Sarge, I seen him before when he come in the station. He was always coming in the station, bothering the detectives."

The fat cop folded up the chart, got to his feet, steadied himself. "You William R. Drake of East Boston?"

The boy's hand tightened on the gaff, then relaxed. Two against one, both of them armed, what could he do? "This is private property," he said. "No trespassing."

The fat cop laughed. "You got that right, Billy boy. We got a notification of eviction here, says you got twenty-four hours to clear out your stuff."

"That's wrong," the boy said. "I been to court about that. The title is in dispute, it ain't been settled."

The launch drifted in closer to the pier. The cop at the helm had a line out, ready to wrap around the piling. "That's fine, Billy boy," the fat cop said. "We're not here to argue with you. All we're gonna do, post this eviction notice. Which we *will* do. So keep your hands clear of that gaff."

The boy got out of the lobster boat, took the line from the launch. He put his hand out to take the paperwork, but the fat cop shook his head. "I said we got to post it," he said. "That's the law." Grabbing a piling, he hauled himself out of the launch, then swore when he found his hands coated with fresh creosote.

"A little gasoline'll take that off," the boy said, but the fat cop just glared, stomped on down the pier.

The island was a five-acre rock with a little scrub pine above the high-water mark. Boards laid over the rock and seaweed made a path to a shingled fishing shack that had recently been erected on the ridge of the island. The fat cop stomped up the boardwalk, used a handy stone to nail the notice to the door. In less than a minute he was back down to the dock. Pretty well satisfied with his performance of duty, he glanced around at the rickety pier, the barren rock, and said, "Two thousand bucks for this? You gotta be kiddin' me. You can buy a beachfront lot for five hundred bucks, down the Cape. Nice clean sand and a road going by."

"We never sold it," the boy said. "That was a mistake. It was a lie said by Sugar McKane."

"Come on, Sarge," said the cop at the wheel.

"That bastard McKane is trying to steal it away," the boy said. "That's not right."

"You been legally served," the fat cop said. He lowered himself into the launch, unwrapped the line.

"What happens next?" the boy said as the launch backed away, leaving a rainbow-streaked oil slick.

The fat cop said, "That's up to you, asshole."

The boy, Bill Drake, age eighteen, walked up to the shack and peeled off the eviction notice. Calmly and carefully he tore it into small pieces, crushed the pieces in his hand, tossed the clump onto the bare rock. Let the wind take it away. Inside the shack—one room with a potbelly stove, two bunks, a card table and two folding chairs, a shelf of canned goods—he cracked open the hinged window, let some of the summer heat out. The place still smelled of the whiskey his brother, Roy, had spilled—it was a stink that just wouldn't leave. It clung, that smell, and the clinging made the boy feel strong.

He sat at the table, looked around the shack. He and Roy had knocked the place together after a winter storm had swept over the island, cleared off the old buildings. Nothing lasted very long out here except the island itself. You could find it on the oldest charts, a hunk of rock far enough out of the shipping channel so it was not a navigational danger, never came to the attention of the Coast Guard or the old Lighthouse Service, the folks who had taken over some of the other fishing islands by federal decree. Over the years several of the little islands had been blown up to widen the channel, others built over with navigational beacons. Drake Island stayed as it always had been, back two hundred years or more, a seasonal fishing outpost for the Drake family, their place, their little island forever and ever, for as long as the rock lasted. As a kid he'd always felt that fierceness of pride, knowing a piece of the harbor was named for him.

Now his brother, Roy, was dead and the lying murderer McKane was trying to steal the island away. Things were all out of kilter and wrong. Sitting there with his head in his hands, the boy decided that when the time came, someone would have to die to make the balance right. There was really no alternative.

Eight

The Genius of the Leucotome

There were shapes in the mist on the reservoir. Deirdre watched without fear, secure behind the wire mesh. Formless shapes that echoed in her memory: Salome in veils of mist, dancing, dancing, her limbs the color of early light, or morning water, or the whiteness of sky above. Figures trudged along the fairway, black against green, a glint of reflected light as the golf irons arced into the turf.

"Daddy," Deirdre said to herself alone, "is that you?" as a quarter mile distant, the figure trudged, turned, vanished into the roiling mist.

Behind her a key turned in a lock. She felt the air move as the door opened. It was nice, plump Dr. Parkay and a nurse pushing an empty wheelchair.

"Good morning, Miss McKane," the doctor said.

Deirdre did not voluntarily move from the window, but she did not resist when Dr. Parkay gently pried her fingers away from the mesh and guided her into the wheelchair.

The nurse pushed the chair. Dr. Parkay walked beside her, letting his clipboard bounce against his thigh.

"Dr. Freeman is waiting," he said. "He's come all the way from Philadelphia by train, just to see you.

Deirdre did not respond. Why bother? Dr. Parkay always knew what she was thinking. Sometimes he put his stethoscope to her heart and picked up the signals from her mind.

"Dr. Freeman has been on the cover of *Time* magazine," Parkay went on, very chatty this morning. "He has cured hundreds of people. And he finds your case of particular interest."

In her chair, Deirdre smiled inwardly. She wasn't listening to the doctor, exactly, she was letting the noise from his mouth resonate inside her head, where it resembled the warbling of a bird. A plump blue jay, strutting and talking. Deirdre closed her eyes and concentrated on the humming of the wheels of the rubber-tiled floors: *Hmmmmmmmmmm. Hmmmmmmmmmmmmmm.* It was soothing. It filled the emptiness.

Select staff had been allowed to assemble in the shock-therapy facility, also known as the rubber room, because of the thick rubber mats on the floor. Electroconvulsive treatment was by now routine at the clinic—virtually all regressive or unresponsive cases were put on a cycle of three convulsions per session for a specific number of sessions, a minimum of six and as high as twenty-eight, usually at two sessions per day. A full cycle took an average of fourteen days, after which the patient was re-evaluated.

"It is my pleasure to introduce Dr. Walter Freeman," said Dr. Parkay, gesturing to a tall, almost completely bald gentleman who wore round, wire-rimmed glasses and a salt-and-pepper goatee. Standing in his white lab coat, with his hands folded at his waist, Freeman had the look of an athlete in repose. He appeared to be slightly bored.

"As you know, Dr. Freeman is renowned for his advances in psychosurgery," said Dr. Parkay, "and in particular for the transorbital lobotomy, which he himself perfected. He has most graciously agreed to demonstrate this technique here today. Dr. Freeman?"

The great surgeon scratched the lobe of his ear, glanced at the patient with no particular expression. "Would you be so kind," he said, "as to read me her case history?"

The patient, mildly sedated with a dose of Phenobarbital, lay quietly on the gurney, her wrists enveloped in canvas restraints, while Dr. Parkay read from her file.

"The patient, age twenty-one, has a long history of compulsive sexual behavior, beginning in early adolescence. Outpatient treatment has been almost continuous since the age of thirteen, and has not succeeded in moderating her behavior for any significant length of time. Approximately six weeks ago she was admitted to this clinic in a state of acute manic distress, hallucinating freely. After a full cycle of convulsive therapy, the patient experienced the expected level of memory loss and some lessening of manic emotional outbursts, but her compulsive symptoms continued unabated. We have reluctantly concluded that her condition is chronic and may require long-term institutional care.''

Dr. Parkay coughed and closed the file.

Reaching into the pocket of his lab coat, Dr. Freeman withdrew a small instrument case and began what was obviously a rote lecture: ''It has been established that this patient may benefit from an interruption in the ventral and medial areas of the brain. According to statistics compiled over the last five years, there is an eighty percent chance that the procedure will prove beneficial, a better than fifty percent chance that she will improve to the degree that she can be cared for in the home.'' Dr. Freeman approached the gurney and signaled for an attendant to wheel up the electroconvulsive equipment. ''As you will observe, the entire procedure takes less than ten minutes and does not require anesthesia. As some of you are no doubt aware,'' he said with a sly smile, glancing at the copy of *Time* magazine that had been circulating among the nurses, ''I have successfully demonstrated this technique on as many as twenty-five patients in a single day. Properly performed, the mortality rate is—and I do not exaggerate—zero.''

He nodded at the attendant, who applied a conductive ointment to the patient's temples before slipping on the electrode yoke. The patient, by now inured to the routine, and in any case already mildly sedated, did not resist as a nurse gently positioned a wad of cotton between her teeth and tongue.

Dr. Freeman placed his instrument case on the gurney behind the patient's head and continued, ''Between two and five convulsive shocks will be administered, enough to maintain a state of coma for about five minutes. Dr. Parkay, would you care to do the honors?''

After assuring himself that all the equipment was in order, Dr. Parkay asked the nurses to step back. The attendant carefully placed both of his hands on the insulated handle of the electrode yoke and indicated that he was ready. The patient's body arced in the first convulsion. The device was activated four more times in rapid succession. The electrode yoke was removed. The patient was deeply unconscious.

"Excellent," said Dr. Freeman. He opened his instrument case, withdrew a small metal hammer and a white-handled device that resembled an ice pick. "Nurse, please cover the patient's nose and mouth with a towel. Very good. That prevents contamination by nasal secretions. Now observe: I begin with the left eye, pinch the upper eyelid between thumb and forefinger, and lift it away from the eyeball. I then insert the transorbital leucotome," he said, holding up the ice pick, "and insert the point into the conjunctival sac, thusly." He inserted the probe into the eye socket and then paused as the staff crowded eagerly around. "You must take care not to touch the skin or lashes—contamination danger—and now I am moving the point around until it settles, there, against the vault of the bony orbit. I will now drop to one knee beside the table, in order to aim the instrument parallel with the bony ridges of the nose."

He went to one knee beside the gurney. With his free hand the surgeon reached for the small hammer, and with one quick move he tapped it sharply against the handle of the leucotome—the ice pick.

"Now the orbit is breached and the leucotome may be inserted directly into the brain, to a depth of five centimeters from the margin of the upper eyelid, as marked on the blade." Slowly he rose from his knee, gripped the ice pick in both hands. "Lateral left," he said, pushing the handle to one side. "Now lateral right. There. The lobes are now severed. I will withdraw the instrument, keeping pressure on the upper eyelid to control bleeding." Pressing his thumb against the patient's eyeball, he withdrew the ice pick and presented it to Dr. Parkay, who handled it gingerly.

"For the right eye we will use a freshly sterilized leucotome," said Dr. Freeman, reaching into his instrument case, "and proceed in exactly the same manner."

A little more than a minute later, Deirdre McKane was fully lobotomized. In less than a hour she was conscious and had been returned to her room. It was Dr. Parkay himself who noticed that she no longer seemed interested in the window. Perhaps, he concluded, because of the temporary swelling in her eyelids.

She did not, he was pleased to report to the nurses, attempt to raise her gown.

Nine

Pledging Allegiance

Jack Fitzroy was sitting in the big Packard, smoking a cigarette, half listening to the ball game on the radio. Jim Britt announcing, the Braves were beating the Dodgers, second game of a doubleheader, take a pair from New York and Boston would be three up, solid in first place. That would make Mike happy—Jack didn't really care one way or the other. The old man had been a devoted Boston Braves fan until the day he died. Maybe that's what Mike was doing, carrying on the family tradition.

With the car window rolled down, you could smell the waterfront. Different kind of smell here in East Boston, at the old Emmett Street docks. Diesel and heavy oil and the iron taste of rusting hulks, barges that had foundered in the mud. The stink of sewage, that was a given, live here and you got used to it, he supposed. The shipping business was confined to the big piers close by the main channel. Out here on the windward end, where the mud had filled, only shallow craft could make it into shore. No longshoremen here, no teamsters, no unions at all—not even an active railroad spur. This was end of the line in Eastie, home to a few local fishermen—and one particular fisherman, if his information was correct.

Headlights on the street. It had rained earlier, a passing shower, and in the glittery blackness the approaching vehicle appeared elongated. By the time it came to a stop, motor idling, headlights dimmed, Jack recognized the Ford coupe.

" 'Lo, Jack," said the hatted, rain-coated figure who emerged from the coupe.

"Hello, Bob."

Bob Cogan, presently a detective with the Safes & Lofts unit. Might or might not come on full-time with the firm, he hadn't made up his mind yet. Jack found himself thinking of it that way lately: the firm. Cogan came large, must be two hundred and fifty pounds of him, and that was why Jack had picked him for this assignment. Also he was a guy who knew how to keep his mouth shut when it counted. Jack got out of the Packard, stood on the running board—that made him about even with Bob Cogan.

"This one is off the books," said Jack, pinwheeling his cigarette into the darkness. "Fifty bucks, a flat fee."

He heard Cogan's quiet laughter. "I won't kill nobody for less than a hundred," the big man said.

It was a joke, of course. Cogan knew he'd been called in for a muscle part. He also knew Jack Fitzroy well enough to guess that no serious mayhem was involved. It was one thing for an active cop to moonlight, quite another to hire out as leg breaker, or worse. "You want to throw a scare into this guy, that it?"

"Maybe," Jack said. "We'll take it one step at a time, see what he has to say for himself."

"He there?" said Cogan, indicating the docks.

"If I got the right guy, yes. That's a thing we have to be sure of, that he's the right guy."

Cogan shrugged. Jack guessed he'd worn the raincoat because the padded shoulders made him look even larger. If so, it worked. "How do we play it?" Cogan asked.

"Like cops," Jack said. "Just do what comes natural."

He could feel the old pier move as Cogan lumbered along the planking, reminded him of the goddamn Revere Beach roller coaster, only slower and no one was throwing up on his shoulder, not yet. Pilings jutting up from the black water like old bones, or jagged teeth, parts of another, even more ancient pier rotting away, slime-slick hulls settled on the bottom—this was a dead place, or dying.

The only source of light, other than the dimness of the clouded stars, came from a boat lashed to the ragged pilings at the end of the pier. A bare bulb hanging by wire from the wheelhouse or whatever it was—Jack had no particular feel for boats, had endured Mike's runabout out of politeness and as a means to bump knees with Miriam—the naked light was illuminating a torn-up cockpit, a hatch cove askew on the transom, the signs of a man at work.

He and Cogan came to the end of the pier and looked down. About a six-foot drop there, and only a toothpick ladder to get down. "Ahoy, the *Irene*," Jack said. All he could see under the exposed engine was a bare foot resting on the hatch combing. "We're looking for William Drake, the owner."

No response. Jack went down the ladder first, just in case it wouldn't hold Cogan. As he landed, the boat shifted under his weight and a loud curse came from the vicinity of the engine.

"Go to hell, you bastid! Look what you made me do!"

Now Cogan was coming down the ladder, moving lightly for such a large man, taking care as he shifted his weight onto the boat. A lobster boat, Jack could tell that much, painted lead white and with a winch block near the wheel so that a man could run the boat single-handed, if necessary.

The bare foot shifted away and with a groan a figure emerged from under the engine. The grease-stained face made the blue eyes even more vivid, eyes that glared. Eyes that were, Jack was pleased to see, registering fear.

"Who the hell are you?"

He was upright now, a thin boy in coveralls, younger than Jack had expected—he'd have trouble buying himself a drink, this kid. Jack took his time looking him over, noticed the kid glancing at Cogan's bulk, and tapped a cigarette from the pack.

"Careful with the match," the kid said. "Gas all over the bilge."

Jack tucked the matches away, kept the unlit cigarette in the corner of his mouth. "You Bill Drake?" he said.

"I think you should get off my boat, is what I think."

Jack looked at Cogan. "Find if he's got some ID. Maybe a wallet."

As Cogan started to move, the kid backed away and said hastily, "So what if I am? Who the hell are you guys, huh? Are you cops?"

Cogan stopped where he was, his huge hands relaxed at his sides. Doing his silent but deadly act, letting Jack speak the lines. "What do we look like, son?" Jack said.

"I already talked to the cops," Drake replied. "I done nothing but talk to cops."

Jack opened his mouth to ask what cops, thought better of it. Better to play like he knew. "What you need to do," he said, "you need to sit down and relax."

He could see the kid deciding what to do—he could jump over the side, thrash around between the pilings, maybe get himself shot, or he could do as he was told. With big Bob Cogan looming, the options were limited.

"Sit," Jack said.

Billy Drake leaned against the side of the boat and folded his arms. That was his idea of a compromise, apparently. Jack let it slide for the moment.

"We're going to have a conversation," he said. "You start first."

"What?"

"Tell us why we're here."

"I don't know why the hell you're here."

"Think about it," Jack said. "Think about why we'd come all the way out to this shithole dock in Eastie on a Saturday night, we've got better things to do."

Drake opened his mouth, shut it, let his eyes flick nervously at Cogan. Clean him up, Jack decided, he'd be a good-looking kid. Didn't fit the picture of a poison-pen type, but you never knew. "We get very offended, somebody commits a crime, Bill. So offended we give up our Saturday night."

"What?" the kid said. "You're going to arrest me? For what?"

Jack turned to Cogan. "Did you hear that?"

Cogan made a noise deep in his throat, sounded like a Doberman on a choke leash. Jack was surprised and pleased—this was a touch he hadn't expected from a plodder like Cogan, and he could see the reaction looming in the kid's eyes. The way he was clenching himself, expecting to get hurt.

"Let me tell you what's required here," said Jack, taking out his matches. "What is required, Bill, is a confession. We'll all feel better, you confess your crime."

Jack glanced from the matches to the engine, saw that Drake got the message.

"You're nuts," the kid said. "What crime?"

"What do you want," Jack said, waggling the cigarette with his lips, "a hint?"

"I got no idea," the kid said. "No idea at all."

Jack turned to Cogan. "Take him inside."

He didn't add "out of sight" because there was such a thing as laying it on too thick, and the kid was frightened enough as it was. He'd crack as soon as they got inside there, all of them bunched up tight on the little bunk inside the tiny cabin. Rain gear and ropes taking up most of the space. Cogan bent over almost double to squeeze inside, his thick arm wrapped in mock-friendly fashion around the kid's shoulder, the kid averting his face, his eyes getting wilder as the minutes passed.

"We're waiting," Jack said, tossing the matchbook from hand to hand. He wrinkled his nose—it was foul in here, a damp, unpleasant odor.

"Are you going to kill me, too?" the kid finally blurted. The tears intensified the blue in his eyes.

"I want your confession," Jack said. "Go ahead, it's good for the soul."

There was the whine of a distant motor. A minute or so later the boat began to rock hard against the pilings as the wake came through. Another noise, higher up—a DC3 coming into the airport. Jack would know that sound anywhere. He'd flown all over Europe in those old Dakotas, take off in a cornfield if they had to.

The kid was crying now, his face all knotted up. Jack felt a little queasy, must have been the smell. "You bastids," the kid said, trying not to blubber. "You get everything. You just take it. Anything you want."

Jack made a sign to Cogan, who eased up, loosened his grip on the kid. "Come on, Billy," he said. "Tell us why you wrote those letters about Mr. McKane."

He could see the kid's eyes go blank with panic. "Letters?"

"Lies," Jack said. "Slander. You could go away for ten years, writing things like that."

The kid gulped, got his breath back. "I don't know what you're talking about."

As an MP in Army Intelligence, Jack had interrogated his share of prisoners, sometimes with a .45 aimed at the head just for effect. Later, as a police detective, he'd spent many long hours grilling suspects. He had, he be-

lieved, a feel for how men lied when they were frightened, and how they told the truth. The feeling—not always reliable, he knew—told him that Billy Drake was
telling the truth.

Jack put away the matches, dropped the unlit cigarette
to the grimy deck, and took a notebook from his pocket.
He folded it back to a blank page, held it out.

"Take this," he said.

Drake looked at him, uncomprehending.

"Go on," Jack said, shaking the notebook.

The kid took it. Jack handed him a fountain pen and
said, "I want you to write something down. You know
the Pledge of Allegiance?"

"What?"

"You heard me. Write it down."

"Are you serious?"

"Dead serious," Jack said.

The boat nudged violently up against the pilings again,
another wake coming through. Cogan was giving him a
look, he wanted to know what was going on. Jack
shrugged him off. Meanwhile the kid held the notebook
on his knee, tried to get a grip on the pen. "I can't
remember," he said. "I really can't."

"I pledge allegiance," Jack said, starting him off, "to
the flag . . ."

The kid nodded, wrote down that much, then seemed
to remember the rest. When he finished he looked up
and said, "Are you FBI, is that it? Because you've got
the wrong guy."

"Never mind who we are," Jack said. "Just turn over
the page and write it down again."

When the kid was finished, Jack took the notebook and
the pen and crawled out of the fetid cabin. Cogan was
behind him, working his big shoulders through the narrow door. Drake stayed on the bunk. "Come on out of
there," Jack said.

The kid emerged from the cabin, looked ready to bolt,
take his chances in the water. "Get back to work," Jack
advised him. "Finish what you were doing."

Cogan went up the ladder first. When it was Jack's
turn, he had some trouble getting his bad leg to hold on
the rungs, and when he looked back the kid was staring
at him with those hard, wet blue eyes. Didn't say any-

thing, just staring at Jack's bad leg like he knew the FBI didn't employ cripples, nor did the police department.

Back at the cars, Bob Cogan took off his raincoat and threw it into the front seat of the coupe. It was hard to make out his expression, but Jack figured he was smiling from the sound of his voice. "That was for a handwriting sample, huh?" Cogan said. "All that bullshit about the Pledge of Allegiance, that was to throw him off."

Jack held out the notebook and the pen. "Could you write it down, the Pledge?"

"Hell, no. I never took you for such a patriot, Jack."

"It came to mind is all."

"So, you get what you came for?"

"I don't know," Jack said, getting into the Packard. "We'll have to see about that."

Ten

Let's Be Happy

Sugar in his music room, listening to the NBC Symphony Orchestra, broadcasting live from New York. Sugar had his eyes closed, his great head resting on a wing back of his favorite chair. His face sagged in repose. Only his lips moved, a slight, rhythmic puckering that followed Schumann's *Spring Symphony*. Music had always been a basic need for Sugar. He understood the joy of it, sensed the sadness beneath the joy, all those alternating currents of sad-happiness that were bound up in a classical theme. When the mood was right and his concentration was complete, as it was now, he could feel each note in his bones, the singing of each musical voice, and on his best days he still utilized that understanding in his rhetoric, honed the instrument of his own voice accordingly, to compel an emotional response. Music, like politics, was driven by emotion, not intellect—this was, for Sugar McKane, a fundamental truth, a source of power.

He was on the verge of forgetfulness, of bliss, when his daughter came into the room. Miriam in a linen skirt, white satin blouse, white purse hanging from a strap on her shoulder. She went to the sideboard, where he kept the ice bucket and the soda syphon, withdrew a pint of gin from her purse, and poured herself a drink.

Sugar closed his eyes, tried to recover the forgetting, but he knew it was no use, not with Miriam back from her visit.

"That's nice," she said. He opened his eyes to see her pointing the gin glass at the radio console. "What is that?"

"Schumann," Sugar said. He did not get up from his chair by the radio. "Conducted by that scoundrel Toscanini."

"No opera?"

"Later," he said. "The Verdi starts at nine."

"I know you hate this," Miriam said, rattling the ice cubes in her glass. "Me drinking in your house. Pretend I'm drinking seltzer water."

"I'll do that," Sugar said. "So, how is she?"

"Give me a minute, Daddy, will you?"

Miriam sat down in the chair opposite, kicked off her heels, *clump-clump* on the carpet that covered the hardwood floor. She sighed, averted her face, lifted the glass to her mouth with both hands. The summer skirt rode up at her knees, there were wrinkles working into the hemline, dark spots under the arms of the white satin blouse. Her stockings bagged at the ankles. He knew she would never let herself be seen like this, not by anyone other than himself. It was a message of sorts, from her to him.

"I'm sorry," he said. "You know I can't go there. It gives me the heebie-jeebies, seeing her in the loony bin."

"I know, Daddy."

"Did Mike go with you?"

Miriam shook her head. Her hair had come unpinned, a dark wave covering one eye. "Michael was busy. And he's no help at all, you know that. Acts like he'll catch a disease going in there."

"Like his brother with the polio."

"Something like that, I suppose. It has to do with his mother dying of tuberculosis when he was just a boy. He hates hospitals of any kind. Or that's his excuse."

The music swelled, starting to soar now, but it was losing him, beginning to sound like mere noise from a radio—he was aware of the static, the hum of the vacuum tubes, the coughs from the audience on the sound stage. Aware of the gin in Miriam's glass, of whatever had compelled her to do that, here in his house, in this room.

"You ought to put in air conditioning," she said.

"Gives you a fever," Sugar responded. "Bad for the liver."

"It's the gin that's bad for my liver, Daddy. Not air conditioning."

"Whatever you say." McKane heaved himself up from the chair, walked slowly to the sideboard. His large hands drifted by the gin bottle, closed around the soda syphon. A squirt of charged water in a tall glass, no ice. The sting of the soda bubbles was a stimulant to the mouth, or so he believed. All the pick-me-up a man needed, if his mind was clear. Another of his Rules to Live by.

"Jack Fitzroy was here today," he said.

Miriam did not respond.

"Full of anger, still, at his misfortune." Sugar drained the glass, patted his lips with a hankie. "How well do you know the man?" he asked.

Miriam shrugged. She seemed to have shrunk into herself. He was aware that he was standing between her and the gin, and that if she got up he would move away, give her room. Let her have her way on this special occasion. But she did not move, she did not stir from the chair.

"Mike thinks the world of him," Sugar said. "What do you think?"

"I'm not thinking about much of anything right at the moment."

"Try," said Sugar.

"As you say, Michael likes him."

"I'm interested in your opinion."

"Why?" she said wearily, her expression blank, exhausted.

"Because I've decided to rely on the man. I'd like to know if he can be trusted."

"Ask Michael."

"We're back to that, are we?"

"I'm all used up for now. Maybe later."

Sugar returned to his chair. The symphony had just concluded, and the applause of the studio audience sounded like surf breaking in the distance. Miriam seemed to be waiting, and so he gathered up his strength and said, "How is she?"

"Quiet," Miriam said.

"Oh? Quiet? What does 'quiet' mean, exactly?"

"It means Dee Dee wasn't screaming, Daddy."

Sugar nodded. "That's good, then. You think she's better?"

"That fat little doctor who runs the place thinks she is."

"And you don't?"

Miriam put her head back, closed her eyes. Her voice was flat, deadened. "I don't know," she said. "Really, I couldn't tell. But Dr. Parkay says she's much improved. His words, Daddy. Much improved."

Sugar switched off the radio. "We should be happy then, for Deirdre."

Miriam in her dead voice said: "Why not? Let's be happy."

Eleven

The Shooting Gallery

They were almost at the peak of the first incline, the cars ratcheting upward, when Robby said, ''Can we see Mom from here?'' and tried to stand up, look over the rail of the Cyclone toward the beach. Jack grabbed his collar, yanked him down so hard the kid looked like he was going to cry. More out of surprise than pain. Seven years old and he'd never been spanked by his old man, Doris took care of that. Jack, remembering his father's razor strap, had opted out of the whole business—he didn't want the boys to remember him with his hand in the air. ''Take it easy,'' he said, drawing David tighter, making sure they were both under the safety bar. ''Stand up on this thing, you could get your head taken off.''

''Really, Dad?'' Robby had recovered quickly. ''You could lose your whole head?''

''Sure,'' Jack said uneasily. They were almost at the top now, Revere Beach spread out like a toy along the boardwalk, and he wasn't so sure the roller coaster was a good idea.

''What do they do?'' Robby wanted to know, tugging his sleeve. ''What do they do with all the heads?''

There was just time for Jack to say, ''They keep 'em in the fun house, in jars,'' when the cars went up and over, and suddenly they were falling headlong down the track, wheels screaming, the kids screaming, Jack having a few screams himself. What an incredibly stupid idea, bringing his sons on this contraption. You could feel the tracks shaking with the weight of the cars, hear the fastenings working loose, like the whole thing might explode into kindling.

Somewhere up over the first big turn, riding up so you could see the beach again, glimpse the neat white curl of waves along the shore, David coughed up his frankfurter, a hot mess on his father's neck, no way to clean up until the ride was over.

It seemed to take forever, the cars shaking against the turns, the wind dampening the screams. When the cars slowed on that last incline back into the platform, Robby begged for a repeat ride. Jack said, "Another day maybe," and watched his older boy use the bars to pull himself out of the car, almost doing a chin-up—what a strong little guy—and grinning, as if he hadn't really expected to win another go-around.

"Come on, Dad," he said. "You know what we could do? We could go to the fun house."

"Honey, I need to get a napkin or something," Jack said. David was tugging his hand as they walked away from the roller coaster. Tossing up his lunch hadn't dampened his manic three-year-old energy level one bit.

Robby wanted to run ahead, save a place in line for the fun house. Jack told him to calm down, they were making a pit stop. "What's a pit stop, Dad?" "It's where I sit down for a couple minutes, catch my breath." "I could go in the fun house by myself." "No," Jack said firmly. "I want to rinse off, then we'll think about what to do next."

They sat at a table in Rudy's, the boys drinking from cups of Leary's draft root beer while Jack cleaned himself up. The smell of grilled pepper steaks was so compelling that he regained his appetite, ate a big sloppy pepper steak sandwich while Robby tried to decide what he wanted to do most, go in the penny arcade or the fun house. Jack made it clear it was one or the other.

"I guess the arcade," the boy said. "You can shoot guns in there. Even kids get to shoot guns."

"Who told you that?"

"Mom said so."

"Your mom won't let you shoot cap pistols in the house, isn't that right?"

"In the arcade it's legal," Robby said very solemnly. Obviously he'd given the concept a lot of thought, the weight of law in his own mind.

They passed the Frolics, recorded music trumpeting from loudspeakers. "WOODY HERMAN TONIGHT ADVANCE TICKETS NOW ON SALE" up there on the marquee, and Jack hurried the boys along. He didn't want to answer any silly questions about big bands. It was bad enough that Doris had wanted to go. We could just sit there and listen, she had said, her expression going soft—once upon a time they'd been great dancers. Give her credit, one look from Jack and the campaign ended, she didn't mention it again.

In the arcade he cashed in a dollar, made Robby cup his hands to receive his quota of nickels. "How many, Dad?" "Count 'em yourself, see what you think." "I got *ten whole nickels*, Dad!" Little David tugging, holding his hands out, amazing how he mimicked his older brother, and Jack was ready with pennies, there were still a few of the older games that hadn't gone up to a nickel, tame things that would amuse a three-year-old. Robby so pumped up with excitement he was almost breathless, saying, "Dad! Dad! What can I spend it on?" and Jack tousling his son's soft brown hair, saying, "Anything you want, honey. You decide."

Jack pushed pennies into a dancing marionette machine—it seemed to hold David's attention—while Robby worked his way around the arcade, announcing each time he'd selected a game. Ball Smasher! Pick-Me Up! The Treasure Crane! Jack calling out, "Fine, enjoy yourself," because the boy seemed to be seeking his approval.

The shooting gallery was three shots for a nickel, and Robby insisted that his father go first, handed up one of his sweaty little nickels. "Go on, Dad, I want to see you shoot stuff." This said with such intensity that Jack was given to pause, looking into the dead serious eyes of his oldest son, and he had to wonder, where had *that* come from, this overwhelming desire to see the old man fire a gun?

"I'll bet you can shoot anything, Dad. I'll bet you never miss."

"I don't know about that," Jack said. He raised the light little gun—hell, it only fired a pellet—and missed the first duck, knocked down the next two, ping-ping, no kick to the airgun.

Missing that first duck didn't seem to disappoint Robby, who fumbled out his nickel, insisted that his father show him exactly how to shoulder the gun, and be damned if the kid didn't hit one duck out of three. Little

David screaming with laughter and jumping up and down as he watched his big brother take another three shots, using his last precious nickel, concentrating with a fierceness Jack had never seen in the boy and hitting two out of three ducks this time, as good as his old man, and Jack said it aloud, "As good as your old man," and was truly astonished to see that Robby's eyes were glassy with tears. What had gotten into the boy?

"It doesn't matter," Robby said, taking his father's hand. "Not if you can shoot good."

"What doesn't matter, honey?"

"Your leg. Anybody says anything mean about you, we'll just shoot 'em, Dad."

Jack opened his mouth to reply, thought better of it. What could he say to a seven-year-old boy who had, it was now obvious, a secret mind of his own?

Finally, clear of the arcade, he said, "I'm fine now, do you know that?"

Robby squeezed his hand, kept his eyes downcast.

"We don't need guns," Jack said. "Not as long as you're on my side."

A strange thing happened on the beach. Jack walked right by his wife without recognizing her. This curvy woman in a sun hat, dark glasses, and a tight black swimsuit smiled at him from under a rented umbrella and he smiled back, just a friendly guy on the beach with two kids in tow. Little David kept yanking to get free, and as Jack turned to gather up the boy—where the hell was Doris?—the sand draining into his shoes, weighting the cuffs of his trousers—the curvy woman stood up and he recognized those dimpled knees, the way her hips cocked.

"Jesus," Jack said, letting the boys go so that they could run to the shade of the umbrella, get their toys from the canvas beach bag. "This sun is bright. I couldn't see."

Doris smiled, seeming very pleased with herself. She extended both legs, pointed her feet. "Do you like the new suit?"

"Very nice," he said, still unsettled. Doris unfolded another rental chair and he sat, untied his shoes, feeling the sun on the crown of his head, burning a hole into his brain. What had he been thinking? Who had he expected to see?

"I was going to get one with the little skirt, you know? And then I thought no, I'll try on this *maillot*—that's what it's called, I suppose that's French for something or other. How was the Cyclone?"

He told her about David losing his lunch, vowed he would never take them on that damn rickety ride again. "I swear," he said. "I could feel the boards shaking loose."

"Next time maybe the bumper cars," Doris said. She poured a Dixie cup of lemonade from the Thermos, handed it over. "Go on, drink up," she said. "You look funny."

"Funny?"

"Sick funny."

"I'm fine, Dottie. All those onions on the pepper steak."

"Where'd you go, Rudy's?"

He nodded, drank the tart lemonade, tasted almost like medication but maybe that was just Doris saying sick, made him think of medicine and hospitals. His leg was fine today, maybe a little numb from the exercise, a little slow to respond, he'd had to think about it, making the leg work as he trudged through the sand, but no pain at all. The boys were down at the water's edge with their buckets, Robby on his knees, working on a sand castle, David squatting, watching water come out of his bucket. What a gleeful kid he was, looked a lot like Doris, the shy way he smiled to himself.

"I've got your trunks in the bag, you could change."

"Naw."

"A swim might do you good. A real swim, not that exercise in the pool. I know you hate doing that."

"Just let me sit." As a concession he rolled up his trouser cuffs, worked his bare toes into the hot sand, thought of something to say. "Sugar says I should get a bicycle. And don't scrub the vegetables."

"What?"

He described his visit to the McKane residence, leaving out the poison pen letter, the real reason Sugar had summoned him. Doris had yet to see the inside of the big house—they'd never received a social invitation to the

Hyde Park residence. It had always been business, or something to do with Mike, and Jack was aware of how much his wife resented the exclusion. When she was feeling especially irritated about the social gulf between the two families, Doris called him ''Digger McKane'' or just ''the undertaker,'' although she was well aware that Sugar hadn't been actively involved in the funeral business for twenty years or more. In person, of course, he was charming as hell, and Doris couldn't seem to help herself, she responded to that charm.

''He's given Mike a line of credit,'' Jack said. ''Enough to expand, cover the payroll for a year. The trouble with legwork for lawyers, they don't pay right away, or you have to wait until they settle the case. You know, cash flow.''

''I know what cash flow is, Jack,''

''Well, I'm not sure I do. Anyhow, Sugar has it covered. Mike says give us five good years, we'll be as big as Pinkerton—the office in Boston, anyhow. They're making me an equal partner.''

''They?''

''Mike, I mean.''

''And you don't have to invest?''

''I'm investing my expertise, he says. And my connections on the force. And all the dumb cops I know want to moonlight as investigators. Doug Donnelly is coming on full-time.''

''Yeah? Dougie? He's giving up the pension?'' Doris seemed impressed. Doug was what she would call a level-headed guy, known to all the cop wives as a good husband, which meant he didn't drink much, had never been known to gamble away his pay envelope without calling home first.

''There's a captain he doesn't get along with, maybe it's the best thing,'' Jack said. ''Doug thinks so. Mike wants every man an ex-cop. He says it makes for a better impression with the law firms, like we're a private police department.''

Doris titled her chair back. ''The boys okay?''

''They're fine. David is covered with mud, but he looks happy.''

''It'll rinse off.''

He stole a glance at her, lying back in the chair in her

new swimsuit. Had almost forgotten those nice legs. That was the first thing he'd noticed about her, the slim calves extending from the white ruffled waitress skirt in Brighams, bending down to scoop ice cream. Doris McLaughlin at eighteen, just graduated from high school, she and her mother doing volunteer work for the war effort, helping to promote scrap-metal drives, Jack giving them a hand just so he could be in the same vicinity. Playing grown-up at twenty, he was still something of a kid himself, still working in his father's South End grocery, driving the delivery wagon, his mother by then long dead. He'd first kissed Doris McLaughlin in that old Ford wagon, the smell of bread around them as he cupped her breast. Or was that another time—she'd made him wait, he remembered that now. He'd never touched her there until they were engaged. By then his father was dead, too, and yes, it was right after the old man's funeral it happened, his hand on her breast.

He lay back himself, let the heat of the sun bake his legs. He began to let Miriam flow into his mind. A few minutes later he nudged his wife and said, "I've got to work tonight."

"Oh?"

"For Sugar," Jack said. "A little business problem he's having."

It was amazing how easily he lied.

Twelve

Local Boy Makes Good

Morning on Mount Vernon Street. Miriam was lying in the bathtub with her eyes closed. That perfect, oval face in repose. So peaceful-looking, she could have been asleep except she was humming something, a melody her husband didn't recognize.

Mike Fitzroy watched her in the mirror as he shaved, using a Gillette safety razor. King Gillette, a local boy who had made good, invented a way for a man to clear away his beard with a trembling hand, if necessary. Shake like this with one of those old straight razors, you'd cut your own throat.

"That second cup," he said. "I gotta cut down on the coffee."

"Try cutting down on the whiskey," Miriam said.

Her eyes, he noticed, remained closed.

"One before bed, that's a nightcap."

"Whatever you say."

He liked the way her breasts seemed to float on the water, that fleshy pinkness emerging from the glistening delicacy of the soap bubbles. Funny how she wouldn't always sleep with him but he was allowed in here, watching her bathe, an intimacy that after eight years of marriage still made him feel light-headed.

He rinsed his face, patted dry, and sat on the closed lid of the toilet, partially dressed in trousers and undershirt.

"Look at me, Miriam." When her eyes opened, green and luminous and to him mysterious, he waved hello and said, "Scrub your back?"

"I want to just lie here, Michael."

Her knees like islands above the surface of the water. He couldn't help it: he wondered where exactly her hands were under all the bubble bath, what she was touching.

What she was thinking. He'd given up trying to guess. There was a time when he'd thought he knew what was going on inside Miriam's head; now he figured he'd been kidding himself. What could anyone know about another person? Really know.

"You didn't ask, but it went well," he said, folding his hands in his lap just to keep them still.

"The meeting with Daddy."

"He's been good about the whole thing, really," he said. Meaning the disbarment and all that had followed.

"Daddy promised."

"I know, but—"

"No buts," Miriam said. A small splash as she turned in the water, draping a slim, soapy arm over the rim of the tub. Looking at him now, languid, almost sleepy. "Daddy said he'd come through and he did."

"Yes."

He discovered that it was unsettling, at this particular moment, to be reminded that her eyes were shaped like Sugar's eyes, if you looked hard enough, imagined them darker, older.

"I was reading in the paper," he said, glancing away, focusing on the sink, "that Russian spy they got. Eisler?"

"What about him?" said Miriam, apparently interested.

"Nothing about him, exactly," Mike said. "It made me think of the Russians. You know they have a thing they call a five-year plan?"

Miriam nodded. He was aware of soap suds dripping from her fingertips, pooling not an inch from his bare feet.

"I was thinking it's not a bad idea, planning five years ahead. That's what we're doing, with the firm."

"The firm?"

Miriam said it in such a way it convinced him she wasn't taking him seriously. When that happened he had a tendency to talk faster, trying to make his case. Mike was aware of this reaction—he'd learned a lot about himself in the last eight years, the precise limitations of his pride—but he couldn't help it. He still wanted to sell her on the idea, he wanted Miriam on his side.

"I could petition the bar for reinstatement next year, you know," he said. "I doubt I'll bother. That's how confident I am, we can make this work. With Sugar behind us, get us rolling. These old gumshoe outfits, they're so limited—no competition. All they got, a few warm bodies, real plodders, the best they can manage is going door to door, take a few notes. Most of the stuff they get hold of can't even be used in court. For instance, their idea, a deposition—I'm talking these old-style guys now, the hats—they depose a witness, some civil case—they stand there and threaten the witness, like it was a felony case and they're still on the cops. So of course the witness gets on the stand, denies the substance of the transcript, it was under duress or whatever, and the attorney who paid for the deposition is left holding the bag. The thing is, unlike these old-timers, we know what we're doing, how to get it right in court. Depositions, locating the hostile witness, I figure that alone will account for twenty-five percent minimum, our billings.''

He was aware of how his words were tumbling, sounding hard and urgent against the tile surface of the walls. There was a time when Miriam said she loved to hear him talk—she was a woman used to hearing a man talk, a great man—and he'd basked in the idea of his words alive in the same way that Sugar's language came alive. Now, sneaking glances at Miriam perched sideways in the white porcelain tub, her pale hip showing above the water, an expression on her face that was so neutral, so uninvolved it made the breath tight in his chest, it made him want to talk even faster, win her undivided attention, that particular look in her eye that meant they were connected.

''The thing is, we can deliver the goods,'' he said. ''Jack, he runs an investigation, it's really beautiful, airtight. I mean a work of art. The kid hadn't been a detective, he would have made a great lawyer. Sometimes he intimidates, or he gets very cool, but whatever it takes he asks the right questions. He gets everything down there, the transcript, which of course is what the job is all about, right? This service we provide.''

''If you say so,'' Miriam responded. Now her fingers were tapping the side of the tub, keeping the beat to that melody she'd been humming, the one he didn't recognize.

''All I'm saying, we can do the job better than anybody else currently in the business. Better than Pinkerton—we've already proved that, the Hannaford case. No comparison in size, not yet, but like I say, the five-year plan. Five years we'll be billing out as many hours as Pinkerton. You know the reason? They're just a regional office. The guy in charge, he'd rather be in New York or Chicago, that's his focus.''

Miriam said, ''I've never been to Chicago.''

''And the regular, grind-it-out detective work?'' Mike said, ignoring the Chicago jibe. ''The bread-and-butter stuff? We've got some of the top guys coming aboard. Doug Donnelly? Skinny little bald guy, doesn't look like a cop, but you turn him loose in a neighborhood, every housewife gives him coffee and donuts, I guess they want to fatten him up—and if there's information pertains to the investigation, Doug gets it. Pinkerton, one of these other outfits? They could put ten guys in there, that little neighborhood, they couldn't get what Doug gets in an hour. This time next year we'll have a dozen guys of that caliber, another five or six doing nothing but divorce work. Hale and Barney, they specialize in big-money divorce, they've already given us a couple of cases, sending over another file this morning. We keep getting results, they'll give us all we can handle.'' Mike paused, took a deep breath, found the courage to look his wife right in the eye, a searching look, he didn't know exactly what he expected to find there. Something, anything. ''So anyhow, Miriam, that's my five-year plan.''

She turned, splashed, still contriving not to let him see her pubes. She'd gotten shy about that, just lately. ''Michael Fitzroy a communist.'' she said. ''I better tell my congressman. Can a wife testify against her husband? 'He sat right there on the loo, Your Honor, and told me about his five-year plan he'd gotten from the Russians.' ''

''You don't call a congressman 'Your Honor,' '' Mike said. ''Look, about lunch, I was thinking Locke-Ober.''

Miriam sat up in the tub, shook her head. ''But I'm getting my hair done at Carado's,'' she said. ''Can't we go someplace nearby? Please?''

There, he'd finally come up against something she cared about. Where they had lunch.

''Anything you want,'' he said, trying not to look at the slick wetness of her breasts, feeling, for some reason, just a little sick. ''Name the place.''

Thirteen

Snake Pit

In the dim basement corridors under Boston Police Headquarters the walls were sweating. Jack Fitzroy could feel that moisture of condensed, street-level heat slick underfoot as he trudged carefully along, balancing two cardboard cups of coffee and a bag of sugar crullers. The smell down here, that hadn't changed. A musty pong of carbon paper, mimeograph fluid, old newspapers. All the files down here being slowly consumed by bacteria mold, or whatever it was that ate paper and ink, turned things old and crumbly.

He came to a familiar door, pushed it open with his right foot, slipped through before the closer wheezed shut. "Hey, Danny?" Jack put the coffee down on a counter clogged with evidence bags and envelopes.

A toilet flushed. A moment later Detective Daniel Stearn emerged from around a partition, checking his fly. His expression was blank, the mask he wore for strangers, and it wasn't until Jack grinned and held up the bag of crullers that Danny Stearn recognized him.

"Sorry, Jack. By God, you look healthy. I was expecting—" Stearn paused, uncomfortable, and ran a hand through his wiry red hair.

"You were expecting a wheelchair or crutches," Jack said. "And here I am, fit as a fiddle."

Danny picked up the coffee cup, sniffed to see was the cream fresh. "I heard you were a goner. Paralysis, the whole bit. Then they said your brother gave you a job. I figured, you know, in the office."

Danny Stearn had been made a forensics detective because of his college degree in organic chemistry and because with his freckled complexion, blue eyes, and red hair he'd been mistaken for an Irishman. He was, as everybody in the department now knew, a Jew, and damn lucky to have got on the cops through such an outrageous subterfuge of confused appearance. As the butt of many kike jokes he often responded, somewhat wearily, that his ancestors had migrated from County Jerusalem, which always got a big laugh. Stearn had a reputation for remaining unruffled while giving expert testimony, no matter how acrimonious the defense attorney—he was a man at all times deeply in control of himself. Few were aware, as Jack Fitzroy was, that Danny Stearn had applied for a position in the FBI crime labs and been rejected after a background check revealed that hair color was no guarantee of ethnic integrity.

"I'm fine now," Jack said. "A miracle recovery. I guess you were praying for me, hey, Danny?"

Stearn selected a cruller, licked the sugar before taking a bite. He watched as Jack withdrew an envelope from his breast pocket and dropped it on the counter. "Prints?" he said.

Jack shook his head. "The suspect has been identified. I just want to know, did the same guy write both notes?"

Stearn slowly munched the pastry, sipped his coffee as he contemplated the two handwriting samples. The threatening letter forwarded from the newspaper and the Pledge of Allegiance penned, under duress, by William Drake of East Boston.

"This guy," he said, tapping the Pledge. "He's in school? What is this, his homework?"

"Could be," Jack said. "See where he copied it twice? That's in case he was trying to make it look different."

"So he knew you were getting a sample?"

"I think he did, yes. Does that make a difference?"

Danny used a paper napkin to clean his hands, his eyes never straying from the two notes. "It might, he was a master forger maybe. Which he obviously isn't. I had to guess, I'd say he was scared shitless when he wrote this. See how the pen almost cut through the paper?"

"What about the other letter?" Jack said.

"Different hand," Danny said immediately. "Another person altogether."

"You're sure?"

Danny nodded. "You knew that already."

"Yeah, but I wanted to hear you say it. Can you tell

anything about whoever wrote this?'' he asked, indicating the threatening letter.

Stearn studied the letter again. ''My best guess? A woman, definitely a female hand. And that old spiky style hasn't been taught in public school for forty years, so she has to be what, at least fifty?''

''Anything else?''

''Yeah,'' Danny said. ''She hates Sugar McKane.''

At two in the afternoon Jack bought a ticket for *The Snake Pit,* starring Olivia de Havilland, at an air-conditioned theater in Scollay Square. A cartoon was playing as he climbed the stairs to the balcony, sounded like Bugs Bunny going nuts, a lot of guns going off. The muffled thud, maybe it was anti-aircraft fire, a war cartoon. He got to the top of the stairs, saw Elmer Fudd dressed like a hunter, and thought, *Oh yeah, shotgun.*

Miriam was waving a white hat from an inside aisle, way back against the wall. Not too many customers here in the muggy dark of the balcony, where the air conditioning had plainly failed. Jack shrugged off his suit jacket, folded it over his arm before taking a seat next to Miriam.

''You know what?'' she whispered. ''Popcorn smells like dirty socks, you ever notice that?''

The cartoon segment was over and a March of Time newsreel was playing, cutting from Harry Truman in the White House to diplomats gathered around a table in Europe, something about the North Atlantic nations standing together against the reds. Made it sound like another war in the making, but Jack had his doubts—that was just the way newsreels liked to play it, make everything dramatic. He'd seen a newsreel crew in Germany actually yanking corpses around, improving on a scene—dead wasn't dead until they had the bodies just so. It was all fake, he'd realized, even the combat footage, once it came out of the camera.

Miriam kissed him and he tasted gin.

''So you had lunch with him, huh?'' he said, surprised to find he was not really in the mood, physically. The climb up three flights of stairs had taken the wind out of his sails.

"You know where? This little seafood joint on Tremont Street, you could see into the kitchen."

"Let me guess," Jack said. "Dini's Grill. A lot of fat-cat politicians? Mike loves that place."

"Yeah, well, he never took me there before," Miriam said, settling against him. "I nixed Locke-Ober, so I figure the fish was punishment."

Jack adjusted, slipped his arm around her slim shoulders. "I don't think so. He was showing you off. Sugar's beautiful daughter."

Miriam nudged him. "Shut up and kiss me."

That was a line from another movie, another theater. Joan Crawford, or was it Bette Davis? Didn't matter, it was Miriam's line now. He did as he was told, no longer aware of the gin taste of her mouth but unable to shake the picture of his brother in Dini's Grill, shaking hands and slapping backs on the way to his table, that was a given. The picture going out of focus as Miriam's hands moved under his shirt, teased the tuft of hair on his stomach, and finally he began to relax, letting everything in his head fade away. Mike in the grill, working the pols, that was another world. They were safe in the cloying dark, nothing counted here, it was all make-believe.

"There's this other movie playing down the street," Miriam was saying, sliding away from his lips. "*Sexcapade*. Maybe we should have gone in there."

"You wouldn't like it, believe me. A place like that, it doesn't smell like popcorn or old socks."

"You'd know, huh?"

"I know everything," he said. His hands—it was amazing really, how his hands had a mind of their own—were working the buttons on her blouse, encountering an inner layer of silk.

"You think anyone can see us?" she whispered. "I don't care if they do."

Her skirt was tight, keeping her knees close together. He suggested she take off her nylons, and Miriam said, you do it for me. Her breath hot under his chin and her hands quiet now, not touching him. The feature film was on, faces as big as the sides of buildings, and he had to keep looking around by the light of the movie, making sure they were really alone, or alone enough. Miriam not helping at all, but making it clear she wanted him to do everything, letting herself go limp in her seat.

His fingers, unclipping her garter snaps, encountered latex rubber.

"You're wearing a girdle," he said, surprised.

The last time they'd done this in a theater balcony, she'd been wearing nothing underneath, had gone into the ladies' room and stuffed it all in her purse. He could see just enough of her expression to know this was supposed to be a game, the girdle.

"You're a clever man," she said, squeezing his hand with her thigh muscles. "Find a way."

The prolonging, he discovered, the effort required to fight his way through the layers of clothing, it all added to the urgency. And not only himself: Miriam was slick and wet and biting her lips to keep from groaning when they finally joined on the sticky floor, crammed between seats, their movements restricted into a kind of unbearable, cramped tightness. Jack so out of breath by the time they were done that he felt faint and woozy, his knees trembling as he slipped back into his seat, hardly enough strength in his hands to buckle his belt.

"Jesus," he said, "like kids. Your skirt must be ruined."

"I'll buy another," she said. "Change before I go home."

It was ridiculous, he knew, considering what he'd just been doing, but the phrase *before I go home* made him feel even more out of breath, as if there wasn't enough air in the theater, in the whole city. After a while the feeling passed, and he realized that he did not feel dirty or depraved. The breathlessness was the same thing he'd experienced running a track race at English High: the exhilaration of finishing, that's what made his heart slam against his ribs. Himself inside his brother's wife was like crossing into a room of secrets so terrible, so awesome, that he couldn't concentrate on anything but the feeling of being alive.

Beside him, Miriam quivered. He saw that she was staring at the screen, that she had been disturbed by something in the movie.

"What's wrong?" he said.

Miriam covered her face and said, "Get me out of here, please?" Her voice had tightened.

He got her up standing, brushed and straightened her clothing as best he could. Going down the balcony stairs she clung to him, and he had just a glimpse of Olivia de Havilland, huge on the screen, struggling in a strait-jacket, her giant movie star eyes blazing with madness: spectacularly, beautifully insane.

Outside, in the full light of a June afternoon, the noise and fumes of Scollay Square, he said, "What is it, you're worried about your sister, Deirdre?"

The slap caught him by surprise. Hard enough to make his face sting, his eyes water.

"Idiot," Miriam said before bursting into tears, falling back into his arms, "don't you know I only worry about me?"

Fourteen

The Taste of Ink

Irene Drake woke up on the floor, her cheek burning with the short burr of the old burgundy wool rug. The rug smelled of socks and feet and the perfume of her lying there—it wasn't the first time she'd laid down on the rug for a little nap and come to in the early hours of the morning, her thoughts jumbled up with her dreams.

What woke her, she decided, was the propeller drone of an airplane. That familiar insect noise of wings buzzing against glass. Mostly she never noticed except sometimes the noise invaded her sleep. Something about her dead son Roy tapping his fingers against the window, wanting to come in out of the rain. *Let me in, Ma, I'll be good.*

Roy who could not rest because he had been murdered, his beautiful face eaten by crabs.

Irene rolled over and sat up. This was her bedroom, crammed with furniture from the big house. The four-poster—a wedding gift—and the small upholstered divan that used to be in the music room of the big house, the mahogany linen chest, the burled-oak wardrobe, the three-mirrored vanity, the knee-hole secretary desk, the matched rockers, the set of upholstered chairs stacked there in the corner these last few years, since the day himself had died, all of it jammed into a space that always made her feel anxious with the weight of things.

Huffing and out of breath, for she was a large, big-hipped woman of fifty, Irene hooked her left hand on the arm of the heaviest upholstered chair and hauled herself to her feet. Right, she'd been at her desk, sipping her medicine and composing a new letter to the newspapers when the need to lie down had overwhelmed her.

The desk lamp remained on, illuminating the mottled green felt and the pile of newspaper clippings. Irene went to the desk, drew back the chair, and sat down. Medicine in the lower right-hand drawer. She poured a generous dollop of Mr. Boston brandy into the tooth glass and sat back in the chair, breathing heavily through her nose.

The clippings were of a single subject, taken mostly from the *Transcript.* The dishonorable Sugar McKane. The great orator, hypocrite, and liar. In one of the accompanying photographs Sugar was shaking hands with a South Boston fire chief, the both of them pretending that the check McKane had just presented was for the welfare of widows and children, a likely story indeed. Among the clippings were political columns mentioning Sugar, usually in the context of a nominating procedure or election. A meeting of the Ancient Order of Hibernians was documented, and a portion of Sugar's lecture on ''Clean Living & the Rewards of Abstention'' was reproduced. One already yellowed clipping showed a grinning, formally attired Sugar about to enter Symphony Hall, having contributed generously toward the purchase of a new concert piano that cost more than an average house, and certainly more than the house Irene now occupied. Not all the stories and articles mentioned Sugar by name. Many of them merely documented his pervasive and corrupt influence. Notices of auction and foreclosure, funeral notices emanating from the Costello Funeral Homes, police logs noting the arrest of Irish thugs and criminals—all clipped or sometimes torn in rage from the newsprint, pieces of the puzzle.

Irene sipped her medicine—she believed it lowered her blood pressure—and stroked her fingertips over the green felt of the desktop until the brandy brought, as it always did, a certain inner clarity.

More was required than merely writing letters of accusation to various newspaper editors, all of whom were undoubtedly secretly employed by the ward boss Mc-Kane. Somehow she had to find a way to haunt him, as her own son was haunting her, in dreams of crab-chewed fingers tapping the rain-spattered window glass.

Calmly and deliberately she selected a clipping. Sugar at Symphony Hall. Look at him holding his ridiculous old-fashioned top hat, smiling with his strong animal teeth. Look into his newsprint eyes and you saw nothing, it was like falling off a cliff.

Irene tore a strip from the newsprint, rolled it up into a ball, and placed the ball in her mouth. She swallowed it. She tore another strip, and another, swallowing, swallowing, until the clipping was gone, consumed.

See a demon and eat him, this was her secret new religion.

Fifteen

Polaroids

A day in June, streets blurred with heat, the Fenway green and blooming, dinghies on the river, sails white in the sunlight. Jack came into the office aware that his hair was wet and smelling of chlorine—it wouldn't come clean in the feeble shower. Twenty laps at the Y, kicking the weakness from his legs, he'd find himself pulling mostly with his arms, the antiseptic bleach stinging his eyes, filling his nose. He hated the pool, hated the need for special exercise. Like homework, do it or suffer the detention hall of pain.

In the shaded office suite of the newly renamed Fitzroy Security, a cooling breeze from the window fan, the smell of coffee. Rosemary was not at her desk, the switchboard was unattended. He could hear the commotion of Mike's voice from the inner office. Laughter. A crowd in there, being charmed and entertained from the sound of it.

First things first. Jack tapped a mug of perked coffee from the urn, added a cube of sugar. Then entered, the mug raised hot to his mouth, and was blinded by a flash of light. Stars in his eyes and his brother saying, ''Hey, Jack, that was beautiful! Sixty seconds, boys, start counting.''

Mike, gadget-oriented ever since Jack could remember, had bought himself a new toy. The suddenly famous Poloroid instant camera, you couldn't open a paper without seeing the ads, turn on a radio without hearing that smarmy, know-it-all voice pitching Dr. Land's incredible invention.

Jack, curious despite the spot of coffee on his shirt, watched in good humor as his blurred image was unpeeled, releasing a faint chemical smell.

''What's the trick, Snap? How does it work?''

Mike was conferring with Clarence ''Snap'' Edwards,

a police photographer who'd retired early to join the firm. The firm, yes, that's what Mike called it and that's how Jack thought of it, too, this new enterprise financed with Sugar's money and Sugar's network of connections.

"It's all in the film," Snap said. Dark and big-gutted, with Arthur Godfrey racoon pouches under his eyes, he had the Polaroid brochure in hand, seemed more interested in the printed material than the camera itself. "Like a miniature darkroom in each film packet," he said, reading. "Patented, of course."

Rosemary Phelan, her tightly permed hair the color of gun metal, was inspecting an instant photo of herself surprised, as Jack had been. "I can't see the resemblance," she said, touching her penciled-in eyebrows. "This is a goldfish, maybe. This is not me."

"Can you use it on the job?" Jack said, indicating the expensive camera.

"Maybe," Edwards said, eyeing Mike, his new, untested boss. Snap had been hired for his expertise in photographic and electronic surveillance, an absolute necessity in the settlement of high-income matrimonial disputes. Motel work, he called it, and best accomplished with an assortment of telephoto lenses, wire recorders, and crystal microphones, most of the gear courtesy of the Boston Police Department, out the back door as Snap retired, making himself a useful present. "Use it for effect, I guess, show 'em what we got," he said, tapping the brochure. "The shysters'll still want clear, indentifiable shots of the parties involved. And negatives, too, just for insurance."

Mike put down the camera, brushed back his thinning hair. A gesture Jack recognized as prelude to big brother speaking his mind, getting serious. "Snap?" Mike said. "Dougie? Tony? This is important."

Doug Donnelly, until last week a detective with the Lost and Stolen Property unit, picked his skinny butt up from the desk where he'd been perched, a moist Polaroid print curling in his hand. Bright and witty, a talented clown in social situations, Donnelly had for a time been Jack's closest pal on the cops, and had risked leaving the force largely on Jack's assurance that the firm, backed as it was by Sugar's political machine, would make good.

Today Doug looked a little worried. His large, pale

gray eyes squinting, his expression tight and self-contained. Having, Jack surmised, second thoughts about the big move. He and his wife were trying to adopt an infant girl—it was a tricky thing, giving up the security of an eventual city pension. Made somewhat easier, Doug had readily admitted, by an immediate raise of fifteen hundred a year.

Tony was Anthony Grazi, who'd quit homicide to sign up with the Fitzroy brothers. Grazi was a small, dapper man with large hands who'd transferred from the Irish-dominated arson bureau of the city fire department, believing an Italian-American would get a better shot with the elite homicide unit. Grazi had realized his mistake almost immediately when he was made official translator of, as it was known in the department, ''guinea gossip'' extracted from North End snitches. A third-generation native of Cambridge, where his father was chief custodian of Harvard's medical school, Tony Grazi knew enough Italian to order from a menu, that was it. If all went as planned, he'd be handling arson and fraud investigations for the insurance companies.

Mike, having got the attention of his new employees, made his pitch: ''I know you've all heard me refer to my legal brethren as shysters. Which a lot of them are, the bastards. But from this moment on I want us all to stop using the word. This firm is billing several very prestigious law firms, and it wouldn't do, they think we think they're shysters. So, please, make it *attorney-at-law* or just plain *attorney*. And the staff here, you're all investigators, okay? I don't want to hear the work *dick* or even *detective*. Investigator, or if you want to sound really impressive, security consultant.''

Snap looked pleased, preened by sucking in his gut. ''Hey, I never heard that one. Security consultant? So now I'm a security consultant?''

''Surveillance expert,'' Mike said with a grin. ''That's your specialty. And that's what it'll say on your business card.''

Dougie had a look, Jack read it like this: *Who are you kidding, a business card is equal to a detective's shield? Come on.* And the fact was, they'd all given up the potent magic of the badge, the buzzer, the flip-it-open power of the police fraternity. This way was a different way, no call boxes on convenient lampposts for Fitzroy investigators, no slack-jawed astonishment when doors cracked open to blues and nightsicks.

Snap and Doug and Tony and others to be hired in the coming weeks would learn, as Jack had learned, that private cops were not cops at all. In low moments he knew himself to be an errand boy for well-dressed lawyers; at best a kind of go-between, carrying vulgar intelligence for interested parties. Basic equipment: cop instincts, the ability to take legible notes, and a sturdy pair of legs. Jack had two out of three and he was working on the third, doing his goddamn homework in the goddamn YMCA pool. Making the best of it.

"Okay, lecture's over," Mike was saying, folding up the camera. "Rosemary has your assignments. Get out there and earn us some money." He caught Jack's eye and said, "Hang on, will you?"

When the others had left the inner office, Mike slipped behind his desk, loosened his belt a notch. "I think maybe I'm getting an ulcer," he said, sounding puzzled.

"So cut down on the booze."

Mike gave him a sly look. "That's what Miriam says."

"Smart girl."

"Yeah, she's all of that." Mike sighed, his hands gently massaging his belly under his starched white shirt. "Listen, I got a call from Sugar last night. For some reason he's got this impression you're not taking his problems seriously."

"That's bull, Michael, and you know it. I got Bob Cogan to scare the piss out of that kid."

"Yeah, well, I guess he got another letter, Sugar did. I think you better go over, make him happy."

"He wants me out there, Hyde Park? Right now, I suppose, when I've got a hundred better things to do."

Mike nodded. "Humor him, would you, Jack?"

Jack started to speak his mind on the subject, thought better of it.

"I'll do what I can."

Jack parked by the carriage house and walked into the garden, expecting to find McKane tending his rose bushes, or making compost, or whatever the hell it was he did out back. It was getting on toward noon and the light was blinding, broken into rainbows by the mist of sprinklers.

"Sugar?" Jack lighted a cigarette, a new menthol brand that managed the trick of tasting hot and cool at once. He heard a window crack like a pistol shot behind him, and he turned, startled into a fit of coughing.

"Up here, my boy!"

Sugar's voice emanated from a silhouetted figure at the window, the light behind him, glinting off the brightness of glass. Jack sighed, trudged to the flight of stone steps that went from the sloping garden up to the main, street-level floor. A puff of menthol for each step, a small act of defiance. He was surprised, really, at how little it bothered him, advancing up the steps. An electrical twinge, nothing that qualified as pain. Not real pain.

The side door was open, the screen unlatched. Jack let it snap behind him, felt the wind of it ruffling the damp hair at the back of his neck. Sugar lumbered into the kitchen exactly as Jack entered, grinning hugely and clapping his big hands together, as if Jack was an intimate friend returning from a long, arduous journey.

"Mrs. Riley is preparing sandwiches," he said, searching for Jack's hand, enclosing it briefly with his own two hands, cool and dry.

At one time McKane had employed a full staff of household servants, including a shuffling leprechaun of a man who'd been trained in Dublin as a butler. After his wife's death, in the year his daughter Miriam had married, Sugar had let them go, found them other situations, retaining only a single housekeeper. Mrs. Riley was new to the position, an apple-cheeked widow from Southie whose late husband had some vague relationship to Sugar or his business partners, the Costello brothers. Cheerful, bright, and efficient, she was, in Jack's opinion, an improvement on the previous housekeeper, Annie O'Hare, a furtive old woman whose arthritic fingers seemed perpetually entwined in her rosary beads, and whose brogue was so cream-clotted with the homeland that Jack could never quite make out her rambling, self-directed conversations. The old bat had recently been "let go," was all Sugar would say about her, and good riddance.

Lunch was served in the kitchen alcove, which had a

view of the garden. Jack sitting in the walnut dinette booth opposite his host, who poured glasses of lemonade from a frosted pitcher, having squeezed the lemons himself, as he was quick to point out.

"I leave it with just a tang of bitter." McKane indicated the sugar bowl. "Don't be shy if you want it sweeter."

"This is fine," Jack said after taking a sip, feeling the clean sting of it spread through his mouth.

The sandwiches were ham and cheese, with the bread fresh baked and cut thick by Mrs. Riley. "The woman is a wonder," Sugar said, loud enough to be heard in the pantry, where the housekeeper was stocking a delivery of S.S. Pierce canned goods. "Maybe I'll marry her and save the salary," he added, winking elaborately. From the pantry came a peal of laughter, pleased and flattered.

Jack knew better than to raise the subject of Sugar's concern here, where they could be overheard. Instead he talked of his two boys, Robby and David, and Dot's plans for summer. This year they would return to the beach cottage, a welcome resumption of family tradition after last season's disaster with Jack in the hospital and Doris, fearing the worst, hunkered with the boys in the heat of the three-decker.

"A fine woman," Sugar said. He had stopped chewing and swallowed. A careful eater and never a man to be seen with food in his open mouth. "I get the impression she doesn't like me."

Jack hesitated before responding. "Dottie is shy," he said.

Sugar held up his hand, shook his head. "I'd never hold it against her, not liking me. There's many that feel the same way, Jack, including yourself."

Jack almost choked on his ham, felt the spicy mustard burning in his nose. Where was this coming from? Surely Sugar McKane didn't care a damn for the regard of Jack Fitzroy and wife.

Sugar said, "I've found this often to be true: there are those I regard with great fondness who curdle at the sight of me." He smiled, daintily wiped his large jaw with the corner of a linen napkin. "You might say it is my curse," he added. "More lemonade?"

"I'm fine, Sugar. Jesus."

A look, reminding him that blasphemy was forbidden in this place.

"I mean jeepers," Jack said, making a face. "Jeepers creepers, is that okay? I mean, can I say that here?"

"I say it myself," Sugar said. They were sitting close enough so that Jack could smell the meat and yeast on his breath, and something else, some deeper, aging smell, not unpleasant. "I knew a man of that name. Jeepers McGee. Ruined by horses."

"I heard of him," Jack said, embracing this new subject. "He owned a saloon in Scollay Square."

"I owned it," Sugar said. "Jeepers ran it for me."

Jack sat back against the warm wood of the booth. "You owned a bar? But you're a teetotaler."

Sugar shook his head slowly. "Jack, Jack. A man can own a saloon and not drink liquor. As it happens, Jeepers ruined saloons for me. Had his hand in the till."

"The horses."

"The very same. He stole from me and gave it to four-legged animals. And when he died, I buried him just as grand as can be. You can steal from Sugar McKane, but you can't make him disrespect the dead. Not in an election year. Which it was."

Jack, thinking they'd got away from the uncomfortable subject of Sugar's unpopularity with Doris, or with himself, asked who had won the election.

"The incumbent," Sugar said. "James Michael Curley. He's another of those who dislike me."

Jack grimaced. His stomach clenched as he remembered his brother's admonition to humor McKane, who seemed determined to stir up trouble.

"You've always backed candidates against him," Jack said. "So the mayor has a pretty good reason to, um, dislike you. He hates all the ward bosses, and they hate him. Been that way for years."

The big head nodded, black bushy eyebrows cocked wild, drawing Jack to the clear darkness of his eyes, cunning animal eyes in a large human face. "Exactly my point. Curley has a reason to despise me, but you do not. No logical reason. What have I done to earn this enmity, can you answer?"

"Sugar, please . . ."

"No. You listen. I've taken your brother into my

bosom, loved him like a son. Presumably you love him, too. But ever since Michael had his little troubles, you've looked at me with loathing.''

''Little troubles?'' Jack's heart was thudding, his hands weak, trembling, the sure signs of his temper rising. ''Mike was disbarred, Sugar, on account of some scheme of yours. I believe you forged a property deed, isn't that right?''

''I did, yes,'' he said. ''A business miscalculation. But when Michael took it upon himself to cover for me, did I turn away from my responsibility? No, I did not. Does Michael hate me for the shame of his disbarment? No, he does not. Why, then, should you?''

Jack got a hold of the black rising, closed the fist of his mind around it, forced himself to be calm. ''You want us to be friends. Is that what you want?''

Sugar was quiet for a moment. He looked away, focused through the window to his garden, bee-full and blooming in the new heat of June. ''What I want is this: that you not sit at my table and sneer at me. That you not twist my name into a word that sounds, from your mouth, contemptuous.''

Jack pushed his plate away, the sandwich half eaten. ''I'll try,'' he said.

''Not an unreasonable request, given the circumstance.''

''No,'' Jack said. ''Tell you the truth, Sugar, I didn't think you cared what I thought.''

''Well, there you're wrong because I do. We needn't be friends—you can't force a friendship—but I require something less than revulsion from you. I require, at the very least, respect.''

''You've got that,'' Jack said. ''You've always had that.''

The big man turned his bulk from the window. ''Have I?''

''Sure. You scare the hell out of me, Sugar, you always have.''

''Fear is not respect.''

''You've got that, too. I know who you are, what you can do.''

''I don't want your fear, Jack. You have no reason to

fear me. None whatever. And in any case I don't believe it, not for a minute. You never feared me, or anyone.''

Jack shrugged. ''I said you scared the hell out of me, sometimes. That's maybe not quite the same thing as fear.''

''No,'' Sugar said. ''It is not. If you're not sure of a word, Jack, you should take the time to look it up.''

Jack couldn't help it, he laughed. This was too much, getting the dictionary lecture from Sugar McKane. His great belief in vocabulary builders, the possibilities of self-education. That unshakable certainty of McKane's that his way was the best way, the only way, and that to deviate or doubt was somehow immoral, or at the very least unintelligent. How had Miriam, living from moment to moment, come from this man, this house, this garden of fixed beliefs?

''Who are you backing this time,'' Jack asked, ''against His Honor the mayor?''

Sugar made a sound in his nose, as if he'd smelled something offensive, pursed his lips with a bad taste. ''I may keep out of it altogether this year,'' he said. ''Sonny McDonough has come sniffing around, he wants me to buy him a truck with a loudspeaker device. The idea being that no one can escape voting for him if he makes enough noise.''

''That's it, Sonny McDonough? He's the only one with guts enough to run against Curley in the primary?''

Sugar laced his fingers together, as if in prayer, raised his chin, improving his already upright posture. ''The scandal of James Michael Curley has exhausted the party,'' he said. ''Sonny is the best we can do, and that is a very sad failing indeed. If the do-gooders put up a reform candidate, they'll win. Unless Curley finds a way to steal it—and those vote-stealing days are mostly over. He's an old man who lives for trouble, Jack, and he's had his way for so long he's worn us all out.''

Jack understood that by ''us'' McKane meant the ward bosses who had opposed Curley from the very beginning of his career, because he had threatened to end their patronage system and replace it with one of his own, a threat he had made good on over the years. ''You sound like you're ready to retire,'' Jack said. ''Give up the party.''

McKane made a gesture of dismissal. ''Not at all. But

I'll focus my attention elsewhere, to others in need. Congress, the governor, the state assembly. Let the liar Curley play mayor one last time, if he can. If not, so be it. There'll be no tears for him in this house.''

Feeling himself safely away from more sensitive areas, Jack wanted to keep the subject on politics. ''You should run yourself,'' he said. ''Show the mayor who's the real boss.''

He'd expected Sugar to be flattered. Instead he bristled, a man deeply insulted. ''Swim in that sewer? He'd be calling me the Undertaker, you know, in his very first radio broadcast. Digger McKane, that's what he called me years ago, and he never forgets his own insults. Nor would it matter I haven't been actively in the funeral business for all these many years. Oh yes, his dishonorable Honor would have a fine time with the likes of me. Remember what he did to poor Tom Eliot? Have you ever seen that mouth of his up close? Those Curley lips? It makes me shudder to think where that mouth has been, the lies it has spawned. Never, ever would I put myself in that position, Jack, to have that foul little man's foul little mouth making lies against me. Never.''

''My mistake,'' Jack said uneasily.

''My road was chosen long ago,'' Sugar said, his voice in full stage resonance, almost rattling the ice cubes melting in the pitcher, and certainly rattling Jack's peace of mind, such as it was. ''I have acted selflessly in these matters, for the sake of the party, for the sake of the city, the state, the Commonwealth. Indeed, I've always tried to act for the good of the nation, Jack. Can you believe that of me?''

''Sure, of course.''

Sugar opened his mouth, ready for another rush of rhetoric, then thought better of it, his great teeth snapping shut, cutting himself off. ''You touched a nerve there, Jack Fitzroy.''

''I guess.''

''Never mind. Come into my parlor, said the spider to the fly. We've got some sticky business to attend to.''

As Jack got up to follow, he could hear the rustle of Mrs. Riley's apron in the pantry, the click of canned goods set in place. Sugar's ''parlor'' was the walnut-paneled library where he kept his gramophones and his radio and the grand piano that had never, to Jack's knowledge, been played by anyone since McKane's wife had passed away, taking with her the only real musical talent in the family.

Sugar went directly to a rolltop desk, unlocked it, and withdrew a piece of paper from a pigeon hole. Gravely he handed it over. "Forwarded by a smirking fellow from the *Boston Post*." he said.

> *If you pursist in ignoring the evidence that the ward boss McKane is a murdering, thieving, raping monster, something terrible will happen. Does McKane or the Irish Jews own this newspaper, is that why you won't print what he did? The cops know what he did make them say it or else whatever happens is your fault.*

"I think it's the same hand," Jack said. "I can find out."

"I don't care whose hand it is. Just take care of it."

Jack folded the paper, slipped it into his pocket. "I checked out the boy you mentioned, Bill Drake, and got a handwriting sample. He didn't write the other letter, I doubt he wrote this. Most likely the writer is a middle-aged woman, so they tell me."

Sugar loomed closer, his expression unreadable in the dimness of the library. "I don't care who it is, just make it stop."

"You could file a complaint, have the police investigate."

"I don't want the police brought into this, Jack, I thought I made that clear. The mayor gets wind of this, he won't let go, not in an election year. You know how he likes to run against the big bad ward bosses. You just take care of it for me, that's a good lad."

"I'll do what I can."

McKane's massive hands were suddenly on Jack's shoulders, gently kneading the poplin of his summer-weight suit jacket. "Not what you can, Jack. Whatever is necessary. That's a very different thing. If you don't believe me, look it up."

Sixteen

They All Scream for Ice Cream

There was music on the grounds of the Parkay Clinic, the fine, sweet music of stringed instruments, and if you stared hard enough you could actually see the music in the air, flowing like honey.

This is what Miss Deirdre McKane believed as she lay on her bed, peering through a corner of the window where she'd pulled the screening away, sucking on her thumb and thinking: *I see it, I see it, that's why everything vibrates when I stare at it too long, that's what makes my voice sound wrong when I hear it talking, all the music in the air from all the radios in the world, notes like mosquitos all around, all around.*

These thoughts occurred not as words, or the coherence of memory, but as a series of jagged images and unrelated emotions, the consequence of her surgery.

They had given her a new room, no bars on the windows, no locks on the door, a pretty room decorated for a young lady and painted in pink frosting that reminded her of Pepto Bismol smeared on a spoon. She had been encouraged to join in the clinic games and group activities, but the noise of the snapping cards and the goony, spittled lips and the darkly bruised eyes of those who huddled at the tables made such visitations unbearable.

Better to lie here and watch the music. See it glimmer like translucent jelly, the zim-zim zing of the strings.

Deirdre sucked the heat from her thumb until her hand felt cold, until her mouth ached, and when the hand began to crawl down from her mouth to the pillow, and from the pillow to the sheet where she lay, she made a silent, jaw-slackening scream and jerked herself up from the bed. Standing on one foot in the center of her new, sick-pink room, she let herself turn, a pirouette with her arms raised, responding to the gyroscope inside that wanted to spin, an upright compass that hummed from the middle of her being, from so far inside that the string-buzzing bug notes of the music could not penetrate.

A gyroscope in her bones, spinning the marrow, sparking like static in the dark interior of herself. And now, as she saw it, the music began to form a familiar picture, or made the picture of what she saw in her mind intensely familiar, and so the secret gyroscope drew her out of the room, down the pale yellow emptiness of the hallway, and out through the open French doors to the new-mown lawns of the clinic.

Through the jungle green of the trees she glimpsed the hot reflection of the Brookline Reservoir. The leaves so full on the branches that she could no longer see the country club or the prowling golfers with their flashing sticks. All of it, in any case, blurred by the insistent visual noise of the concert and—yes, she could see it now—the bright bug chatter of the lunatics who had been assembled on folding chairs for the afternoon performance. To be followed by servings of cake and ice cream.

Deirdre floated, the grass like cool breath exhaled on the soles of her feet, and came around the corner of the building on a trajectory that took her out, unseen as she ventured into the trees, into the sanctuary of heavy boughs and new leaves drenched with chlorophyll.

From here she could see the quartet, four neatly attired females sawing industriously on their instruments, pretending to make music that came, Deirdre was convinced, straight out of the air. Fooling the poor loonies who didn't know any better, and who sat with their turnip heads turned to the sun.

She crouched, aware of the cool grass, the fragrant, budding leaves, and behind her, forming and reforming like clouds boiling in the sky, the ominous shadow things extruding from the base of the tree. Prior to her operation such manifestations would have terrified her; now she was detached, an observer-Deirdre, alive in a small corner of her mind, processing images.

In another, entirely separate compartment of her mind, a desire made itself known. This desire-creature demanded physical exhilaration. It wanted leaping, movement, the thrill of grace and beauty. It wanted air against the skin.

Observer-Deirdre, content to remain where she was, had no means of resisting this dimly perceived urgency. She let her hands entwine themselves in the hem of her thin cotton sundress, pulling the material up, unpeeling itself from her body. These same detached hands managed somehow to remove her slip, roll down her nylon underpants, unsnap the plain white brassiere.

The purity of being naked was not in itself enough to silence the urgency. It screamed, from the screaming part of her mind, for movement. *Do it do it do it do it* and so she did it, she allowed herself to be levitated from her place on the cool grass, passing through the membrane of leaves directly into the hot, dry kiss of the sunlight. Running light and fast down the slope of the hill to where the concert was underway, her short-clipped hair alive in the wind she made.

Dancing, dancing, responding to the honey-thick currents of music. A music so powerful and compelling that she was not aware of it ceasing, nor did she notice the stunned expressions of the young musicians, bows held daintily, tentatively aloft, and then in defensive positions, as if her naked, bare-limbed frenzy was an assault upon themselves.

At first there was little reaction among the assembled patients. A few covered their eyes, a few more grinned lewdly or made noises. Then an elderly woman, blind in one eye, shrieked a word: *Ice cream!* and that was enough—the demand for ice cream became a chant.

Ice cream! Ice cream! Ice cream!

Deirdre dancing faster, her fine, slim legs thrusting her into a series of leaps as the members of the quartet—students from a nearby women's conservatory—backpedaled, clutching their instruments, sheet music all aflutter in the stillness of the air.

Out of the clinic, trotting, one hand keeping his wire-rimmed spectacles in place, came short, tubby Dr. Parkay, accompanied by two orderlies, one of whom carried a canvas restraining device, the other a folded blanket. Restraint was unnecessary, for at the first human touch—Dr. Parkay with his hand extended—Deirdre froze in her pose of dancing, a knee lifted, exposing for all who cared to look her soft pubic places.

The doctor, murmuring concern, draped her with the blanket.

"A relapse," he said as the orderlies lifted her up. "Most unfortunate."

A nurse appeared, awaiting instruction. The chant for ice cream continued.

"Better feed them," said the doctor.

He followed the orderlies inside, ticking off the pharmaceutical options, thinking that it could have been worse, that it *had* been worse—this time poor Deirdre McKane had not actually abused herself, at least not in view of the other patients.

All in all, it was an improvement.

Seventeen

Person Unknown

Finding the address was as simple as looking up the family name in the appropriate directory, then dialing the East Boston operator and asking, in his best cop voice, if a William Drake resided at the same residence.

"Billy? Yeah, sure, he lives there with his mom. You want me to ring it, the home number?"

"No, thank you, ma'am."

There was short burst of laughter, thick with the adenoidal buzz of Eastie. "That's a miss, not a ma'am."

"Sorry."

"Anytime, honey."

A girl, Jack decided, trying to sound older, more worldly—and succeeding. For some reason the sound of her voice kept replaying in his mind as he drove through the narrow cobblestone streets into the harbor tunnel. And in the tunnel, driving down through what always reminded him of a tiled, nightmare bathroom, never ending, deeper and deeper and ever more airless, he heard her voice quite clearly, saying, *Anytime, honey.* This was accompanied, incongruously, by an image of Miriam standing in the doorway of the suite she had rented earlier that day at the Parker House. Under her own name again, or anyhow as "Mrs. Fitzroy," just to see his reaction. Wanting him to share her intoxication with taking chances.

Which, admit it, he did.

Miriam. On her way out of town, gone up to Rye Beach for several days to get the summer house ready. He'd wanted to meet her there, imagined her strolling naked through rooms draped with dust sheets. Hands on her sex-cocked hips, giving him a look that meant she would do anything at all, anything he had the courage to suggest.

I want you to miss me, she'd said, stroking the same cheek she'd slapped when he'd made the mistake of mentioning her crazy sister. *Go on and play with yourself, just so you're thinking of me.*

An idea so repulsive, coming from her lips, that he'd recoiled. Miriam, amused by his reaction, reiterated her refusal: he was not to sneak a visit to Rye Beach.

The summer house is off limits, verbotten she'd insisted, *so just put it out of your dirty mind.*

As if *he* had the dirty mind. And why, he continued to wonder, why of all places was the shingled mansion at Rye Beach inviolable? Because it was Sugar's place, and Miriam and Michael summered there at his invitation? Because Mike had proposed to her on that great, ostentatious porch overlooking the sea? Or was it because the marriage reception had been held there, under a rented tent, with entertainment by a sixteen-piece dance band whose leader had owed Sugar McKane a favor? A reception most notable at the time to Jack because it was the occasion of his last celebratory drink before he left to go overseas, and because the bride had kissed him deeply, giggling and coy as her tongue probed to find his, just a tickle before she withdrew. And himself married already for more than a year.

He'd carried this with him to bomb-cratered Germany: his brother's new wife whispering, *I can't resist a man in uniform—or out of it. . . .*

Jack fought the big Packard, the unruly wheel and linkage, as he backed into a fire-hydrant space a few grim blocks from the waterfront. Waiting there in the heat of the parked car until he was no longer tumescent with desire for Miriam—a grown man unable to control his thoughts, what was happening here? You had to laugh. An ex-cop with gimpy legs, as hard as a pimple-faced kid.

He found himself grinning all the way up to the stoop, chosen because it was near the address in question. An old house stained chocolate brown, windows heavily curtained, shades drawn, shutting out the sunlight and heat and sewer stink of the harbor.

He knocked on the glass, watched a flake of putty drop from the window, and he thought: what am I going to say if someone answers the door? He'd been so full of

Miriam that he hadn't given it much thought, what ploy to work the neighborhood.

Sure enough the door unlatched under his hand and it came to him in that moment: insurance.

Stepping back on the stoop, he removed his hat and waited.

"Yes?" This from a woman of forty or so, dressed in baggy, colorless slacks, her head covered with a scarf. There was a wet string mop upright in her left hand, a glint of sweat on her work-reddened cheeks.

"Sorry to disturb you, ma'am. I'm with New England Life and Equity. We're doing a survey."

The mop wavered. She was, he decided, on the point of shutting the door in his face.

"I'm not a salesman," he said, attempting to put her at ease. "No salesman will call. All we want to know, what risks we take for policies issued in this neighborhood. On this street in particular."

"You just want to ask questions?"

"Just a few questions," he assured her. "I'm not empowered to make a sale, even if you wanted to buy insurance."

"We already have insurance. My husband . . . what kind of questions?"

"Nothing personal, ma'am. What we call statistics. Questions about how long people live in this neighborhood. Age groups. Frequency of crime reports, fires, that sort of thing." Jack was riffing all this from the top of his head, and he could tell by the way her expression softened that the lady was buying. Convinced by the technical sound of "statistics," or the deferential way he held his hat in his hands.

"Not in the house," she said. "The house is a mess."

"Here is fine," he said, taking out his notebook.

"Around back."

Around back was a narrow yard, enclosed by buildings that were not quite tenements. Mrs. Ruth Cushing did him the courtesy of removing her scarf and shaking out her hair as they sat opposite on wood-slatted chairs, in a patch of shade. There was a small, scruffy-looking vegetable garden, already overgrown with weeds, a reflection of the neighborhood decay. Every few minutes, in a rhythm that defied expectation, the propeller drone of unseen aircraft. Mrs. Cushing, used to the noise, did not even bother looking up.

"I didn't know insurance companies did surveys," she said.

Jack explained the necessity, indeed, the importance of surveys, for how else could a company set its rates?

"Statistics, Mrs. Cushing. They love 'em back at the central office."

"I wish my husband was here. He works inventory at the Navy Yard, knows all about statistical things."

"You'll do fine, Mrs. Cushing. These are not technical questions."

On the cops there had been none of this posing-as-someone-else nonsense, having to lie to get information about a neighbor. You simply pushed through the door, instilled a little fear of authority, mouthed threats if necessary—when all else failed you pulled out the cuffs, made it very clear the next stop was downtown, all those scary rumors about what happened in interrogation rooms.

Never mind. Jack discovered, sitting in the shade of the tenements with this pleasant, lonely woman, that he rather enjoyed being an imposter. In the course of thirty minutes he learned more than he had ever wanted to know about Monmouth Street and the families who lived there, the Drake family in particular.

"The poor woman," Mrs. Cushing said when the flow of conversation finally took her in that direction, as natural as a leaf in the current. "Her husband died before the war, just dropped dead right at the supper table, his heart, and then a few months ago her older boy drowned. Royal, they called him Roy, and very handsome, too. Looked like a movie star, that boy, although he wasn't the type. Very nice and polite and looked out for his mother. They're an old family, the Drakes."

"Really?" Jack pretended polite disinterest. "Are there a lot of old families in the neighborhood?"

Mrs. Cushing shook her head. "Not like the Drakes. There've been Drakes on this side of the harbor since the Pilgrims almost, my husband says. Of course, they haven't always lived on Monmouth Street. They had a big place out on the point before the airport went in. The bank took it, I heard. Irene—that's Mrs. Drake—she always said that's what killed her husband, losing the big house, rundown as it was."

"Hard on a man," Jack said. "Losing a house."

"Hard on everybody," Mrs. Cushing said. "I don't suppose the older boy had any life insurance?"

"I wouldn't know."

"Be nice if he did, help out his poor mother."

"I could check with the other insurance carriers, see if he had a policy," Jack said. And he intended to do exactly that, if only to see who might have profited from his sudden death.

"Could you? It's killed her, losing that boy. It seems to have affected her mind. Talking to herself, that kind of thing. You can tell something's wrong and it's more than poor Billy can handle."

"Billy?" Jack said innocently.

"Her youngest, the only one left. He's taken over the brother's lobster business. They've always been like that, the Drakes, mostly fishermen. Living hand to mouth, you might say. My husband says they're swamp Yankees, whatever that means. It's not a bad thing, is it, to call them swamp Yankees?"

"I don't think so, Mrs. Cushing. I'm not really sure."

"But you'll check about Roy?"

"I'll check."

"It would help, I'm sure, if he left his poor mother a few pennies."

The best part of the day was walking into Homicide, the hero's welcome he got there.

"Hey, whattya know! Hey, it's Jack Fitzroy!"

That was Corky, Detective Forever Lawrence Corcoran, the two-finger typist who handled most of the paperwork. Corky, a screw-up away from his desk, rarely went out on a case and seemed content with the situation. Nor had he been disturbed by how quickly Jack had advanced in the ranks. And now here he was up on his bandy little legs, pumping Jack's hand and grinning like a mad leprechaun.

"Hey, way to go, buddy. Way to go."

Jack was puzzled. What had he done?

"You and your brother. The detective business. The guys are talking, okay? So we heard."

"Heard what, Corky?"

"You know," Corky winked. He had to scrunch half his face up to do it, but he winked. "That ward boss fella, McKane. With him involved you can't fail now, can you?"

"I guess not," Jack said.

"You guess not. You guess not." Corky was vastly amused. "Money'll stick to you boys like gum on a shoe. It'll be like the private FBI, they say. You got a spot for me when I get my twenty-five in?"

"Well . . ."

"You know me, Jack. You know my work."

"We'll see what we can do, Cork, comes the time."

After Corky there was Lou Moakley, he'd just made lieutenant. Big Lou was in line to take over the squad when Delaney finally retired. And then Captain Francis X. Delaney himself, Jack's mentor when he first made detective—all of them genuinely happy to see him, happy for his good fortune, which for some reason had been grossly exaggerated by the department grapevine. He finally ended up in Delaney's office, sipping good Irish whiskey from Dixie cups, which was a real honor, drinking with Francis in his office.

A barrel-shaped man with sloping shoulders and a flattened nose from when he'd boxed with the department club, Delaney had kept his teeth somehow, big white choppers he liked to flash. He was, like many of the better-connected captains, a member in good standing of the Ancient Order of Hibernians, and took care to keep a little of Ireland in the way he talked, although he himself had never actually visited the old country. Still, he had a way of letting you know the professional Irish stuff was all blarney, a necessity of position, and not meant to be taken seriously.

"Well, this is a fine thing, Jack," he said, raising his Dixie cup. "You've landed on your feet and I'm glad of that. Didja know I spoke to that polio doctor?"

"I did, yes."

"He told me, the man did, you'd never walk without a cane."

"I guess I fooled 'em, Captain."

"You know it wasn't a personal thing, the department decision?"

Jack shrugged. Getting the word he was out had been

almost as bad as hearing the original diagnosis. Another way of cutting his legs out from under.

"It's the same with the T.B.," Delaney said, rushing his words, embarrassed to be speaking of such things. "We can't fight a chest X ray, can't fight the polio. Regulations. Nothing personal, you were one of the best, I said. You can ask anybody, I said, I told everybody who'd listen, the man was here but three short years and yet we all knew he would have my job in the fullness of time. For certain you'd have made captain one fine day if you'd stayed on."

Jack nodded, sipping the heat from his Dixie cup, wondering how best to get off the subject of his recent illness and back to the business at hand.

"Maybe it was a blessing," Delaney said. "Got out while the getting was good. While you're still young. There'll be a new governor next year and that means we'll have a new commissioner. A shake-up for certain."

"You'll be okay," Jack said. "They'd never touch you."

"Maybe not." Delaney reached in the drawer for the bottle, retrieved it with surprisingly nimble hands. "Maybe not. I heard Doug Donnelly went with you, and that smart little wop we had here, what's his name?"

"Tony Grazi."

"Yeah, him. It's become a topic of discussion, Jack. You're paying big money, they say."

"Not big money. A decent salary."

Delaney chuckled, his small eyes warm with the whiskey. "Very decent, I'm sure. Well, that's fine. And you'll have only your own kind, is that true?"

"Every man an ex-detective," Jack said. "Mike insists on that. They hate to admit it, but lawyers are impressed with cops. Or maybe afraid."

Delaney grinned. He obviously liked the idea of frightening members of the bar. "Well, your brother Mike the lawyer is impressed with you, I'll go that far. Did you know he came into this office and threatened to sue me personally, I didn't see you kept your position? I can tell by your look you didn't know that, Jack. I see no harm in telling you now. This is when you were still inside, of course, the hospital."

"Mike did that?"

"He did. And when I said it was out of my hands, he asked me to step outside and put up my dukes."

"You're kidding."

Delaney was laughing now, starting to hiccup. "I swear," he said, putting his hand on his heart. "Put up your dukes, he said. Let me tell you, I didn't dare laugh because the man was so serious. He'd have busted my jaw for certain, but Lou came to the rescue. He couldn't be mad at Lou like he was at me."

"I'm sorry, Cap. I didn't know."

"Sorry? And why should you be sorry? With a brother like that?"

Later, a little worse for drink, he'd managed to get Lou Moakley aside, and Lou was more than happy to pull the jacket on Royal Leighton Drake, late of East Boston, and share what little he knew.

"It was a float job," he said. Lou was a little deaf, the result of artillery duty, and sometimes his voice boomed. "You know the drill. They pulled him out of the water all tangled up in a rope."

"Who?" Jack asked, attempting to concentrate, clearing the whiskey fog from his head. "The Harbor Patrol?"

Lou turned the page, checking, and satisfied himself. "Nah, it was the kid brother found him. The kid pulled up a lobster pot and that's where he was, tangled up in the rope."

"Jesus."

"You said it. Anyhow, I got the call and went over there, the docks. The kid brother was crazy with grief, it was a terrible thing really. I had to wait there with that body an hour or so until Gleason finally got there, the lazy bastard."

"Gleason? He's what, a medical examiner?"

"Right, I guess he's come on since you left. Lot of new faces. Anyhow, Gleason estimated Drake had been dead, he says here, 'several hours,' that's the best he could estimate. All those crabs in the harbor, you can imagine."

In his day Jack had logged a number of floaters. So he knew about the crabs and what the water did.

"No indication of foul play?"

Lou shook his head. "Water in the lungs, pulmonary edema, a classic death by drowning. It happens more often than you'd think, a guy falls out of his boat and drowns. The deceased was boozed up pretty good, that showed in the blood work, which makes it even easier, he fell out of the boat accidental."

"Autopsy?"

"Yeah. And that was the funny part."

"What funny part, Lou?"

The big man leaned away from the file, remembering. "That there was an autopsy. A death by drowning, we don't always bother. Usually the family doesn't like us cutting up their loved ones, they're worried there maybe won't be enough left to bury. But the kid brother insisted. He's been a real pain in the ass, that kid."

"He requested an autopsy?"

"That's what I'm saying, Jack. He demanded we check out the remains, his brother. Claimed person unknown had been responsible for the death."

"Person unknown?"

Lou was cagey, avoided making eye contact. "That's what I put down here in the file: person unknown."

"Did the boy name a suspect?"

Lou paused, fiddled with his pencil. "He was crazy with grief, Jack. You know how people get."

"I do, yes."

"Something bad happens, they want to blame somebody."

'Lou? Who did he blame, this kid? Who did he say drowned his big brother?"

Lou nipped at his pencil eraser and grimaced. "I didn't write it up because there was absolutely no evidence and because the victim was dead the result of accidental drowning, open and shut."

"Lou?"

The big man sighed, lowered his great booming voice until it was soft, husky soft. "This nutso kid, Billy Drake? He said Sugar McKane must have did it. He didn't know how, but he thought McKane was somehow responsible. He's crazy on the subject. Came in here regular for a while, demanding we investigate."

"And did you? Investigate?"

"What's to investigate? Yeah, okay, we checked it out

finally, just to get the kid off our ass. Nothing, a complete zilch. McKane has absolutely no connection to the victim. Which is why, you look at the file, I didn't think it necessary to put his name in there.''

''Person unknown,'' Jack said.

''Yeah, keep it simple. We get this sometime, a poor jerk wants to blame the mayor or the governor or whatever. We had a guy once, you remember, he said Cardinal O'Connor put a curse on his wife, she died in her sleep?''

''I remember,'' Jack said.

''This is like that,'' Lou said, spreading his hands, shaking his head at all the sad and crazy people in the world who tried to blame the innocent rich. ''You can tell Mr. McKane it ain't nothing to worry about.''

Eighteen

Salt Water Taffy

In the gravel lot of a Socony filling station in Newburyport, forty miles north of Boston, Michael Fitzroy sat in his brand-new Cadillac convertible, his hands locked on the wheel, his gaze fixed at the sign of the flying horse. The way the light hit the white-winged horse he almost expected to see the creature free itself from the red background of the sign, fly off into the darkening sky. Big smoke-gray clouds boiling up like the world was on fire somewhere over the horizon. So spooky it made him feel light-headed.

"Hey, mister? Your change, mister?"

Black fingernails displaying three damp one-dollar bills.

"Two bucks to fill it," the boy said. He was close enough that Mike could smell the spearmint gum on his breath. "You give me a fiver."

"Uh, thanks." The bills were cool and greasy in his hand. On impulse he put the money in the glove compartment—too dirty for his silk-lined billfold.

"You okay, mister?"

"Yeah, sure."

" 'Cause you look at this sky, you just know we got rain on the way. You want a hand putting up the top?"

"What?" Mike wasn't paying attention. From inside the shack a cheap table radio was blaring "String of Pearls" and the kid was humming alone, nodding his skinny head to the beat like a real hipster.

"Nice leather seats," he said, snapping his fingers. "The rain'll stain 'em."

Mike closed his eyes and thought, *Snap out of it.* Think too much about winged horses and the world on fire and he'd start crying, embarrass himself in front of this kid.

"Right," he said. "Rain on the way."

Mike got out of the car and began to unsnap the cover for the white convertible top. Every button an effort, getting his fingers to work the canvas. The kid, watching him with curiosity or concern, wiped his hands clean on a rag and then stood opposite, helping him raise the top, snap the locks into place over the windshield.

It wasn't until Mike crossed the bridge into Salisbury that he realized he hadn't tipped the boy. He'd make it up on the way back, give the kid a silver dollar, make sure he never forgot the absentminded gentleman in the bright yellow Coupe DeVille. He could imagine, as the first fat drops of rain made soft puttering sounds against the canvas top, the bebop kid with the black fingernails saying, *The guy had class.*

The first shower came and went within a half mile, the two-lane blacktop steaming with the rain. The sky was the color of wet slate, looming and close to the earth. As he crossed the state line into New Hampshire, a slant of late afternoon sunlight broke through, making the white motor-court cottages appear luminous and unreal, pale Chinese lanterns tacked up with novelty siding and strewn near to the road.

Bide-a-Wee, Ocean View, Kitty Lou's, Sea Mist, the sleepy names, the brightly painted shutters, the neatly parked automobiles outside each numbered door, all of it seemed to unfist inside his belly, a kind of vertigo that made him grip the wheel and squint, having to *think* about steering the car.

The tires thumped across another low bridge and suddenly he was in Hampton Beach, a boardwalk resort town that seemed, after the brief deluge, to be slightly below sea level, with water pooling in the streets, creating an instant archipelago of shacks, for the most part unoccupied. Tar-paper islands for rent at five bucks a night, precarious on cedar posts.

He pulled over to the side of Ocean Boulevard as the rain came harder, almost a squall this time, blowing white caps from the blackened sea, and he laid his head against the cool glass of the side window, feeling the Caddy rock with the wind, and wondered again just what the hell he was doing, following Miriam up to the beach house.

A dirty, nervous thing, setting out after Miriam. Wanting and not wanting to catch her. Hence the queasy stomach, the inability to concentrate on something as simple as steering, or gassing up the car. Lover's vertigo—and husbands were not lovers, exactly, so where did that leave him?

Between squalls—the little storms marched in from the sea, violent, fitful, and brief—he found shelter on the boardwalk, under the wooden awnings of the penny arcades. The winter storm shutters had been taken down, the gaudy signs put up, but only a few of the joints were open. Most would await, he supposed, a season that began the first day of July and ended, just like that, on Labor Day.

After a creaky perambulation of the boardwalk, dodging leaks in the far from impervious awning, he found a soda fountain open for business and sat there on a wobbly stool, drinking a vanilla frappe to fill the uncertainty in his belly. The frappe was watery—too much milk and syrup, not enough ice cream—and sweet enough to make his teeth ache. From his stool, nursing the last few slurps from the metal cup, he watched a machine spin out saltwater taffy, a small miracle of ingenuity, stretching and snipping and cutting and spitting out the paper-wrapped twists of candy, smelling of industrial-strength peppermint oil.

There was a pretty girl behind the counter, boxing the candy. She wore starched whites and a little white hat, and she looked tentative, uncertain, he decided, as if fearful that the flailing arms of the taffy machine might reach out and grab her, weave a paper ribbon into her fine brown hair. Mike decided that she was an April or a May or possibly a June—anyhow, named for a spring month—and that she had not yet kissed a boy, a condition that would not possibly survive the coming summer.

He fully intended to ask the pretty girl her name, just to settle the bet with himself, but when the moment came he lost courage and simply paid for a one-pound box of the taffy and left. His stomach was cold, his throat was hot, his head was wet, and in his heart cowardice bloomed like a red, red rose.

He parked behind the carriage house of a neighboring estate, where he had a view of McKane's summer mansion, an enormous gray-shingled monstrosity with more eaves and roofs and beach stone chimneys than could easily be counted. Miriam's two-tone Olds coupe was there, under the portico that extended from a wing of the house, out of the rain. Sugar had acquired the place for, as he put it, ''a song'' just before Roosevelt got in the first time. Picked it up, Mike had later learned, after the property failed to sell at auction, the previous owner a Chicago margin trader whose paper fortune had vanished in less than a year. There was no truth to the persistent rumor that the ruined man had hung himself in one of the mansion parapets, or anywhere. Mike had checked that out, too, more out of curiosity than any dread of sleeping under the same roof as a suicide.

His nose pressed to the blurred side window, he stared at her car, the Simonized colors flattened by a yellow bug light shining down from the portico. He recalled, with a thrill of anguish, the day he'd bought both cars from a Commonwealth Avenue dealership owned by one of Sugar's golfing companions, and how Miriam had insisted on the two-tone model because it matched her maroon-and-cream pumps. How, in that same car, demonstrating her driving ability—undoubtedly the equal of his own—she'd pulled off the road and reached for him, slipping her hands beneath his belt and snatching hold, her fingers so hot he'd felt scalded. Miriam lifting her skirt and saying, *Go on, I dare you* and himself, more the fool, afraid of a passing policeman, declining with regrets that she would not, for a week, forgive.

Idiot. Cretin. Fool. He was all of those things, and another, a stuttering beast of a word, *cuh-cuh-cuckold.*

That unutterable fact having long been established, after a series of assignations that began shortly after their marriage. Tennis pros, flyboys, actors—did it really matter who, or precisely where and when? The answer, sitting alone in the rain, gobbling peppermint taffys as he played Peeping Mike on his own wife, was obviously yes. It did matter.

The mansion windows, boarded up for the winter—a task that took a local handyman the better part of a week—had been unboarded, although the curtains and drapes remained drawn. From here he could follow her by the way she lighted each room. He'd arrived to find the whole place ablaze and assumed, with a sick feeling, that another car would soon arrive: Miriam making her lover welcome. Dinner by candlelight, then—and this was the sick part, because he couldn't help but be stimulated by the thought of it—Miriam showing a vodka smile as she undressed, quick with need. Miriam naked on her hands and knees. Miriam looking over her shoulder, her eyes like hot sparks as she mouthed those dirty, dirty words, *Go on, I dare you.*

Several of the lights went off in order. A brisk walk through the rooms, he supposed, clicking off the electrified chandeliers. He could imagine the delicate tick-tock of her high heels, her agile, elegant carriage. The way she moved inside her clothes. Now only an upstairs wing was lighted, several rooms, including her father's suite. And still only her own car in the drive. Was her newest lover a local lad, then, sneaking in through a back door? This seemed unlikely somehow—Miriam expected her men to be well scrubbed and monied or at least, by his own example, exceedingly ambitious.

Mike lighted a paper match, checked the clock on the dash. Aware of peppermint fumes on his breath, the sweet ache of too much candy, kind of a shaky feeling from the sugar and a headache that made him want to sleep. At some point he dozed off, then awakened cold and clammy from a dream he could not remember, and saw that the sky had cleared. Stars up there, the sliver of a moon, and the mansion dark. So dark he couldn't see under the portico. Was that another automobile nudging close to Miriam's Oldsmobile? Low-slung, possibly a foreign-made roadster, he couldn't quite make it out.

His hands were numb and trembling as he got out of the car, unable to stand up straight without making an effort, cramped from his nap. Standing, he soon realized, in a puddle that lapped over the edges of his shoes, soaking his socks. He could hear the waves crashing, the dull roar of gravel dragged into the undertow, and he could easily imagine what the beach looked like, black and seething, from Sugar's grand summer porch.

There was, he determined, no extra vehicle under the portico, or anywhere in the vicinity. No roadster—he'd imagined it there, shaped it from shadows.

Miriam was alone.

As he crawled into the backseat of the Cadillac and made a pillow of his hands he felt two things: relieved and disappointed.

* * *

He jerked himself awake with sun on the window and the leather seat hot under his chin. His heart was racing and his neck was swollen tight against his shirt collar. Something was taking his breath away.

As he sat up, groggy and suffering from blurred vision, the thought and the fear became clear. *Another car was not necessary.* It was quite possible, indeed probable, that Miriam, cunning Miriam, would transport her lover in her own car, slunk down in the Olds doing God-knows-what to her as she drove.

They were in there together, slick with love sweat at this very moment, stealing the air from his lungs.

Panicked, Mike fumbled, got the car door open, and slumped into the sunlight. He loosened his collar, drank hungrily of the warm, salt-drenched breeze. Gulls wheeling against the pale sky, everything green and soft and wet from the rain. There, on his knees in the damp grass, he experienced a wave of self-loathing so fierce and repugnant that his stomach emptied.

He knelt beside the car, coughing, and cleaned his mouth with a handkerchief. Thinking, *If the boys could see me now.* Meaning his list of client law firms, all of them dependent on the Fitzroy expertise, the ability to coordinate investigations with various police departments, provide depositions of crucial witnesses, organize the discreet gathering of intelligence with the help of every modern technical convenience—all points italicized on the elegantly printed promotional brochure of Fitzroy Security.

What would they think, these client law firms, if they knew that Mr. Michael Fitzroy himself couldn't accomplish what any boozed-up, flophouse gumshoe could do in a few hours—namely, identify who exactly Mrs. Fitzroy had been screwing lately.

They'd laugh like hell, he decided, getting to his feet, that's what they'd do. Just prior to severing any contractual relationship. And why not? You had to laugh, or anyhow smirk, at the idea of big-talking Mike, well-connected Mike, disbarred-but-undaunted Michael Fitzroy gorging on saltwater taffy and sleeping in his car like an anxious, lovesick boy.

He decided then and there to enter the big house and see for himself. Ignore the tugging sense of dread that made his feet heavy, his hands bird-light. Display for Miriam, as best he knew how, the truth of himself.

Go on, he thought, *I dare you.*

No doughboy stood up from his trench and charged with more courage than Michael Fitzroy approaching the front entrance of the house where his wife had spent the night. The door was, as he'd expected, unlocked. Miriam who had trouble with keys, rarely locked a door. He stood there inside the entrance hall listening to his heart boom in his ears, aware of the musty odor of a place closed up for the winter. A dried seaweed smell. A coolness in here and a kind of absolute stillness that, if you let it get to you, terrified.

Gravely he knelt to unlace his shoes. Then, his head light, he walked in his soiled socks up the curving staircase to the second floor, looming like a theater balcony over the great central room, big enough to stage a dance. Birch logs stacked unlit in the beach stone fireplace. Carpets yet to be unrolled, furniture still draped with ghostly sheets. The feel of the place was empty—so empty he began to wonder if Miriam's car was really there under the portico, or if he had imagined it just as he'd imaged the phantom roadster, projecting some need to demean himself with sick fantasies.

He found her asleep in Sugar's bedroom, in the rooms he kept to himself as a kind of private apartment within the larger house. Her overnight bag open on a trunk, clothing scattered. As he came into the room, near silent in his stocking feet, Miriam sat up and screamed.

Pulling the quilt up to her chin she blinked, blind with sleep, and clearly frightened until he spoke his name.

"It's me, Miriam. Michael."

Now she could see him and he could feel her eyes surveying his unkempt suit, his soiled cuffs.

"My God," she said. "What happened?"

"I had to change a tire."

"But what are you doing here?" Then, suddenly, and with fierce concern: "Something's wrong. What is it? Tell me what's wrong."

Mike slumped on the edge of the bed and found that he could not look into her eyes. Instead he stared at the floor and said, "I don't know. Really, I've no idea."

Nineteen

Me and Fibber McGee

The old woman prayed by the light from the small window, head bowed as she sat in her upholstered chair. A word in God's ear. Would he hear? All those other prayers rising like a symphony, yes: an etching in a catechism manual, God's ear in the picture glowing with love and wisdom and the superimposed image of a beatific Jesus, an Irish Jesus from the look of him, the soft spit curls of his Donegal beard, all knowing, all wise, ready with a small joke to ease her pain, soothe her fear.

Come, walk with me, Annie, yes, in a voice like warm wind, a wind voice alive with the smell of cut grass in Heaven, of hay drying in the Garden of Eden.

This she believed, all of it, every hand-colored picture.

Soon, she prayed, *I will ascend with Thee, my Lord Jesus.*

Outside, the noise of children playing on tenement porches. A neighborhood of dirty faces, broken glass. Not the Sheehans, of course. Her new people were top-of-the-block, a clean and proper house with a detached garage and two fine, white-walled sedans to fill it. Surrounded on all sides, though, by Italian three-deckers, a dark little face in every window, the fumes of diaper pails, clotted milk, rotting tomatoes wafting in the heat to her room over the garage.

Privacy, Sugar McKane's grim undertakers had promised, and that she had, a place to herself alone, alone, not made to feel welcome except in her capacity as house cleaner, at certain designated hours, and of course for supper, which she ate by herself in the kitchen, kept company by radio shows.

Mr. Sheehan was, she reminded herself, a fine and gentle man, coming home from his salesman's work with his tie still firmly knotted, shoes freshly polished. The missus, now, that was a different thing altogether, and to be expected. Mrs. Sheehan had a way of checking the rugs after Annie had run the vacuum machinery, a certain critical look in her eye, in the way her small and pretty mouth poised. Lipstick to match her big, shiny earrings. Still, not an unkind woman, no, you couldn't say bad about her.

But it wasn't the same, was it, as the fine mansion in Hyde Park? The hushed silence of that great house, in those fine days before she had come to know what unspeakable things happened there, in the sight of God. She put her rosary beads into the small purse, slipped the purse into her bag, centered the bag on her lap.

Put it from your mind, Mrs. Annie O'Hare.

What the new priest had said, hearing her confession, a man of half her age born in this country, his voice thick with the honk of Boston. *There are sins that must not be discussed except by those who made them, do you understand?*

Yes, Father, you want me to shut me old gob.

Not at all, he'd said, the fearful, nervous breath of him rattling the confessional screen, *that's not what I meant at all. Keep in mind that McKane is a powerful man and what you say is slander. For your own protection, speak of it only to me, or to God.*

Yes, Father, I promise.

Below, a garage door was being opened, the rumble of it tickling her slippered feet. The missus going into the city to shop. Annie's offer to accompany on such expeditions had been gratefully, and instantly, declined. Services not required.

Her eyes found the wind-up clock on the table by her bed. Counting the hours to supper with Fibber McGee. Fibber made her forget all about the terrible secret of Sugar McKane and his yellow-haired devil daughter.

The old woman sliced the cold pork cutlet into small cubes, added a ladle of applesauce from the white bowl of it left out for her. Mr. Sheehan had taken his wife to a restaurant, and after that for dancing at a ballroom on the beach. Mrs. Sheehan had come back from the city with a new dress, had showed the flounce of it to Annie as they took their leave.

"Too young, do you think, Anne?"

"Now, you're not too young for a dance, are you, Mrs. Sheehan?"

A puzzled look, then a small, startled laugh of recognition. "I meant the dress. All the girls are wearing these."

"How they stay up is a miracle. Very pretty, I'm sure."

"There's a plate for you in the Frigidaire. I hope you don't mind."

"I never mind, missus."

Cold, the broiled cutlet tasted of pig fat. The applesauce helped. That and a teacup of clear cooking wine borrowed from the larder. On the radio Molly was telling Fibber what a fool he was.

"Just like a man!" Molly shrieked.

Sipping her wine, the old woman smiled with her eyes shut. It was true, they were all the same.

Twenty

Nailing Keegan

Inside a vacated storefront, Jack put on the wire-recorder headphones and heard the torch grunting in satisfaction, smacking his fat lips, breathing heavily through his nose.

The torch had a street name, Stinky, and he ate two meals a day in the same place, an Automat on Causeway Street where the lemon meringue pie was a dime a slice. Everything was a dime, including factory-made sandwiches on bread so thin you could see the mystery meat right through it.

The arsonist loved every mouthful.

"Stinky does business there, the Automat," Tony Grazi had explained when they were setting up the stakeout. "I guess he figures it's cheaper than an office, plus he can stuff his face. He keeps all these dimes in a little change purse like a woman carries."

"Can we get a kid inside?" Jack had asked him.

"I'll do it myself." Tony had been cocky, having a good time on his first really sizable assignment. "We put a kid in there, busing those tables, you never know, old Stinky might smell a rat."

"You sure the guy can't make you?"

"Don't worry. Understand, Stinky is not real bright. The sharp guy we gotta handle is Jimmy Keegan, the landlord.

The stakeout was really about the landlord, not the lowlife arsonist with a taste for ten-cent pies. Keegan had a business: he bought up vacant warehouses, fixed paper to make it look like the buildings had been renovated and leased, then hired a torch. The insurance companies never settled for the inflated evaluation, but even at fifty cents on the dollar Jimmy Keegan made money.

The Fitzroy brothers had gotten involved when Commonwealth Mutual found itself in court fighting claims totaling almost a hundred thousand dollars. Evidence of the landlord's complicity in the arson was worth thirty percent on a contingency basis, the fee to be equally split with attorneys representing the insurance company.

Fifteen grand for linking Keegan and his torch.

Large money, as Mike had said, inking the agreement. Well worth the risk of investing in a stakeout scheme. And Tony Grazi, who knew the players from his days on the arson squad, could prove his worth and then some to the new firm.

The prospect of a fifteen-grand fee was why Jack found himself hunkered down behind windows whited out with Bon Ami, keeping his fingers crossed because the wire recorder was a finicky piece of equipment and because it was by no means guaranteed that Stinky Doyle would select the right booth to conduct his business. Tony was in there, playing busboy (the regular busboy presented with five bucks and a grandstand seat for the Red Sox game, a died-and-gone-to-heaven deal) the idea being that Tony would steer Stinky into the booth they'd miked from the storefront.

Snap Edwards, who had set up the wire recorder, had wanted to put a microphone in every booth, cover all the possibilities, but Jack had decided on just the one, keep it simple.

"Drill eight holes in the wall, somebody is bound to notice," Jack had said. "We spook this guy, we lose him, maybe for good."

Snap was situated in a bread truck parked directly outside the Automat, ready to photographically document Keegan meeting with the torch. Before taking his position he'd given Jack last-minute instructions on the care and handling of the wire recorder:

"Just make sure the spool is turning, okay? Very important. And keep an eye on the levels here, shows you the transmission is actually being transferred to the wire. The only worry, if we get a lot of background rumble from the trains."

The Automat was located within spitting distance of North Station. So far, listening in the headphones, Jack hadn't noticed any problem with the trains. A little screech or hiss now and then, very minor when you compared it with the noise of Stinky Doyle smacking his lips. Sounded like a poodle in there, snuffling around his bowl.

They had the torch in the right place, miked and ready to have his picture taken. Now it was a matter of waiting for Keegan to show. According to Tony, the landlord made all his payoffs on Thursday, from city building inspectors to the fire marshals. Although Jack hated, just hated the idea of a fire marshal on the take, exposing graft was not the thrust of the investigation—that was a felony crime, police business. The whole point was to deliver the goods to the attorneys, who would use evidence of insurance fraud to secure a no-payment decision in civil court.

Stick to your own business, he kept telling himself. Focus on the fifteen grand. Let the cops handle their own.

It was getting to the sticky end of June and hot as a bastard in the closed-up storefront. Jack had taken off his suit jacket and necktie, rolled up his sleeves, and he was hoping the humidity wouldn't short out the hidden microphone. Stinky slobbering so much, anything could happen. Jack could hear the brittle noise of dishware and assumed that was Tony busing the tables, at this point functioning as a potential witness to any transaction between Stinky and Keegan, assuming the landlord showed.

Jimmy Keegan did show, but not before the torch had nosily consumed most of the available pastry, slurped several cups of muddy coffee. What with the heat and the stuffy air, Jack was on the point of nodding off when the landlord finally arrived.

"Here, take this and wipe your filthy mouth."

The voice boomed in his ears and Jack jerked to attention, his hands reaching to activate the wire recorder. Copies of the conversation, in transcript form, were later provided to the insurance company lawyers and the Arson Squad of the Boston Police Department's Bureau of Criminal Investigation.

KEEGAN: Keep the hankie. Believe me, I don't want it back.

DOYLE: (*indistinct*)

KEEGAN: For God's sake, wait till you've swallowed. You know what you look like, eating? Like a cow getting ready to crap.

DOYLE: You know about cows, Jimmy? I didn't know you knew about cows.

KEEGAN: Forget it, let's stick to business. Take the envelope and don't open it here, you moron. It's all there, two and a half.

DOYLE: You said five yards.

KEEGAN: The rest after you do it. Which I keep telling you. It don't seem to get through your fat head.

DOYLE: Yeah, okay, relax, why doncha? Pie? They got this—

KEEGAN: Shut up about the pie. You think I'd eat this crap? Take a look in those little mailboxes they keep the food in, you can see flies buzzing around in there. Disgusting.

DOYLE: I never seen that. Not one fly, Jimmy, honest.

KEEGAN: Forget it, okay? Just forget it. We gotta problem here, I gotta get this settled right away. That place I told you, on Lewis Street Wharf, you recall the building?

DOYLE: Yeah, sure, over in Eastie.

KEEGAN: It's the one got the new sign up, East Boston Cargo, can you remember that? It's blue, the sign.

DOYLE: A new sign.

KEEGAN: Right, just remember that. New. Because you gotta do the right building this time and you gotta do it soon. Like tonight, okay?

DOYLE: You gotta key?

KEEGAN: Never mind the key. This time you make it a break-in, bust the door or whatever.

DOYLE: You always give me a key, Jimmy. That's the deal.

KEEGAN: Well, the deal changed. I got these insurance companies on my ass, from now on we make it look like a break-in. This one, the East Boston thing, I got it covered with a different company, we're like turning over a new leaf here. I level the building, settle for whatever, then I got a buyer for the property. It's beautiful, the way I got it covered.

DOYLE: I don't get it.

KEEGAN: Never mind. Just bust in the door and do it, can you do this for me?

DOYLE: The place on the wharf, there, Eastie. You sure

about the pie, Jimmy? I can get you a piece, it ain't
had flies.

KEEGAN: Don't call me, whatever you do.

DOYLE: You never give me a number, Jimmy, how
could I call?

[Transcript ends with the departure of Keegan.]

They had a little celebration, there in the storefront.
Warm Ballantine ale, it was the best they could do. Snap
Edwards, not much of a suds drinker, ended up coughing
like crazy, foam coming out of his nose.

"We got the bastards cold," he said after playing back
the wire spool. "That bastard Jimmy Keegan is cooked.
I got a really nice shot, him handing over the payoff."

"So tell me," Jack said, clinking bottles with Tony
Grazi. "How'd you do it? Make sure Stinky took the
right booth?"

Tony was grinning, shaking his head. He was still
wearing his busboy apron. "It was so easy. You might
even say it was a piece of cake."

"You're kidding," Jack said, hooting with laughter.
"You gotta be kidding me. The guy fell for that? You
left a piece of cake on the table? No, wait a minute, it
was pie, am I right?"

"Lemon meringue," Tony said, nodding happily.
"And you know the touch, to make it look for real? It
was only half a slice. He can't resist, that, Stinky, finishing off the plate."

It was funny, hysterical, as close to good police work
as they were ever going to get now, working as civilians.
Worth, they decided, another quart of warm Ballantine.

"What this is," Snap Edwards said, holding the bottle
aloft, "this is piss, is what this is."

"Get used to it," Jack said, and for some reason,
maybe the heat or the alcohol, that did it. They broke
up, laughed so hard, all three of them laughing to the
point of breathlessness, that they had to take turns
pounding each other on the back.

Jack was so hot on the idea of really nailing Keegan
that he persuaded Michael to let him contact the arson
squad, set up a police stakeout of the East Boston warehouse, catch Stinky in the act.

"It's perfect," Jack said, selling him the idea. "We give 'em the time, the place, the perpetrator. They'll owe us."

Mike was at first uneasy with the idea. He'd been moody lately, almost skittish, and often came into work with the faint perfume of last night's drink on his breath, overpowering the medicinal smell of his stomach medicine. Jack knew what the trouble was, but he didn't like to think about it, and so what he talked about with Mike now was business. He never even glanced at the picture of Miriam on his brother's desk. He didn't want to risk thinking about her when Mike was there to maybe pick up on it.

Keep to business, and that was easy enough because business was good and getting better.

"Okay, what have we got?" Jack said, ticking off the points. "We've got the wire recording, we've got pictures, we've got two witnesses can put Keegan and Stinky together. Which, like you say, is enough for the lawyers."

"It's good, Jack, really," Mike conceded, fingers laced protectively over his troubled stomach. "I mean great, are you kidding? They're going to love us. I bet we get more potential billings out of this one case than anything else we've handled so far, and that includes the Hannaford embezzlement thing."

Jack nodded. Solving the Hannaford swindle had opened up a world of accounting-related cases. Mike was considering hiring a full-time CPA to coordinate investigations. It was scary, sometimes, how fast the client list was expanding. It meant hiring more investigators, the necessity to keep getting bigger just to cover the overhead.

"Okay, what I'm saying, let's take it a step further," Jack said. He was perched on the edge of a wooden office chair, the wire spool safe on Mike's desk. "The cops nail Stinky in the act, he's sure to rat on Keegan. So then we'll have a criminal prosecution, a felony act. I'm not sure how it works, but wouldn't the insurance companies be able to go after Keegan, try to recover money they've already paid out? Kind of a bonus situation?"

Mike shook his head. "They'll never find the money.

A professional sleezeball like Jimmy Keegan, he's got it buried out in the woods or whatever.''

''But they'll have the opportunity. It can't hurt, we get the both of them arrested. A little extra, our way of saying thank you for the fifteen grand.''

Mike agreed. ''If you think it helps us with the cops, sure, why not?''

''I'll give Timmy Collins a call, the arson squad.''

''And I suppose you'll want to be there, they nab this creep in the act?''

Jack nodded his head, stared at his fingernails. ''Sure. Are you kidding? Not that they'll let me. I'll be there, though, the station house, when they bring him in. Just to see the bastard's face.''

Mike grinned. ''And to remind the boys who made it all possible.''

''That, too.''

Twenty-one

The Bondsman

Jack drank hot black coffee from a chipped mug, leaning on his elbows to take the weight from his leg as McGinley dealt solitaire. The cards were so thumb-worn and smudged you could barely tell the suits. McGinley, a night-shift desk sergeant at Berkeley Street, had made his rank the previous summer, and therefore was not familiar with Jack Fitzroy, except by reputation. That was enough to enforce a stiff politeness—the sergeant did not, his manner implied, work for Homicide, or answer to Captain Delaney, or any of Fitzroy's old friends.

Jack said, "He's been in there what, an hour?"

The cards were soft and pliable, and made a slight, lip-smacking sound as McGinley dealt them. "I ain't been watching the clock, Mr. Fitzroy," he said without looking up.

"Jack. Call me Jack."

"Okay, Jack. An hour is I guess about right. You want more coffee, help yourself to the urn."

Jack said, "I'm swimming in it, Sergeant. You know Detective Farrell, right?"

The sergeant dealt, nodded.

"What's his routine, he come back down here after he books a suspect? That what he does?"

The sergeant said, "Depends."

Jack shook his head, smiled to himself. He was a stone, this desk sergeant, you couldn't squeeze him. Detective Farrell was with the arson squad, had been the ranking officer on the stakeout that caught Stinky Doyle in the act, hauling five-gallon tins of kerosene into the East Boston warehouse. Jack had wanted to come along for the show, but Farrell, a stickler, had declined the pleasure of his company.

No civilians, Fitzroy, I'm sure you understand. And he

was correct, Jack understood. It didn't matter that he'd voluntarily divulged information that was leading to the arsonist's arrest, he was now a civilian, just a guy from the old days who knew a few other heavyweight detectives like Delaney. Connections and friendships were understood and deferred to within the department, but it still didn't get him on the stakeout, or into the interrogation room with Stinky Doyle, which is where he wanted to be, hearing the little weasel name Jimmy Keegan as his accomplice. That would be sweet.

"You could take yourself home, Mr. Fitzroy," the desk sergeant suggested. "I'll tell Detective Farrell you were here."

"Thanks for the coffee, Sergeant. I'll just wait a bit."

Jack took his mug away from the desk and left the sergeant to his solitaire. He settled into the hard curves of the wooden bench and stared out the big glass doors—not a thing moving out there on Berkeley Street. Four in the morning, light would seep into the city soon. He hoped Doris had been able to get back to sleep. She'd been very edgy when he left after midnight, had wanted to make sure he wasn't carrying his service revolver, as if she suspected he had secretly gone back to work for the police in some nefarious capacity that might put him in harm's way.

I'll bet your brother is safe asleep in his bed, she'd said, tugging at his collar, and the statement seemed so incongruous—where the hell had that come from?—that Jack had been speechless. You had to wonder what thoughts went through the woman's mind, made her say a thing like that. Why shouldn't Mike be safe in his bed, and what did that have to do with Jack following up on a job well done, seeing it home?

In the pre-dawn dimness of Berkeley Street, paired headlights came around the block and slowed to a stop. A Caddy from the shape of it, and parking right there in front of headquarters, had to be a ranking detective thought he could get away with that and not get the bumper on a hook. A figure emerged from the automobile and Jack recognized him instantly, just from the distinctive way he moved, but he refused to believe his eyes until Sugar McKane came up the steps and into the lobby. Dressed, despite the warm humidity, in a full suit and poplin raincoat and carrying an umbrella, although the street was dry.

"Morning, Jack," he said, not in the least surprised to find him seated there. "Gonna be another hot one, they say."

Jack stood up, feeling suddenly quite queasy, had to be all that coffee. "Sugar," he said. "What the hell."

After saluting the desk sergeant with the umbrella, Sugar came up close and pitched his voice low, intended only for Jack's ears. "I heard you set this up for your old friends on the force," he said. "Very commendable. Mrs. Doyle called me with the sad story not an hour ago."

"Mrs. Doyle?"

Sugar nodded gravely. His breath smelled of toothpaste. "Stinky's mother," he said. "The old girl phoned me in a panic. He's been her cross to bear, young Stinky has."

"Excuse me," Jack said. "I don't get it."

A look of faint surprise passed over Sugar's face. He then nodded thoughtfully to himself and placed a hand lightly on Jack's shoulder. "I buried her husband years ago," he said. "I know it's hard to credit that a mongrel like Stinky had a father, but take it from me, he did. Also I once took back a mortgage for the late mister, God rest his pickled soul. Never mind, all that matters is that poor Sadie Doyle wants her wretched boy bailed out of jail again."

"You're posting bail for Stinky?"

"In a manner of speaking," Sugar said. "I'm a bondsman, you know."

Jack knew and had forgotten that McKane had once been a licensed bondsman, or really, he had assumed that McKane had long since let the license lapse, since he certainly wasn't active in the sleazy business. The current bonding rate was something like ten percent plus collateral, so bail set at two thousand would cost two hundred in cash plus, typically, a signed-over mortgage or note to ensure that the bailed individual made it into court at the appointed hour. Bondsmen often ended up holding paper, and for some of them that was the whole point of the business, a way to acquire mortgages and properties on the cheap. McKane had done a bit of it in his early days, long before the war—not lately, as far as Jack was aware.

Jack's mouth was dry. "I figured Keegan maybe."

"Keegan?"

"The creep Doyle works for. Keegan might try to spring him. That's who I expected. Keegan or his lawyer."

"Ah," Sugar said. He smiled, patted Jack again. "Mrs. Doyle mentioned the name. A hoodlum, no surprise. Poor Stinky, it sounds like they caught him redhanded."

"Dead to rights."

"You'll excuse me, Jack, I have to see a man called Farrell. Do you know him, Detective Farrell?"

"Slightly," Jack said.

"I hear he's a good man," McKane said. "Straight as an arrow." He paused. "A teetotaler. And very polite he was, over the telephone."

Sugar approached the desk and Jack slumped to the wooden bench. McKane was acquainted with many Irish families of a certain class, why not the South Boston Doyles? Of course he knew the Doyles. Young Stinky had been going wrong since grade school, probably tried to light a nun on fire, or worse. Mrs. Doyle would naturally align herself with a man revered as a cradle-to-grave fixer. And yet the coincidence of McKane intruding himself at this hour, in this particular circumstance, made the back of Jack's neck tingle—it was a warning, a sign that he mustn't pursue this particular case, that Doyle and Keegan were off-limits.

Nothing said, but he knew, as surely as he knew that if Sugar McKane carried an umbrella it was guaranteed to rain. And sure enough, as he stepped through the glass doors he was greeted by a crack of thunder and fat spatters of summer rain that clung to his face like gobs of warm spittle.

Twenty-two

The Twelve-Inch Philco

Two days after Stinky Doyle was released on bail, Michael Fitzroy made a delivery to the Jack Fitzroy household in Jamaica Plain. A block of decently maintained three-deckers, their identical porches strung with clotheslines. Like signal flags on wooden arks, he decided, all of them hard aground.

Mike had the top down and a cardboard crate taking up most of the backseat of his Coupe DeVille convertible, and he was feeling, well, quite jubilant for a change. Flying high. The big insurance payoff meant that the firm was, after less than a month of expanded operations, in the black, turning a slight profit.

Prospects unlimited.

He pulled to the curb, the fat white walls squeaking, and sounded the horn. Robby came running from out of nowhere, as if jerked by a string, his hands up and waving—what was that, a squirt gun?

"Unka Mike, Unka Mike!" The handsome little kid grinning and waving the gun. "I squirted a dog, he ran away!"

By the time Mike had gotten out of the car, Doris was descending the porch steps, the littlest, David, taking cover behind her skirt. It was hot, there had been thundershowers earlier in the day, and her hair was damp, kept back in a ponytail that made her look, at first glance, like a teenager. Two kids and she still had that fresh cream look.

"Jack around?"

Clearly Jack was not around because the big Packard was nowhere to be seen. Mike had noticed but asked anyhow, just to make conversation. Years had gone by and Doris still made him nervous whenever they met. The tension would pass, he knew from experience, within a few minutes. They'd learned how to make friends quickly, although they had to keep at it, make an effort.

"He called. Said he'd be home late. Some errand for Sugar."

"Ah," Mike said. He'd knelt, opening his arms, and now David was coming forward, bashful and smiling.

"He said it was important," Doris said, waiting for him to confirm.

"Then it must be," Mike said. He didn't feel like discussing any of the McKanes, not at the moment, not when he felt so good. "Come on, David, I want you and your big brother to see this."

He hoisted little David into the Cadillac, let him stand up on the seat. Robby had already scrambled inside, squirt gun leaking in his back pocket as he pried at the corners of the cardboard crate.

"Mom, it's a present, Unka Mike brought us a present!"

"Get down, Robby. You've got mud on your shoes."

"It's okay," Mike said. "He can't do any harm."

"What is it Michael?" Her tone questioning, critical.

"Jack's bonus," he said, patting the top of the crate. "A console, Doris. Philco, they make a good set. I got the twelve-inch screen."

"Mom, a television! Can we keep it, Unka Mike?"

"Michael," Doris said in a warning tone.

"I got a deal at Berman's," he said hastily. "Big sale. You're gonna love it, Dottie."

"But, Michael, the money."

"Because, we *made* money, okay? Can you let me do this?"

Doris, hands on her hips, about to speak, then shutting her mouth, shaking her head. She was starting to smile, though, he could see that much, couldn't help but respond to the excitement of having a television in the house. Maybe the first on the block—he sure as hell hoped so.

The fancy car and the crate and the prospect of something new had begun to attract a crowd, mostly youngsters from the neighborhood, and by passing out a ready supply of small change Mike was able to effect the transportation of the television to the second floor.

Doris, by now into the spirit of cooperation, supplied

glasses of cold grape-flavored Zarex to the kids who had helped, all of them sweating and proud and fingering their coins in anticipation of penny candy, kites, comic books. Shooed from the apartment as soon as the Zarex was consumed, a thundering herd retreated down the back stairs.

"They'll buy cigarettes," Doris said, giving Mike the eyeball, "the older boys. You didn't have to pay them."

"I wanted to pay them," he said. "You know me."

"Yes," she said, handing him a glass of cold beer. "I do."

Mike used a single-edged razor blade to cut away the cardboard. Exposing, to the excited shrieks of the two boys, the glittering gray eye of the Philco. A twelve-inch daylight screen, state-of-the-art. It was a project setting the thing up, exactly the sort of task Mike reveled in, his gadget mentality. As there was only one electrical outlet in the living room, and that behind the sofa, Doris had to borrow an extension cord from a neighbor. Meanwhile Mike used a butter knife, supplied with silent pride by the grinning David—that trusting smile nearly as big as his head—to screw down the leads of the rabbit-ear antenna.

"Will this blow the fuse?" Doris wanted to know, handing over the extension cord.

"Only one way to find out. Boys, stand back. Better yet, sit down on the sofa. Very good. Dot, you do the honors. Just turn this knob to the right."

"Like that?" Gingerly, as if expecting to receive a shock.

"It takes a few minutes to warm up the tubes," he said. "We get a picture, then I'll adjust the antenna, improve the reception."

Mike stepped back, finished the beer while the set warmed up. As the image came slowly into focus, little David stood up on the sofa, shouting. "Injuns! Injuns!"

On the glass, the flickering, a picture of an Indian chief: this was the test pattern, and under it a banner proclaimed

TRANSMISSION DIFFICULTIES PLEASE STAND BY.

Mike switched to the other channel and discovered that it, too, was off the air, scheduled to resume programming in the evening. The children did not seem greatly disappointed—David insisted on watching the test pattern, pointing his finger at it like a gun and shouting, "Pow! Pow!"

Doris, leaning in the kitchen doorway, was giggling, her eyes moist. "Michael, if you could see your face."

He shrugged. "You can watch Arthur Godfrey tonight."

"Of course we can."

"What's so funny?"

"I'm sorry. That look you had when the picture wouldn't come in. Like a kid who got a lump of coal for Christmas."

Mike squeezed past her into the kitchen, aware that he was blushing. "I just wanted, you know . . ."

Doris nodded. "I didn't mean to laugh. It's very nice, really, having a television. The boys love it already."

He wanted another beer, decided against it, mostly because Doris expected him to have another. Surprise her by requesting coffee, that was the strategy.

"Too hot to turn on the stove, Mike. How about iced tea, I've got a pitcher in the icebox."

"Iced tea is fine."

And so they sat at the kitchen table, chatting fairly comfortably and making conversation while the boys whooped it up around the new television, playing cowboys and Indians with fingers for guns. There were kitchen goods stacked neatly in boxes, ready to go. Doris was packing up beach stuff, getting ready for the summer migration the first of July, the same cheap little cottage they'd been renting since she was pregnant with Robby, and she was, quite understandably, eager to get away from the heat of the three-decker.

"It'll do Jack good," she said, looking away. "Get him up there on weekends, maybe he'll soak his legs. The sun will help."

Mike realized he and Doris had not discussed Jack's bout with polio since he had been released from the hospital—Jack sure as hell didn't want to talk about it. He was reminded, sipping the sweet iced tea, that Doris never forgot it, not for an instant.

"He swims at the Y," Mike reminded her. "Therapy, build up those muscles."

"Yeah, but he hates it. I want to get him in the salt

water, get him to relax, you know? You think it's possible, get a Fitzroy to relax?''

Mike smiled, shook his head.

''So it's going good, huh?'' she asked.

''It's going great. Better, you know, than any of us expected. We put on six new guys in the last two weeks and we'll need to double that, the way business is coming in. I figure we'll have maybe four guys do nothing but handle the insurance investigations. This time next year, we'll have twenty-five full-time investigators, minimum.''

''It seems very . . . fast.''

Mike leaned forward, intent on convincing her. ''Dottie, we don't hire unless we have the business, I promise you. And we have the business. The office next door goes vacant in August, I'm leasing it. We need the extra space.''

He knew that look—he'd been getting it since Jack met the girl, an expression of stony distrust that always made him feel like some scheming hustler, a look that said, *Who are you kidding, with your fancy car and your smart talk? No matter how much money you throw around, you can't fool me, you came from the same place I did.*

Usually he ignored the look, remained polite. Today, however, he wasn't going to let it slide. He was going to win Doris over, convince her that Mike Fitzroy was for real, no schemes or hustles.

''Don't you get it?'' he said. ''This is going to change your life, the firm. Jack is going to make a lot of money the next few years. You'll be able to move out of this place, the very least.''

Doris sat up, her voice low, her expression almost savage. ''There's nothing wrong with this place, Michael. It's a decent flat in a decent neighborhood.''

''Hey! I didn't say there was anything wrong with it. Are you kidding? Compared to where we grew up, over the store, this is beautiful. But, admit it, you can do a hell of a lot better. Nice place in Brookline or Newton, the schools are good. The boys would have a nice big yard to play in. Jesus, Dottie, what's wrong with that?''

''And who's going to pay for all this? You? Your father-in-law?''

Mike couldn't help it, he was grinning because that's

exactly what he had expected her to say. Like the prospect of success was some kind of scheme or trick, you couldn't trust it. "So that's what you think, this is all Sugar's money?"

Doris folded her arms. She was hot, she'd had a long day, she had no patience, her posture indicated, for a lot of Michael Fitzroy's highfalutin nonsense.

"Let me explain how it works," Mike said. He wasn't going to let her get to him. He was going to reveal the fabulous truth, open her eyes. "Sugar provided the start-up financing and a line of credit, what we needed to cover overhead and salaries for the first few months, when Jack was getting back on his feet. He also—and I'm not saying this wasn't important—steered some business our way. Anything wrong with that?"

Doris shrugged. Deliberately she refilled his glass of iced tea, letting him know he would continue to receive hospitality in her household even if she didn't believe him.

"Sugar helped. He's still helping. But the reason we're staring to get a lot of clients on our own is me and Jack, okay? *Our* connections. All the lawyers I know, all the cops Jack knows. Mostly *what* Jack knows, who to hire and how to run a professional investigation. These old gumshoe outfits, they can't compete. Couple of years from now it won't matter that Sugar McKane backed us at the start."

Doris, exasperated, muttered a few words. Mike, his hearing acute for insults, caught them.

"I know you think the old man is a crook," he said, "but what Sugar is, Dottie, and it's a different thing, he's a politician. Really, more like an engineer in the political machine. Oiling the machinery, making sure it runs, and in politics in this town, that means raising money."

"I've heard that before," said Doris. She was keeping her voice low so that the boys couldn't hear the edge, her restrained anger. "You know what it sounds like, Mike? Pardon my French, but it sounds like bullshit. Sugar McKane bullshit. You say he's not a crook, but he got you disbarred, didn't he?"

Mike sighed. This wasn't working, she just wouldn't listen to reason. "That's over and done. I made a deal and I stuck by it, okay? I don't expect you to understand.

But it doesn't matter now because we've got a good thing going here. We'll both of us make money. More than I made as Sugar's personal attorney. A helluva lot more than Jack ever made on the cops, even if he had made captain someday.''

Robby came into the kitchen, skidding on the linoleum, his eyes big with excitement. ''There's a man on television, he's got a clown face! And a little dog that jumps!''

''Go and watch him, honey. And no squirt guns in the house, I told you.''

''Come and see him, Mom!''

''In a minute.'' Doris stood up, put away the pitcher of iced tea. After closing the refrigerator she took a deep breath, gave him a wary smile. ''I'm sorry, Mike. Didn't mean to give you such a hard time.''

''I know what it is. You think Jack will get into trouble like I did, is that it?''

She nodded. ''He's doing secret things for Sugar, he won't tell me what.''

''Doris, all I can tell you, it's a legitimate investigation. Jack isn't breaking the law, not even close. And what are you worried about? Jack is Jack, right?'' Mike raised his hands, wanting her to see the absurdity of the idea, Jack Fitzroy breaking the law. ''Right?''

''Right,'' she said at last, and made a face. ''What am I thinking?''

''Things are looking up,'' he said, rising from the table. ''Get used to the idea.''

On the drive back into the city it rained. He didn't bother stopping to put the top up. What the hell, the rain felt good and if it ruined the leather upholstery he could always buy new seats, or trade in the car. It was great, feeling like this, king of the mountain, top of the world, and he decided to keep the feeling, no matter what happened with Miriam when he got home.

Twenty-three

Bottom Feeders

Lunch at the Ritz-Carlton. Jack had dressed for the occasion, his new seersucker and a straw boater that felt silly, the way it perched on his head. A target, he was convinced, for the army of pigeons patrolling the Public Garden.

Jack had commandeered a wrought-iron bench near the Arlington Street entrance, his eyes peeled for a little cane-wielding man in spats, surely there couldn't be more than one. It would have been easier, or more dignified, to meet the reporter on Newspaper Row, take him to a chowder house or maybe the Thompson Spa, but the man had been insistent, he wanted the Ritz.

The reporter's name was Hamish J. Higgins and he had been writing a State House gossip column for the *Transcript* since Hoover was in office. According to Sugar he was a small, black-haired gentleman in his late fifties: a dapper, old-fashioned dresser famous for his waxed moustache, sleek gray spats, white gloves, and the knobbed cane he carried like a baton on his rapid, health-faddish walks through the Public Garden.

A colleague writing a column for a competing newspaper had likened Higgins to a Boston tourist attraction, faster than the nickel swan boats and—this was the point of the barb—cheaper. Never in all his years as a newspaperman had Higgins ever been known to pay for his own lunch. Or that was the way Sugar told it, anyhow. Sugar knew him from the old days, when Democratic clubs ran the West End and Hamish J. Higgins was a young reporter covering ward politics, poorly paid and always on the lookout for a free meal.

"The good Lord broke the mold after he made Hamish," McKane had said, his voice booming over the telephone, so loud that Jack had had to hold the receiver away from his ear. "A good thing, too. The best way to handle this, let him order off the menu. Humor him. He wants stroking, Jack."

"I'm not much of a stroker."

"You'll do just fine."

There was no doubt at all when Higgins came strutting into view. Marching like a band leader, ramrod straight, knees up, hut-hut. When Jack stood up and—he couldn't help it—raised his straw boater in greeting, Higgins saluted with his cane, then paused to daintily mop a sparkle of perspiration from his brow with a large monogrammed handkerchief that he kept, of all places, up his sleeve. After use, the hankie was tucked neatly away, hidden by a heavily starched shirt cuff.

The strange thing was, Jack didn't have to fight any impulse to laugh. As absurd as the little man might appear by reputation, in the flesh there was nothing comical about Hamish J. Higgins. On the contrary, he made Jack feel slightly soiled, sorry he hadn't worn a more conservative suit and tie. The columnist had a confidence, a presence that made you take him seriously.

But the white gloves. Who was the last man to wear dress gloves in public? Jack found himself considering the glove question as he shook hands, Higgins doing his bow of greeting, a discreet dip of the head.

"Mr. Fitzroy, I presume?"

Jack admitted as much. Introductions complete, they crossed Arlington Street and entered the hotel lobby.

A shallow flight of marble steps divided the entrance from the foyer, no big deal, except that Jack's left leg for some reason decided to play dead and he had to stop, reach down, lift his foot up to the top of each step. Like he was manipulating a marionette, yanking the strings. He could feel the angry blush burning his collar, a surge of temper that made him want to spit and curse, but this was the Ritz. All he could do was snap his teeth and grin like a dog.

Mr. Higgins waited, a man of infinite patience, at the top of the stairs. He did not comment on Jack's physical distress, other than to offer his cane.

"I'm fine. This never happens."

Jack was dragging the foot, it wanted to turn sideways,

strangely numb at the ankle and yet thrumming with a pain that ran like a knife blade up the back of his calf.

Higgins nodded, ever courteous, and turned to the elevators, avoiding the curving staircase. At the second-floor restaurant, an elegant room of high ceilings and tall windows that overlooked the Public Garden, Higgins was greeted by name and led to, as the maître d' put it, "Your usual table, sir," an atmospheric location with good light and a lovely view.

Jack eased himself down as the maître d' slipped the chair under his backside.

"I'll be having wine with the meal," Higgins announced, "but for now my companion requires a very dry martini."

"Right away, Mr. Higgins."

"I hope you don't mind," Higgins said, unfolding his napkin with a snap of the wrist. "I think you'll find a good martini does wonders."

Jack, catching sight of himself in a wall mirror, saw a hollow-eyed stranger pale with pain. When the drink arrived, he took it as intended, like a dose of medicine, and sure enough, felt better almost at once.

Higgins meanwhile discoursed on the weather.

"Unusually fine air for June," he said, eyes directed at the artificial tranquillity of the duck pond. "Already it has the feel of mid-summer. I'm quite sure this is the first time the *Transcript* has run an egg-on-the-sidewalk story before, oh, mid-July."

"Egg on the sidewalk?" Jack, checking the mirror, saw himself returning, like an image taking form in one of his brother's instant photographs.

"As in 'hot enough to fry an egg,' " Higgins was saying. "A traditional *Transcript* story, you understand. Like the L Street Brownies taking their annual winter swim. Usually assigned to a young reporter because if he fails to deliver, we can always run last year's story. Never varies by more than a few sentences. Tradition."

Jack nodded. It was amazing, hearing Higgins speak. Was that an English accent? Didn't sound quite like the Brits he'd come across in occupied Germany, but those boys were mostly Cockney, and that was like a foreign language: all you could do was smile and nod. This, Higgins's clipped manner of speech, was something else again. Snotty except that the old gent didn't have a snotty attitude. Very self-contained, as if he was visiting from another and better world but rather enjoyed consorting with the natives.

Maybe it was the chilled gin, but Jack found himself liking Hamish Higgins, and grateful for the man's polite deference. Sugar had said let him order off the menu and that meant a lobster salad plate and a bottle of pre-war white wine that cost, Jack was stunned to discover, twelve dollars, triple the cost of the lobster itself.

He'd taken fifty from petty cash, signed out by Rosemary Phelan, and impulsively he decided what the hell, this was Sugar's idea, on his tab, why not have the cold beef platter and another soothing martini, really put a dent in the fifty.

"So you know Sugar from where, the old Ward Eight boys?"

Higgins patted his lips dry, sat erect as he responded. "I was introduced to Mr. McKane by the Mahatma, Martin Lomasney."

"Oh yeah," Jack said. "Sugar has a lot of Mahatma stories. He loved the old guy."

"Many did," Higgins said. "Mr. Lomasney was a remarkable man. Sugar was an apprentice, you might say, at Martin Lomasney's clubhouse. If you ever heard the Mahatma give a speech, you'll know that Sugar learned from him. That great rhetorical flourish, reliance on old-fashioned themes of self-improvement, and so on. The Mahatma was always excessively polite, always astonishingly loud, whether on stage at a rally or presiding over the old Hendricks Club. Lived like a monk. No booze, no women. Quite a character, the Mahatma. Of course, your father-in-law has developed his own style over the years."

"He's not my father-in-law," Jack corrected. "My brother, Mike, is the one married the daughter."

"Ah," Higgins said. "I see. A stunning young lady, smart as a whip. Looks a bit like that young film star, what's her name, Elizabeth Taylor. Big eyes like that."

Jack found himself muttering in agreement, not wanting to be too hasty about changing the delicate subject of his brother's wife and what a stunner she was, maybe give something away to a well-known newspaper columnist who just happened to have certain connections to Miriam's father. God forbid. As for Higgins, he did not seem inclined to pursue the matter, nor did he give any indication of suspecting his host of anything more serious than a disinclination to discuss family matters.

"Have you an interest in politics?"

"Not really," Jack said. "I was a cop."

Higgins nodded. "A homicide detective. Before that a decorated military hero. And you're just thirty years of age. Wouldn't be a bit surprised if Sugar persuades you to run for office."

The martinis insulated him from embarrassment. "That was my brother again," Jack said, "who Sugar wanted in office. Only Mike got disbarred, so forget about that now."

Higgins held the wineglass delicately, a crystal flower blooming from his manicured hands. "A spot of trouble with the state bar association would not necessarily preclude a career in public service," he said. "Not with McKane behind you. Behind your brother, I mean."

"Is that what this is about? Mike running for office?"

Higgins smiled, shook his head. "Forgive me, that was merely a conversational gambit. I see that it has failed."

"Oh." Jack was confused.

"Mr. McKane asked me to show you certain documents I received through my office at the *Transcript*."

"Yeah, that's what I figured."

"Not the sort of thing gentlemen would discuss prior to eating. Best examined on a full stomach."

"Eat away," Jack said. Amazing how the gin had gone to his head, two lousy drinks. "Take your time."

After dispatching the last morsel of lobster the newspaperman ordered a sherbet and coffee. Jack had two quick cups, wanting to sober up before he had to limp out of this place, maybe fall and make a fool of himself if he wasn't careful, betrayed by his goddamn polio leg, all that goddamn swimming at the goddamn YMCA was no goddamn guarantee.

"What's that?" Higgins was saying, a look of concern lifting his mustache. "Is the coffee bad?"

"Fine," Jack said, waving a hand over the cup. "Pay no attention to the man behind the screen."

"What?"

"Wizard of Oz, never mind."

"Oh yes, I quite see." Higgins's bright little eyes were amused. "A wonderful movie. Judy Garland was in this very hotel only last month, I think it was. Charming young lady. Inclined, they say, to dipsomania." He spooned up his sherbet, allowed Jack time to regain his composure, a gentleman acknowledging the awkward effects of a medicinal martini, or in this case a double dose of high-octane gin. Eventually the coffee seemed to compensate and Jack felt the rug lift from his tongue.

"I guess you better show me the letters," he said.

Higgins produced a manila envelope, slid it across the table. "They continue in the same vein as before," he said. "From the spelling and the tone one assumes the writer has little formal education. Lack of schooling does not preclude, as you already know, an active imagination."

"Right," Jack said, opening the envelope. "Imagination is one way of putting it."

Why do you keep stalling? Tell the truth about that great bastard Sugar McKane who raped his own daughter and killed a man. Is it becuse your owned lock stock in barrel by Irish Jews like he is and stealing from the dead right out of there coffins. Uther wise this is the story of the centry how him the no good grave robbing bastard had a man killed over a lousy two thousand dollers and got away with murder. If you wont write it your an Irish Jew bastard like him.

Jack looked up and said, "A regular broken record."

"I would say the individual is disturbed," Higgins said. "That 'Irish Jew,' I haven't heard that in years." Seeing that Jack was puzzled, he hastened to explain. "The old rumor about Mr. McKane being half Jewish. No truth to it, of course. Beyond the fact that he deals in second mortgages."

"Sugar doesn't care about that, being called a Jew. It's the other thing bothers him."

Higgins, engaged in polishing his dessert spoon with a linen napkin, nodded thoughtfully. "There was a time, not so many years ago, when a man involved in ward politics would admit to rape before he'd confess to Jewish blood.''

''Come on.''

''I exaggerate, of course, but not by much. The anti-Semite Father Coughlin didn't preach to the wilderness, he had a following. A very large following here in Boston. Many believed that Roosevelt himself was secretly Hebrew.''

Jack shook his head. ''I don't know why Sugar's getting hate mail, but it's not about hating the Jews. That's just a word, an insult. Doesn't mean a thing.''

Higgins had finished polishing the spoon, was hard at work on the salad fork. ''Respectfully, I must disagree. Words are important, particularly words spoken—or in this case written—in anger. I agree, Mr. McKane is not even remotely Jewish, but the point is, this person, this hateful, crazy-sounding person believes he is. You're the detective, surely that suggests something about the character of the letter writer.''

''Maybe,'' Jack conceded. ''I don't know what.''

The mustache twitched. ''For starters, I think we can conclude this person is neither Irish nor Jewish. Thus rendering innocent about three-quarters of the city.''

Jack smiled. ''That narrows it down to a hundred thousand or so.''

Higgins shook his head. ''The first few letters were hand-delivered to the *Transcript*, left in our letter box. This one, which arrived day before yesterday, came through the mail. Postmark, East Boston.''

Jack wasn't sure how much information he should impart to Hamish Higgins. The idea of taking him to lunch had been quite the reverse, *extracting* whatever tidbits he had, including the latest threatening letter. Just as clearly Higgins, who after all had refrained from publishing the threats, expected some sort of exchange.

''Look,'' Jack said, ''a certain person from that neighborhood made similar accusations to the police—the murder part, not the rape—but there's no evidence that any crime occurred. It was an accidental death, a drowning, no reason to suspect anyone, let alone Sugar.''

Higgins nodded thoughtfully. He'd finished polishing the silverware and the empty wineglass and seemed content to sit with his hands folded. "Whatever Sugar McKane may be," he said, "he is not a killer. Nor would he engage to have anyone killed, for any reason. I say this having known the man for many years. Many years. Take advantage? Oh yes, he'll take advantage of a situation, depend on that. But he lives by a code of his own devising, and whatever that code may allow in the way of financial shenanigans, it forbids the mortal sin of murder. Or, for that matter, of incest."

Jack found that he had no response. He did not share the newspaperman's confidence in the limits of human depravation—not Sugar's limit and not, as he'd been demonstrating lately, his own. Whatever he'd learned from Miriam, it touched on this unknowable truth: no man can know for certain what another person will do, least of all himself.

"Financial shenanigans?" he said finally, just to say something.

Higgins was for the first time uncomfortable. "Excuse my rhetoric. Like Sugar McKane, I love the sound of my own voice."

Jack leaned forward, keeping his voice low. God knows what the waiters heard in here. "Mr. Higgins? My brother got himself disbarred covering for Sugar McKane, remember? So I know he's no Boy Scout. And I'm working for him right now, spending his money, so what does that make me? Do you get my point?"

"I do, yes."

"All I'm saying, you know anything might concern this East Boston connection, tell me. Don't spare my feelings, or Sugar's. He trusts me, so can you."

"I dare say."

"Shenanigans, I believe you said."

Higgins sighed. A hand fluttered to his face, adjusted the points of his mustache. "In my business one hears many rumors, and one soon learns that most rumors are merely untruths made to sound attractive. Pretty lies."

The old man paused, his eyes drifting again to the window, the swan boats pedaling over the duck pond. Lovely to look at from here, Jack decided, but close up, on a hot day, the smell would wrinkle your nose. Higgins had a look like that, as if he'd just gotten a whiff of something unpleasant.

"I'll leave you with this, young Mr. Fitzroy: there are rumors about certain real estate transactions that have occurred recently in East Boston."

Jack tried wheedling, cajoling, wanting to know if the rumors touched on the arsonist landlord Jimmy Keegan, or Sugar McKane, or both, but Hamish Higgins refused to elaborate. He did add, as they left the dining room, Jack trying to hide the way his foot dragged, "Thank you very much for the fine lunch, Mr. Fitzroy." And then, after a pause, his small eyes alight. "You'd never know from the taste that lobster feeds on the bottom."

Twenty-four

The Mahatma's Boy Wonder

Sugar McKane had the place of honor, supreme high judge of the sack race. For this solemn office he was given the traditional green starter's flag—a piece of crepe bunting—and a top hat that had supposedly been worn on a much more previous occasion by then mayor John Francis "Honey Fitz" Fitzgerald.

The top hat, being too small for McKane's massive head, was propped on a pole designating the finish line. The contestants, all under the age of twelve, stood waiting in flour sacks supplied by a South Boston bakery. A variety of smiles peered from above the flour sacks. Not all of the grinning kid faces were Irish, Sugar noted with a grunt of approval. Children from the Italian-dominated West End and North End wards had been bussed in for the event. And, God bless them, there were undoubtedly a couple of Jewish kids in there, cuckoos in the nest.

The Castle Island picnic was an annual affair, sponsored by the Ancient Order of Hibernians. Of all McKane's organizations, the Hibernians was the most influential when it came to the twin power sources of church and politics. Rare was the high-ranking cop or the pol or the upwardly craving city employee who didn't seek membership. Why, even that hawk-faced Brahmin, Henry Cabot Lodge, Jr., had been made an honorary Hibernian, although it was widely known that McKane himself had sponsored Senator Lodge just to tweak the beard of Curley's goat, as it were.

Castle Island was attached to the mainland on the easternmost reach of South Boston, overlooking the harbor on one side and Southie's shallow bay on the other. The "castle" was an old fort built to defend the harbor, and during the war it had been manned by civilian wardens. A scurvy bunch of hens, as Sugar recalled, proud of their badges and government-issued binoculars. At the height of the scare it was not unusual for nervous lookouts to report German submarines in the harbor, only to have the "periscopes" confirmed as lobster buoys or dozing sea gulls.

On this, the last Saturday in June, with the war four years over, the shallow bay, protected by a breakwater, was alive and screaming with children afloat on black inner tubes and Navy surplus life rafts. Hundreds of screaming kids, gleeful with noise. Sugar, who'd been up since dawn, overseeing the organizational details, was pleased with the results.

"Ready on the sack line!"

That his voice was clearly audible over all of this hullaballoo was a testament to Sugar's lung power, of which he was immoderately proud. Yes indeed, he thought, here's a man can make himself heard in a hurricane. A great thunderclap of a voice, look at the children jump to attention.

"Go!"

Down went the arm with a flash of green bunting. Down also went a majority of the sack racers, most of who had not mastered the art of remaining upright while at the same time going forward. Cute, a pony-tailed girl in there reminded him of Deirdre long ago, before the troubles started.

"Will you look at them wop kiddies," said the fire chief, situated a yard to the left of McKane. "Ever seen maggots trying to wiggle out of a trash pail?"

"Are you saying they'll hatch and fly away, Freddy?" Sugar had taken his rightful place at the finish line, ready to eyeball the first three contestants to cross, which from the look of things was going to take some time.

Freddy Neeson, the fire chief and a great florid man pumped like a sausage into his splendid dress uniform, remarked that the dark children of Sicily were more likely to hatch into job applicants for Murder, Incorporated.

"I believe it was a Jewish gentleman ran that organization," Sugar said, "and, Freddy my lad, you're best advised to button your lip about wops. Our Italian friends are sensitive to insult."

The chief's red face darkened by several hues. "By

Jesus, McKane, you've got your nerve telling a man to keep his trap shut.''

''As you say, Chief,'' Sugar said. ''I've got my nerve.''

From where he stood, McKane had had a clear whiff of the booze on Neeson's breath, and he saw no reason to mask his disapproval of a man who would sneak whiskey at a children's picnic. The fire chief had his office by virtue of the current mayor, the aged scoundrel and jailbird James Michael Curley, and although McKane made an effort to maintain cordial relations with all city employees, he drew the line at boozing and name-calling.

Nowadays the Italian wards were crucial, and not only for votes. In recent years the North End business associations wooed by McKane had contributed generously to the party coffers. A drunken fire chief who muttered about guineas and organ grinders was a throwback to the old days, an embarrassment that might, in the long run, prove expensive.

''Well,'' said the chief, hooking his fat thumbs in his belt, ''I can see why the top hat don't fit.''

''Here they come,'' Sugar said, ignoring the jibe, ''the little dears.''

The wiggling flour sacks were approaching the finish line, spilling children, some of them rolling and bobbing like kittens in a bag, and all of them screaming.

Sorting out the winners was impossible, as it happened. McKane picked the three sack racers closest to hand and saw they were given ribbons. The races concluded, all of the children—and they'd come by the hundreds—were treated to ice cream, a problem of logistics and supply that would have stumped Eisenhower, but was handled rather neatly, McKane decided, by a variety of city vendors who understood the importance of pleasing the Hibernians.

''Freddy, there're none of these kids on fire, you're free to go.''

The chief's eyes went hard and small, chips of mica set in flour paste. ''Are you ordering me off, is that what you're doing?''

''I'm suggesting,'' Sugar said pleasantly, turning to face the man, ''that your duties are complete here. I heard a siren just now, over to Roxbury Shore I think it was. No doubt you're wanted there.''

"You know what's wrong with you, McKane? You're afraid to take a drink."

"Please lower your voice, Freddy. The kids."

"I hate the brats. Jesus, a man can't hear himself think."

"In your case, there's not much to hear," Sugar muttered, signaling for the chief's driver. It was time to take control of the situation, remove Neeson from the scene.

"What?"

"Go on, Freddy, we'll see the kids are taken care of."

That children had become the focus of the outdoor activities was largely McKane's doing. Before Prohibition the Castle Island picnic had been a kind of beer-garden affair, horse-drawn vats of the stuff brought in by brewery teamsters and distributed free of charge. In those days the rule of thumb was this: a man would be served so long as he stood on his own two feet—after that he'd send his children with a pitcher. It was understood that the free beer and clambake were provided by the ward bosses as an encouragement to vote early and often, come the fall elections.

In recent years the elaborate clambake had been scrapped in favor of a more popular weiner roast—these war-boom kids seemed to hate anything to do with fish—and crates of bottled tonic had replaced the old beer wagons. Alcohol was still consumed, of course, but on the sly now, and there was not the wallowing public drunkenness that had for years been loudly and repeatedly denounced by Sugar McKane as the curse of Ireland, a specter no less hideous and harmful than the ghost of Cromwell—supposed by many in the crowd to be a despised brand of British beer, a misapprehension that secretly pleased him.

With the fire chief disposed of, McKane returned to the area of tables set up behind the stage, away from the crowd. There was a brass marching band on stage now, soon to be followed by a collection of costumed accordion players, and the ward leaders were able to converse among themselves without danger of being overheard. Thus the traditional placement of the picnic tables.

Not that it really mattered, Sugar knew, what a keen

ear might hear. Take, for instance, Fat Charley Monk in his iron mike, the hard-shell derby he wore to protect his bald, empty head. Sugar was always amazed, looking at Monk, simply amazed that the cigar-smoking fool, barely literate, actually considered himself the sage of Dorchester.

"Hey, Sugar! Hey! Here, have a seat, take a load off yer feet. Dija try the tater salad, man, it's first-rate. Come on now, we saw yuz givin' poor Freddy Neeson the grief, whatja do there, put out the man's fire?"

"He's gone home to sleep it off."

"That's what you think." Fat Charley's laugh was somewhere up his nose, wet and snuffling. "Freddy's off to the Shamrock to finish what he started."

Pushing aside a plate of weirdly discolored potato salad, Sugar announced that he didn't care where the drunken lout of a fire chief soaked his brain, as long as it wasn't in broad daylight in the sight of innocent children.

At this several of the ward leaders, including Fat Charley himself, nervously clutched their beverage cups, as if fearing closer inspection. Sugar smiled, for he well knew that the boys did not fear him as much as they loathed enduring his famous half-hour lecture on abstinence.

"And what, pray tell, has been under discussion on this fine day?" he asked, looking around the table, focusing on each ward captain in turn. "Any business I should know of?"

"We been shootin' the shit, Sugar—excuse me, throwin' the bull."

"Telling lewd stories, I suppose."

"Couple dirty jokes, what could it hurt?" said Jimmy Harris, bail bondsman and South End captain. The youngest of five brothers, he was the only one of them not on the cops. "We had a priest come by, pay his respects, he knew a good one about three nuns in a rubber boat."

"I've heard it," Sugar said, although he hadn't.

In practice, little political business was actually conducted at the annual picnic. The truth was that Curley had finally succeeded in replacing the old ward patronage system with his own self-serving method of awarding favors. You wanted a city job or a contract, you went directly to the mayor, standing in line with other citizen supplicants outside his home. Curley cut his own deals, made good on his own promises. The ward bosses, broken by Curley's so-called reforms, could now deliver little more than a simple majority of votes in any one district. Gone were the days when Martin Lomasney could nominate a paper boy to Congress simply to demonstrate his wit and power.

Many of the boys still clung to the old ideas, confident that their influence would return with the long-awaited demise of James Michael Curley. Sugar, acting as the party's chief fund-raiser, knew better. The Mahatma was dead and gone, so too the voters who blindly obeyed district captains. The seemingly simple and pliant men of the working-class wards had gone off to war and come back greatly changed, skeptical of stogie smokers and back-slappers. Many of the young veterans seemed eager to start life over in new places, out of the city, beyond the reach of the ward bosses and old parish priests, or even Mayor Curley himself.

It was a brave new world where citizens rallied to radios and television. Oh, there were still rallies, to be sure, and noisy orchestras and stirring speeches, but the old political caucus didn't count for much now. Roosevelt had changed that forever, with radio speeches that made him seem a friend to those who'd never met him. That's what counted now—the broadcasts that determined how the people voted. A distinction not understood by all those at the annual picnic, in Sugar's strongly held opinion.

Oh, the voters went to the polls, delivered as of old by the ward bosses, that part still worked. But when they got there, these modern and ungrateful citizens voted as they pleased. You wanted to put your man in office today, you had to get inside those not-so-thick citizens' heads. Advertising. That meant money, and lots of it. In the past buying votes had been easy. Now, in the modern way of doing things, you had to buy opinions—a much trickier undertaking. Far too complex a notion to penetrate the stony skull of Fat Charley Monk, for instance.

"Sonny gave a fine talk," Fat Charley offered. "If you could hear him over the brats."

McKane did not react. He had no use for Sonny McDonough, a man of the old school, a throwback, and in Sugar's opinion a certain loser come the fall. Let the man harangue the neighborhoods from his sound truck, let him make his case with the voters, the newspapers, the ward leaders; Sugar would see that McDonough got a token contribution from the party coffers, but no major investment in a city election that was surely going to the reformists come fall. Better to conserve now, disburse funds at the state level next year, when it might do some good.

"The man is wasting his time with this crowd," McKane offered. "By the time most of those in attendance are old enough to vote, Sonny will be in heaven. Or possibly elsewhere."

"Florida!" a ward leader shouted.

This was followed by loud, smoky guffaws. Fat Charley Monk was so overcome with amusement he spilled his drink—it being well known that he himself had recently purchased a red-roofed ranch house in Pompano Beach.

"Sonny'll do okay," Monk said, pawing at his stained shirt front. "He's due for a win. He'll take the primary, watch him."

"We'll be watching, Charley."

"Hey, I'm serious here. McDonough wins."

"Ya takin' bets again, Charley?"

Every man at the picnic tables knew that Monk had once been partnered with a notorious bookie. His adroitness at extracting himself from the partnership prior to certain arrest was legendary. Supposedly he'd bribed a police captain to destroy crucial evidence—a bank book, initialed betting slips—but the truth as Sugar knew it was this: the bookie had ditched Fat Charley for taking the wrong end of a Boston College football game that he claimed to have fixed but hadn't. So he was dropped, and lucky for him, as the bookie went down soon after.

"Watch yer mouth with that talk." Monk was suddenly sober, serious, his small, fat eyes gone dangerous. With the FBI on a crime-busters rampage and wiretaps in vogue, references to illegal operations, no matter how long expired, were to be refuted.

Sugar smoothed over the gaffe by airing an old anecdote about his hero and mentor, Martin Lomasney. ''Sonny, when the day comes,'' Sugar began, ''he'd do well to pass out the combs.''

''The combs, Sugar?''

They all knew the tale to follow, of course, had heard him tell it a hundred times, but McKane expected a certain level of listener involvement, and he got it. ''The combs. Very important, the combs,'' he said, warming to his own rhetoric, feeling his voice lift. ''Martin had them manufactured at a little plant out in Roxbury. The price was a dollar a hundred, I believe.''

''A penny apiece, Sugar?''

''I believe that was the price, yes.''

''Cheap combs.''

''Cheap,'' Sugar agreed, ''and priceless.''

''I suppose he passed them out, did Martin, these cheap combs?''

''He did,'' Sugar said. ''A comb for every man and woman of an age to enter the polling place. Even bald men got combs. Especially bald men, of which there were quite a number, as I recall, in the old West End. Enough so the glare might blind a man, looking down from a rally stage.''

''Hats? Hadn't they hats, Sugar, to cover their heads?''

''Of course they had hats. Scalley caps and iron mikes. I meant, of course, when they took off their hats to cheer. Which they always seemed to be doing at a Martin Lomasney rally. Hence the sudden glare.''

''Cheering for you, I suppose. The Mahatma's boy wonder.''

Sugar shrugged modestly. ''Cheer they did, that's all I'll say. And after the cheering, Martin had his lads pass out the combs. With instructions on how to use them, come voting day.''

''A pretty dumb crowd you'd gather, who didn't know how to use a comb.''

''Not dumb,'' Sugar corrected, shaking a large finger. ''Illiterate. And bear in mind that's not the same thing at all. A man can be dumb and know how to read, I think you'll all agree. Sonny McDonough can read.''

Laughter, even from Fat Charley, who was backing McDonough.

''Remember how it was,'' Sugar went on, ''how it was

in the old times, when a man put his shoulder under a hod at dawn and carried it until the moon rose. No time for book learning, no time for reading even if you had the knack, no money for books even if you had the time, and no lanterns bright enough if by some great miracle you found the time *and* the books. Hence, gentleman, the Mahatma's comb.''

''Lomasney had a head like a cue ball, Sugar. Why'd he need a comb?''

''Ah, but the comb was a gift, boys, and like the best of gifts it gave both ways. Because the secret, you see, the secret was in the tines.''

''The tines, Sugar?''

''The tines. Certain tines were missing, gaps in the comb, and so when your illiterate gentleman placed the comb over the ballot, he could see what names to mark.''

''Like a sample ballot, then.''

''In a manner of speaking, yes. But unlike the old sample ballot, with the names already checked off, the Mahatma's comb was not illegal to carry into the voting booth.''

''The man was a genius.''

''He was a great man,'' Sugar agreed, expecting and getting a chorus of agreement. ''A great man indeed.''

There was no time to bask in the pleasure of an old story well told, however, because Jimmy Harris, the South End captain, was on his feet and waving, his wide, wet mouth twisted into a sickly grin. ''It's him, the bastard, come to ruin the day,'' he said. ''Him in his bleeping convertible car.''

Groans went up from the picnic tables, for the most part good-natured, because an appearance by Mayor Curley was not exactly unanticipated. His Honor was, after all, a man who'd cheerfully run over widows to get to a funeral, a famous party crasher who'd conquered many an unwilling audience with his bombast. He was, in addition, an officer of the Hibernians, and could not be denied attendance at the annual children's picnic.

What he could be denied, and Sugar had already seen to this, was access to the microphone. By prearrangement, Curley's appearance coincided with the failure of the public-address system. All that could be heard now, as the mayor's Oldsmobile convertible boated

slowly through the crowded picnic grounds, was the unamplified wheezing of the all-accordion orchestra.

"Let's be civil," Sugar instructed the ward bosses.
"Put your hands together."

He demonstrated by applauding noiselessly, his big
hands not quite meeting as he made a show of clapping.

"The old fraud's got a megaphone," Fat Charley
warned. "He remembered from last year."

"Let him bellow," Sugar said. "What's the harm?"

Curley did indeed have a megaphone, and more to the
point he knew how to use it, spacing his words to take
advantage of the echo. A white-haired man in a beautiful
suit, standing erect in the rear seat of a white convertible—quite a sight, a vision that made Sugar want to close
his eyes, maybe take a nap right then and there. But the
fat wheels of the car came to rest not ten yards from
Sugar's picnic table, and it was no coincidence that the
horn of the mayor's battery-powered megaphone was
aimed directly at Sugar, who could see the glint of petty
triumph in Curly's lizard eyes.

"Gather round, kids. Your mayor brings gifts. Come
and get it."

The stampede was immediate and overwhelming. The
children, already alerted by the appearance of the flashy
convertible, instantly converged on the area in back of
the stage. The trunk of the mayor's automobile was
thrown open, and his lackeys were passing out comic
books and lollipops as Curley, standing nimbly on the
rear seat, continued his carefully elocuted harangue.

"Have no fear, Mom and Dad. These are not ordinary,
mind-polluting comic books. Read them and see."

With that the mayor surrendered his megaphone, got
out of the automobile, and began to glad-hand his way
through the crowd, showing his elegantly tailored backside to the ward bosses he so famously despised.

Wearily—he hadn't slept well the previous night, or for
many nights running—Sugar retrieved one of Curley's
comic books and inspected the gaudy monochrome cover.
The Red Menace was, he soon discerned, a political/
religious tract in the form of poorly executed cartoons.
The gist was this: a pack of neighborhood children work
together to expose communist subversives who wanted
the kids to stop going to church every Sunday and come

to their "World Youth Organization" meetings instead. The communists were no match for the patriotic kids. In the last panel the atheistic villains were led away in FBI handcuffs and the kids were being praised by parents, priests, and policemen.

"Hey, this ain't bad," Fat Charley commented. He'd tucked a few free lollipops into his shirt pockets and was now smearing *The Red Menace* with his plump, oily fingers.

"Look familiar to you, does it, Charley?" Sugar asked, tossing a comic book on the table.

"I dunno," Charley said, looking worried. "Should it?"

"The cardinal got 'em by the crate," Sugar reminded him. "To be passed out in the parochial schools. Must be twenty thousand copies over there, the Hibernian basement."

"Oh, yeah." Charley had unwrapped one of his lollipops, tucked it into his fat cheek.

All Sugar could do was shake his head and smile ruefully. The old thief had done it again. Half the kids and most of their parents would now go home thinking the whole picnic had been a gift from the mayor himself. Nothing to be done about it. Hadn't he enjoyed the games with the kids, judging the sack race? The brief vision of a child Deirdre smiling from the starting line. Something to savor there, for that alone he could be grateful. Why, he'd even had the dubious pleasure of reminiscing with a sweet-sucking moron like Charley Monk.

What ruined the day for Sugar McKane was not, as it turned out, His Honor the jailbird mayor. What ruined the day, what curdled the juice in his belly, was the arrival of an all-too-familiar limousine. Black and gleaming, funeral flags in unmistakable display on the fenders. The limo stopped at the entrance, and the long-legged, black-suited figure of Leonard Costello emerged.

Sugar hurried from the picnic tables.

"What is it, Leonard?"

Costello, a professionally dour man with deep-set, Raymond Massey eyes, seemed uncharacteristically agitated.

"She been there again," he said, rubbing a bony hand

on his long face. "That Drake woman. Followed us right to the cemetery."

"She's a nutcase," Sugar said.

"I know that. Don't make no difference, does it, to the grieving family. Standing there shouting those terrible things, it's upsetting to everyone."

"I've got a man working on it," McKane said. He was trying to back Costello into the limousine, wishing the man had had the common sense to remove the funeral flags before arriving at a children's picnic. "What else can I do, Leonard?"

Costello didn't want to meet his eyes. He was fidgeting. "Liam says—" he said.

"What did your brother say?"

"Liam says maybe we should call the police, have her arrested. It's not right, her accusing you in public."

Sugar reached out, opened the limo door. "Go on," he said. "Get in."

"Liam says—"

"I know what Liam said. You go back there and tell Liam there'll be no calls to the police, is that clear?"

"But, Sugar, the woman."

"It'll be taken care of soon enough. Remember, no police."

He shut the door, leaned in the open window, and gripped Costello, skin and bones in his black suit.

"No police," Costello agreed. Sugar's touch seemed to calm him.

"She *wants* to get herself arrested, Leonard. That's her plan. You just go on about your business, do the best you can. And tell Liam."

"We thought you'd want to know."

"I appreciate it," Sugar said. "Really I do."

Twenty-five

Three in the Head

Doris was on his case early, from the moment he got up late.

"Jack, you promised."

"I got tied up, honey. No way I could make it back early."

The deal was, he was supposed to help her with the packing, get everything stowed away for the beach. He'd never seen her so intent about the move, you'd think it was the first time, and it should've been old hat by now. There wasn't time for him to pitch in, make good on the promise. There hadn't been time last night and there wasn't time now.

Jack squinted into the mirror over the bathroom sink, trying to find his face without having to confront his bloodshot eyes. "I'll help tonight. Be home early, I, uh, promise."

Doris, behind him with her arms folded, dressed in old demin trousers and ready to get down to work, snorted. Sounded like a filly when she did that, except she never stamped her foot. "You're not kidding me, Jack Fitzroy. Coming home stinking of booze and perfume."

He froze, the safety razor cool and slippery in his fingers.

"You were out at a bar," she said, her tone flat, a statement of fact.

He relaxed inside, holding himself poised, trying to act just a little bit sleepy, although he'd never been wider awake. He lowered his hand, dipping the razor into the water. Amazed at how steady he was, a time like this. Hands like a surgeon.

"We were on a stakeout," he said. "And, yeah, we stopped in for a nightcap after."

Her voice was low, barely carried, though he heard it clearly enough, no problem there, none at all. "You pick up a girl, Jack? Is that what you did?"

He wiped a clear spot on the steamy mirror, looked at her that way, through the glass. "Couple of quick drinks, Dottie. With Tony Grazi. No girls. Jesus, can't a guy have a pop after work?"

"What's a 'pop'?" she asked, suspicious.

"Drink. A shot."

"I thought, maybe, you know, a 'pop' was like a hooker."

"Hooker? Come on, Dottie. Even in the army I never did that."

"So you say."

"Because it's true," he said. "What's the problem here? You're mad 'cause I didn't help you pack up? I was on a late stakeout, then I had to check on Snap Edwards, this divorce case, he'd got two guys covering some crummy hotel out in Revere. So the last guy I see is Tony, he's working this warehouse thing out to the Fort Point Channel, he says buy me a drink. So I do."

Doris came a little closer, her voice no longer certain. "Where there girls in the bar? Those kind of girls?"

"Maybe. I guess so, sure. That time a night, bound to be. I wasn't paying attention."

"They pour it on, the perfume, those kind of girls. All you have to do, be in the same room.

"Well, you got me, then," he said, lifting the razor to his face. "I was in the room."

Later, after a stand-up coffee, he left the apartment on the double, fighting the impulse to actually run. Wanting—and this was the crazy part, the part that made him feel maybe he was losing his marbles—he wanted to laugh out loud. Not because there was anything even remotely funny about almost getting caught, but because the whole thing was so gruesome, so awesomely stupid and self-destructive.

There was a creepy kind of humor, though. You couldn't get away from this: What would Miriam think of Doris mistaking her perfume for a whore's?

The really clever thing, though. He really had had a drink with Tony Grazi, just to cover his ass.

* * *

Doug Donnelly was the inside man on the Fort Point warehouse investigation. Working as an inventory clerk, where he had the opportunity to confirm or reject the insurer's allegations that items went missing here at the warehouse and not further down the line, the result of normal teamster pilferage, as the warehouse owner alleged.

Snap Edwards was nearby in his favorite surveillance vehicle, a milk truck.

"It's big enough so I can stand up, stretch my back," he'd explained when requesting the truck. "Also, it's cool in the summer, and you know how I hate the heat. What it does to my cameras, the film."

Now, coming up to the stake a good thirty minutes late, Jack found himself rapping his knuckles on the rear doors of the milk truck, rat-a-tat-tat. Snap inside there wearing striped milkman's overalls, he almost looked the part. Maybe a little too large and thoughtful. More like a high school science teacher who coached football on the side, combination of smarts and bulldog determination. That part, the bulldog smarts, that was true.

"Whatta we got?" Jack said, settling onto a canvas stool inside the dim interior of the truck. It smelled faintly of sour milk, no surprise.

"Got the warehouse owner backing a beach wagon up to the loading dock," Snap said, his voice husky. They were speaking very quietly. It wouldn't do to have a pedestrian pass, wonder what was going on here, a talking milk truck.

"What's he taking?"

"Radios," Snap said. He had his eye to the spy hole, a Leica ready to shoot. "Table models. Must have stowed fifty in there, the beach wagon."

"There's a helluva lot more than fifty radios gone missing."

"Right you are," Snap agreed. "The way I figure, if the owner is copping the little boxes, he sure as hell knows about the big boxes."

"Good point."

"Can't hurt, we get him on film. Probably gives those little table models to his friends, or sells 'em cheap. He likes to play the big shot, this guy. Dougie says he talks like a bigtime gangster."

"He's not," Jack said. "What he is, is a thief."

The insurance company was pushing this not because there were huge amounts of money involved, but because they wanted to get the message out about fraudulent claims, particularly in the freight business. Convict one warehouse owner of felony theft and insurance fraud, it got around.

Jack wasn't concentrating too well—he and Miriam had been drinking room-service Rob Roys, the sugary booze always made his head thick the next day—and he missed the bomb the first time Snap Edwards dropped it.

". . . our old friend Stinky Doyle," he was saying, talking out of the side of his mouth as he kept his eye to the spy hole. "Three in the head."

Jack said, "What?"

Something in Jack's tone made Edwards back away from the hole. "I assumed you knew."

"Knew what?"

"About what happened to Doyle."

"He got bailed, that's all I know. Except the arson squad detectives swore he never said a word about Keegan."

Edwards let the camera rest on his belly, held by a strap around his neck. He fished in his shirt pocket for a pack of Pall Malls, shook one out. Used a Zippo lighter that came with some bullshit story about saving his life in Iwo Jima. He always laughed when he told that story, so you never knew if it had any truth, or maybe the truth made him nervous. He *had* been in the Pacific, a Marine photographer, Jack knew that much.

"Yeah, well, maybe Jimmy Keegan didn't buy that," Edwards said. "Anyhow, somebody didn't trust Stinky, because he never made it back into the Shamrock."

"The Shamrock on D Street?"

Edwards nodded, inhaled, wreathed his round face in a cloud of smoke. Not a lot of air here in the milk truck. "The way I heard it, Stinky was getting a buzz on, which why else would you be in a shithole like the Shamrock, right? Anyhow he's got a new watch and he's showing it to everyone at the bar. A genuine Timex, right? Like he thinks that makes it especially valuable. And the reason he's got this valuable new watch is so he won't be late for this very important appointment."

"God damn it," Jack said. "I don't believe it."

"The watch? Oh, you mean what happened to Stinky. Nine o'clock he leaves the Shamrock, says he'll be back for last call, buy a round for the house. Never happened. Midnight a patrol car reports a deceased male in the vicinity of Bunker Hill. Sitting on a bench, I guess he was, right under the monument."

"Shot?"

Edwards nodded. "Three in the head."

"Who'd you get this from?"

"Delaney's missus is pals with mine. She was on the horn first thing with all the gory details. I got it with my poached egg."

"Keegan did it," Jack said. "Had to be Keegan. Afraid that Stinky would point the finger."

"Sure. Except Jimmy Keegan has the perfect alibi."

Jack said, "Come on. There's no such thing."

"Sure there is, if you're in jail. Keegan beat the shit out of some guy in Jake Wirth's bar yesterday afternoon. Claimed the guy stiffed him on a bet. Anyhow, he assaults the victim in full view of about thirty witnesses, he gets cuffed on the spot and he's in the Charles Street Jail eating supper off a tin plate when Doyle gets ventilated. Ironclad alibi."

Jack said, "Keegan hired it done."

Edwards agreed. "Of course he did. And he got away with it, too."

"Is he still in jail?"

Edward stirred uneasily. He'd sucked the Pall Mall down to the glowing end, was in danger of burning his fingers. "Nah, he got bailed."

Jack gave him a look. "I can guess who bailed him," he said.

"You heard it was Sugar, huh?"

"I didn't have to hear," Jack said. "Who else would stand up for a bastard like Keegan?"

PART TWO

Rye Beach, New Hampshire

One

The Pagoda

Ten minutes on the beach, setting up the big umbrella and the canvas chairs and the toys, ten minutes of squirming the bottoms of her feet into the lovely warm sand, and Doris realized that of all the women staking out chairs and blankets in front of the Pagoda Cottages, she was the only one who wasn't pregnant. Shel, Babs Marcotte, and even that skinny-hipped ninny Patsy Doulin, they were all pregnant. Bella Flynn she knew about already, she was pretty far gone, Bell would give birth before July was done, no question there. Make it her third in three years, that bastard Joe with his lewd jokes about keeping her knocked up until he had Flynns by the dozen.

First couple of summers Doris had felt herself to be an outsider. Most of these families had been coming here for years, since they were kids themselves. The single-story cottages were propped on cedar posts, the beach starting right where you stepped off the porch. White-washed novelty siding, leaky old iceboxes, bare light bulbs, a few sticks of wicker furniture—you lived out here, on the beach or on the screened-in porches, a summer-long drinking party that moved from cottage to cottage and got jazzed up pretty good on the weekends, when the working husbands were up from the city. Things a bit quieter weekdays, but these girls loved their cocktails, put the kids into their creaky beds before the sun was quite down and then got together, sharing some of the lewdest stories Doris had ever heard. Worse than cop jokes, and everybody a good Catholic, you missed a Sunday Mass here and everybody knew about it, gave you a sorrowful look like you might die of sunstroke and not go directly to heaven.

Behind the beachfront cottages, set almost directly on

the road—locals called it ''the boulevard''—was the Pagoda itself, a big cedar-shingled building with a false front. Inside, a small, sunny room served as a lunch counter, the rest of the place taken up by a dim, pine-paneled dance hall that had at one time been decorated with Chinese lanterns, a style for some reason popular in the time of Prohibition. Fewer lanterns every summer, Doris had noticed, the pagoda theme was fading. Couple of gas pumps out front, surrounded by a lake of white gravel—at night the whole place glowed and the yellow lights of the dance hall windows gave it the look of a ship at sea.

First time Jack had taken her dancing there was the summer before they got married. Jack absolutely insisting that she and her mother come up to Rye Beach for a weekend, he wouldn't take no. All very proper, too. He'd found them a room at the Gray Gull, on the other side of the boulevard, a room so narrow that two thin beds bumped all four walls. Bathroom at the end of the hall, cobwebs in the window, but God in heaven what a weekend that had been, the flush of love, the real thing this time, and the thrill of Jack's excitement as he showed her off to his friends.

Dance music loud on the Pagoda jukebox, a big old Wurlitzer that made the floorboards quiver. Close your eyes, Benny Goodman was right there, crooning that sweet clarinet just for you, perfectly pitched to the sleepy gravel-hiss of the surf outside. Or it might be Glenn Miller's machinelike, never-miss-a-beat orchestra compelling you to lift your feet. There was Dorsey and Stan Kenton and Artie Shaw. The great Negro bands her mother hated, Ellington and Basie and Hampton, all the hard-to-find recordings, and late at night the forbidden, dirty-mouthed lyrics of zoot-suited Cab Calloway. Mother, who always had the same response to the wicked thrill of a big band tune: *There's none of 'em can sing like a good Irish tenor*—for her music began and ended with John McCormack. Who was not there on the Pagoda jukebox, although Jack had offered to find a McCormack record, an offer Mother had politely declined and then, with a stiff but knowing smile, made a show of going early off to bed. Crossing the boulevard with a heavy tread and leaving her daughter alone to repel the anticipated advances of handsome Jack Fitzroy, about to become a rookie patrolman with the Boston Police Department. A job well regarded in the world of John McCormack lovers. Oh indeed, yes, her mother had ached for the news of engagement, legitimizing this proper and yet somehow scandalous weekend financed by the spendthrift prospective groom.

It had happened, as Doris knew it would, that very night, on the post–dance hall stroll along the beach. A night of stars, no moon at all, and so dark you could barely see the faint white lace of the waves curling up neatly at the shore. Two in the morning, for God's sake, and Jack, full of his big brother's whiskey, sounding very knowledgeable about the possibility of U-boat surveillance. A delicious sensation of danger that made his embrace seem necessary—as indeed it was necessary—and when his hot hands somehow slipped into the back of her dress and imprinted palm-shaped desire on her naked back, she did not protest, although she quite stubbornly refused to lie down in the sand so as to present less of a target to the imaginary U-boats and their leering, yellow-haired captains. Letting Jack touch her as they walked, keeping him moving, dizzy with her own deft manipulations and the feather touches of his questing fingertips—very clever hands had young Jack Fitzroy, too clever by half.

They had walked as far up as Straw's Point, where the sand ended and the rocks began, Doris unaware at that precise moment that Jack had dated the Straw girl, the pretty one, and no doubt had trod these very sands with her on a previous summer night, whispering who knows what kind of lies about Nazi submarines. Jack at one point running into the water up to his knees and shouting her name, whooping it up, pretending to be drunker than he really was, and somehow Doris was not the least bit surprised when he emerged, new shoes clotted with seaweed, and with a starlit grin said, *Doris McLaughlin, will you marry me, Doris McLaughlin, will you marry me, marry me, marry me,* repeating it again and again and shaking clumps of wet seaweed at her until she said, *Yes, yes, yes.*

Night of a lifetime, yes, eight years and a million years ago.

"He's just the cutest little man," Patsy Doulin was saying. Standing over Doris with her pleated swimsuit distended by her pregnancy, one hand touching her own baby-proud belly while the other gestured at little David, sitting on his butt in the sand and contentedly manipulating the scoop of his toy steam shovel, a present from his uncle Mike.

"September, is it?" Doris said, eyeing Patsy's lump, pretending an interest she did not feel.

"Labor Day, you get it?" Patsy giggled and lowered herself into a canvas beach chair, edging it into the shade of the umbrella. She chattered on for quite a while, and Doris responded to her litany of light-headed remarks without really paying attention, until this jumped out: "You must be sad, Dottie darling, about no more babies."

Doris had been craning her neck to keep an eye on Robby, who was wading in the tidal pools, turning over rocks with several of the other boys, and it took a moment for the comment to strike home. "What *are* you talking about, Patsy dear?" she said.

"Oh, you know. What happened to Jack. The poor, poor man."

Doris stared at this pretty little numbskull and said, "You mean about Jack getting the polio virus? Is that what you're talking about?"

Patsy nodded happily, pleased to be understood. "We were terribly worried last year, all of us. You should have heard us, Dot, it was all we could talk about. A big, strong man like your Jack getting crippled. It was so unfair, after he won that medal and all."

"Excuse me, Patsy? What was it you said about no more babies?" Doris fighting to keep her voice under control.

Patsy finally tumbled to the fact that Doris was angry, and it made her uneasy. "You know," she said. "The, uhm, thing thing."

"The thing thing? What the hell are you talking about, Patsy, can you tell me? Thing thing? Jesus."

Patsy fiddled with her straw sun hat. "Dottie dear, you know it makes me feel creepy inside when people take the name in vain."

There was a fist-sized rock a few inches from her right

hand, and Doris thought about picking up the rock and banging Patsy Doulin on her hard little head. What she did do was get up from her chair, loom over the pregnant, cringing woman, and say, "Jesus Christ! God damn! How do you like them apples, you dumb little bitch?"

Doris marched right down to the tidal pool and grabbed Robby by the hand and yanked him, protesting and finally crying, back up to the sand, where she hefted little David, toys and all, up on her hip.

She put the boys in their bedroom—the both of them by now frightened into obedient silence by her anger—and sat in the knotty-pine dimness of the cottage interior and smoked three quick cigarettes, her eyes as hot as small stones left out in the sun, until Babs Marcotte came through the screened porch and knocked tentatively on the open door.

"Dot?"

"Come on in, Babs."

Babs, tan and lean despite her baby belly, her hair cut boyishly short, dropped into a wicker chair and lighted a cigarette. Crossed her firm tennis player's legs and said, "Come on, Dottie, she's a moron, pay no attention."

Doris shook her head. The sisterly, intelligent presence of Babs made her eyes feel salty. "Jack has this little limp, okay? A bum leg, that's all the polio did to him."

"I know, Dot. He was lucky. You were both lucky."

Doris took a deep breath, didn't bother to brush away her tears. Keeping her voice low, so the boys couldn't hear through the thin walls of the cottage. "Patsy thinks it means he can't make a baby."

Babs made a sound in her throat, shook her head in disbelief. "She said that?"

Doris nodded. "The 'thing thing.' That's what she calls it."

Babs sputtered smoke through her fine thin nostrils, turned her head to cough. Laughing as she coughed.

"I know," Doris said, "it should be funny, except it made me so angry."

Babs was convulsed. Her voice, normally a throaty baritone, was up there in the thin soprano range. " 'Thing thing' ? She said 'thing thing'?" Her laughter, always infectious—Babs was a life-of-the-party type, would lift up the hem of her dress and Charleston after she'd had a few drinks—began to work on Doris, who was soon having her own fit, she didn't know if it was laughing or crying or just plain temper letting go.

When Babs had recovered enough to speak clearly, she said, "Where's the booze, kid?" and poured them each a tot of straight whiskey, there was no ice because they'd missed the morning delivery.

"Let me tell you something," Babs said, settling down with her drink and lighting a fresh cigarette. "Patsy is a little confused as to how she got pregnant."

"What?"

Babs was grinning over the whiskey glass. "I mean it. She's not really sure about the actual act, you know? The thing Dennis does to her when she's fast asleep, or pretending to be fast asleep? So it's no surprise Patsy thinks polio makes men sterile, or whatever it is she thinks. The poor girl hasn't got a clue, honey, and that's a fact."

Rita Donnelly arrived with her new baby late in the afternoon. Her white-haired mother was hunkered down behind the wheel of an old Nash that sounded like a cement mixer, you could hear it coming for half a mile down the boulevard.

"It's a miracle," Rita exclaimed, emerging from the vehicle. "Mother had her eyes closed the whole time, didn't you, Mother? We ran over a man in Seabrook. He was laughing so hard when he heard us coming, he fell down in the middle of the road."

"Now, Rita," said her mother.

Later, with the baby freshly changed and in her crib and her mother unpacking, Rita trudged through the sand and made a great show of dragging herself up the steps to Doris's screened porch. "I swear I pushed that car all the way from Lexington."

Babs, who liked to play bartender, made her a cocktail.

"Thought we'd never make it," Rita said, flopping into a chair and lighting a cigarette. "Doug might have to work this weekend, is that true?"

The question was addressed to Doris, who wasn't really paying attention. She was watching the boys, a whole pack of kids out there running through the tall beach grass and shooting cap pistols. The trace of exploded powder smelled like summer, and for the first time today she felt perfectly at ease. "What?" she said. "Oh, the weekend. Jack's real busy, I know that much. He said they'd try to make it."

"Money, money," Babs said. "Let 'em work."

"Not on the Fourth, though. I mean, Dot, they'll have the Fourth off, won't they?"

Doris sipped a beer. "Jack said he'd be here for the fireworks," she said. "He doesn't tell me much."

"You know about the dead guy, right? Gee, he really *doesn't* tell you anything, does he?" Rita dragged on the cigarette. Black hair, dark eyes, an Italian married to an Irishman, she was impishly pretty, had a brassy laugh that filled a room. She and Babs were a team, clowning and cutting up, the brightest and funniest twosome who ever crashed a boozer.

Doris, a small ache of dread in her bones, made herself ask, "What dead guy?"

"The one who liked to play with matches. Doug said they caught him red-handed, trying to set a fire. East Boston warehouse job. Doesn't ring a bell?"

Doris shook her head. Moody now, the sense of ease had evaporated.

Rita turned to Babs. "They get the guy, right? Dougie says a couple hours later he's back on the street. Next thing you know, he's on a park bench in Chelsea, watching a parade. Except he wasn't watching it because he's dead as a doornail."

"That's terrible," said Babs.

"Yeah, but the boys made money, and that's what counts."

"Rita!"

"Hey, I didn't mean it that way. I meant they got paid off by the insurance company even though the guy got killed. Not because he got killed. Or anyhow, that's what Doug said. Mike gave everybody a nice bonus, and you'll never guess, we're buying a new car this fall. Brand-new. Maybe a Buick, Doug says."

"You're kidding," Babs said, happy to change the subject. "A brand-new Buick? That's swell."

After a while Doris got up and went into the meadow

of beach grass and took the cap pistols away from Robby and little David, who was barely big enough to pull the trigger. "You can be the Indians," she told the boys. "Pretend you have arrows."

Two

The Straw Man Deal

"What it is, it's a straw man deal," Jack said. He and Mike catching a quick Saturday lunch at Dini's Grill on Tremont Street. The place was relatively quiet—the fat cats were out of town, the State House business closed down for the long holiday weekend.

Mike paused with a fork full of deep-fried haddock raised from his blue-plate special.

Jack said, "Look, Jimmy Keegan has been buying up property all over East Boston. Being lovable Jimmy, he's been clearing the lots by torch, but the insurance scam isn't the point."

"Oh?" Mike said. He set the fork down on his plate, had the look of a man who knew what was coming next.

"All these lots he's bought up, a total of four hundred acres, he's deeded everything over to a real estate trust. I had a helluva time getting through the smoke, Mike, but what I finally established is this: Sugar controls the trust. Keegan has been acting as his straw."

"So?"

Jack gave him a look. "So? Is that all you have to say, I tell you this—so? Come on, Keegan is a crook. No, I take that back, he's a killer. A killer and a crook."

Mike folded his hands. You could tell, if you knew him, his stomach was acting up, it made his lips soft, deepened the look of his eyes. "The point is, Jack, it's not our concern. That's Sugar's business, he wants to get involved with a creep like Keegan."

"He bailed him out, Mike."

Mike shrugged it off. "Sugar's a bondsman, he can bail a guy out if he wants to take the risk. That's what bondsmen do, get crooks out of jail."

Jack shook his head. His stomach wasn't feeling so good, either. Maybe he was catching big brother's ulcer.

"You know what I'm worried about. He did you once, now he'll ruin the both of us."

Mike reached out, tapped Jack on the wrist, making his point. "I wasn't ruined, okay? Let's keep that in mind. So I stopped practicing law, so what? We've got a great thing going here, Jack. Take a look at the books, you don't believe me."

"I believe you." It was true, they'd just hired five more operatives and were keeping all of them busy, billing hours to major law firms. Divorce, fraud, industrial theft—these were growth industries, boom times in the post-war recession. "What I want to know," Jack said, "what the hell is Sugar up to? I know that, maybe I can figure a way to cover our asses, Michael. Help me do that."

Mike looked up and studied the tin ceiling, rubbed his belly with soft hands. "You'll have to talk to him yourself, little brother."

Jack made a face. "Hey, Mike? Sugar won't tell me a damn thing. You know how he is. I'm checking out this poison-pen thing for him, which may or may not be connected to this real estate scam, he's lying about that, too."

Mike lowered his voice. Quiet as it was, you never knew, the mice had ears at Dini's grill. "You know for a fact he's lying?"

"He's evading the truth, is what he's doing," Jack said. "Sugar knows damn well why that family hates him, and he won't tell me. Just handle it, he says."

"And you need to know?"

Jack nodded.

"You're the detective. Go back to Sugar, get him to talk. Do whatever you have to do."

Jack started to reply, then hesitated. Sometimes, looking at Mike with his stomach troubles and his unfaithful wife, he wanted to blurt out a confession. Tell him all about Miriam, as if Mike could somehow advise him on the subject. Crazy idea, insane, and yet it kept rising within him, this urge, tickling his throat. What he said was "He might be playing me along, Mike. Setting me up."

"Yeah? Setting you up how?"

"I don't know. Like maybe he wants me to be the fall guy this time. It's this feeling I have."

Mike said, "Jesus, you're giving me the creeps here, Jack. I know about your instincts. All I can say, watch your back. I'll watch it, too. The problem is, we can't just tell the man to go to hell. You know that."

"I do, yes."

The way Mike had it figured, and he'd been right so far, they'd have thirty men on the job by this time next year. Bill for all of those hours, that was big money. Right up there with the monster law firms, taking slices from all those, rich, rich pies. And without Sugar's connections, the weight everybody seemed to believe he carried, none of it would be happening, not on such a large scale or so quickly. Give the Fitzroy brothers a few years, really establish the firm, maybe then they wouldn't need Sugar McKane. Right now he was essential.

"Look, the man is in business with Jimmy Keegan and Keegan just had a man killed. Keegan will walk away—they can't tie it to him. But what happens if some other line of evidence is developed and Keegan rolls over on Sugar? It could happen."

"You're ruining my lunch, Jack." He removed his horn-rims, began to polish the lenses with a paper napkin.

"This is serious, Mike."

"No kidding, I get the message. You don't really think Sugar was involved, getting Stinky Doyle rubbed out?"

Jack shrugged.

"Come on," Mike said, leaning forward, his voice a husky whisper. "Sugar has his shady side, like every ward boss in this town, but he never sheds blood. I *know* this. He fuzzes the edges, okay? Finesses a deal, like whatever he's doing over there in Eastie, buying up land, but he doesn't have people killed."

"Not to make money, no."

Mike squinted, puzzled. "What other reason is there?"

"I don't know," Jack said. "And that's what scares me."

Three

Hot Pennies

Miriam arrived, windblown in her two-tone convertible, at one in the afternoon. Mrs. Michael Fitzroy, sleek and tanned in her white cotton tennis shorts and her little white rayon top that didn't quite cover her waist. The thin white band of her Playtex bra strap showing through at the back. That made her a shameless hussy according to Patsy Doulin, who stood blinking in the sun, apparently unaware that her own bra strap was showing.

"Shut up, Patsy dear," Babs Marcotte said under her welcoming smile, as she waved gaily to Miriam. "This is a holiday. We're supposed to be nice to the rich folks on holidays, didn't your mother teach you that?"

Patsy said, "Huh?"

Miriam, meanwhile, had opened the convertible trunk and was beckoning to the three women in the sand, Babs and Patsy and Doris Fitzroy, pausing with canvas chairs in hand, on their way down to the beach.

"What's she got in there?"

"The Lindbergh baby," Babs said, pitching the comment to Doris. "Or maybe Judge Crater."

What Miriam had was a brand-new twenty-gallon picnic cooler loaded with frosty cartons of Popsicle sticks, orange and grape and lime flavors, and stacks of Hoodsy cups. "For the kids," she said. "Michael said candy bars, but I said the Fourth of July is ice cream and Popsicles."

The four women carried the big, ice-heavy cooler into the dark shade of Doris's screened porch, and the children streamed up from the beach unbidden, chattering with excitement as they filled the porch, maybe twenty kids from two to twelve years of age, hushed into a stunned, reverent silence by the sight of cool steam rising from the treasure chest.

"Holy cow," Robby whispered. "Where did you get all that stuff, Aunt Miriam?"

Sweet, smiling Miriam knelt by the cooler, lifted out a Popsicle stick, the color luminous through the waxed-paper wrapper. "Who likes orange?" she asked, and a dozen small hands went up like battle flags.

Later, when they were under the beach umbrellas, drinking from Bab's thermos jug of vodka-collins cocktails, Patsy Doulin kept edging her striped canvas chair closer to Miriam, chatting on and on about movie stars and fashion trends and that crazy Milton Berle. At one point Babs nudged Doris and said, sotto voce, "Patsy's in love, look at her," and it was true, Patsy was flirting with Miriam, there was no other explanation for the way she kept squirming in her beach chair, batting her eyelashes, trying desperately to impress the unimpressible daughter of Sugar McKane.

For the first time in a week Doris felt some sympathy for Patsy. The little fool had no idea what she was doing or why, beyond the urgent need to make friends with an exotic woman who summered in a huge, cedar-shingled mansion that her notorious ward boss daddy condescended to call a cottage, all twenty rooms of it. Forget it, Patsy, Doris thought, you'll never be invited to those exclusive dinner parties, and even if you are invited you'll be made to feel like the invitation was a gift bestowed by the great beauty and socialite Miriam McKane, excuse me, Mrs. Michael Fitzroy. Oh yes, *Make yourself at home, Dottie dear,* but all Doris could think of that night, looking furtively around at the delicate crystal chandeliers and the Spode china and the uniformed kitchen staff during her first and only society dinner party, was *You lace-curtain bitch, you're just like your bastard father,* deep veins of jealousy and resentment and simple, killing envy that made Doris feel ashamed of herself. Ashamed of her family, or her ignorant and spiteful mother, her petty, coal-smudged father. Hating the smallness that was apparently distilled in her family blood, no escape. No way to carry herself like moneyed Miriam even if Jack was to become—what a crazy notion—as wealthy and powerful as Sugar himself. Invisible dirt under her fingernails, you could never scrub that away.

"There he is," Miriam was saying, standing up from

her chair and waving her sunglasses. ''There's that man of mine.''

Michael Fitzroy came down through the dune grass, looking tall and plump and pale, holding his wingtips in hand as he strolled barefoot through the sand, the wind fluttering his tie. Sky blue seersucker suit pants rolled up at the cuff. The expression on his face when he saw his oh-so-beautiful wife gave Doris the sympathetic creeps. It was the look of a spaniel pup who knows he's about to be petted, and that's just what Miriam did, she reached up and ruffed his thinning hair, good boy, and he looked so damned grateful, so pitifully happy, that Doris had to glance away. Thinking: *You poor dumb bastard, you haven't got a clue.*

Later, when Michael had taken a chair and accepted, with extravagant charm, a tall cocktail tumbler from flirty Babs Marcotte, Miriam wandered off to play with the children. Getting the seat of her white cotton shorts wet as she crouched at the shore, showing David how to apply frosting-like mud dribbles to his sand castle. Absorbed by the pure delight of his response, Miriam laughed—chimes in the sea breeze that made her husband shiver—and lost her balance, sitting back with a splash and then laughing louder as her fine, slim hands patted her firm buttocks, a move that riveted every eye on the beach, male or female.

Mike sighed and fussed his bare feet into the sand as he sipped from the sweating tumbler. ''Jack said he'd make it,'' he assured Doris. ''He'll be here for the fireworks.''

''Hot in the city?'' she asked, simply to make conversation, distract herself from the vision of Miriam and her wet fanny.

''Not too bad. Jack's over the registry of deeds, looking up a few things. Paperwork,'' he added vaguely, as if he felt obliged to explain his brother's absence, and keep on explaining until his sister-in-law let him off the hook.

''On Saturday?'' Doris said. ''The registry? I assumed the whole city government would be shut down, a holiday weekend.''

Mike grinned, his eyes blue slits in the sunlight. ''You know Jack. He always finds a way.''

They left it at that. Doris knew better than to ask what was so important about a property deed, it had to be looked up on a holiday weekend. Probably Michael himself didn't know—he was the money side, the business side, Jack did the legwork. Something to do with McKane's underworld, some sleazy scheme of Sugar's, she'd bet the ranch on that.

Miriam came back up from the mud castle with David clinging to her, reaching up for the thigh-high hem of those damp shorts, not getting it when everybody laughed just a little nervously, the kid acting on impulses, doing what every man on the beach wanted to do, grope that lithe and sensual figure, but Miriam seemed as oblivious as the three-year-old, intent on something else.

"Come with me," she said to David, taking his hand. "I know a secret."

Miriam's secret was in the picnic cooler, which she dragged out of the screened porch, easing it down the creaky steps into the direct sunlight. Doris watched her with small hawk eyes, this exotic creature seducing her son, who followed her every move, fascinated as his fairytale aunt tipped out the block of ice. This odd activity attracted the other children, who wandered up from the shoreline wet from splashing, coated with fine layers of white beach dust, hands still sticky from the ice cream treats.

"Watch this," Miriam said to the children. "My father taught me a magic trick once upon a time, and now I'll teach it to you."

Reaching into the rear pocket of her damp white shorts, Miriam withdrew a shiny new penny. "Hold this in your hand," she said, giving the coin to David. "Like this—make a fist."

She showed the boy how to make a fist, and he laughed, looking around at the other children, proud of himself. Doris, coming up from her beach chair, could see his expression as bright as a hundred-watt bulb, his delight at being the center of all this attention, as proud of the fist as he was of the penny.

"Now put it there," Miriam said, touching the block of ice. "Go on, honey, this is the magic part."

David didn't want to unfist the penny until Miriam tickled his wrist and showed him how to hold the penny on top of the ice, balanced upright under his index finger, glinting hot in the sun. ''Now just hold it there,'' she urged him. ''The magic will start to happen.''

Years later Doris would remember the sun reflecting off that bright new penny, and the look of wonder in her little boy's eyes as the coin slowly penetrated the ice. This was Miriam's trick, her secret, and David crouched in his little boy body, watching the hot penny descend into the center of the glistening block of ice, holding his tiny fists tight as if that was part of the magic. Not a peep out of him, just an intensity of expression that made you know his mind was in high gear, taking in the penny, the ice, the other children, and Miriam, beautiful Miriam wanting to please him with all her considerable charm.

Doris wanted to pick the boy up, carry him off with some excuse—too much sun, he needs a nap—and found to her surprise that she could not make herself disturb the moment, or startle the wonder from David's face, not even if it meant letting Miriam share him.

The older children wandered away, easily bored, but David waited quietly until the block of ice was reduced to a small, watery lump, and when the coin at last came free, he insisted that Miriam help him bury it in his mud castle. The two of them laughing and dripping wet sand over the penny until a wave came in and washed it all away. David started to cry and then suddenly stopped when Miriam cupped her hands to his ear, whispering.

That's when David came running up to Doris, eyes wild, and said, ''Mommy, Mommy, guess what! Aunty's is going to marry me! She promised!''

Miriam came up and dropped into a chair and stretched out her perfect legs. She smiled at Doris. ''I hope you don't mind,'' she said.

Four

Fireworks

The Packard had a loud personality, a distinctive clunk and wheeze as the big straight-eight engine shut down, and an unmistakable two-ton thud when the driver's door was slammed. So an arrival was announced, like it or not. Jack was not a yard from the vehicle, pausing to light a cigarette, work the kinks out of his legs from the cramp of a stop-and-go drive up the coast, when the kids exploded from the back door of the cottage, whooping like a couple of serial Apaches.

"Daaaaa-deeeeeeee! Daaaaaaa-deeeeeee!" That was Robby, leading the charge, and little David supplying a high-pitched scream, sounded like a teakettle on the wheeze, holding his arms straight out for a hug.

"Lo, boys," Jack said, rolling the cigarette to the corner of his mouth, squinting against the smoke, reaching down to tousle their freshly scrubbed heads, still damp from the bath and smelling of Johnson's baby shampoo. "What's all the excitement?"

As if he didn't know. The air-shudder of small explosives detonating in the long summer twilight, a preliminary to the much larger barrage that would greet actual darkness, and the horde of cottage kids shrieked with each whomp of a cherry bomb.

Robby had his cap pistol, showed it to his father as they climbed the steps to the porch. "Mom said I could shoot off all my caps tonight," the boy said, hefting the pistol. "Once *you* got here."

"All at once, huh?" Jack said.

"That way it's almost as good as having firecrackers," Robby said in his sober way, clearly having given the matter a lot of careful thought. "Mom won't let us touch firecrackers."

"We're in complete agreement on that, your mom and I," Jack said. "No firecrackers."

"Because we might blow off our fingers."

"Kid with no fingers can't play marbles," Jack said, easing down into a creaky wicker porch chair, ignoring the twinge of pain in his bad leg.

Little David ran inside from the porch, returned a few moments later with a bottle of Pabst, cool and damp from the icebox. He held it out to his father, saying not a word, hugely pleased with himself.

"That's pretty cute, kid," Jack said. "Now go fetch the bottle opener."

The three-year-old already had that covered, except the opener was stuck in his rear pocket and he needed help extricating it. "Hey, Dottie, who taught this kid to fetch beers, huh?"

Doris came out to the porch then, making an entrance, all dolled up in a new summer dress that showed off her tan. Dark red lipstick, kohl blue eye shadow, her thick reddish-brown hair held up on one side with a silver barrette, like something she'd seen in a movie magazine. Rita Hayworth in the tropics. "Who do you think taught him that, carrying beers in?" she said, hands on her cocked hips, her earrings jangling. "His uncle Mike, that's who."

"Nice," Jack said, standing up to greet her, getting a smudge of lipstick on the cleft of his chin.

"Mommy took a whole hour to get dressed," Robby said, obviously impressed. "She made us play in our room."

Jack came close to giving it all away right at that very moment, unwittingly revealing his infidelity in front of the children. It happened like this: wanting to compliment his wife, let her know he appreciated the effort, he was about to remark on her familiar perfume. It was on his lips to say, *You know how I love that smell* when Doris saved him by her anxious way of asking, "Do you like it?"

There was something faintly naughty and forbidden in her tone that made him react carefully. "Is that new?" he asked.

Doris nodded. "It's Miriam's," she said airily. "She changed her clothes here and I guess she was trying to be nice, you know how she is. But I thought, why not take it? She gave me the whole bottle, Jack, I'll bet it cost twenty bucks.''

He moved back so his wife would not feel his heart slamming. So close! A rush of adrenaline, it was like being under shell fire. Because he'd almost said it was his favorite perfume. Dottie would have known in that instant, no doubt about it, plucked the awful truth right from between his lying eyes.

''That was okay, I guess,'' Jack said. He succeeded in convincing Doris, by the tone of his voice, that he wasn't keen on the way his wealthy sister-in-law dispensed small gifts to the less fortunate. ''You can buy anything you need,'' he added, summoning up a pride he did not, could not feel. ''You know that.''

''She was just trying to be nice,'' Doris said. ''The point is, do you really like it?''

She offered her neck. Jack made a show of sniffing her. ''Yes,'' he said, kissing her carefully on the lips. ''Matter of fact, I do.''

The holiday celebration, underway since early afternoon, gained new momentum in the long twilight. The revelers streamed from the rows of summer cottages, joined by their weekend guests, as well as hundreds of flinty Rye natives drawn to the shore, cars and farm trucks and beach wagons parked bumper to bumper along the boulevard. The sea, dark and slick under the airbrushed sky, lapped lazily against the hard sand flats. A few white-hulled boats lay quietly at anchor off the Beach Club, where the fireworks were to be launched—this now annual tradition paid for, without fanfare or even his actual presence at the clubhouse, by member-in-good-standing Sugar McKane.

Jack and Doris and the two boys eased along the crowded beach, weaving around crackling driftwood fires set alight in the white sand. The Fitzroys kept close together, the boys and Doris going barefoot. Jack breaking in his new leather sandals, pleased that a couple of beers had eased the throbbing of his damaged sciatic nerve. Taking it slow, no hurry, he was pretty sure the limp didn't show, not that any of these boozers would notice, or dare to comment.

"On the radio they said maybe thunderstorms," Doris said, searching the sky. "I don't see it, not tonight."

She had looped her arm through his, her new dress the color of glowing embers, looking more youthful than he'd come to expect of her. Jack slightly surprised to discover that he liked it, Doris making an effort to please him. They walked south toward the Beach Club promontory, edging around the gawkers. The pungent smells of seaweed, seared marshmallows, and exploded firecrackers overpowered the illicit scent of Miriam's perfume, and for this he was grateful.

"Robby? Hold on to your brother's hand, that's part of the deal."

The boys were being as good as they could be, keenly aware that their father was perfectly capable of ordering them to bed if they disobeyed his specific instructions regarding their behavior on this night of all nights. Or anyhow Robbie knew enough to be good, and made an effort to keep his little brother out of trouble. Both kids humming like small transformers, radiating force fields of excitement.

"I know a rock, Dad," Robby said, tugging at Jack's wrist. "It's big enough we could all sit on it."

"Okay," Jack said. "Show us to it."

The kid wasn't exaggerating, he'd scouted an area of flat-topped boulders, exposed by the low tide, just beyond the Beach Club. Within sight, Jack noticed, of where the rocket-launching tubes were banked into the hard sand, objects of intense fascination for the boy.

"Is it too close?" Doris wanted to know.

"We'll be okay," Jack said.

And so they were, sitting under the arc of fireworks that began to blaze upward a few minutes later, ignited by a couple of torch-wielding beach-clubbers who were, from the look of them, more than a little the worse for drink. Stumbling about in Chaplinesque panic as the launch tubes coughed and the bright trail of sparks whizzed high overhead, bursting into other, smaller blooms of color, a delicate and momentary perfection.

At the height of the barrage Robby raised his toy pistol in a salute, pulling the trigger methodically with both hands, firing off his full roll of paper caps, as sober and serious as if he was participating in a military opera-

tion—in his own mind, maybe he was, Jack decided—
while David squirmed into the safety of his father's lap,
his small pink cheek pressed against Jack's chest, his
wide little-boy eyes sneaking glances as the sparkling
flowers opened overhead, followed, a heartbeat later, by
the thud of each sequential explosion.

It was over in ten minutes, all the larger rockets ex-
pended, and the torch men were staggering back to their
clubhouse in search of rum before the cheers had quite
faded. All along the length of the beach, two miles or
so, the smaller, hand-held fireworks were still going off:
Roman candles hiccoughing little balls of multicolored
flame, the crisp muzzle flash of cherry bombs thudding
satisfactorily inside tin cans, and the spark-thin engrav-
ing of tiny bottle rockets scratching up, up, never quite
getting there before fading suddenly away.

Beyond the rocky promontory, one of the white-hulled
boats had launched a parachute flare. For a long time the
incandescent flare hung nearly motionless, kept up by a
puff of rising air, suspended between the sea blue sky
and the sky blue sea. The searing flames burned into
Jack's eyes, stunning his retinas, but he could not look
away, not until the white-hot thing at last extinguished
itself and he heard Doris sigh and say, "Well, that's that.
Let's get these Katzenjammer kids to bed."

Later, with the boys heavily asleep in their narrow cottage beds, Jack walked barefooted Doris back down to
the beach, where the big bonfire was starting to burn out,
part of it already covered by the rapidly advancing tide.
Babs Marcotte saluted them from her perch on a driftwood log, her cigarette glowing like a distant taillight.
She looked moody, distant.

"Where's Hank the Shank?" Jack whispered to Doris,
referring to Babs's husband, a high school principal.

"Who the hell knows," Doris whispered back. "He
knocked her up again, his homework is done, I guess."

Doris had made it clear she wasn't interested in so-
cializing, not even with a dear friend like Babs. She
wanted to be alone with her husband, and Jack allowed
himself to be steered around to the distant side of the
bonfire, where she had already picked out a likely spot.
Jack watched his wife bending to spread out a beach
towel, the firelight making her new dress glow like a

paper lantern, her fine, sturdy legs silhouetted through the material. He grinned to himself in the dark, recalling other nights on this very beach in those last few intensely lived weeks before he had been shipped overseas. The small noise Dottie had made the first time, and the way she cried, and the way she giggled and said: *Don't worry, I cry for everything, weddings and funerals and Christmas and now this. . . .*

He was not at all surprised when, sitting hip to hip on the blanket, she entwined her hands through his and gently, tentatively ran her fingertips over the underside of his wrist. Dottie's signal, because she could never bring herself to speak the word.

Jack brushed back her hair, touched his lips to her ear, and said, "Right here?" as he slipped his hands down the back of her dress and in one dextrous move—he was not a man who struggled with women's undergarments—unsnapped her bra strap.

"Not here," she breathed, turning her face up to meet his, opening her mouth to him.

They left the towel on the sand and hurried back to the cottage, where, Jack discovered, Doris had already given some thought to the squeaky bed spring problem. The solution, she said, keeping her voice low so as not to wake the boys, was to put the mattress on the floor. Jack shook his head, amazed by her ingenuity, by the fact that she had planned this all out: the new dress, the romantic cuddle by the bonfire, and what to do about the distraction of the noisy, steel-sprung bed frame.

When the mattress was on the floor, Jack pulled the chain, clicking off the bare light bulb, and indicated that he wanted her to stand in the very center of the mattress. Doris complied, her eyes glowing moistly, and Jack knelt and slipped his hands up under her dress and found that she was already, as he knew she would be, damp with desire.

"Jack," she whispered, sliding down to meet him, "do you really love me?"

"You know I do," he said, and right at the moment, entering her, he meant it.

Later, much later, he awoke with a start and pawed the floor beside the mattress, searching for his wristwatch. Found it, held it up at an angle, trying to read the hands. After two in the morning, Christ almighty, and he'd actually fallen sound asleep.

Doris, aware of him, turned, her voice thick with sleep. "Honey?"

"Cramp in my leg," Jack said. "I'll walk it off."

"Oh, honey."

"It's okay, no big deal."

He dressed quickly, favoring the leg, and limped from the bedroom. Outside he was surprised by the moonlight, bright enough to cast shadows in the sand, making the asphalt glitter on the cottage roofs. While he was sleeping, the air had changed with the tide. It was cool and dry now, and the surf was rolling pretty good, dragging back rocks, making quite a racket, hushing and hissing as the waves unfolded against the shore.

He walked slowly down to the beach, favoring the leg—it did actually hurt a little—and saw the bonfire wrecked like a ship, charred timbers strewn by the now retreating waves, and when he saw a cigarette glowing above a driftwood log he thought for a moment it was still Babs Marcotte out there.

Then Miriam stood up and dropped the cigarette, and Jack hurried to her because it was like high noon, all this moonlight, and it was important that he ease her out of sight, somewhere far down the shoreline.

"I'll bet you were screwing Dottie" was how she greeted him. Miriam was smiling and her white teeth flashed and her hands went down to her slim hips and inched up the thin cotton of her knee-length, flowered dress. "You were screwing her and you fell asleep."

"Miriam," he said.

"I'm glad you were," she said. The little dress was climbing upward, revealing more of her well-tanned thighs. "Doris is a sweet woman, and she deserves a good screwing every now and then."

"We have to take a walk," he said, catching her.

"Can't move," she said, extricating her hands. "I've been here so long my feet are rooted."

"Look, I'm sorry."

"Sssh," she said. The smile seemed genuine, but with Miriam it was always hard to tell. "You're going to make it up to me, lover man. Right here."

The little dress came up over her head and flew off, settling into the sand, and Miriam was standing there with her legs apart, naked and ready. Two-toned, creamy white and coffee tan, sleek hips cocked.

"Fuck me right now or I'll start screaming," she said in her huskiest voice. "You know I'll do it."

He believed her, but that part didn't matter because his head was already pounding with breathless desire and he wanted exactly what she wanted, this crazy, high-wire fuck in the moonlight, two-for-one on the Fourth of July, screwing like dogs knee-down in the sand, no time to find the blanket he'd cleverly left in place. Nothing mattered but Miriam rutting herself against him, hair down and talking in her dirty, husky voice, luring him on, telling him exactly where she wanted it and how hard, using words so obscene he'd never heard them spoken aloud, not even by her.

They were still coupled together, pausing for breath, when Miriam swiveled around to face him, cocking her hips in such a way that he remained inside her.

"Smell me?" she said.

He nodded.

"Not that," she said, smirking. "The perfume I'm wearing. I got it from Dottie, we exchanged bottles."

Jack tried to pull away—this was crazy stuff, it was dangerous lunacy—but Miriam cramped up, wouldn't let him go. "You know why I did that?" she said. "Gave her my scent? To make it easy for you."

"I don't get it," he said.

"When you're screwing your wife."

"Okay, but I still don't get it. And we really need to get out of here, Miriam, please? Someone is bound to wander down."

Miriam licked her index finger, touched it to his mouth. "Because when you're fucking Dottie you think about me. You told me that, remember? So now you can close your eyes and smell me when you do it to her."

"Jesus, Miriam."

"Jesus has nothing to do with this, baby." She lifted her hips, started pumping him, never taking her eyes from his, staring hotly into him, boring holes in his mind. "I want you to fuck her a lot," she whispered urgently.

"Fuck her every night and think about me for the rest of the summer."

"Oh, Jesus."

"Cause this is our last screw until Labor Day, lover man."

"Jesus."

When he came that time it ached like a wound and hurt so good, so good, and then Miriam, wild and crazed, was after him with her mouth and he almost couldn't stand it and he thought, *I may actually die from this. Actually die.*

For just that one terrible moment, the thought pleased him.

Five

Bogey Golf

Michael Fitzroy on the porch of the Abenaqui Country Club clubhouse, pitching dimes with the caddy master, a local boy who was a clever cheat. The lad had a cunning way of swiping up the coins before his opponent could get a good look, keeping both dimes and winking sagely as he said, "You're getting closer, Mr. Fitzroy, but not quite close enough," and Mike kept pitching those dimes because he loved it, the way this kid lied without a twinge of conscience.

"You could be an attorney," Mike said when the last dime vanished into the caddy's ferret-quick hands. "Give it some thought."

"Need a lot of dimes for that, hey?"

"You're on your way, kid. Keep up the bad work." That quip just to let the kid know that Mike was on to his game. It wouldn't do to play the unwitting sucker for a country club lackey. Being proved a fool among members was like getting a bad rash: you could keep scratching at it, but it would never quite go away.

"I put your foursome with two of my best boys," said the kid. "Doubles okay? We're shy this morning, some of these little jerks took the day off."

"Two boys will be fine."

" 'Cause I sure wouldn't want to disappoint his honor the guv'nah."

"Mr. McKane was never a governor," Mike said.

"Well, he shoulda been," said the caddy master, flashing a big, phony grin. "He's sure got the moxie."

Sugar would like that, being mistaken for a governor. He was back there in the locker room now, showering. The old man always cleansed himself before a round of golf, scrubbed his flesh raw under cold water, it was a fetish. Time was when Michael felt obliged to do likewise, following his father-in-law's lead, shivering under the cold tap, but lately he bathed like a normal man, after working up a good sweat. And bank on it, Sugar would make him sweat, find a way to get under his skin. Might not have to say a word, just a look like they'd exchanged earlier that morning, when Miriam had returned in the wee hours, acting giddily drunk, but—and this was strange—not smelling of alcohol. To make matters worse, to really screw the knife home, she'd then staged a confrontation by requesting that her faithful husband—that was the phrase she used—vacate their bedroom, saying, *Oh, faithful husband, be a sweet boy and do me this favor: go roost with the roosters or something, I need to be alone.*

Just a glance from across the dim hallway as Michael, gray with inexpressible anguish, made his way to one of the guest rooms. That's all it took from Sugar, a flinty glance that said: *We both know there's nothing we can do about this, no point discussing the situation.*

Mike was on the practice green, sighting putts, when The Voice boomed from the clubhouse porch. "Perfect day for it, lads."

Sugar, pink as a baby, and wearing, as was his custom, a cuff-linked white shirt, green silk tie, and freshly pressed gray-checked wool knickers. Mike had sworn off knickers when he got his first pair of long pants, somewhere back around second grade, but on Sugar McKane's massive frame the knickers looked somehow fashionable.

Accompanying him, blinking like a tall, mournful rabbit in the harsh slant of morning light, was McKane's weekend guest and frequent sidekick, Liam Costello, who had slept through Miriam's noisy pre-dawn return, or in any event had refrained from letting on that he'd been disturbed. It was the long, fleshy ears that gave him the rabbit look, Mike decided, and the nervous habit he had of rubbing his pale, freckled hands together. The Costello brothers, Liam and Leonard, were from the old days, bound to McKane by financial and personal obligations so complex that not even Michael, privy to much of it, really understood exactly who owned what or how much or how many of the half-dozen funeral homes the brothers either co-owned or managed for McKane, and of course for themselves and innumerable affiliated relatives. Sugar periodically claimed he had sold off his interest in the ''padded box business,'' as he called it, but if this was technically accurate, there still remained deeper ties that could not be severed, and the small matter of mortgages on each of the funeral homes and the actual homes occupied by various Costellos and their in-laws.

It was Liam who asked after Jack. ''That brother of yours, he's making up the foursome?'' he asked craftily.

''Jack'll be right along,'' Mike said, glancing at his wristwatch.

''Ahhh,'' Liam said. He rubbed a hand on his skinny neck and swallowed hard, as if digesting the information. ''Ahhhh, that'll be fine, then, we need a word with the young man.''

Something to do with that ugly poison-pen business, Michael decided, as Sugar made a show of pulling out his pocket watch, studying the time.

''By heaven, the man is late,'' he announced, swiveling his great head to search the parking lot. ''Tee-off is eight on the dot.''

''They'll hold it for us,'' Mike said. ''Don't worry about that.''

''Do you suppose it slipped his mind?'' Sugar asked, in the falsely aggrieved tone a parole officer might use when a notorious parolee failed to report. By Mike's watch it was still a minute before the hour, typical of McKane to be fussing already. ''I don't suppose anything has ever slipped Jack's mind,'' Mike said. ''Why don't we loosen up, take a few swings?''

''Never practice on the tee,'' Sugar advised. ''Throws off the internal gyroscope, ruins the center of balance.''

Mike opened his mouth, decided comment was futile. The internal gyroscope bit was a new one, a crackpot theory the old man had picked up somewhere or other, and there was no dissuading him from his latest theories, any more than you could convince him that being a minute or two late was not really late by conventional standards; the only standard was Sugar's standard, you just had to accept that, deal with him on his own level.

The big Packard boated into the parking lot at four minutes after the hour. Jack got out, saluted, and began to saunter very slowly toward the tee. He was wearing dark glasses, a short-sleeve, soft-collar shirt, and an old, comfortable pair of pleated trousers. Walking slow to cover his slight limp, or because it was bothering him this morning, Mike assumed. Whatever, his whole posture was somehow defiant, typical of the way he handled social engagements with McKane.

Sugar eyed him and, out of character, refrained from commenting on the late arrival. There would be, Mike intuited, no lecture on this fine morning, and for this he was grateful, whatever the reason. Little brother was not easily lectured, had already expressed a distinct lack of enthusiasm for resuming golf, a game he'd taken up only to please Mike and because, as he said (not entirely in jest), he liked hitting things.

"Liam," Jack said, hands in his pockets, not offering to shake. "So how's business?"

"Business is good. I hear the same about you boys."

"We'll see," Jack said. "Check with us this time next year, that's what Mike says."

"You're looking well, Jack my lad," Sugar commented. "We're pleased you could make it."

Jack raised the dark glasses, winked a bloodshot drinker's eye. "I'd have been a couple minutes early, Sugar, instead of a couple late except David fell out of bed and bumped his head. It threw me off."

"Nothing serious, I hope?"

"Just a bad dream. Somebody else go first, I'm going to need at least three strikes."

Jack played with the set of clubs Michael had given him, stored away all of last summer. A whiff of paste wax was released as he pulled off the covers. "Hey, these look brand-new," he exclaimed, waggling the driver and disturbing Sugar, who was addressing his ball on the tee. "Sorry, Sugar, give it a poke, huh?"

Mike winced. Jack and his attitude, you could tell he was pushing, trying to get a reaction out of McKane. A kid poking at a snake, poking and poking, wanting the thing to strike. Mike tried to flash a warning at his brother, get him to lay off, but Jack was ignoring him for some reason, he seemed to have an agenda of his own. All you could do, when Jack was like this, was go along for the ride, try to smooth out the bumps.

They all got to the first green more or less together, Jack shooting out of the grass bunker and somehow clearing his ball under the big elm branches, getting lucky right away, which was sure to irritate the hell out of Sugar, Mike knew that much. McKane was a plodding, down-the-middle golfer who firmly believed all deviation from the course was ill-conceived, if not actually immoral. And there was brother Jack grinning and waving his seven iron as he approached from out of bounds. "That's what I needed, I guess, a year off," he said, then added, "Sweet suffering Christ on the cross," for emphasis.

Sugar grunted.

"Nice shot," Mike said.

Jack was away, the first to putt. Mike obliged by holding the pin and watched the damn ball roll right over thirty feet of close-cropped green and drop tidily into the cup.

"Birdie," said Liam Costello. "The hard way, too."

Jack threw up his arms and dropped to the grass. He lay there flat on his back, laughing. "I don't believe it," he said, rolling over and propping himself up on his elbow, blades of new-mown grass sticking to his clothing. "Maybe I should turn pro, huh? What do you think, Sugar, I got what it takes?"

"Sure you've got it," Sugar said. He was trying to line up his putt, his huge face expressionless. He missed the cup, short by two feet, and bogeyed the hole.

As they came up to the second tee, Jack said, "Maybe if we laid a bet, huh? Gambling concentrates the mind." Mike interrupted, "Hey, Jack? Please, okay?" but Sugar intervened. "Jack has something he wants to say, isn't that right, my boy? Isn't that where you're going?"

Jack, bending gingerly to tee up his ball, leveled his gaze at McKane and nodded. "The house in Eastie, Sugar. I know about the house. I know about the mortgage you held on it. I know why that Drake kid hates your guts, and if I know, then you know. Which means you've been jerking me around on this situation."

"Drake?" Sugar said airily. "Am I supposed to know that name?"

Jack shook his head. He had the club in his hands and his arms were flexing, and for a moment Michael was afraid he was going to swing the club at Sugar, take a divot out of the old man's massive skull. "I checked it all out at the Registry of Deeds," Jack said. "A real puzzler, the way you move paper around. Anyhow, the point is you held a second mortgage on a home that had been in the kid's family for a couple hundred years. Twelve-room colonial, three acres of harbor waterfront. Few years ago you pulled a fast one, decided to force a foreclosure."

Sugar shrugged his big shoulders. "If I remember correctly, and I think I do now you bring it to my attention, they had failed to make payments for quite some time. I was within the law there, I'm sure of that."

"I don't give a damn why you did it, Sugar," Jack said. The club was down now, resting lightly on the grass. "What pisses me off is you didn't tell me about it. I ask why would this family hate your guts, and you never told me you foreclosed on their property."

"Go ahead and hit," Sugar said. "There's another foursome coming up behind us."

"I'll hit when you answer me," Jack said.

"I didn't think it had any relevance to this particular situation," Sugar said. "There's your answer. Now hit the ball."

"No relevance?" Jack said quietly. Michael knew that was a bad sign, it was never good when Jack got quiet and angry at the same time. "No relevance? The old man dropped dead, did you know that? Dropped dead at the dinner table a week after you gave him notice."

"That was a couple of years ago," Sugar said. "This, um, ugliness didn't begin until quite recently."

"Slow fuse," Jack said, shrugging. "The older brother gets himself drowned, they decide that must be your fault, too."

The way Sugar nodded to himself, his eyes hooded, Mike got the impression he was somehow satisfied by the exchange, as if it proved that young Jack only knew so much about this particular deal, so much and no more. It was just an impression, you never really knew what the old man was thinking.

"Maybe this discussion should wait until after the game," Mike suggested. "Out of earshot," he added, indicating the two young caddies, who were nervously hanging back, put off by the display of adult anger.

"I'm not the one raising his voice," Jack said carefully, enunciating each word.

"Hit your ball or I'll go out of turn," Sugar threatened. His face had gone a deep red and his eyes seemed to be receding darkly into his head.

"I'll hit the goddamn thing," said Jack, taking a swipe that hooked the ball into the rough.

"Do you want a mulligan?" Sugar said. "We'll agree to give you a mulligan. Take another shot."

"Screw your mulligan," Jack said. "I'll play my ball."

Mike caught up with Sugar, who as usual had hit a modest drive right down the center of the fairway, no distance to speak of but straight as an arrow. "Take it easy on him," Mike said, pleading. "You know how Jack gets."

"Take it easy on him?" McKane's complexion had gone back to pink, he was recovering his temper, his blood pressure was falling. "He's a hothead, Michael. How can I trust a hothead with my business?"

"You can trust Jack. You know that."

"Do I?" Sugar said. "Do I?"

"Level with him, Sugar. It's the only way."

"Oh? That's your advice, is it? What makes you think I'm not doing that very thing?"

Michael watched a white ball arc neatly out of the rough and bounce rapidly down the fairway, landing within chipping distance of the green. He cupped his hands around his mouth and called out, "Nice shot, Jack!"

On the green Jack two-putted, saved a bogey. Sugar, putting with hands of stone, missed the cup three times. The two caddies, who knew McKane and his famous temper by reputation, stood well back from the green, clutching the bags. They looked frightened.

Finally Liam Costello nudged Mike and said, "Make the peace, it's up to you."

Well, he was trying, but with bullheaded individuals like Jack and Sugar it took more than simple diplomacy. At this point, replacing the pin and heading for the third tee, the two weren't speaking. Each step was an angry step, and the anger was building into something potent and dangerous.

"Jack is just trying to do right by you," Mike said to Sugar. "Isn't that right, Jack?"

A nod from his brother. A grunt from McKane.

"He feels he deserves your complete trust," Mike said. "And I've got to say this, I think he's right about that part. Tell him whatever he needs to know, Sugar. It's the only way, and it's the right way."

McKane sat heavily on the bench, clutching his hickory-shafted driver with both hands. "I buried the man for nothing. Gratis," he said, staring at his club, not making eye contact with anyone, not even his toady, Liam. "Do you think I was happy about that, the poor gentleman dying after I had to take back his property? Do you think I *wanted* to be the cause of a personal tragedy?"

"It wasn't the father dying set the kid off," Jack said. "It was the brother. The one who drowned."

"So I'm to blame for everything that happens to that family?" Sugar asked.

"That's what I need to know," Jack said. "What set him off? The kid brother, the one I interviewed. Why's he suddenly got it in for you? And who's in it with him? I know he isn't writing the notes himself, or calling the newspapers."

Sugar shrugged, waggled the club. "It's the mother, I suppose," he said. "She's a crazy woman. Out of her mind with grief. Also, it's apparent that her brain is addled with alcohol. Ask Liam about her."

"What?"

Sugar turned to Jack and smiled, fully recovered, seemingly amused. "Tell him, Liam."

Costello obliged. "The woman has been disrupting our funeral processions. Making a fuss and screaming out terrible slanders. Leonard was going to have her arrested, but Sugar said no, that wouldn't be right. Jack'll take care of it the right way, he said, without the poor woman going to jail."

Jack kicked at the grass, shook his head. "Why the hell didn't you tell me about this?"

"I'm telling you now," Sugar said. "And I want you

to do something about it first thing tomorrow. But right now what I what you to do is hit the ball.''

"Somebody else go first,'' Jack said. Mike could tell that the wind had been taken out of Jack's sails, his brother's anger was blown out for the moment.

"No, you're up,'' Sugar insisted. "That's how we do it around here. We play by the rules.''

Six

Widows and Veils

The thing Jack noticed was the way everybody ignored the aircraft. They came along every few minutes, filling the sky, mostly DC-3's so low in the sky you could count the rivets on the fuselage, hear the flaps squeaking as the pilots lined up for the runway. Prop wash kicking up gusts of wind that lifted the veil on the widow's black hat. And nobody seemed to notice.

Live with a thing like this, the constant presence of noisy aircraft, you went deaf and blind to it. There was a lesson there, Jack decided: Don't live near the god-damn airport, that was the lesson.

Liam Costello had insisted that he wear a dark suit and hat, so as not to offend the mourners. Jack decided the hell with it as he peeled off the tie, unbuttoned his collar. The hat was baking his brain under the hot sun, and he took it off and used it to fan himself. Not even a patch of shade here at the Calvary Cemetery in East Boston, unless you wanted to stand under the small portable awn-ing with the widow and the priest as they waited for Leonard Costello and his assistants to position the hearse, a tight job in this overcrowded burial ground, not an inch to spare. Polished chrome bumpers grazing the stone markers as poker-faced Leonard stood ramrod stiff in his coal black suit and directed the vehicle with gray-gloved hands, himself apparently impervious to the stunning heat.

Get this stiff in the ground quick, Jack prayed, before it ripens. He'd more or less decided that his vigil at the cemetery was a waste of time. The lady wasn't going to show today. Crazy or not, she was evidently too smart to come out in weather like this.

Counting chickens, that's what it amounted to, be-cause the subject did indeed make herself known as the casket was sliding out of the hearse into the sweaty hands of the waiting pallbearers.

It all started with an ear-splitting scream:

"God knows the truth! He knows!"

Jack squinted into the sunlight and saw a sturdy, big-hipped woman lurching out from behind a granite mausoleum. Loose flesh of her arms flapping as she stomped clear of the mausoleum, hands held high, as if for some bizarre ceremony of benediction. The woman was barefoot, Jack noticed, her feet splayed in the close-cropped grass of Calvary's perpetual care. A raggedy flower-print dress showing thin in the light, might have been an expensive item when new, but that had to be sometime before the war from the look of it. Her broad-boned, fleshy face was mottled red from her exertions. A high-blood-pressure type, Jack concluded, possibly a heavy drinker, there was that in the ponderous way she moved, as if struggling for balance.

"God knows he did it!" The woman screamed again, a wordless shriek. Her eyes rolled back and she grimaced, showing her teeth. "Damn every one of you bastards to Hell!" she shouted. "Damn Sugar McKane, the lying Jew bastard who killed my son!"

Already the Costello employees were advancing rapidly through the lines of grave markers, cutting her off. "Jew McKane!" she ranted. "Child killer McKane! Rapist McKane! Bastard! Murderer! Leave me alone, you shanty Irish bastards! And screw the Pope, too!"

Jack had to smile. Oh yes, that last bit made quite an impression on this crowd. Matter of fact, the widow had already fainted into the arms of the priest. You wanted to disrupt a Catholic funeral, that was the way to do it. This bunch happened to be mostly Italian, so the shanty Irish insult didn't stick, but my oh my, our Holy Father the Pope, that got their attention.

Jack sighed, put his hat on, shoved his tie into his suitcoat pocket. He strode purposefully into the fray, caught up with the tangle of limbs just about when the woman broke free, her lips spraying spittle as she fell headlong onto a grave site. Rolling and kicking, her dress flying up to reveal grayish knee-length bloomers of a type Jack hadn't seen since long before the war.

What he decided to do was make a stand, put himself

on her side. Taking up a position near the prostrate woman, Jack raised his fists to Costello's puzzled men. "Now, just you back away from here, you Irish bastards!" he roared. "Leave this poor woman alone or I'll bust your thick skulls, get me? Get me?"

The "get me" was for the boys, hoping they would indeed "get it" and leave the woman to him. It was Leonard Costello who quickly and correctly assessed the situation, called his men off by clapping his gloved hands together smartly.

"Get out of here, the pair of ya's," Costello advised, backing away from the scene. One eye closing in a droll, nerveless wink. Was there a much repressed sense of humor lurking under that lugubrious exterior? Jack wondered. Helping a woman up from the ground—he had to get her on all fours, work from there—he said, "We better skedaddle, miss. They'll sic those damned cops on us."

Up on one knee, swaying, she looked at him with glazed eyes. Tried to speak, couldn't make the words come. There was a strong smell of alcohol about her, a peculiar medicinal scent. Vodka, Jack decided, the secret drinker's elixir, not odorless at all when taken in quantity.

"I could use a drink," he said, urging her up. Keeping his voice low, two conspirators against the mob. "And we really must get away from here. I don't trust the police in this town, they're all related."

"Yes," the woman said, her eyes focusing. "Yes, that's true. You know about that, do you?"

"Sure, I know," he said.

"Shoes," she said. "Need my shoes."

He retrieved her scuffed brown pumps from the base of the granite mausoleum and soon had her under way. Using her momentum to steer her bulk through the white maze of headstones, heading for the back gate. A real sense of urgency, too, he didn't have to fake that part, you never knew when a crowd might start reacting as a mob, get truly ugly. For instance, pick up stones, that's how they did it in the old country, righteous women in black shawls stoning the blasphemous.

"Do you have a car here, miss?" Jack asked, fairly certain she did not own a vehicle or drive one.

She was panting, leaning heavily against him as she forced her swollen feet into her shoes. Her broad face glistening with sweat and tears. "I hate them . . . so much," she panted. "Keeps me . . . alive."

"Here, I'll take you home," Jack said. He worked her around to the running board on the passenger side of the Packard, where she slumped and sat, exhausted. "Miss?" he said. "I'm John Cabot Lodge, by the way, no relation to the senator. Can I give you a lift?" The idea, don't let her pass out here, have to deal with lifting all that dead weight into the car.

To his surprise she seemed to sober up right before his eyes, an astonishing act of willpower, pulling herself into focus. "I'm so sorry," she said, right hand splayed on her bosom. "I've hurt your leg."

Jack hadn't been aware of his limp until she mentioned it. "Not at all," he said. "It wasn't you did that."

"I suppose you were wounded in the war?"

"Let's not worry about my leg," he said firmly. "Let's worry about getting you home."

"What did you say your name was?" she asked, shading her eyes, looking him over.

"Lodge," he said. "John Lodge."

"John Cabot Lodge, I think you said."

Jack grinned, shook his head ruefully. "My dear mother, rest her soul. She admired the senator. And she *was* a Cabot—alas, not the money Cabots." He indicated the somewhat battered Packard as proof of relative impoverishment. "Lodge, well, I suppose my father was related somehow or other, nobody is really sure."

"Mrs. Irene Drake," she said, offering her hand. Almost coquettish as she added, "Much obliged to you, I'm sure."

Mrs. Drake was able to stand on her own while he opened the door, then took her arm, and assisted her into the seat. One of her shoes slipped off and he had to get down on his knees, fish it out from under the running board. Rising to his feet, his bad leg cramped, making him stagger. Mrs. Drake looked quickly away, not wanting to cause him embarrassment.

He eased the Packard away from the curb before delicately clearing his throat. "I really could use a drink,

Mrs. Drake, do you mind? Don't normally take one this time of day, but those men back there . . .''

Staring straight ahead, Irene answered, "I'm not sure we keep any liquor in the house."

"No, no," Jack said. "Wouldn't dream of imposing."

The fact was he didn't want to take her home just yet, and risk being recognized by one of the neighbors he had already interviewed, or worse, run into Billy boy, her son. Best thing to do, keep her on neutral ground. Mrs. Drake rejected his first choice of saloon. "No, that's a bad place. A terrible place," she said, and Jack understood that she was known there, and possibly banned. Fair enough, he drove a few blocks north, toward the Revere town line, and found a suitable bar and grill located on the new traffic circle.

"Sorry to trouble you," he said. "But my nerves feel a bit shaky."

Irene, maintaining an air of polite civility, responded that it was quite all right with her. Shaky nerves required medication, that was a fact of life.

The bar was air-conditioned and virtually devoid of customers. Irene sighed deeply, contentedly, as they slid into a red leather booth, into the near-blind comfort of perpetually dim lights. "Bourbon, soda back," Jack said to the instantly hovering bartender. "Would you join me please, Mrs. Drake? Make an exception for the early hour—I do hate to drink alone."

"What's it called," she asked coyly. "A vodka collins?"

"That's what they call it," the bartender said. "Coming right up."

They waited. Irene swallowed hard, tried not to look at the bar.

"Terrible things," Jack said. "Funerals, I mean."

"Terrible," said Irene, and now she couldn't help it, her eyes locked onto the bartender as he set up the glasses.

"Displays of grief," Jack said. "I suppose it's a necessary thing."

It was no use, Mrs. Drake wasn't going to converse until she had that glass in her hands. Fortunately, the bartender was quick and efficient, had recognized a need for urgency. Jack sipped gingerly from the shot glass of raw-tasting bourbon, covered his reluctance by drinking deeply of the soda.

The proximity of the alcohol eased the lines of tension in Irene's face. No gulping, she wasn't that kind of drinker. Slow, careful sips that made her shudder with relief. "I suppose it must have looked all wrong to you," she said. "What happened."

Jack shrugged. "All I know is, those men were menacing a defenseless woman. That's not right."

Irene was savoring her medicine, and her eyes glowed with contentment. "They were menacing me, that's true." She eased the glass down, holding it cupped in her plump hands, and then her eyes narrowed. "What were you doing there, Mr. Cabot Lodge? Friend of the deceased, I suppose."

Jack quickly shook his head. "Visiting a gravesite. Young man under my command . . ." He paused, let it sink in, what a noble thing he was doing, paying his respects to the war dead.

"So you weren't with *them*," she said, twisting the word.

"Certainly not."

Having the drink in hand made her confident, and also skeptical. "I suppose you know *him*, though. You must."

"Him?"

"McKane. Him that's behind it all. Him that owns those men who chased me. Sugar McKane, he's a famous bastard, pardon my French."

"Ah," Jack said vaguely. "Familiar name. Wasn't he the mayor once upon a time?"

Irene shook her head vehemently. "Never the mayor, or the governor, or anything but a big blowhard of a ward boss. Though you'd never know it to hear him talk so big. The man's never been elected to anything. What it is, see"—here she leaned forward and lowered her voice to a conspiratorial whisper—"he's afraid of what might come out. Because a lot of us know about him, all the terrible things he's done. Unspeakable things. I'm not the only one who knows. Not by a long shot."

Jack smiled and said, "I'm afraid you've lost me. Was he there at the funeral today, this Sugar McKane?"

Irene shook her head again. "He's hiding from me. He's a coward at heart. All of them are. The Jews and the Irish. They're in charge of the city now, and they won't let us forget it. Just try to find a bit of truth in the newspapers, you'll see I'm right. They're on his side, every one of them. Those kinds protect each other. And the crookedest villains of all are the cops, because they're all Irish.''

"I suppose they are," Jack said. "Look, these cocktails are pretty small, I'm going to have another."

A crafty exchange of glances acknowledged that they were in this together, secret sharers with a need. "Just to be polite about it," she said airily, signaling expertly for another round.

Bad idea ordering shots of bourbon, Jack decided: you couldn't hide it, and the stuff was going right to his head, made him almost dizzy enough to think that this crazy lady was making sense. There *was* a conspiracy. It wasn't an Irish conspiracy, exactly, and it didn't include every institution and newspaper and police officer, but surely it involved Sugar McKane. Right up to his size-seventeen neck in an East Boston land grab that had spanned, Jack was beginning to think, the entire decade.

"Leighton was a weak man," Irene said. "My late husband, Leighton Drake, he was—" She stopped and looked around, made sure no one was there to overhear. "Can I say something in confidence, Mr. Lodge?"

Jack nodded.

"My husband gambled. He had a good bit of money when we married, enough to live decently. The Drakes had land, you see, and they'd sold most of it off in the Twenties, and old Mr. Drake was too smart a man to just leave it fallow. Municipal bonds, that's what he bought with his money. Invest in the city because there'll always be a city, I must have heard him say that a hundred times. But then what happened, he died and Leighton got hold of the money and he began to speculate.''

"Ah," said Jack, trying to sound sympathetic. For his trouble he got a sharp look.

"I don't mean horses, Mr. Lodge, if that's what you're thinking. My Leighton never stooped to that. No, what he did was invest in things. Inventions. A thingamabub to core an apple, he wasted nearly two thousand dollars trying to get a patent, only it turned out somebody else had already invented it.''

"He was an inventor, your husband."

"I didn't say that." Another sharp look, as if she had reason to doubt his intelligence. "I said he invested, okay? Say you have an idea for a thing, a device of some kind, you'd come to Leighton and he'd put up the money to develop the idea and pay for the patent search and so on."

Jack felt he should stick up for the dead husband, put in his oar. He let his voice slur a little—that was easy. "Sounds like a pretty good business proposition," he said. "Quite a reasonable thing to do, if you have money to invest."

Irene sighed deeply. "Oh, I thought so, too, for a long time. Leighton made it all seem quite reasonable. But he had a way . . . he didn't like to worry me, you see? He was a good man, really. He tried so hard."

"Yes?"

"The one really bad thing he did was borrow money from that shylock McKane. That's how it all started. That's how he got his hooks into us." Irene's eyes had started to shine in the dimness, glittery and jumpy and inward-looking. "All the lies. That's what made him want to ruin us, because he got Leighton in his power. And then Leighton died and he had the rest of us to squeeze. He's part Jew, you know, that's what makes him so cunning when it comes to money."

"I didn't know that," Jack said. He signaled for another round of drinks. He wanted to keep her talking while he had the chance, maybe she'd stumble on something he didn't already know.

"You can always tell a Jew," she said. "They try to hide it, but you can always tell. My poor dead boy never believed that. Roy was too nice a boy to see the evil in anybody, and look where it got him. Look at *his* reward."

Irene stared at him, waiting. Jack shifted, it was an easy thing to make out that he had no idea what she was talking about. "I don't know what to say," he said. "I'm sorry about your troubles, Mrs. Drake."

"Do you have any children, Mr. Lodge?"

"Unfortunately, no."

The drinks had arrived. Irene waited until the bartender retreated. "Lucky for you, maybe. Bring 'em into this rotten world, filth and garbage taking things they've no right to. Putting on airs. Acting so high and mighty. It makes me sick what they did to us. What they did to my poor, beautiful son. What they made him do.''

Jack waited until she'd had a good strong swallow of the fresh drink, nothing delicate about the way she slurped it down now. He said, ''What did they do to your son, Mrs. Drake, the one who died. What did Sugar McKane do?''

He thought she was going to chew the glass, that's how hard her teeth snapped. ''It was her,'' she said in a voice thick with booze and malevolence. ''Her that killed him. That lunatic daughter. The crazy girl. She tricked Roy. That little witch, fogged his mind. The father was behind it, though, he was the one made her do it. He made her do all kinds of terrible things, that's what she told Roy, just before the little witch killed him.''

''Do what, Mrs. Drake?'' Jack said. ''What did Sugar do to his daughter, exactly? And how did she kill your boy?''

That was when young Billy Drake entered, carrying a tire iron. ''Mother, please get away from that man,'' he said. His voice was high and excited, and he was smacking the iron against his open palm. Sounded like a baseball smacking into a glove. ''He's one of them, didn't you know?''

The old woman finished her drink, and then she balled up her fist and hit Jack right between the eyes, as hard as he'd ever been hit in his life.

Seven

Pillars of Light

Deidre kept catching glimpses of the ring. It was somewhere under the bed, hiding in the shadows that lurked
there. Shadows like black tongues. Dr. Parkay said it was
silly to be afraid of the shadows, but there were a lot of
things Dr. Parkay didn't understand. He couldn't see
through things to the other side like Deirdre could, and
sometimes that made him stupid. The fact was, the shadows were trying to dissolve the ring because the shadow
tongues needed precious metal, just like humans need
vitamins and medication and lots and lots of sleeping
pills.

Lying flat on the floor, keeping herself at what she
believed was a safe distance, Deirdre watched the smoky
fog of shadows pulsate under her bed. There! A glint of
gold. It was always difficult for her to concentrate—ever
since the operation her thoughts were like butterflies, and
if you touched them the wings sometimes dissolved—but
the ring was very important and so she focused all of her
energy on finding a solution to this dilemma: how to get
the ring out from under the bed without having to touch
the shadows?

At ten in the morning, wearing an ankle-length blue
cotton robe that tied up in the back, so she would be less
likely to fiddle the belt open and engage in the impulsive
self-exposure that bothered Dr. Parkay and his staff, if
not the other patients, Deirdre McKane approached the
first-floor nurses' station and handed the duty RN a piece
of folded paper.

The RN unfolded the paper. It was blank.

''What do you want, Dee Dee?'' the nurse asked. It
was not the first time this patient had delivered blank
paper to the nurses' station. Dr. Parkay said it was her

way of announcing that she wanted to communicate, and his explanation made as much sense as anything else.

Deirdre made sweeping motions with her arms and smiled her beautiful smile.

"You want a broom, Dee Dee, is that what you want?"

Deirdre nodded.

"Staff cleans the room for you, dear. Remember?"

Deirdre shook her head, stamped both feet, and made furious sweeping motions.

The nurse sighed. Two hours to lunch and already it had been a very long morning. "What harm could it do?" she said aloud. Work in this place, it was not unusual to develop the habit of talking to yourself, or directing inner comments to patients who clearly could not comprehend.

The nurse gave her a broom and Deirdre snatched the nurse's hand and kissed it. There were tears in her eyes. She really was a sweet girl, the nurse decided, wiping her hand on her starched skirt. A stunning beauty, too. Mad as a hatter, of course, despite the experimental surgery.

Deirdre ran back to her room with the broom. Her intention was to go after the ring immediately, before the shadows could do any more damage, but her attention was diverted by the window. Light coming in. Shapes of light that made cool-breeze sighing noises like the nice nurse. Dr. Parkay had ordered the heavy wire screen removed as a reward when Deirdre seemed to agree to wear the back-belted robes, and so she could look out the window now without having to press her cheeks to the screen.

They were out there. The white shapes. Molten blobs of light, that's what you saw at first. Until you really concentrated and squinted, and then you could see *inside* the light. See *them*. The Beautiful Creatures.

It was happening too soon, though, this wasn't fair. She needed more time. Deirdre opened her mouth. Nothing came out, but inside her head she was saying, *No! Please wait!* because you didn't need to speak out loud to the Beautiful Creatures, they didn't like noise and you could scare them away. They were timid that way. Make a sudden sound and they'd sometimes disappear for hours, or for days.

Deirdre was torn. She longed to watch the shimmering lights and yet she needed to get the ring that had somehow been taken by the shadows, because *they* needed the ring. Not even the Beautiful Creatures could have a wedding of light without a ring.

Deirdre assumed she was going to be something like a bridesmaid. Of course, it was a very different kind of wedding, and she was still a little vague on exactly what the differences were, but one thing was very clear—she had to get the ring out from under the bed.

In a panic Deirdre tore herself away from the window—all the lovely pillars of light were gathering out there and she was going to miss the ceremony!—and threw herself to the floor. She extended the broom, swept it flat under the bed. Closing her eyes because it was very difficult to look at the shadow things when you've been in the presence of the Beautiful Creatures.

She jerked the broom around blindly for a while, before deciding that she *must* open her eyes and look for the ring. There it was, shimmering pale gold, bigger than she'd remembered. With exquisite care she extended the broom and pushed it forward by the handle. There, it was touching the ring. Had to be. Deirdre extended leverage, holding the broom flat against the floor. Grunting with the effort, she pulled the handle toward her, easing the broom out from under the bed. Dragging the ring along with it.

When she turned over the broom and could not find the ring, the sense of urgency increased. She had to get it! And there it was, only in a different place under the bed. The shadows could move it around now! This was a new development, a new power, and the idea of it frightened her. If they could move the ring, what else could they do?

Deirdre began to cry. Wailing with dry eyes. Soon enough an orderly heard her and came to investigate.

"What's the matter, honey?" he asked. Kneeling down, he looked under the bed. "Bogey man under there, is he?"

Deirdre covered her eyes and made mewing noises. This wasn't good. The orderly put in a call for Dr. Parkay, who was on rounds in another ward. When he finally arrived, after a delay of nearly thirty minutes, he seemed to have a pretty good idea of what was going on.

"She's lost her ring again," he told the orderly. He

turned to the patient, who was sitting on the floor and rocking. "Is it your ring?" he asked kindly.

She wasn't able to respond. She kept hugging herself and rocking.

Dr. Parkay got down on his hands and knees and looked under the bed. "Hand me that broom, please."

The orderly handed him the broom. A moment later Dr. Parkay had the ring in his hand. "Get someone to dust under that bed," he said to the orderly, and then he went to Deirdre, holding the ring in the palm of his hand.

"You must remember to keep it on your finger, Dee," he said. "Like this." He slipped the ring onto her finger. "Keep fiddling with it and you'll keep losing it. There, do you feel better now?"

Deirdre looked at the ring on her hand and nodded. "Thank you very much," she said, her voice thin and hoarse, but audible.

"Hey," the orderly said. "She talks to you."

"Of course she does," Mr. Parkay said. "We're good friends."

As soon as the doctor and orderly had left the room, Deirdre took the ring off her finger and put it in her mouth. She made the sign of the cross and then she swallowed. The ring was cold going down, like a chip of ice, but it felt good because she knew that this was the only way to keep the ring safe. Leave it on her finger and the shadows would have it off while she slept.

Deirdre went to the window. No shimmering lights, no Beautiful Creatures. They were gone, frightened off by all the noise. They'd come back, though, Deirdre was pretty sure about that. All you had to do was be quiet and wait.

Eight

Miriam Makes a Promise

"You're joking."

"Swear to God," Jack said. "She knocked me out cold."

Jack and Mike were sitting in the screened-in part of the back porch of McKane's huge, gray-shingled summer home, overlooking the rarely used tennis court and beyond that, just visible through the landscaped yard, a white-capped sea. For all the grand elegance of the summer estate, the numerous guest rooms, the double kitchens, the banquet-sized formal dining hall, and the sweeping, chandeliered stairway, it was a fact that the property did not actually abut the Atlantic. All of the mansions of this exclusive promontory were cut off by the lazy curve of the sea-abiding boulevard. Cut off, but also protected from hurricane floodwaters; high ground made the land more valuable by far than the beach-level acreage, where cheaply built cottages were propped up on cedar posts, offering little resistance to the occasional storm tides that swept over the boulevard and back into the salt marshes. Of course, the sheer proximity of the beach—they virtually lived upon it—made it easy for the summer cottage dwellers to roll out of their creaky camp beds and wander out to the white sand, simple as that.

The McKane estate, in contrast, was on dry ground, well above the bluff, and if guests wanted to wet themselves they waded at the Beach Club. Sugar had refused to put in a pool, as many of the other estate owners had done, because he thought an unattended pool dangerous to small children and—this was the real reason, Jack had decided—because he himself did not swim.

Jack was thinking about the pool, or the lack of one, because he dreaded his twice-weekly therapy sessions at the Boston YMCA, and because his bad leg was causing him distress right at that moment, even as he made light of the assault.

"What about the kid?" Mike wanted to know. "He hit you with that tire iron?"

Jack shook his head. "He grabbed the old lady and took off. What bothers me, Mike, is that he found me at all."

Mike, sipping leisurely from a pilsner glass of beer, uncrossed his legs and crossed them the other way, trying to get comfortable in the stiff porch rocker. Wearing crisp white duck trousers and a short-sleeved Banlon shirt and new white buck shoes that were as yet unscuffed. Looked born for this place, Mike did, with those Ivy Leaguer horn-rims framing his intelligent eyes, you'd think he'd been trust-funded at birth. He had good color from the holiday weekend, too, a golf-pro tan, and he was about as relaxed as he ever got; or he had been until Jack arrived with his unsettling report. "Must have been one of his mother's watering spots, I guess," Mike said. "Went looking for her when she didn't come home."

"He went looking all right," Jack said. "But that bar and grill was no local. What must have happened, he recognized my car."

"That's not good," Mike agreed. He lifted a pack of Pall Malls from the porch table, tapped out a cigarette, and fished a Zippo—a gift from Jack, as it happened—from his trouser pocket.

"No," Jack said. "The kid bothers me, and I don't just mean the tire iron."

"Time you bought a new car," said Mike. His eyes were bright and he was smiling—he loved to talk about buying things.

"A new car won't fix it. The kid is on to me."

"So we put someone else on him. How about Doug Donnelly? Doug would be perfect. Or one of the new boys, take your pick."

"That's not the point, Michael. The point is we've done all we can. We've identified who has been sending poison-pen letters to the newspapers. It was the mother. And she's just a crank. Loony but harmless."

Mike chuckled. "Harmless? How many times you been knocked out with one punch?"

"I hit the back of my head on the booth. I wasn't ready."

"Still, I wouldn't want to try it, taking a poke at you."

"Go on and do it," Jack said, lifting his chin. "I'm easy."

"Sure you are. And so's Gene Tunney. You're back in the ring like Tunney, am I right?"

Jack shook his head. It was apparent that Mike had been having more than a few beers, and possibly a bit of hard stuff. McKane didn't stock liquor himself, so boozing at the summer estate tended to be on the sly, or when Sugar was out thrashing his way around the golf course. "Let's drop the boxing bullshit, okay, Mike? It's nice you think your kid brother is a tough guy, but that's not getting us to the real problem."

Mike was smiling to himself, finding just the right place for his cigarette, keep the smoke from his eyes. "Which is?" he said. "What problem?"

"Whatever Sugar did to give old lady Drake such a hotfoot. She mentioned his crazy daughter. I'm thinking that Miriam's little sister might have been involved."

"Deirdre? Come on, Jack. I thought you knew about Dee."

Jack sat back in his chair, glad of the sea breeze. It seemed to be easing his headache, heightened his awareness of where he was, who he might see here. "I know she's Section Eight," he said. "But that might fit right in."

"How so?" Mike said doubtfully.

Jack leaned forward, kept his voice low, there was no one else around but you never knew. "Look, she had a problem, right? Chasing after everything in pants? Liked to strip her clothes off, play with herself, didn't care who was around? I heard the stories, Mike."

Mike shrugged elaborately, and that made Jack sure he'd had quite a lot to drink, even though his voice wasn't slurred. He could hold his liquor, but that didn't mean it didn't affect his thinking.

"What if she had something going with Mrs. Drake's son?" Jack suggested. "The one who drowned?"

"What if she did?" Mike said. "Poor Dee was naughty with lots of guys, Jack, you get my drift. Only she never really knew what she was doing—it's this compulsive thing, she can't help herself. Dee never hurt anybody that I heard of. Basically she's a sweet kid.''

Jack hesitated. "I was thinking maybe you could ask Miriam. Maybe she'd know.''

Mike looked away, sucked deeply on his cigarette. ''Nah,'' he said. ''We're not getting along too grand right at the moment. Better ask her yourself.''

"You don't mind?''

"Why should I mind?'' Mike said. "I gotta warn you, though, she's very touchy about her sister.''

"Sure.''

"I mean it. The subject is not discussed in this house. The old man, he gets this hollow look sometimes, I know he's thinking about her. It kills him, having to put her away.''

"I'll be diplomatic.''

"Yeah, be diplomatic, but, Jack? Be ready to duck, pal, okay?''

He was sitting under the portico, smoking a cigarette he'd cadged from his brother, when Miriam returned from her tennis lesson. She came in fast, as she always did, spraying gravel around under her two-tone convertible. The engine of the nearly new Olds was knocking, sounded low on oil.

"Better check the dipstick,'' Jack said, standing up as she switched off the motor.

Miriam stayed in the car, hands gripping the wheel, looking straight ahead. "Where's Michael?'' she said without inflection.

"Driving over to the harbor to get lobster. I waited around.''

"Michael know that?''

"Take it easy,'' Jack said. "This is business.''

Miriam gave him a who-are-you-kidding look.

"On my honor,'' Jack said. "I've got a couple questions I need to ask you. And I'm serious about checking the oil on this rig. You'll run it dry.''

"What if I do?'' Miriam said loftily. She made no move to get out of the car, kept her hands on the wheel.

Jack opened the door. "Just play along,'' he said under his breath. "I'm your brother-in-law, remember? Being friendly to your brother-in-law is allowed.''

Staring straight ahead, not shifting in the seat, Miriam said, "I thought I made myself clear on this, Jack."

"Right," he said. "Believe me, I'm looking forward to Labor Day like I've never looked forward to Labor Day. But this isn't about that."

"Everything is about that," Miriam said, swiveling her legs out to exit the vehicle. Her little white tennis skirt rode up high, and she did not attempt to conceal herself. "I thought you knew."

Jack followed her inside, carrying her tennis racket and a small canvas duffel bag. "They still don't have a shower room for the women members, can you believe that?" she said, peeling off a lemon-colored scarf, shaking her hair free. "I guess you noticed, huh? You're sniffing at me like a horny bloodhound."

"Jesus, Miriam," he said, looking around for eavesdropping servants.

"Oh, give it a rest. I told you not to come here, you're getting what you deserve."

Jack seized her wrist, made her face him. "Take it easy, for chrissake," he hissed.

"Screwed your little wife lately?" Miriam said sweetly. "I'll bet she keeps her eyes closed, am I right about that?"

Jack let go of her.

"Sorry," Miriam said. "I'm tired and I need a bath. Not to mention the fact my father is due back any minute. Unless, of course, you want to quiz him, too."

Jack shook his head. Wouldn't be smart to let Sugar see them together, not the way Miriam was acting. "This won't take long."

Miriam reached up, patted his cheek. "You poor kid. I'm being a bitch and you're just trying to do your job, is that it?"

"I didn't say you were a bitch."

She smiled. "Well, I am, and proud of it, too. All you bastard men in the world, we need a few good bitches to balance it out."

"It's about your sister," Jack said, and he watched her face close up, like a fist being squeezed shut.

Miriam slumped into a heavy decorative chair in the paneled hallway, let her head thump against the wall. Her eyes were closed and when she spoke her voice was distant, without inflection. "What about my sister?"

This wasn't how Jack wanted it to play out. He needed to ask Miriam a few questions, yes, but he had intended to do so with more intimacy than she was willing to allow him right at the moment. An intimacy that might, admit it, lead to the physical contact he craved like a drug whenever she entered a room, or his thoughts, or managed to distill her essence into that damned bottle of perfume she'd given to Doris.

Face it, he needed her like he'd never needed anything in his life, and he couldn't wait six more weeks, not if he was going to retain his sanity.

"I can't do it," he said. "I can't be without you."

Miriam opened her eyes. "What is it about my sister?" she said. An edge in her voice now. She'd snapped her knees together, catching the pleats of her tennis dress, and her fists were balled up in her lap.

Jack took a deep breath. More than anything he wanted to touch her again. Just feel that cool-hot, soft-hard flesh under his fingertips, driving him crazy with impossibilities made real, made super-real, remembered images and sensations so powerful he sometimes thought that gravity itself might fail, that he'd cut loose his moorings and bump up against the ceilings like some swollen, mindless balloon of a man.

"Are you trying to torture me?" Miriam demanded. "Is that your intention?"

"East Boston," he began. "Did Deirdre ever date a man from East Boston?"

"Date or screw?"

"His name was Roy Drake. Full name Royal Leighton Drake. Twenty-four years old. Good-looking, so I'm told."

"Was? He's dead?"

Jack nodded. "Drowned. He was a lobster man, got tangled up in his trap lines. Accidental death."

"Dee saw lots of men," Miriam said. She had crossed her slim, tanned arms over her chest and she wasn't making eye contact. Instead she stared at a vase of roses on a fancy mahogany end table, into the mirror that was mounted behind the vase to show off Sugar's prize flowers.

"So I've heard," Jack said. "I don't care about that. What I need to find out, did she ever have anything to do with the late Roy Drake?"

"East Boston? That dump?"

"I heard she liked to slum."

"Screw you, Jack."

"I'm not judging her, Miriam. I barely know the girl. I remember her from your wedding, saw her around the beach a few times, that's it. I don't care what she did or with who or how many times, except it's very important that I know what, if anything, she had to do with Roy Drake."

Miriam put her finger to her lips. "Hmm. Let's check her social calendar, shall we? Oh, right, she's been locked up in a loony bin for the last two months. Do you think she met your man in there?"

Jack tried to ignore the sarcasm, but with Miriam that was impossible, really, she poured it on like hot tar over the ramparts, scorching everything, taking no prisoners. "Drake drowned in April," he said.

Miriam shook her head violently. "The answer is, I can't give you an answer, okay? Can you live with that? What I can remember, Dee was still more or less okay until sometime in May. She was back living at home with my father, and she was talking about going to modeling school. Just talking. She really wasn't well enough to handle school, but we thought it was nice if she had a goal, you know? Something to think about other than whatever the hell it is that gets inside her head and makes her loony."

Jack said, "If it helps, the Drake family had financial dealings with your father. It's possible that Deirdre met Roy through your father."

Miriam shook her head, incredulous. "Then I guess you better ask Daddy about that. Why the hell are you badgering me about it?"

"She's your sister, I thought—"

Miriam stood up, smoothed out of the pleats of her little skirt. "Oh, I know exactly what you were thinking, lover man."

She moved closer, so close his head was spinning, so close he could smell her heat. She lifted her face and leaned her breasts against him and then she wet her index finger and placed it on his lips.

"Don't come around here," she said huskily. "When I can't stand it anymore, I'll come looking for you."

There was the sound of fat tires spitting gravel, the thud of a car door, a loud halloo. His brother, Mike, was back with a crate of lobsters, making enough noise to wake the dead.

Nine

Personal Favors

Rosemary Phelan wore a crisp new summer-weight linen suit to work, in recognition of her promotion, and Michael Fitzroy, watching from the vicinity of the coffee urn, heartily approved of the confident way she gave instructions to Mrs. Harrigan, who had replaced Rosemary as office manager.

"Keep two girls on the switchboard Mondays and Fridays," Rosemary was saying. "That's when we log the most calls. Tuesday through Thursday you can usually leave it with one, let the other girl work on files. Of course, if we get swamped, you'll have to make adjustments. But keep in mind that Mr. Fitzroy wants each call pegged by the second ring. The files can be attended to after hours, if need be."

As Rosemary tick-tocked away on her sensible heels, Mike set an interception course, handing her a mug of heavily creamed coffee. "Go get 'em, General Phelan," he said, grinning. "How goes the battle?"

"We've every man on paid assignment, Michael, isn't that grand?"

"Indeed it is," he said, following her into the small room that now functioned as her office. "All the troops well deployed, are they?"

Rosemary gave him her stow-the-blarney look, but she was clearly in a fine mood. She had devised a magnetic bulletin board for work assignments, and it dominated the wall next to her gun-metal gray desk, which was always kept in a state of tidy readiness. "I've been clearing all of this with Jack," she said, "but he keeps telling me to use my own judgment."

"That's the whole point," Mike said. "With you in charge back here, deciding what's the most efficient way to utilize personnel, Jack can be out there on the front lines, making sure the boys are doing it right."

Rosemary sipped from her coffee mug. Her eyes were on the assignment board, and he could almost sense the tumblers clicking over in that fine brain of hers. "I'm getting the hang of it," she said. "Sizing up each man."

Mike chuckled and winked lewdly.

"Not like that, Michael Fitzroy."

"Sorry, Rosemary."

"Deciding which man is best for each type of assignment, that's the key. Some of it is obvious, of course. Mr. Edwards is responsible for all the photo surveillance and wire work, and he's just taken on an assistant. As you know, the insurance companies seem to prefer Tony Grazi for the arson investigations—I wish we had two or three of Tony. The new red-haired fellow, Danny Stearn, he handles forensic evidence—I had to go and look that word up in the dictionary, I'm ashamed to say—and anyhow most of his hours will be taken up preparing expert testimony for our industrial clients. I suggested he buy himself a little pillow, those courtroom chairs are so hard? He said he just might do that."

"Did he now?" Mike said.

"He was teasing me, sure, just as you are."

"I'm not teasing, Rose, honest. It's a load off my mind, you getting the place organized."

Rosemary gave him a hard look, then softened. "I'm grateful for your confidence, Michael," she said. "It means a lot."

"Are you kidding? Eisenhower had you deciding what army to put where, the war would have been over in 1942."

"Oh, please. This isn't a war, Michael."

"My question, Rose, in your judgment do we need to bring in more investigators? Maybe make a couple of the part-timers full-time? I was planning to do that in the fall, but if we're shorthanded we can do it now."

Rosemary thought it over. "This week I'd say yes, we could use at least two more men on the industrial assignments. But then it looks like there may be a bit of a lull toward the end of the month, unless you scare up a few more clients."

Michael grinned. "Working on it. Dunning, Chase has been putting out feelers, they may want us on retainer."

"Dunning, Chase?" Rosemary made her eyes go wide, acknowledging what would be a major coup. "Big firm, Michael. Top of the heap."

Indeed they were, with a stable of blue-blood attorneys who represented a wide range of old-money families, trusts, and corporate clients. Most of Dunning, Chase's investigative work had been going to Commonwealth Detective Agency, basically a half-dozen gumshoes equipped with flash cameras. Broken-down heavies from the old push-it-in-their-faces school, and that lack of finesse had recently lost the law firm a major client. Mike was taking the senior partner to lunch, and he was going to impress the hell out of him with Fitzroy Security's modern, high-tech savoir faire. No kicking down motel room doors, flash bulbs going off like hand grenades. Why bother, when you had high-speed film, discreet wiretaps, and investigators who could provide sober, methodical testimony without terrifying a jury?

"How's the new man working out?" Mike asked, fiddling with his glasses, trying to make it look like a casual inquiry. "The big lug."

"Bob Cogan? A real gentleman. I've got him backing up that warehouse surveillance in Quincy. Getting his feet wet. He'll be fine."

Michael nodded. "Sure, he'll be great. Listen, when he calls in, tell him I'd like a word before he punches out."

"We're not using a time clock, Michael. You know that."

"Figure of speech. Just tell him, would you please? Thanks." Mike headed for the door, turned back just as he was about to exit. "And, Rosemary? This is on the Q.T., okay?"

"Everything is on the Q.T.," said Rosemary, studying him. "That's a given."

When Cogan sat down, the chair simply disappeared. He'd put on a new necktie, Mike noticed, and hadn't gotten the knot quite right. Must have been hasty, wanting to make a good impression after the standard Fitzroy

Security lecture about employees wearing business suits whenever possible.

"Is everything okay, Mr. Fitzroy?" he asked.

Just a little nervous, Mike noted, and who could blame him? He'd given up a lot—ten years as a lost & stolen property detective, his city retirement—in exchange for a higher salary and the chance to establish himself with the new firm. Probably having second thoughts right about now.

"Call me Mike, please, everybody does. I just wanted to say, Bob, that I'm delighted you came aboard. Jack has great things to say about you."

"Yeah? I mean thanks."

Mike fiddled with a glass paperweight, holding it up to the light. "What I'd like to know, Bob, would you be interested in a little overtime? Off the books." He hesitated, put the paperweight down. "I mean cash, of course."

Cogan shrugged his enormous shoulders. Take a deep breath and he'd hatch right out of that suit. "Sure, why not?"

"This is a surveillance job," Mike said. "Discretion is important."

Cogan nodded.

"I'd like you to keep tabs on a certain person," Mike said. "And report directly to me."

"So who is the certain person?"

Mike opened a drawer, withdrew a small photograph, and handed it to Cogan.

"Hey," the big man said, looking uncomfortable. "I know this broad." Then it dawned on him and his face went crimson.

"That's Miriam," Mike said gently. "My wife. This is a personal favor, Bob. I'd really appreciate it, if you can find the time."

Ten

Hate Therapy

The stench of chlorine rising from the pool couldn't quite
mask the underlying odor of mildewed lockers and dirty
socks that permeated the YMCA gymnasium. Jack wore
goggles to protect his eyes, and he was thinking about
getting one of those nose plugs. Make him look like an
idiot, swimming with a thing on his beak, not that he
cared. Twenty laps twice a week, he kept at it because
the neurologists insisted it would do him, quote, a world
of good. These were doctors who did not, he assumed,
have to face the indignity of stripping nude and bathing
in an essentially public pool. Public pools being the
source, rumor had it, of the summer polio epidemics,
although no infection had ever been traced to this particular pool, nor had he been frequenting the damn place
when he contracted the disease. Jack assumed there was
enough chlorine in the water to kill even the most hardy
virus, or the humans who used it if they swallowed
enough of the bleach-tainted water.

The fact was, he'd probably gotten the disease from
one of his sons. As it was explained to him, many children contracted mild forms of the poliomyelitis virus,
built up an immunity, and were never damaged, never
even knew they had more than a bad cold. Which did not
mean that a previously uninfected adult exposed to a recently infected child would get away unharmed. Witness
Jack's own experience, coming down with what he
thought was the same spring flu the boys had, only to
find one fine morning that he couldn't stand up. Fell right
to the floor beside his bed, both legs twisted up with
muscle spasms as he screamed for Doris to come quick,
and that was the beginning of the two worst months of
his life. Kindly physicians squeezing his frittering calf
muscles and murmuring ever so politely about irrevers-

ible nerve damage and core muscle atrophy, and how fortunate he was that the virus hadn't settled into his lungs.

Of course, the boys weren't ever to know that one or both of them might have been the carrier, not even Dottie knew that. The doctor who'd mentioned the possibility was sworn to secrecy—Jack's strong right hand pulling the poor man down by his stethoscope, making his point. No, never a possibility there. Terrible thing for a kid to grow up thinking he might have turned his old man into a gimp.

And so Jack swam his twenty, using his anger, his unspeakable, unreasonable, teeth-clenching fury to propel him, lap after excruciating lap, through the piss-warm, bleach-tainted water. Both legs burning with exertion, the left leg actually throbbing to the quickened beat of his strong heart, the virus-damaged sciatic nerve stretched like a hot piano wire through the meat of the calf muscle, electric tingles of pain discharging throughout his lower body.

Twice a week. He was going to stop this self-inflicted punishment as soon as the summer was over. From then on his gimp would have to look after itself. An argument that had sustained him at various intervals—two months, four months, six months, setting a limit so he had something to strive for. Setting a new limit when he achieved the old, but you didn't think about that until you got there.

Jack hauled himself out of the pool and rested on the tiles for a minute or so, getting his breath, letting the muscle tremors subside. Aware of the heat funk in the old building, air virtually as wet as the water, he couldn't wait to get back to the clean, dry heat of the street, let the sunshine burn away this bleak mood.

His knees were always weak when he limped into the shower stalls after a session, and today was no exception. Felt like the fragile joints might actually unhinge if he didn't take care to step very carefully on the slick concrete of the shower room.

He was head down, concentrating on his footing, when the voice startled him.

"I know about you."

Jack looked up and he saw the gun. Saw the man attached to the gun. More boy than man, that was his next impression, although he was concentrating on that gun, he saw that it was a big old .45, the Colt army-issue semi-automatic. The boy had to be pretty strong just to hold it like that, unwavering, pointing it right at his guts.

"Ah, shit," Jack said, because now he recognized the man-boy with the steady hand. William Drake of East Boston. Billy Boy.

"Keep your hands where I can see 'em," the kid said, echoing a line he must have heard in the matinee westerns, it sounded so rehearsed.

Jack looked down at his hands, back up at the kid. "I'm stark naked," he said. "You want me to hold my hands up?"

Billy kept the Colt steady on Jack's midsection. He said, "Sit down on that bench and don't move."

"Sure, anything you say," Jack said, easing himself onto the bench. The butt-smoothed wood was slick and moist against his bare skin. It was eighty-some degrees in here and he was getting goosebumps.

Rows of beat-up lockers were arrayed on either side of the bench. Some of the doors were open, and Jack was furtively scanning the open lockers, wondering if maybe he could fit inside, but really he knew it was pointless—a .45-caliber slug wouldn't be stopped by a few millimeters of rusty sheet metal.

"So how'd you get in here, Bill?" Jack asked, trying to make it conversational.

The kid wasn't buying any friendly chitchat. "You shouldn't have done that. Got Mother drunk."

Jack had very carefully placed his hands on his knees, he didn't want to make that trigger finger squeeze involuntarily. In his M.P. days he'd seen a German looter gutshot with a .45, looked exactly like the model in Billy's fist, and the looter had bled to death in about thirty seconds, spouting like a fountain. Going *ug-ug-ug* because he knew he was already dead.

"I felt like a heel, taking advantage of the lady," he said. "Really, I did."

"You're a liar," said Billy. Large sea blue eyes looking like they might spill right out of his face.

"You're right," Jack said. "I'm a liar and I lied to your mother and I got her drunk."

"So you admit it."

"Sure I do," Jack said. "You want to know why I did such a rotten thing, is that why you're here?"

The eye of the heavy pistol did not waver—amazing how steady the kid was, or the part of the kid that controlled the weapon. Jack wasn't at all sure that he himself had the strength to keep a .45 aimed like that, as if it was screwed to a tripod.

"Maybe I'm here to shoot you," Billy Drake said. His voice, unlike his hands, was thin and shaky, on the verge of breaking.

"I sure as hell can't stop you," Jack said, "if that's what you're going to do. But I'd like to get this off my chest first, why I did such a rotten thing to your mother."

Billy hesitated. Never for an instant did his hand waver, but you could see the uncertainty in his eyes. "I'm listening."

"It was that or have her arrested," Jack said. "She'd been disrupting funerals for the last few weeks and they wanted to have her arrested. So instead of letting that happen, I decided to try to find out what was bothering her."

"Don't," Billy said, his voice gone small. He cleared his throat and gulped, showing his white teeth. "Don't pretend you care about Mother."

"I kind of liked her, Bill, if you want to know the truth."

"Mother hit you," he said. "She knocked you cold."

"Exactly," Jack said, trying out a smile. It felt unreal, probably looked that way, too. "She's got guts, you have to admire that."

"I could have beaten you with that tire iron," Billy said in a warning tone.

"Sure you could have. But you didn't. And not because you were afraid, I'm guessing. It was because you didn't want to get your mother in trouble. Whack my brains out, it would have meant the cops for sure."

Drake came a step closer. Not a large person, indeed, he had a youthful, wiry slenderness, and yet he was looming, enormous, enlarged by the black, rust-specked .45-caliber semi-automatic pistol. "So you admit you're not a cop. You said you were a cop. That night you came on my boat and threatened to blow me up."

"I needed a sample of your handwriting, Bill, remember? That's why I had you write out the Pledge of Allegiance."

"That was just to make me think you were the FBI."

"I'm not a cop," Jack said. "I'm not an FBI man, either."

"No," Billy agreed. "You're just a bastard who does dirty work for Sugar McKane. I know that now. I followed you around, you never even noticed. I thought a private detective would see me, but you didn't." He paused, came just a little closer, close enough so a thought flitted into Jack's head, the notion that he could make a move, grab the gun. "What's wrong with you?" Billy said. "What happened to your leg?"

Jack decided to ignore the flitting thought: the kid was nineteen, nerve-quick and frightened; trying to make a grab would be suicide. "What?" Jack said. "What did you say?"

"You a war hero or something? That why your leg is bad?"

"Polio," Jack said.

"You serious?"

"Why would I lie about a thing like that? It embarrasses the hell out of me, you want to know the truth."

"Yeah? Why should it do that?"

"I dunno," Jack said. "It just does."

Billy scowled. "You just think I won't shoot a cripple, that's why you're saying that."

"Okay, I was a war hero, is that better? Will that make it easier? Come on, Bill, think of your mother. You kill me and who will take care of her? She needs help, or she'll get into serious trouble."

Billy backed up a step. The .45 might have been balanced and sighted by gyroscope, the way it swiveled as he moved. The barrel tracked Jack's naked sternum, and the weapon had the muzzle velocity and bullet mass to sever his spine, no question. "You don't know how hard it's been for her," Billy said. His eyes were filmed with moisture, wet and blue and jittery. "First my dad, and losing the big house. Then when she was sort of okay, my brother, Roy, gets killed. It's enough to make a person act a little crazy. She can't help it."

Jack took a deep breath. His hands felt like pieces of

dead meat, no strength in them at all. "You think the way your mother does, Bill? You think your brother was murdered?"

"Maybe I do," he said. "You're saying he wasn't?"

"All I know is what the cops told me. They said accidental drowning, no question about it. That's what the autopsy showed. But your mother thinks McKane was responsible, and she's been sending threatening letters to him, and to the newspapers. That's why he hired me, to stop the slander."

Billy was clearly surprised by this revelation, and for the first time the gun barrel wavered slightly, drifted away before coming back on line. "What kind of letters?" he asked.

"If you want, I'll let you read one," Jack said. "You can tell me if it's your mother's handwriting."

"Just tell me!" he said, his voice kicking up to a higher pitch.

Jack repeated the contents of the letters as best as he could remember, the threats and accusations, and he didn't temper the language because he hoped that Billy would recognize something of his mother's tone, a phrase she'd used in his presence.

"Anyhow, that's the basic idea," Jack said, concluding. "Money-lending Irish Jew. Hints of incest with his own daughter. How he got away with murder. Irene said pretty much the same thing to me that day I got her away from the cemetery."

At first Jack thought his eyes were playing tricks, and then he saw that it was true. Billy Boy was stuffing the .45 in his trouser pocket. Damn thing was so big it stuck way out, and he was keeping one hand on the butt of the gun and using the other hand to pinch the bridge of his nose. Fighting to hold back his tears.

"I didn't know about the letters," he said. "She never let on she was doing that."

"Nobody wants to arrest the poor woman," Jack said. "Least of all me. And I don't know what happened to your brother. Maybe McKane had something to do with it, but if so I haven't been able to find out what, or why exactly."

"You're protecting that bastard."

"The bastard hired me," Jack conceded. "I won't protect him if he's guilty."

"Oh, sure," Billy said. He was weeping freely now, the tears dripping from the end of his nose, and he slumped to the bench. Tried to take a deep breath, get control of himself, but the words came shuddering out of him. "Rigged. The whole goddamn world is rigged. That's how b-b-bastards like him make all their money. C-c-couldn't get Mother to sell the island, so they got Roy drunk, and he signed the deed over, and th-th-then he drowns? And it was an accident? He was all t-t-tangled up in that rope, that's how they must have killed him."

Jack had wrapped a towel around his waist. The .45 was still in the kid's pocket and so he didn't want to move too quickly, or in a way that Billy might interpret as threatening. "You keep saying 'they' killed your brother. Who is 'they,' Bill? Who did it?"

Billy looked up, blinking wetly. He did not seem ashamed of the tears. Maybe they were proof of his grief, Jack thought, proof that his brother *had* been murdered. "Him and the girl," Billy said. "McKane and his crazy daughter."

"What do you know about the crazy daughter, Billy?"

"I know how she came after Roy. Rubbing herself all over him like she was a whore. He told me he didn't care, he wanted to help her." The kid had regained a measure of composure, and his voice had returned to a lower register as he got his breath back. "That's the last thing he said to me: 'The poor girl is crazy, but she needs me.' What a sap, huh? All she cared about, that rich little bitch, was getting him to sign over the deed."

Jack was braced to run, as best he could, if the kid suddenly changed his mind about that gun, but his instincts told him the danger was past, at least for the present, and he wanted to know more, he wanted to know everything the boy knew. "Hey, Bill? I think you said that McKane wanted your mother to sell the island. What island is this? I thought he foreclosed on your house."

"In the harbor," Billy said. "You know, Drake Island?"

"Never heard of it."

"Right there on all the charts. We fish off it, summers. Me and Roy built a cabin out there just last year."

"So McKane had a mortgage on the island, too?"

Billy shook his head. "He just wanted it. People like that, they want something, they just take it."

Eleven

Miriam's Ghost

The filet of sole was a bad idea, Michael decided, because Emmett Dunning resembled a freckled flounder. Look at him face on, the gray, watery eyes were so wide apart that the poor man appeared to be peering in two directions at once. Was it the unusual peripheral vision that had helped him survive as a Navy tail-gunner? Washed out as a pilot, Mike had heard, and crazy enough to volunteer for the torpedo bombers, which meant he couldn't possibly be as mild and nerveless as he looked close up over a Parker House lunch.

"The veal is good," Dunning said, sawing industrially with his fork and knife, dicing the meat into tiny morsels that he carefully arranged on his plate. "Do you know about veal?"

"Pardon me?" Michael said.

"Milk-fed, that's the secret. Makes the meat tender and easy to digest."

"Ah," said Mike, nodding in appreciation. "I see."

"I was never nursed," Dunning explained, smiling with his small, fish-pale mouth. "Mother couldn't, you see. Barley water was the substitute in those days. Maybe that's why I prefer veal now, all these years later. Making up for the lack of milk."

"Sounds reasonable," said Mike, who had no idea what Emmett Dunning was talking about. Mother's milk? Veal? The lad had been too long in the gun turret. But Dunning was heir apparent to the throne of Dunning, Chase, and reputedly an astute attorney and businessman who intended to bring the stodgy old firm up to date, adding corporate clients to the list of bluebloods that had been pumping money into the family coffers for three generations.

The Dunning, Chase account was important to Michael

not only for the potential business—they had billed thousands of hours to several detective agencies last year—but because they had absolutely no connection to Sugar McKane. Long noses, bluebloods, Brahmins, whatever you wanted to call the Choate-ordained, Harvard-trained attorneys, they were a world apart from Sugar and his sticky web of neighborhood connections. McKane's name had not been mentioned in any previous conversations with young Emmett, and Michael intended to keep it that way if possible.

"I mentioned our difficulties with Commonwealth that last time we spoke," Dunning was saying. "Sad to say, it's taken a turn for the worse."

This was not sad news for Michael, no indeed. Commonwealth Detective Agency was Fitzroy Security's principal competitor, in that it was staffed by local retired police detectives, and offered more than simple divorce work services.

Dunning explained his dilemma. "Had a couple of their chaps on a stakeout, this new industrial client of ours? Bay State Chemical and Light, we've handled their patent work for the last few years. Point is, they're in a dither because these Commonwealth chaps roughed up one of the executives. This was in regards to a lawsuit brought by a former employee. I won't bore you with the details. Suffice to say, Comm screwed up rather badly and targeted the wrong man. When he protested at being searched, they took away his briefcase, pawed through the contents—which of course had no relevance, since he was the wrong man—and then actually roughed him up, can you imagine?"

Michael nodded, wanting to convey the impression that he could well imagine Commonwealth screwing up, but he wasn't so impolite as to actually speak derisively of a competitor.

"We effected the usual repairs," Dunning said, frowning in a way that made his eyes seem even more distantly placed. "Rather an expensive mistake, and I've had to assure Chem Light we won't use the Commonwealth ruffians again. Which puts us in an awkward position, as we've relied upon them for years. Father and I discussed adding investigators to our own staff, keep an eye on them that way, but there are cases where we require as many as a dozen men for a rather short period and, well, the in-house investigator situation just isn't practical for us. Father suggested making an arrangement with the Pinkerton people—we've used them on a limited basis now and then—but frankly, I've less confidence in Pinkerton than I do in Commonwealth."

Dunning paused, seemed to be waiting for a response. Mike was about to oblige him, make the case for going with Fitzroy exclusively, when he saw Miriam crossing the lobby of the restaurant, striding purposefully on her high heels. Except this was impossible. Miriam was at the summer house this very moment, and in the next heartbeat he saw that the woman, though radiantly beautiful and of similar build and coloring, was obviously not Miriam. Not even close, he now saw as he focused upon the retreating woman. Was there some sick part of him that wanted to find his wife here, on what could only be an assignation, one more infidelity in a marriage constructed of various infidelities? Did he hunger for humiliation, is that why he still loved her desperately—and there was no other way to love Miriam, except with copious and frequent injections of desperation, this he knew. Michael took out his small notebook and wrote this down: *call bob c.*

"Mr. Fitzroy?"

That brought him back, the tone of voice and the puzzled look in those flounder eyes, and Mike made himself slam the door of the huge room where Miriam lived in his life, and focus his attention on the very important business of making the right impression on Emmett Dunning.

"Have you had a chance to read our brochure?" Mike said.

Dunning nodded. "Very impressive."

"You're wondering how much of it is true, I suppose," Mike said with a grin that was for the most part genuine, since smiling came so naturally to his round and fleshy face. "A good prospectus tends to put things in a favorable light, of course."

"Of course."

"All I can really say is that we have very specific goals, and we intend to fulfill them. The core of the organization is in place, providing a full range of services. This includes the normal investigative work, and in addition we have developed an expertise in electronic and photo surveillance, and forensic evidence. That's what differentiates us from some of the more traditional detective agencies. We're looking to science, Mr. Dunning, that's where the future is. Technology. Specialization. For instance, my own special area is in rehearsing our investigators for the courtroom, making sure their testimony is clear and cogent when required—the legal details that can make a case. My brother, Jack, oversees the actual investigations. He's the master detective, if you will."

Dunning said, "Mmmmmmmm," and then, with apparent interest, "He's the homicide man?"

"Jack was an M.P. with Army Intelligence in the occupying forces. Came back, they made him a homicide detective. He has numerous commendations, if that counts for anything and I believe it does. The point is, Jack is a very bright guy—no plodding flatfoot, if you get my drift."

"I heard him give testimony in the Hannaford case," Dunning said with an air of approval. "Very impressive. Cool as a cucumber under cross, and the jury believed him."

Mike nodded. "That's my Jack. All of our men are former police detectives, that's company policy, and we're encouraging them to take law courses at night to stay current." Mike was making the night-law stuff up right on the spot, but it sounded like such a good idea he might even act on it, why not? He was into the swing of things now, the pain of Miriam receding as he concentrated on the task at hand. "As we mentioned in the brochure, our organizational model is the FBI," he added.

Emmett Dunning smiled faintly, as if he found the reference to the Federal Bureau of Investigation amusing. Mike pressed on, selling the idea. "Okay, there are those who think Hoover's men are a bunch of hack lawyers who couldn't pass the bar, and some of them are, but it's the organization itself that's impressive. Look how they're handling these spy cases."

"I've noticed that. Lots of publicity."

"I'm not talking about the publicity angle. What impresses me is their professionalism. How the agents are perceived by the public. That's the kind of service we intend to provide to the private sector: well-dressed, polite investigators who are comfortable in a courthouse environment, and on good terms with local law enforcement. No filthy trenchcoats or brass knuckles. I like to think of it as intelligence gathering, because that's our specialty, providing intelligence to law firms, and if necessary the kind of expertise that makes the right impression on a jury."

"A private FBI, available on retainer?" Dunning's eyebrows went up, and very nearly disappeared into his high, freckled forehead. "That's very ambitious, Mr. Fitzroy. I'm not sure it's possible."

Mike shrugged. "Every company needs a goal. That's ours. How long it will take us to attain that level, I can't say. I can tell you that we're prepared to add as many men as necessary to satisfy the needs of our clients."

Emmett Dunning continued to subdivide his portion of veal, until the morsels resembled colorless ground beef. He seemed more interested in preparing the food than eating it, and he listened to Michael Fitzroy's spiel with the reserve of a banker processing a loan. Filing away each item, each claim, each debit, seeking a balanced risk, preferring no risk at all.

When the plates were taken away and the coffee was served, Dunning added precisely one level teaspoon of sugar to the cup, stirred it three times briskly, and said, "About your own situation, Mr. Fitzroy."

"Pardon me?"

Dunning cleared his throat delicately. "Your little problem with the Massachusetts State Bar Association. Naturally, we looked over your bona fides. Am I correct that the bar acted in response to complaints about the back-dating of a deed?"

Mike put his hands in his lap so as not to let them be seen as visibly shaking. It was not shame that made his hands tremble, it was anger. Anger at himself for getting caught in a lie and then suffering the indignity of being disciplined like a naughty schoolboy, and now, inevitably, having to admit the lie to the likes of Emmett Dunning. "That's correct," he said, keeping all inflection from his voice. "At the request of a client, I did back-date the paperwork."

Dunning nodded to himself. "No need to be embarrassed, Mr. Fitzroy. It is not widely known, but my own father was once disciplined for improper use of an escrow account. He was reinstated a year or so later, I believe. Father is rather vague about it now." Dunning paused, smiling to himself, as if pleased with the notion of his father being disciplined. "In point of fact," he continued, "the word is that you took the fall for your own father-in-law, who actually forged the damn thing without your knowledge. True?"

"It doesn't really matter," Mike said.

"Oh, I think it does. Makes a difference to me. I heard that and I thought, here's a loyal fellow. Sticks up for family and friends and knows how to keep his mouth shut. Very admirable quality. Of course, we'd expect you to apply for reinstatement when the time comes. If it would help, I'd be willing to drop a word in the right ear."

"You'd do that?"

"Might be helpful all around, for the sake of appearance. Appearance counts for a lot in this business."

"In any business," Mike said.

"Quite right. Now then, Dunning, Chase will agree to use the services of Fitzroy Security exclusively for a trial period of six months, on a man-hour basis. After that we'll see about an annual retainer and quarterly billings. Satisfactory?"

Michael looked him square in the flounder eyes and said, "Emmett? We're about the same age, so I suggest we drop the formalities. Mike will do."

Dunning reached across the table and shook hands. "Friends call me Matt. I take a little getting used to, but I do actually have friends."

"You've just made a new one, Matt. By God you have. We could do it like Indians, and co-mingle our blood, or would you rather have a drink?"

"Cognac," Dunning said. "I faint at the sight of blood."

Twelve

Snip-Snip

"Tell him it's urgent. A matter of life and death."

The receptionist gave him a look that said everything was a matter of life and death at the Parkay Clinic—he'd have to do better than that.

Jack leaned over the desk, kept his voice low, knowing the best threat was the quiet threat. "Tell Dr. Parkay that I represent Sugar McKane."

"I already told you, sir. The doctor is on rounds. Can't be reached for another hour. If you'll please wait, or come back later."

Jack pointed at the telephone. "Use it," he suggested. "Just try it out, see what happens. The alternative is that I go in there and find him, and then you'd have to call the cops and nobody wants that."

That was the difference. Old days, all he had to do, flash the badge. No need for threats, they saw the buzzer and complied, did whatever you asked. Mattered not if it was strictly legal, the good citizens of Boston didn't argue with police detectives. Taught to them as small children, at home, in school, in church—do what the cops say, no complaint, or you're bound for a world of hurt. It was true, too, the jails and prisons were full of wiseguys who'd started out exactly that way, giving lip to the cop on the beat, forever after targeted as troublemakers, potential felons, fall guys.

Without the magic of the badge, all he could rely on was attitude, and this time it worked. Twenty minutes after entering the clinic grounds, a round little man with wire-rimmed spectacles was escorting him into an elegantly appointed office.

After laying down his clipboard, the doctor turned uneasily to Jack, who had already moved to the big, multipaned window that overlooked the clinic grounds. There were a few people strolling on the lawns, or sitting under a yellow-striped canvas sun umbrella, and they did not appear to be obviously loony. Were they dangerous, was someone keeping them under observation? And then, yes, he spotted a couple of burly, white-jacketed gentlemen standing cross-armed in the shade of a chestnut tree, had the look and posture of no-nonsense orderlies.

"Nice place you've got here, Dr. Parkay. First-class."

It was, indeed, a lovely place for a hospital, a far cry from the polio wards of Boston City Hospital. Never know you were only a few miles from downtown, set up on this pleasant hill overlooking the green fairways of The Country Club. They said it that way in Brookline, as if their country club was the original, and for all Jack knew, maybe it was.

"You say Mr. McKane sent you?"

"I'm representing Sugar on a certain matter, Doc."

A surprise, the mild-mannered psychiatrist bridled at that, puffing up his pink little cheeks. "I don't like 'Doc,' " he said. "Sounds like something that cartoon rabbit would say. Make it either Dr. Parkay or just plain Leo."

"Leo the lion, huh?"

The doctor sighed, threw up his hands, and settled into an upholstered chair behind his gleaming desk. "Make it quick," he said, "whatever it is. I'm a busy man."

"Sugar's crazy daughter," Jack said. "Tell me about Deirdre."

He turned from the window and perched on the edge of the mahogany desktop, looming over the doctor. Wondering if he was playing it correctly, coming on this strong. Jack's experience with physicians—and he'd had a lot recently—was that you had to establish an equal, or even better, a superior footing. Otherwise you were shut out, excluded from any real communication.

"Tell me who you are," the little man demanded. "Why you think you can come in here and act like this."

Jack introduced himself.

"A private investigator?" Dr. Parkay was skeptical. "You mean like a detective? That kind of thing?" He was shaking his head and his eyes flitted toward the intercom on his desk. Trying to decide whether to call the bluff, Jack assumed, except it wasn't a bluff.

"We're handling a very delicate matter for Sugar McKane," Jack said. "We have reason to believe it may concern his daughter Deirdre. I understand she's being treated here."

The doctor was obviously flustered. Small specks of steam appeared on the lenses of his spectacles as his nostrils flared. "I really should clear this with Mr. McKane. I can't possibly discuss his daughter without his permission, and even then I'm obliged to maintain confidentiality. That's the law."

"I know the law, Leo," Jack said. He'd picked up a pencil and was testing the point. "There's no law that prevents you from discussing a patient with a friend of the family."

"Now you're a friend of the family?" said the doctor. "A moment ago you were a private detective. Which is it?"

"Both," said Jack. He dropped the pencil, pulled out a new pack of Pall Malls, stripping away the cellophane. He'd decided to try Mike's brand for a change, and he offered one to Dr. Parkay, who hesitated before accepting.

Jack lit the doctor's cigarette first, then his own.

"Okay, I guess I should have made it clear," Jack said. "Sugar came to me because he wants to keep this, ah, 'situation' in the family."

"But what makes you Deirdre's kin?"

"I'm her—that is, my brother, Michael, is married to Deirdre's sister, Miriam. Does that ring a bell?"

The smoke seemed to relax Dr. Parkay, his eyes were no longer searching for the intercom. "It does, yes, now you mention it. Which reminds me, I really should phone Mr. McKane. He's legal guardian as well as next of kin, and we should have his permission before we go any further with this discussion. Law or no law, that's a clinic rule."

"If you feel you have to bother Sugar, go ahead," Jack said. "But first I'd like you to read this."

He withdrew the *Transcript* letter from his breast pocket and placed the envelope on the corner of the desk.

"My God," the doctor said, scanning the contents. He dropped the letter to the desk as if he expected the paper to ignite. "This can't be true. Whoever wrote that is very disturbed."

"Letters like that have been sent to most of the newspapers," Jack said. "All with similar allegations. I found out who was writing them and tried to talk her out of it, but so far it hasn't done much good."

"No newspaper would publish that garbage."

"You're right," Jack said. "They won't. But there's more than just the one person involved. This morning her son came after me with a .45. The old army Colt they issued as a sidearm? Looks like a piece of field artillery when you're stark naked, let me tell you. The boy came pretty close to blowing my guts out, I think. And if it had been Sugar he caught up with, he might have done it."

Dr. Parkay was now sucking nervously on the cigarette, making it burn like a fuse. Jack put the pack on the desk. This was going to be a smoke-filled interview, no question. Hang a stethoscope on Leo and he could do one of those Paul Mall testimonials, "the choice of more physicians" or whatever.

"Sounds like a police matter," said the doctor. "You could have the man with the gun arrested."

"He's a boy, eighteen years old, but sure I could have him arrested. Except that won't stop it. My guess, we touch the boy and his mother goes completely bonkers, causes more trouble. More to the point, McKane wants this kept quiet. Going to the police is the last thing he wants, for a lot of reasons."

"I really don't see how I can help."

Jack nodded, satisfied. They were finally back at the beginning, ready for a brand-new start. "Tell me about Deirdre," he said.

Dr. Parkay glanced at the folded letter, pausing in thought before responding. "If you mean did Mr. McKane have, um, relations with his own daughter," he said at last, "the answer is no, absolutely not. There is no indication of anything like that."

"Okay," Jack said, "but that's not what I asked. Just tell me about her, we'll go from there."

Leo Parkay reached for another cigarette, lit it from the expiring butt in his mouth. He took off his steamy, wire-rimmed spectacles, leaned back in his chair, and closed his eyes. With the smoke swirling from his nostrils he looked like a tiny, white-coated dragon. "A very sad situation," he said after a while, without any further prompting from Jack. His small, gentle eyes blinked open. "I first examined her shortly after her mother died. I suppose Deirdre was fourteen or so at the time. . . ."

As the psychiatrist explained it, the girl's reaction to her mother's death after a long bout with cancer was "peculiar." Well beyond the parameters of normal mourning. A morbid fixation exacerbated by inappropriate behavior and periods of random verbal disassociation symptomatic of a schizophrenic interlude.

"In plain English, please," Jack said. "Remember, I'm just a dumb detective."

"Oh, I seriously doubt that," Dr. Parkay said, squinting his eyes in amusement. "What happened is that the girl, on the cusp of adolescence, began to show signs first of manic, then psychopathic behavior. She refused to believe that her mother was actually dead. She stayed awake for days and talked to her dead mother, is what she did."

"That doesn't sound so peculiar," Jack said.

"Yes, but she firmly believed that her dead mother was hiding in her clothes closet, Mr. Fitzroy, and that is quite peculiar. It was obvious the girl was experiencing auditory hallucinations—hearing voices. I sedated her, of course, and we all hoped this was a passing incident, triggered by extreme grief, but I'm afraid it didn't end there. Within a few months she was indulging in compulsive and inappropriate sexual behavior."

"Come on, Leo. She was boy crazy. Is that really nuts, by your standards? A lot of girls go a little wild."

Parkay sighed. "I have three daughters, Mr. Fitzroy. Believe me, I know how girls can 'go a little wild' for boys at a certain age. My youngest practically faints when she hears that skinny Italian singer on the radio."

"Frank Sinatra?"

"This wasn't anything like that. By inappropriate behavior I mean manic self-abuse. Compulsive masturbation. For hours and hours at a time. To the point where she had to be restrained to prevent actual physical damage to her sexual organs."

"My God," Jack said.

"Such behavior is sometimes symptomatic of a certain type of schizophrenic dementia, although we were all hopeful at the time that it wasn't actual schizophrenia, but a lesser psychosis that might, in time, be cursed. There have been cases like Deirdre's that seem to have been triggered by unusually intense hormonal changes, and when the change is complete—when the individual finally matures—the symptoms may abate, or even vanish completely. Alas, that did not happen. Her symptoms changed somewhat but failed, in my opinion, to improve significantly."

Jack felt a little faint. He moved from his hip perch on the desk to a chair beside it, took a deep breath. "So what happened to her?" he asked.

"After a short interval here at the clinic, she returned home. That was five years ago, when she was sixteen. Her father tried hiring a female companion to keep an eye on her—a registered nurse—who would also act as tutor. That didn't work out, to put it mildly. Deirdre tormented the poor woman unmercifully. Hid the nurse's clothing, poured water on her while she slept, finally placed excrement in her food. That nasty little trick did it. The nurse left McKane's employ, and for a while Deirdre actually seemed to improve."

"Seemed to?"

"Well, she was growing up, and she channeled her compulsive sexual behavior into a slightly more acceptable mode. Rather than abusing herself for hours, or exposing herself in public, she focused her compulsive behavior on men. Having sexual encounters with men, to put it bluntly. Many men."

"You saying she became a nympho?"

Parkay shook his head. "I never use that word. It implies some sort of pleasure or sexual gratification, and I'm convinced that Deirdre never experienced gratification from her activities. Her behavior was compulsive, Mr. Fitzroy. Treating compulsive disorders is a special interest of mine. We've patients in here who wash their hands two hundred times a day. Others who count the number of dishes in the cupboard, or the cracks in the wall. Keep counting over and over again because they can't stop themselves."

"I never heard of that."

"Believe me, it exists. And it destroys lives. So understand that Deirdre McKane is not a nymphomaniac, if such a condition even exists. She suffers from a form of compulsive behavior that in her case is expressed sexually."

"Nothing you can do for her?"

"On the contrary, I think we've done quite a lot for Dee Dee. It is my belief that compulsive disorders are rooted in a deformation of the brain. The accepted Freudian treatment—that is, psychoanalysis, or a study of childhood traumas—has virtually no effect on compulsive disorders. My own observations of hundreds of patients over the last twenty years has convinced me the root cause has to be neurological. Studies of chimpanzees with damage to a particular lesion of the brain will exhibit similar behavior patterns of repetitive sexual deviance."

"Like in a zoo?"

"Different. In a zoo the monkeys masturbate as an aggressive act, or possibly out of sheer boredom. I don't really know about monkeys, Mr. Fitzroy. I do know about human beings. And Deirdre wasn't engaging in this activity because she was bored. She can't help herself, any more than an epileptic can help having a seizure."

"Tearing off her clothes and screwing the paperboy or whatever, that's like epilepsy?"

"I mean it's involuntary. Exactly as epilepsy is involuntary."

"So what can you do?" Jack said. "Besides putting her in a straitjacket, I mean." He was thinking of the movie that had so disturbed Miriam, Olivia de Havilland in *The Snake Pit*.

"Deirdre doesn't respond well to restraints," said the doctor. "Treatments? Let's see, electroconvulsive therapy was somewhat helpful, although the effects were short-term. Similar results with insulin convulsion. The truth is, there wasn't much hope we could offer until Moniz began his surgical experiments on the frontal lobes."

"Moniz?"

"Antonio Egas Moniz. European neurologist. Father of psychosurgical techniques. Here in the U.S. the trailblazers are Freeman and Watts. It was Dr. Freeman himself who treated Deirdre.''

"She's had brain surgery?'' Jack said.

Dr. Parkay nodded eagerly. "Now, here's where it gets interesting. I say 'surgery' and you assume scalpel, knives, bone saws, an operating theater, right? Of course you do. But Dr. Freeman's technique is remarkable. No general anesthetic required, and the whole thing is over and done in less than ten minutes, without having to even cut through the scalp.''

"So it wasn't brain surgery,'' said Jack, somewhat relieved.

"Oh, but it was. Tiny incision under the eyelid, insertion of a leucotome through the eye socket, snip-snip. The connective tissues are severed and the patient's anxiety levels drop dramatically.''

"You mean she's cured?''

Dr. Parkay sighed. "I wish it were that simple. Maybe someday it will be, when the technique is perfected. What the operation means for Deirdre is that she may be able to return home. That's what her father most fervently desires—that she be able to live at home. He can't stand the idea of her being institutionalized.''

Jack got up from the chair and wandered back to the big window. The patients were gone, there was no one under the yellow umbrella. Strange, but he hadn't noticed them leaving—and then he saw them, running down the long, sloping hill. Small figures being chased by the two burly boys in the white jackets.

Dr. Parkay was standing beside him, hands clasped behind his back. "From here they look like children at play,'' he said. "That's because we want it to look that way. The truth is that madness is terrifying and dangerous. There's nothing playful about it.''

"Dangerous,'' Jack said. "Tell me about dangerous.''

"To themselves, I mean. With rare exceptions, of course.''

"Could Deirdre be dangerous?''

Parkay craned his round little head, studying Jack through a blue fog of cigarette smoke. "What are you asking, Mr. Fitzroy?''

"At least two people are convinced that she was involved in the death of a young man from East Boston. A man Sugar McKane had business dealings with. That's where all of this poison-pen stuff got started.''

''You think Deirdre killed someone, is that it?''

Jack was watching the scene unfold at the bottom of the hill. The white jackets had caught up with their charges. It still looked like a game of tag. At play in the green fields of madness. ''Is she capable of violence, Leo? Did she do something really bad, is that why she came to the clinic? Is that why you cut a piece out of her brain?''

The doctor looked up at him, shook his head. He put out his cigarette. ''Come with me, Mr. Fitzroy. There's something you should see.''

Jack followed Dr. Parkay down a sunlit hallway, through a double door. He could smell the fresh wax on the linoleum floor of the hallway, see his dark, unfocused reflection underfoot, and he decided he did not want to be in this place, he did not need to see anything the doctor cared to show him, but it was too late, they were marching in quickstep, Leo the lion and the cowardly detective, on the rubber-tiled road to Oz.

They came to a door. The doctor knocked once, then entered. Jack did not recognize the girl by the window, but he knew it had to be Deirdre, and as he came closer he detected traces of Miriam in that oval face and, yes, something of Sugar McKane in the shape of the eyes.

''Deirdre?'' said the doctor. ''Do you remember Mr. Fitzroy, dear? He's come to visit.''

Deirdre smiled dreamily at the floor as she clung to the windowsill. She was a slight girl, so thin and wan and delicate that the sunlight seemed to go right through her.

''There's something out there she likes to watch,'' Dr. Parkay said, indicating the window. ''I haven't figured out what.''

The girl reached for the doctor's hands, lifted them to her face.

''Deirdre, do you know this man?''

Gently, very gently, she relinquished the doctor's hands and lifted her eyes to focus on Jack Fitzroy. Her expression was fragmented and twitchy, but Jack thought she was trying to smile at him.

"We met at your sister's wedding," he said. "Remember?"

Deirdre nodded. Then she lifted the hem of her hospital gown up over her waist and cocked her head as if to say, Do *you* remember *this?*

Thirteen

Breaking the Mahatma's Cue

He was out with his beach roses, tenderly transplanted
from nearby dunes, when Mrs. Riley came out to the
screened porch at the rear of the mansion and shouted
down to him, where he labored in thorns and delicate
pink blossoms adjacent to the retaining wall that enclosed his summer estate.

A telephone call. Long-distance. Urgent, apparently,
or she wouldn't think to disturb him at his work, that was
understood.

Sugar cupped his hands around his mouth and bel-
lowed: "I'll take it in the billiard room, Mrs. Riley!"

He rinsed his blood-stained hands—the beach rose
thorns were as sharp and numerous as thistle spines—in
the watering pail, dried them on the handkerchief he always carried in the rear pocket of his gardening trousers.
A quick march through the empty tennis court brought
him to the west wing of the mansion, where he entered
the first-floor billiard room. His second-best table
dwelled there, on fat-ankled walnut legs, sister to the
Hyde Park model, although not quite as lively in the
cushions.

A telephone had been installed in the billiard room,
one of three extensions, much to the consternation of the
local phone company. Four telephones in a single seasonal residence! Such extravagance was unheard of in
these parts, where the system had yet to be converted to
rotary from the old crank telephones.

"McKane here," he said gruffly, more out of breath
than he was willing to admit to himself. When he realized who it was on the line, Sugar reached behind him,
located a chair, and sat down. Something about Leo Parkay's voice always made him weak in the knees, as if he
was coming unbolted.

"Asking about Dee Dee? I never told him to do that, never." Sugar held the handset slightly away from his ear as the doctor droned on. Justifying his lack of discretion, that's what the man was trying to do. Such attempts at rationalizing always made Sugar feel a deep, abiding irritation, but in a situation like this it was important that a man not lose his temper and shout things into a telephone. What good would that do?

"Listen to me, Leo," he said, interrupting. "He had no business disturbing Dee Dee. I'll have a word with the lad, rest assured. He's confused about a few essentials, is what he is. He's heading down the wrong road and we'll have to set him right. My Dee Dee has nothing to do with the vile, ignorant witch who wrote those letters." Sugar paused, let the doctor babble on for a while, making excuses. "Yes, well, I don't know what got into Jack, he should know better. He comes around again— he gets anywhere near my daughter—you bar the door and I'll come over there and handle it myself, is that clear?" Sugar, his hands trembling, started to put down the phone, then thought better of it. "Two things, Leo. Forget you saw that letter. And don't you *ever* forget who holds the mortgage on that luxury loony bin of yours."

Down went the phone. Up came Sugar McKane out of his chair, reaching for the first sizable solid object within reach. A billiard cue, one of a custom ivory-inlaid set given to him by Martin Lomasney, on the occasion of Sugar's induction into the Hendricks Club.

Without thinking or hesitating, he did something he would regret to the day of his death. His big, strong hands clenched knuckle-white on the cue, and he grunted and brought it down quickly, smashing the heavy end of the perfectly balanced stick, splintering the fine-grained ash against the slate of the massive billiard table.

Gift of the Mahatma, destroyed in a moment of senseless, thoughtless rage. And he couldn't for the life of him decide what, exactly, he was mad about.

Fourteen

Crazy Talk

"No doubt about it," Jack said. "She's crazy as a rabid mink."

They were in Michael's Coupe de Ville, and the top was up because it had been spitting rain earlier and they'd pulled over at a truck stop in Topsfield to hoist the canvas. It had been a long and eventful day for Jack, what with handling Billy boy and a visit to the clinic, and he was sipping Carling Black Label beer from a long-necked bottle and smoking what had to be his fiftieth cigarette, two and a half packs not counting what the shrink had cadged.

Between the butts and all the coffee he'd been drinking, his nerves were shot and his leg was twitching like hell and he was content to let Mike handle the wheel for the two-hour drive up Route 1. The nation's highway, so-called, what a laugh. All the stop and goes at every goddamn intersection, they'd discovered the wonders of traffic lights even out here in cow country. About time they started building real four-lane parkways out of Boston, like they were doing out of Manhattan.

"I wish you hadn't," Mike was saying. "Sugar'll have a fit. I'm telling you, he's not rational when it comes to poor Dee Dee."

"Poor Dee Dee tried to hump me."

Michael was chain smoking, too, but all the windows were down and he had the defrost fan on, so the interior of the big car was fairly pleasant. Humid but pleasant, here in the long twilight of a July evening, heading into a long beach weekend. "Don't mention it to anyone else, okay? Jesus Christ, Sugar hears that, he'll bite off his fingernails, or maybe *my* fingernails. He thinks she's getting better in there, is what Miriam told me."

"That's what the shrink said, too. She's better. All I can say, if that's better, then worse must've been like something out of a carnival freak show."

Mike was braking gingerly, both hands gripping the wheel—he tended to be a cautious driver. A seemingly endless line of red taillights vanished around the long, slow curves of the crowded roadway. Might be more than a two-hour drive at this rate, and that jog through downtown Newburyport could only make it worse.

"It was bad," Mike conceded. "The kid can't help it, though. She didn't mean anything, lifting her dress like that."

"She did it to you?"

"Dee Dee did things like that to everyone," Mike said. "Sometimes it was worse than others, that's all. When she got really bad, Sugar would have her committed. She's been in and out of the bin since her mother died."

Jack was tapping the sides of the Caddy with his free hand, bongo-drumming the door. "The doctor who did the surgery? He was on the cover of *Time,* did you know that? Impressed the hell out of Dr. Parkay."

"Impressed me, too," Mike said. "It's going to be a great disappointment for all concerned if she can't come home again."

After some thought on the subject Jack decided not to mention the .45-caliber nature of Billy's threats at the YMCA pool. Big brother would want to see the boy arrested, figuring that would be the end of Sugar's problems with the Drake family. Keep a lid on it for now, Jack had decided, see how it played out.

"Maybe she did have something to do with it," Jack said, trying out his new theory. "Poor little Dee Dee does the hump act on Roy Drake, he ends up dead."

"Come on, Jack," said Mike, giving him a baleful glance. "You can't kill somebody that way."

"Not directly. But what if Sugar finds them doing the dirty thing, and he grabs hold of the Drake kid and throttles him. Deirdre hasn't got the strength to kill a man, but Sugar sure as hell does. Look at the hands on him, he's strong as a bull. And you said, I quote, 'Sugar will have a fit.' What if he did have a fit?"

Mike was shaking his head in disbelief. "You're crazier than Dee Dee, you know that?"

"It could have happened," Jack insisted. "Let's say Sugar invites Roy Drake to his house to discuss selling that little island the family owns—God only knows why he wants a pile of rock in the middle of Boston Harbor—but anyhow the old man turns his back and out leaps hot little Deirdre. She has one of her famous compulsive disorders, with handsome Roy as the object. Daddy loses his temper, chokes the life out of Drake, and then covers it up by dumping the body in the harbor."

"By himself? You can't be serious."

"Okay, so maybe he got the Costello brothers to help him. They know about bodies. Burial at sea."

Michael was clearly exasperated, braking harder and more frequently. "Jack, would you stop this? It's making me sick to my stomach. I had a great day, signed up an important client, and now you're inventing a way to make it all come crashing down around my ears."

"How's that, pardner?" said Jack. He was a little high on the warm beer, having fun with big brother, getting under his skin.

"Sugar asks for our help and now you want to pin a murder on him?" said Mike. "A murder that isn't even a murder? I mean, there *was* an autopsy, and the cause of death was drowning. You said so yourself."

"McKane is a great little fixer, Michael. As you well know."

"What's that supposed to mean?"

Jack burped into his fist. "Means what it means, pardner."

"Knock it off with that Gene Autry shit, would you please?"

"Sure thing, pard," Jack drawled. " 'Cept you best come up with a new corporate strategy, in case our main financial backer gets himself carted off to the gallows. Man his size, they'd need a mighty strong rope. 'Course, he might be able to get away with it because he probably owns Boot Hill."

Michael sighed and rubbed his belly. "Have a couple more beers, Jack. Keep it up."

Jack shot him a look, wasn't sure big brother could see

it in the dim interior of the automobile. "What'll you do, Mike? Have me committed to the Parkay Clinic?"

'Don't talk crazy."

"I hope that's all it is," Jack said, lighting his fifty-first cigarette. "Crazy talk."

Fifteen

Home Sweet Home

"Where is he? I dropped him off at the Pagoda, that's where he is."

Michael was in the kitchen, drinking milk from a cool pitcher put out by Mrs. Riley, who had since gone off to bed. His father-in-law was in a black mood. His large face had actually darkened with temper, and his great head seemed larger than ever. The man looked to be on the verge of a stroke or a fit, and that didn't help the condition of Michael's stomach. Cooled by the milk, now curdled by the sight of Sugar McKane.

"He was bothering Deirdre today," McKane said, making it sound like the announcement that Pearl Harbor had been attacked and the nation betrayed.

"It's this poison-pen trouble, Sugar. Jack is just trying to make it go away."

"And I suppose that involves threatening Dee Dee's doctor?"

As Mike sipped the milk, he couldn't help but eye McKane's clenched fists. Large, powerful hands. Undoubtedly strong enough to throttle a man. "I wasn't aware that Jack threatened anyone," Mike said. "I'm sure he didn't mean to. He's just trying to get to the bottom of this business for you."

Sugar, noticing the pitcher of milk for the first time, eased slightly. "Your innards in a boil, son? It's that poison you put into your system. Alcohol, nicotine, strong coffee. And the sweets, too—chocolate is the devil to digest."

"I'm sure you're right," Mike said. He found a napkin Mrs. Riley had left out and wiped his mouth, not wanting to look like a little kid when he was dealing with his father-in-law. "Miriam around?" he asked, trying to sound casual and failing, as he saw from Sugar's reaction.

"I believe she's in her room," the old man said. "I assumed she came down to greet you."

Mike shrugged. "Didn't hear me, I expect."

In the shadows McKane's brow furrowed and his huge black eyebrows jutted prominently over his deeply socketed eyes. "Why won't he just come to me?" he wanted to know. "Sneaking off to see Dee Dee behind my back, that's not right."

Brother Jack had been in a belligerent mood for most of the ride, shadow boxing with themes that he knew would rile Mike, and so Michael wasn't especially keen to defend him at the moment, not with his belly seeping acid and Sugar McKane on the verge of a temper tantrum, all thanks to Jack. What the hell, Mike thought, why not simply tell the truth, let these two hotheads sort it out? "He doesn't trust you, Sugar. I don't know why. Sometimes I think Jack doesn't trust anybody. But he's our ace in the hole. You know that."

The big kitchen was cool and dark, the only sources of light a low-watt bulb in the pantry and whatever illumination found its way in from the adjoining hallways. The counters and shelves and cabinets were kept in a state of pristine cleanliness by Mrs. Riley and the housekeeping help she employed for the season. You could smell the lemon oil she used on the doors and paneling, and a faint wiff of bleach from the big steel sinks. The double-doored refrigerator and the propane stoves were industrial quality—indeed, the kitchen would have served for quite a large restaurant, although McKane no longer employed a professional cook either here or in Hyde Park. Still, it was Mike's favorite sanctuary in the summer house, and he often went down to the kitchen when he couldn't sleep, or when he was trying not to wait up for Miriam. Standing in the dark as he leaned against one of the counters, drinking his cool milk and nibbling on cookies, it calmed him. No cookies tonight, though, it was all he could do to stomach the milk.

"He needn't trust me." Sugar was struggling to keep his voice down. With his powerful instrument, trained for unamplified projection over large and boisterous crowds, there was no genuinely quiet register, and even his whispers made the air stir, the glasses rattle in the cupboards. "All the man has to do is make them leave me alone. Which he has failed utterly to do. Did you know that evil woman has learned to use the telephone? Oh yes, she's calling city editors now, promoting her great conspiracy. Saying things about me that are so vile and disgusting that editors can't repeat them for my hearing, and these are not delicate men."

Michael edged along the counter, keeping his distance from McKane, who tended to loom closer when he was trying to make a point. "It's about the land deal you're putting together," he said, screwing up his courage. "Jack thinks you've been less than candid."

"Meaning he thinks I've been speaking falsehoods?"

"He has a point. Apparently you failed to mention the acquisition of Drake Island."

Sugar pulled back his head, as if dodging a blow. "Drake Island, Drake Island," he rumbled. "I'm sick of hearing about Drake Island. You'd think it was a grand place like Nantucket or the Isles of Shoals. Have you ever seen this par-tic-ular locale?" Sugar said, enunciating each syllable. "A lump of rock not much bigger than this kitchen, that's what Drake Island is. No electricity, no water, no hope of power or water. And I paid those people two thousand dollars for it! Cash money! *They* cheated *me*. Held me up like a thieving band of bank robbers, because I'd had the nerve to foreclose a mortgage the sainted patriarch of the family hadn't paid in more than a year."

Sugar paused for breath. Before he could go on, Mike interrupted. "Why did you want it?" Mike asked. "That lump of rock?"

McKane seemed taken aback. "I didn't want it, and that's the truth. It's all part of a package. We're swapping that rotten little island to the Transport Authority—some beacon they want to erect there—and in exchange we're getting a crucial right-of-way to land adjacent to Logan."

"So this is about the airport," Mike said. "That's the package you're putting together with Jimmy Keegan?"

The mention of Keegan made McKane chuckle, a deeply inflected laugh that sounded to Mike's ears like an old engine turning over. "I'd not put a wooden crate together with the likes of Jimmy Keegan, let alone a project as big as this. If you want a honest profit you can't deal with a crooked man, he'll steal from you. As Keegan would if he could. All he's useful for, in this instance, is acting the straw man. To hold down the values, Michael. If word had gotten out that we wanted all that mucky swamp to build warehouses for the Logan expansion, prices would have gone through the roof.''

Mike said, "I didn't know about any warehouse deal.''

"Didn't you, now? After our previous experience in deed transfers, I thought it best to leave you out of this, Michael. I thought it best. Was I wrong?''

Mike shook his head.

"That's the big conspiracy, Michael. I'm investing in the airport, and like any other businessman I'm trying to keep the advantage.''

"Logan Airport. Warehouses. And you needed Drake Island to make it work.''

"I did, yes,'' said Sugar. "And if I hadn't paid the rascals for it, the Transport Authority would have taken it by act of eminent domain and paid, I'll hazard a guess, no more than five hundred dollars.''

"Okay, but why didn't you just say so? Why leave Jack in the dark?''

"I told him all he needed to know,'' Sugar said in his stubborn way. "The deal is done now, we've got the acreage locked up, but a word in the wrong ear and there would have been holdouts, waiting to elevate the prices.''

"The airport,'' Mike said. "That's all.''

"That's all?'' Sugar said, incredulous. He raised his hands, gesturing as he would to a crowd. "The future is jet-propelled, Michael. That airport is going to be more important to this city than all the trains and plains and roadways ever built. It's money, commerce, international trade, and one day soon every Kelly and O'Hara is going to be flying back and forth to the old country the way we commute from here to Boston.''

"What,'' Mike said, "like Wrong Way Corrigan?''

Sugar shook his big head, dropped his unclenched hands to his side. "Oh, go on and have your jokes, Michael. It's your mother's blood coming through, God rest her. The sharp tongue of the Presbyterian Scot, I know it well.''

Mike ignored the jibe, or tried to, and finished his milk, taking the last gulp like medicine. ''I think I'll go look in on Miriam,'' he said.

''You do that. And, Michael? One other thing. Tell Jack to drop it.''

''What?''

''He's to leave bad enough alone.'' Sugar said. ''My business in Eastie, the Drakes, and Dee Dee. Close the file. Is that understood?''

''Anything you say, Sugar.''

Mike was mounting the back stairs when McKane called softly from below. Couldn't see him, but his voice filled the stairway.

''Son? Try a few drops of peppermint oil on the tongue. It settles the digestive juices and freshens the breath.''

An hour later, he was strolling through the crowd on the Hampton Beach boardwalk, under the awnings of the casino, a white monstrosity that housed fry joints, arcades, indoor miniature golf, and an upstairs ballroom. The band was audible for a mile or more, a local orchestra engaged in a credible impersonation of Tommy Dorsey's big band. ''Marie'' and ''Hawaiian War Chant,'' not too bad. Except for the solos. It always went tin in the solos.

Mike was surprised to spot a few zoot suiters, a phenomenon of style rare enough in Boston, at least in the Boston he frequented—bandy-legged young toughs strutting in absurd-looking trousers with huge pleats pegged tight to the ankle, suit jackets actually extending below the baggy knees. An extreme, cartoonish style made popular by Negro singer Cab Calloway, although none of the toughs was Negro. You didn't see Negroes on this particular boardwalk. No legal booze here in Hampton, either, which meant the Negro bands and the jazz-mad fans that followed them went elsewhere, down to Salisbury Beach or Canobie Lake or Rockingham Junction.

He bought a sack of peppermints at one of the shops. Not quite what his father-in-law had in mind when he suggested oil of peppermint, but the candy seemed to help settle his stomach. Bob Cogan was waiting outside the arcade, as promised, smoking a green cigar and reading a boxing magazine. You didn't know better, you'd think he was a barker for the arcade. He had that slightly dangerous look, even in repose.

"Care for a mint?" Mike asked.

"Naw," said Cogan. "It'd ruin the stogie if my mouth tasted clean."

"We could try a coffee shop," Mike suggested. "Find a seat."

"Not a saloon on the strip," Cogan said, shaking his head in disbelief. "I already checked. What kind of place is this, no saloons?"

"Good, clean fun," Mike said. "That's the slogan."

"It's un-American, not selling beers at the beach. Tell you what, let's just go inside, the noise will give us a little privacy."

The noise inside the arcade was, as Cogan promised, nearly deafening. The ballroom was directly overhead, and a couple of thousand shoe heels tapped out the rhythm to "Begin the Beguine," while inside the arcade the kids were shrieking in sympathy with the pinball machines and the games of chance. Mike had to shout just to be heard.

"How did it go?" he asked when Cogan had found a pillar to lean against, venting cigar smoke at the tin ceiling.

The big man shrugged. "I kept a log, you want to see it?"

"Sure, but can't you tell me?"

"Not much to tell," Cogan said. "Four nights in a row I tailed the lady. More like a stakeout, because she hardly ever left the house after dark. Didn't entertain visitors, only male in the place seems to be her father."

"What about days?" Mike shouted. "You said you could do a few days."

"Uh-huh. Only day I could manage was today. Picked her up at eight this morning, she drove over to the country club, played tennis with three other ladies, what they call doubles. The ladies had lunch right there at the clubhouse. Afterward she drives into this little one-horse town up the coast, Portsmouth, and she goes shopping for an hour or so, didn't buy much of anything, either. After the stores she takes in a movie—I sat a few rows back, and she was all alone in there, Mr. Fitzroy. *Lost Boundaries*, it was pretty good, too, about this colored family passing for white. Then the lady drives back to the beach house and stayed there and so did I—till you arrived, that is, which is when I drove over here like we arranged.''

The pounding cacophony of the stomping feet and the arcade machinery was starting to make his head ache. Mike handed Cogan an envelope of cash. ''I want you to keep on this,'' he said. ''As many hours as you can spare.''

Cogan fingered the envelope, then peeked inside. ''I appreciate this, Mr. Fitzroy. I gotta drop it, though.''

''What?''

''I can't do this for you, sir. Much as I'd like to.''

Mike grabbed Cogan's sleeve. ''You saw something you can't tell me about, is that it?''

The big man was evasive. ''Nuthin' like that, Mr. Fitzroy. I just got troubles of my own, is all. I gotta wife, too, you know, and it ain't easy workin' days *and* nights. That's why I quit the cops and joined up with you guys.''

Mike hesitated. ''Anybody else you can recommend?''

Cogan took the cigar out of his mouth, draped an arm over Mike's shoulder. About to offer his friendly, man-to-man advice. ''You should forget about it. Spying on the lady is bound to backfire.''

''I can't forget about it, Bob.''

Cogan nodded, as if expecting that reaction. ''My advice? Go outside the company. Don't put none of our boys on the spot. Me, I'm just gonna forget the whole thing, like it never happened.''

Sixteen

B.Y.O.B

In a high-backed wooden booth in a dark corner of the Pagoda dance hall, Jack Fitzroy sat drinking whiskey and ginger ale from a waxed-paper cup. The dance hall wasn't licensed to sell alcohol, so you had to smuggle it in, keep the bottle out of sight. In a few minutes the Pagoda would be closing and the last couple would have to stop dancing to the jukebox and leave. You didn't have to go home, the cowlicked kid who ran the place liked to say, but you couldn't stay here.

Jack had no immediate prospects. Might have to sleep on the beach. Five minutes after entering the cottage, Doris had been picking a fight, telling him in no uncertain terms that she didn't want a moody drunk frightening her children.

"They're my kids, too!" he shouted, feeling beady-eyed and mean, aware that the boys were listening from behind the thin door of the dark little bedroom where their mother had stashed them away.

"I don't want them to see you like this," Doris pleaded, setting her hands firmly against his chest and walking him backward out to the porch. "I don't know what's got into you, Jack. But the boys don't understand when you get stoned and feeling sorry for yourself. It scares them."

"I never touch those boys."

"That's not what scares them," Doris said. She kicked open the screen door. "Go on back to the dance hall. Call your brother up, maybe the two of you can cry in your beers. But not in this house."

There was no arguing with Dottie when she got into one of her righteous moods. And very little chance she would change her mind and come looking for him at the Pagoda, although the old cedar-shingled building was no more than a few hundred feet from the cottages. First place they'd ever danced together, to the very same juke-box where ''String of Pearls'' was repeating for it must be the tenth time in the last hour. The same mildly drunk couple kept trying to execute a slow lindy hop and kept failing to get it right, not that they minded. Jack hated the way they were laughing and touching, and right at the moment he hated Doris for kicking him out of his own house—not exactly his, but he *was* paying rent on two, count them, two residences while he worked in the humid, stinking city to support a summer-long indul-gence for the wife and kiddies.

This was the thanks he got. He deserved to get stoned. It was a rare enough occurrence, unlike a lot of the other commuting fathers who remained glassy-eyed for every waking hour of every weekend. Not that Dottie knew what kind of day he'd had, with Billy boy and crazy Deir-dre, and brother Mike. One look at him and he'd been stiff-armed to the door, no time for explanations. Mean as her flinty-eyed mom, more and more of that stubborn, narrow-minded old harridan showing through—you wanted to know what you were getting, check out the mother.

Beneath the table, Jack fumbled with the pint bottle of Seagrams he'd snatched on the way out the door. Slop-ping the last few ounces into the paper cup, more whis-key than ginger ale now, a sweet-tainted concoction that produced a useful numbness. Couldn't feel his toes, let alone the old sciatic. Hell with the beach, he'd sleep on the porch, kick through the screens if Dottie dared to lock him out.

He was thinking about that, bulling his way into the cottage, as ''String of Pearls'' unfurled yet again. Trying to find the rhythm, tap it out with his knuckles, when suddenly she appeared. Vision of Miriam, backlit by the reddish glow of the Chinese lanterns, had to be wishful thinking. Forbidden thinking. And then she was slipping into the booth opposite and dropping her purse on the table.

''They were right, you *are* pissed.''

''Getting there,'' Jack said carefully. Tongue so thick it seemed like a dead thing in his mouth. ''Who says I'm pissed?''

"Your brother, reporting to Daddy."

Miriam was sober and bright-eyed. Wearing tight black capri pants and a silky, burnt-orange blouse that left her shoulders bare. Brassy hoop earrings jangled sweetly as her head moved. She leaned across the table and he could smell her, feel her breath as she said, "I can't stand it any longer, can you?"

Jack looked around at the dance floor. Sparse attendance and nobody was paying them any heed, but even drunk as he was, the sirens were going off in his mind. "Out of here," he said, and he started to get up, bumping his legs on the table.

"What's your hurry?" Miriam said. She was smiling, glowing in the dark, and her hands reached out to caress his wrists, made him sit back down. "This is a bring-your-own-booze, bring-your-own-broad joint, right? So who's to notice?"

"Dottie," he said immediately and sighed, aware of the whiskey fumes rising from every pore of his body.

"Is she here?" Miriam made a show of looking. "Not here. Told you to go sleep it off, is that what she did, Jack? Your dutiful wife?"

He nodded, lifted the paper cup. Miriam's hand snaking out of nowhere, taking the cup away. "Share and share alike," she said, and chugged down several ounces of ginger-flavored whiskey. "Mmmm," she said, patting her lips, blowing him a kiss. "You wouldn't take advantage of a tipsy girl, would you, Mr. Fitzroy? A girl who can't hold her liquor?"

"You can hold it," he said.

As Miriam shook her head her hair came loose, covering one eye. Having fun with that breathless, smoldering look made famous by Lauren Bacall. "Can't," she said in a voice that was as naturally husky as Bacall's, she didn't have to fake that part. "Makes me lose control," she said as her hands entwined with his. "Come on, lover boy. Let's show these farmers how to dance."

Jack pulled his hand away, shook his head.

"Bet you danced here with the little wife plenty of times," Miriam said. "What could it hurt? Can't a guy dance with his sister-in-law?"

"Gimp," Jack said.

"Huh?"

"I'm a gimp. Can't dance."

"Gimp?" Her hands had found his again, and her fingertips were soft in the palms of his hands, soft and promising. "That's an ugly word for such a handsome man. Don't say it ever again, please. Promise?"

Jack nodded. "Out of here," he said. "Take a little walk."

"I'm in your power, lover boy," she said, slipping out of the booth. "Yours to command."

Jack struggled to his feet. Taking a deep breath, he thought: Is it possible to get drunk on the smell of a woman? Because the smell of her was inside his head, not just the familiar perfume, but the intoxicating private scent of Miriam. Salt air, a whiff of vanilla, maybe it was the bath soap she used, but whatever it was, it was driving him crazy, driving him sober almost, and he knew he had to get her out of the dance hall before the lights came up.

Miriam steadied him. He could detect the stiff fabric of her brassiere pressing lightly against his bare arm, so he wasn't all that numb. The sparkle of whiskey was having a very different effect, making his nerves tingle in awareness.

"Mind the step, lover boy."

He came down heavy on his bad leg and felt something give but there was no pain, you couldn't be this close to Miriam and feel pain. His head lolled and he looked up. Either the sky was hot with haloed stars or he was passing out.

"Don't you dare," Miriam was saying as they skittered through the cool white sea of gravel, and then he was tipping forward into the dark mouth of an opening.

Her coupe. The backseat. He was pretty sure he hadn't actually passed out, he was just experiencing a little confusion about time and place, and now the motor was running and where the hell was Miriam? Jack got on his knees, intending to crawl over into the front seat and find her.

"Down, boy," she said, showing her white teeth in the dark.

"Where we going?"

"A place I know," she said, skidding the car through the gravel, wheels spinning for traction. Jack fell back

into the rear seat, laughing. This was *very* funny, speed-
ing away from the Pagoda, burning rubber on the boulevard.

The next thing he knew, the car had stopped—hiss of
waves, they had to be along the beach road—and Miriam
was slipping into the back with him. His hands floated
up and cupped that stiff brassiere. Oh yes, a miracle, her
blouse was gone and the bra was blinding white, head
lamps in the night, and then she was crouching over him
and reaching behind to unfasten the bra strap and her
breasts were spilling into his hands, smooth and firm and
nipple stiff.

"Can you still do it?" she wanted to know. "Can
you?"

He tried to sit up and demonstrate his fitness for this
or any other activity, but she had him pinned around the
waist, grinding her hips against him, laughing as her head
bumped the canvas canopy. Her face loomed dizzy-close
and her tongue found his and then she was sitting up
again and saying, "Let me take care of you, baby."

It was so confusing, so cramped in the back of the
coupe that Jack wasn't sure which way he was facing.
The heel of his shoe squeaked against the window and
his left arm was wedged between the leather seats, and
when he reached with his free hand to find her, she'd
slipped away somehow.

"Hold still," she commanded.

He could do that, he could hold still, no problem, as
her fingers found his belt and opened his trousers, and
then she was inside with both hands hot around him. A
moment later he was aware of the warm, wet enclosure
of her beautiful mouth, and his heart came wildly back
to life, beating against his ribs like it wanted to come out
and join the party. Miriam was making a deep humming
sound as she fellated him, a throat song that threatened to loosen every joint in his body. *Mmmmmm.
Mmmmmmm* as her head bobbed, *mmmmmmmmmmm* and
all he could do was surrender to the sensation. Resonance like a deep note in a pipe organ shaking the pew,
mmmmmmm-mmmmmm-mmmmmmmm sustaining the
pitch, and the whiskey made it easier for him to hold off,
made him think this could go on forever, heavenly music
in this secret place, the First Church of Mrs. Miriam

Fitzroy, oh yes, and the choir was the sound of waves breaking against the nearby shore, and Miriam was tireless, she never lost the beat, never forgot the deep note she was humming as he began to levitate, arching in a spasm that stiffened him from the backs of his heels to the back of his head.

"My turn," she said eagerly, breathlessly, twisting herself into impossible angles as she wriggled out of the tight capri pants, and as he reached for her, Jack realized he'd sprung a leak. He was crying, tears stinging hot in his eyes, because he'd decided, finally, on a solution. He would leave Doris and Miriam would leave Michael and they would go off together, just the two of them, into whatever hell would make this sweetly unbearable heat last forever.

Seventeen

Mother Has a Plan

Mother watched him sleeping. This should have been enough, the comfort of one perfect son, but there was another bed in the room, neatly made, and if she touched the pillow she could still feel the shape left by her first-born son. Taken away in the night and drowned, and those who had done it kept returning in different guises to torment her. The last a handsome, charming liar of a man who'd tricked her out of the cemetery, bought her drinks, encouraged her to speak of private matters.

It was not enough that they had murdered Roy, now they conspired to invade her mind and steal away with her life-sustaining grief. Something had to be done.

Irene edged her chair closer to the bed, and the sound of it scraping the floor startled her surviving son from his troubled sleep.

"Mother?" He sat up in bed, his eyes blinking with the confusion of anxious dreams. "What's wrong, Mother?"

Irene reached out and patted the boy's knee where it lumped under the single sheet. It was hot in the room—it had rained earlier, a fickle summer rain that did not cool the air—and the sheet was damp with humidity and night sweat.

"Your mother has a plan," she said.

Billy sighed, swung his legs around until his feet touched the floor. He yawned, brushed his hair back from his forehead. It was dark in the room, but she could tell by the glow of the street lamps that he was wearing a white T-shirt and boxer shorts, the exact same costume his big brother had always worn to bed. "You should try to sleep, Mother," he said. "Take one of the pills I got you."

"There's a ladder involved," she said. "I can't be climbing ladders at my age."

Billy was plaintive, begging. "Mother, please. Go to bed. I wish you wouldn't sit there in the dark when I'm sleeping, it gives me the creeps."

Irene edged the chair up until her knees were bumping the soft edge of the mattress. Her eyes were luminous and she smelled of sweet brandy and she would not be denied.

"I have a plan," she said in her firmest mother voice. "And you are going to help me."

PART THREE

Incident at Drake Island

One

The Ass End of the Tunnel

Jack was scraping the burn off a piece of toast when the telephone rang. It was seven in the morning on a day late in August, and it was going to be, the radio promised, hot as the very devil.

"Good, you're still there," said a familiar voice.

Jack said, "Who the hell is this?"

There was a deep, resonating laugh. "Nice talk."

"Captain Delaney? I'm sorry, sir." He cradled the phone, reached for a cigarette. "This is a surprise, hearing from you."

For a couple of years of Jack's life, what he was already thinking of as the best years, it had not been unusual to be awakened by calls from Francis X. Delaney, his boss at the Homicide Unit. Always a friendly tone, no matter how early the hour, a sense of contained excitement, although the investigations were rarely that. Out of a thousand or so deaths reported in any given year, less than fifty on average would be actual homicides. Death by falling was invariably more common than murder, as was automotive manslaughter, but each incident had to be investigated, and Jack had loved all of it, from the initial survey of the crime scene to the final report—every day was like cheating death. He'd never been able to make Doris or his brother or anyone outside the fraternity understand that, but Francis X. Delaney knew because he felt the same himself, and he'd recognized it in Jack. When death could be catalogued and quantified and occasionally solved, life made sense because *death* made sense, or anyhow a hell of a lot more sense than what he'd seen of it in occupied Germany.

"No need to sir me now, son," Delaney was saying. "So you're alone there in Jamaica Plain, are you, living the life of a carefree bachelor?"

Jack looked around the empty kitchen. A wisp of smoke from the burned toast undulated in the still air. A strip of fly paper curled from a thumbtack on the wall above the counter—the intermittent buzz indicated an unexpired victim. He could smell the pail of heat-ripened garbage he'd forgotten to put out from the previous night, and the general filth of a home that hadn't been properly cleaned in almost two months.

"Dottie and the boys are still up at the beach," he said. "They'll be back on Sunday."

"That'll be grand, Jack. Listen, there's a thing you should see. Meet me at the ass end of the Callahan Tunnel."

"Excuse me?"

"The ass end, son. East Boston."

Jack went back into the bedroom and changed into his best suit. A silly twinge of vanity, but he wanted Delaney to see him looking prosperous, make sure the captain understood that getting dropped from the unit had actually improved his life. Not that he blamed Delaney for the medical discharge. Well, actually, the truth was that he did blame Delaney, part of blaming the whole department for not making an exception in his case, part of blaming the world for making him fallible.

Cutting through Roxbury to pick up Tremont Street, he thought about stopping to get his shoes polished, really make an impression, but quickly decided that was going too far. A spit shine would only call attention to his limp, a condition that had been aggravated by his drunken gymnastics in the backseat of Miriam's coupe. After three weeks the bone bruises were finally starting to fade away and he no longer winced at every step. Fading like Miriam herself, who had been keeping aloof and out of contact, back on her kick about staying apart until after Labor Day. No way to contact her discreetly, he couldn't trust the phones at the summer place, not with Mike and Sugar there, and anyhow he'd been busy as hell, several new investigations to oversee, new men to break in. There were no dog days in this particular August.

He'd been consoling himself with the calendar, marking off the days in his head. One more weekend of agony, living a lie with Dottie, and then he and Miriam would have to come to some kind of decision, how best to break the news to all involved.

Traffic was fairly moderate on Tremont at that hour, and he was able to reach the North End without difficulty. Which made it all the more surprising to find that the tunnel access was backed up all the way to Faneuil Hall. Stop and go and no way around it. When he finally eased the big Packard down into the sloping tunnel he expected to see flares, or evidence of some accident, but both lanes were moving, albeit slowly.

The cause of the slowdown didn't become apparent until he came up from under the harbor and exited into daylight in East Boston. The inbound lane was partially blocked by hastily erected barricades. Behind the barricade were two cruisers with lights flashing, and an unmarked Ford sedan that he recognized as belonging to Captain Delaney.

"Top of the morning to you, Jack. Cuppa coffee?" Delaney was in high spirits, wearing crisply creased poplin trousers, a starched white short-sleeved shirt, and a wide green tie, no jacket. The cigar parked at the corner of his mouth was unlit, and his eyes were lively and full of humor.

Jack accepted the cardboard cup of coffee, declined the box of sugared donuts. "Somebody die here, Captain?" he asked. He hadn't seen an ambulance or the crime wagon, but it wasn't unreasonable to assume that the homicide commander would be responding to a fatal accident, by far the most common form of death investigated by the unit.

"Not that I know of," Delaney said. "Turn yourself around, son, and look above the tunnel entrance."

Jack turned. He saw nothing but the mouth of the tunnel, the paved embankment, and the stream of slowly moving traffic. Behind him Delaney was chuckling impishly.

"It's the billboard, Jack. Yesterday it was advertising Mr. Boston brandy. This morning it's saying something else again."

The billboard was set at an angle for maximum exposure to the inbound traffic. A thin coating of white paint failed to completely obscure the liquor advertisement, and now that Jack was looking at it he could see where the paint had slopped onto the stones of the tunnel arch and to the roadway below. It wasn't the white paint he was really noticing, though, it was the message hand-painted over the white surface, in ragged black letters six feet high:

BOSS MCKANE & HIS DEVIL DAUGHTER KILLED ROY
DRAKE 4/29/49

It was the billboard the rubberneckers were gawking at, not the barricades or the cop cars.

"Very clever," Jack said to Delaney. "How in hell did they get up there?"

"They tell me there was a ladder bolted to the sign, for maintenance, I suppose, but it's been unbolted and removed by the pranksters."

"This was done last night?"

"Must have been," Delaney said. "Am I wrong to suppose that you might know the culprit?"

Jack finished his coffee, reached in his pocket for his cigarettes. "McKane called me off the case, Captain. Several weeks ago. So this is nothing to do with me."

Delaney smiled and shook his head. "You mean to say that Sugar McKane doesn't mind having himself slandered for all the world to see?"

"Oh, he'll mind," Jack said, eyeing the billboard.

"Yes, I expect he will," Delaney said. "As a courtesy we'll put a man up there to block it out as soon as the ladder truck arrives. There's no love lost between Sugar and Freddy Neeson, the fire chief, so it may take a while."

Hamish Higgins, the *Transcript* columnist, arrived by taxi cab just as Jack was lighting his tenth cigarette of the morning—halfway through a new pack of Pall Malls and he hadn't had a proper breakfast yet.

"Bless my soul," Higgins said, leaning on his cane to keep his balance as he gazed up at the billboard. "Had to see this with my own eyes. It has the look of a banner headline."

"I guess that was the idea," Jack said, surprised at himself because he was actually happy to see the effete little newspaper man again. In his white suit and spats, and with that trademark cane, Higgins looked ready to model for the decoration on a wedding cake. "Would you say 'devil daughter' like that in the paper?" he asked.

"Oh, that's much the best part," Higgins responded. "It has the tabloid ring, coin of the realm. But you needn't worry, this will never make the *Transcript*. Or any of the other fish wrappers. Not a chance."

"I'm not sure that really matters much," Jack observed. "It's getting good circulation right here."

Higgins glanced at the unending stream of inbound vehicles, the upturned faces craning to see the billboard. "Yes," he said. "I suppose it is."

Two

A Family Resemblance

A ticket had been left for him at Symphony Hall.

"You've missed the start," said a woman with pince-nez glasses attached to the end of a very long nose. "This is a special concert performance to raise money for the Shriners Children's Hospital. All contributions in excess of the admission price are tax-deductible."

"Was the ticket paid for?" Jack said testily. It had been a long and arduous day, most of it spent on the road, and he didn't really give a damn about the Boston Pops, even if the concert was in a good cause.

The woman made her disappointment clear as she pushed the ticket through the window. "Your party is at table forty-nine," she said, raising her voice to be heard. "Ask a waiter and someone will show you to the table."

Immediately after entering the main floor of the hall, which had been tricked out like a huge wedding party, Jack realized he wasn't properly dressed. This was a dinner jacket affair and he had on a car-wrinkled business suit and a tie with a discernible grease stain, courtesy of a hurried lunch at a diner in Fall River, where Tony Grazi and his team were undercover on an industrial pilferage job. The summons to the fund-raiser had come over the telephone when Jack had called in prior to going home for what he'd intended to be an early night. The nerves in his bad leg were twitching, as often happened when he was overtired, and he wanted nothing more than to lie in a lukewarm tub and tune in the mindless nonsense of *The Great Gildersleeve*.

He was relieved to discover that Sugar's table was placed well back from the stage, where the sprightly Pops orchestra was sawing away at a waltz-time version of "Yankee Doodle." What surprised him was not the presence of Michael, who often accompanied his father-in-law to these musical affairs, but Miriam, who was supposed to be up at the summer house, not here in the city wearing a creamy white gown. Miriam waving mischievously as he approached.

"Yankee Doodle" ended just as the waiter pulled his chair.

"What a nice surprise," Miriam said, leaning forward to pat his hand. "How've you been, Jack?"

"Peachy," he said. And tried not to notice the deep decolletage, the tight bodice of the thin silk gown, or the fact that her back was exposed right down to her waist, a delicious scoop of tanned flesh.

"Good evening, Jack," Sugar said. His manner was very formal and restrained, but his huge black eyebrows were twitching like the very devil. "Sorry to have extended the invitation so late in the day. I see you couldn't manage a dinner jacket."

"Couldn't even manage my dinner, Sugar. Sorry to be such an embarrassment. Maybe I could sit at another table and you could pass me notes."

Mike chuckled nervously, touching his bow tie. "Now, boys," he said. "Let's not get off on the wrong foot."

"Sorry," Jack said, directing the apology to his brother. "It's been a hellish day."

"How's Tony doing down there?" Mike wanted to know.

"He's managed to get a man inside the factory and another on the loading dock. Snap Edwards is on a forklift with a camera rigged up in his lunch box. It's just a matter of time."

"Good," Mike said. "Excellent."

"And how is your lovely wife?" Miriam said, smiling wickedly.

"She's peachy, too," Jack said. "Everybody is just peachy. Now, I happen to see a waiter carrying steins of beer. You think I could have one of my very own, Sugar?"

"Feel free," the big man said.

"Because I notice the rest of you are drinking lemonade."

"By all means," Sugar said, signaling for a waiter. "Most of the imbibers here seem to favor champagne, but if you prefer, have a beer."

The beer wasn't cold, but it was wet, and Jack drank it quickly and lighted a cigarette. He noticed Mike was smoking, so that particular taboo had already been broken at Sugar's table. The orchestra was cranking away again, sounded like a Gershwin ballad played up tempo, and Jack smoked his cigarette and tried to regain his good temper. It was Miriam who had thrown him off, not Sugar's last-minute summons to the concert. McKane he expected, the old man was sure to have a bee in his bonnet about that billboard, but he hadn't been ready to play brother-in-law to Miriam. How dare she look so desirable when he couldn't acknowledge it? And what the hell was she doing, coming back to the city without letting him know?

Miriam seemed to be reading his thoughts. "Deirdre will be home in a few days," she said brightly. "I'm helping Daddy get the house ready. Isn't that good news?"

Jack was startled. The last he'd seen of little sister, she'd seemed destined for a long stay at the clinic. "That's terrific," he said carefully.

Sugar was giving him the eye, an expression that Jack couldn't fathom. Was it anger? Distrust? A look of pleading? Or was the old man picking up on something else. Jesus, *that* was it, the bastard suspected, he knew what was going on with Miriam. But no, Jack finally decided, as his heart seemed to stutter, this was just paranoid fear, the result of too many hours on the road, too much coffee, too many cigarettes. His mind was fogged with exhaustion. There was no way Sugar could know. He might suspect, the cunning old bastard, but he couldn't know.

How McKane would react when he did learn the truth, that was something Jack didn't want to think about right now. One of a long list of things not to think about in that regard.

"It should have been you who called me," Sugar said grumpily, "not Hamish Higgins."

Jack squinted through his own smoke. "You ordered me off the case," he said. "In no uncertain terms."

McKane looked uncomfortable. He pulled his chair closer to the small table, leaned in such a way that he and Jack could converse privately. "I was worried about Dee Dee," he said, trying to sound reasonable. "Can't you see that? Like any father. It comes to her health, I don't always think straight.''

''But she's coming home now. She's okay.''

''Yes,'' he said, and the smile made his face light up. ''She's coming home at last. And now I can think straight and obviously I was wrong and you were right. Those people must be dealt with. The situation must be resolved. For Dee Dee's sake. We can't have disruptions, she'll need her peace of mind.''

''The devil daughter,'' Jack said.

''What?'' Stung by the words, McKane pulled his head back, a turtle-like move.

''That was on the billboard, didn't Hamish say? McKane and his devil daughter killed Roy Drake.''

Sugar closed his eyes and sighed deeply. His breath smelled of lemons and yeast. ''Take care of this for me, Jack, please? It makes me feel unclean.''

Jack persuaded a reluctant waiter that it would be worth his while to fetch another stein of beer, then pushed back his chair and turned his attention to the Symphony Hall stage. A huge photographic blowup of the proposed new Shriners Hospital had been unfurled under the bank of organ pipes that rose from the rear of the stage. The familiar and beloved figure of Arthur Fiedler was in full Teutonic fury, waving his arms like a madman, as if he was hurling imaginary objects at the orchestra. Unlike McKane, whose sentiments were typical of most musically literate Bostonians, Jack had no particular fondness for Fiedler and his sweet-sounding orchestra. It wasn't the music itself, although he much preferred a real dance band, it was the cop's distrust of a man who chased after fire engines, as Fiedler proudly did. Called himself a fire buff, collected fireman hats. Whenever he saw a picture of the much photographed conductor, Jack always found himself wondering where Arthur kept his matches.

At one point Mike leaned close to him and said, ''Are you okay, Jack?'' an expression of concern so real, so palpable that Jack very nearly recoiled. The next impulse he had, and he knew the response was wild and irrational, was a desire to raise his fist and punch Michael in the face. Bloody his nose.

Instead he said, ''I'm fine, Mike. Just tired.''

''I knew this would happen,'' Mike said. ''What are

you going to do, Jack? Can we make a civil case against the woman and her son?''

Jack shrugged. He really wasn't in the mood to discuss the situation with Miriam so near, so tempting and yet untouchable. The actions of a couple of crazed swamp Yankees didn't matter. What Sugar had or hadn't done to them didn't matter. Not tonight, and not with his brother looming so close, oozing concern.

''I'll handle it,'' Jack said. ''There's a lead or two I never got the chance to follow up.''

''Be careful,'' Mike implored him.

''Of what?'' Jack asked. ''The truth?''

Mike shook his head, patted his younger brother on the knee. ''Just watch your back, kid. That's all I mean. Watch your back.''

At the intermission Jack excused himself and went in search of a rest room. Got his toes stepped on a time or two, fighting his way to the lobby, and very nearly tripped and fell down the stairs to the men's room. Not paying attention, he chided himself, you have to pay attention.

Leaning into the urinal, he closed his eyes, allowed his bladder to ease, and it occurred to him at that exact moment that he was a puzzle even to himself. He should have been pleased by McKane's request for help; he'd resented being told to drop the investigation. Instead he'd been angry all evening. Not at Sugar, he now realized. At Michael, for being in love with his own wife.

You're the craziest one of all, he told himself, resting his forehead against the cool tiles. *You and crazy Dee Dee would make quite a pair. Talk about a compulsive sexual obsession!*

By the time he'd washed his hands in the sink, under the doleful eye of an elderly attendant who was standing by to sell combs and handkerchiefs, the surge of irrational anger had subsided. ''How's it going tonight, pop?'' he said to the attendant, flipping a coin into his tray.

''Yes, sir, I love the Pops, sir,'' the old man said, and bent over creakily to swipe a sponge at the sink.

As Jack came out of the men's room a hand came around and took a grip on his tie. ''Hello there, stranger,'' said Miriam. She pulled on the tie and he followed her into a carpeted alcove outside the ladies' room.

He tried to kiss her.

"Not here," she said. "I draw the line at Symphony Hall."

"If you'd told me you were coming back . . ." he said.

One of the strong and powerful things about his attraction to Miriam was the way her image would diminish slightly when he didn't see her for a while. Diminish in memory, as if he couldn't quite keep her clearly in focus. And then, wham!, when he saw her again her beauty was a surprise. He'd almost forgotten how stunning she was, how those big green eyes looked into the deepest, darkest part of him, an intimacy he craved.

"You need a new tie," she said, wetting her thumb and rubbing the stain.

"I need you," he said, keeping his voice low.

A woman in a sequined gown walked by, clutching her purse, and he could tell she'd overheard his declaration. So what if she did—they were just another pair of lovers and he was feeling dangerous, he didn't care who overheard him.

"Just a few more days," Miriam said huskily. "I'm helping Daddy with Deirdre."

"You remember what I said that night in the car? The last time?"

Miriam smiled and he could see the pinkness of her tongue. He was aware of her body heat radiating through the thin silk. "You were drunk out of your mind, Jack," she said. "I was pretty loaded myself."

"But we love each other," he said.

Miriam quit fussing with his tie and patted him on the chest. "Of course we do," she said. "After Dee Dee gets settled in we can go back to where we were. At least for the next few months. After that it might be a little awkward, but we'll just have to see."

Jack felt light-headed. "What are you talking about?"

She had shifted back a step, and turned to smile at a pair of white-haired women who were exiting the ladies' room. "I guess it isn't obvious yet," she said. Her hands brushed the bosom of her gown. "I thought you'd notice my tits were bigger."

Jack put his hand to his head: he really was feeling dizzy and Miriam wasn't making any sense, she wasn't responding at all the way he'd been expecting. Now she was up close, her lovely face upturned, and she was whispering a word. "Preggers, Jack, preggers. Don't you get it?" and backing away again when his hands tried to slip down the back of her gown.

"I'm with child, Jack," she said. "Pregnant. Wait'll I tell Michael, he's going to be so excited."

Jack felt the need of a seat. There were no chairs available, so he leaned his weight against the wall of the alcove and tried to figure out what, exactly, Miriam was saying. "It's his baby? Michael's?"

Miriam shook her head, amused at the idea. "I never said that, silly. It was that afternoon at the Parker House, I think. That day when I shaved my thing, remember?"

"Jesus Christ."

"Three months," Miriam said with obvious pleasure. "And my tits really are bigger, whether you noticed or not."

"But Michael," he said. "What about Michael?"

"What about him?" Miriam said. "He needn't know who the real father is. Unless of course you want to tell him."

Jack took a deep breath, but it didn't help. He still felt light-headed and dizzy and there was something alive in his stomach. "This is crazy," he said.

"Yes," Miriam agreed. "That's what I love about it. Oh come on, Jack, don't look so worried. You're brothers, so the kid will have a family resemblance. He'll never know."

Black-tied Sugar McKane was holding forth in the lobby, entertaining a former Massachusetts governor and car dealer who shared his interest in music. "That's what we all love about you, Alvin," Sugar was saying. "You could sell ice to an Eskimo. Provided the Eskimo was a Republican."

He caught sight of Jack limping to the doors and hurried over. "What's wrong, lad? Have you taken ill?"

"Just tired," Jack said. "Hit me all of a sudden. Really, I'm okay. All I need is a good night's sleep."

"That'd do you a world of good, I'm sure. I'll make your apologies to Michael and Miriam, shall I?"

Jack nodded, tried to dodge around Sugar. The big

man shifted, blocked his exit. "Jack?" he said softly. "Fix it for me, please? It's the last favor I'll ask of you or Mike."

"Okay," Jack said wearily. "I'll fix it."

He stopped on the corner of Huntington Avenue to vomit up the beer and the remains of the last meal he'd had in New Bedford. After that he felt a little better, promise or no promise.

Three

Annie Gets Her Gun

It was against the law for an unauthorized person to impersonate a police officer in the Commonwealth of Massachusetts, either by verbal persuasion, or by the showing of a badge, or by any means whatsoever.

Jack Fitzroy no longer had a badge in his possession, so after leaving the Costello Funeral Home in East Boston he stopped at a Woolworth Five & Dime and paid twenty-nine cents for a Genuine Dick Tracy Crime Stoppers Detective Shield. It was shiny and it fit inside his wallet, that's all that mattered. The rest of it, the posture and the confidence and the attitude, he didn't have to fake.

The address he'd finally gotten out of Liam Costello took him to a cul-de-sac in the north end of town, not far from the Suffolk Downs racetrack. The neighborhood was mixed, a row of unpainted tenements with sagging porches interspersed here and there with new, postwar homes erected on what had been dumping lots. The Sheehans had one of these new, white clapboard capes, and they'd surrounded it with a chain-link fence, as if girding their home against the creeping dilapidation of the racetrack slums. Hedges planted along the fence line had not filled in yet, their normally rapid growth stunted by the shadows of the surrounding tenements.

The street was the playground here. A pack of tough-looking kids played a version of stickball that used parked cars for bases, and Jack made sure to leave the Packard well away from the action. The ball players eyed him as he approached and then turned quickly back to the game, smelling cop. These were the kids who would keep the Division 7 detectives busy once they reached maturity and passed beyond reach of the juvenile courts.

Jack lifted the latch on the chain-link gate and went up

the neatly kept walkway to the Sheehans' front door.
Name right there above the mail slot, so there could be
no mistake. He pressed the button and heard a gong,
sounded like Big Ben in the background of an Edward R.
Murrow broadcast from London. He kept pushing the
button, bonging the bell. When that had no effect, he
rapped his knuckles sharply against the paneled door—
still nothing.

Something caught his eye. Stepping back, Jack saw the
venetian blinds move. "It's the police, Mrs. O'Hare!"
he shouted, holding up his wallet. "We just want a word
with you, is all!"

A gnarled finger pulled the blinds apart, and he could
see her small, dark eyes studying him. Jack flipped open
the wallet, let the phony badge catch a glint of sunlight.

The old woman unlocked the front door but left the
chain on. "And who are you?" she asked in a lilting
Irish accent that sounded, to Jack's ears, right off the
boat.

"Detective Jack Kelly at your service, Mrs. O'Hare.
Assuming you *are* Mrs. Anne O'Hare, recently of Hyde
Park."

A pause, and then the chain was being slipped and the
door opened. Annie O'Hare, all of five feet of her, shuf-
fled into view and looked him over. It was a very thor-
ough look, commencing with his shoes and continuing
on up until she had studied his face. The old woman
finally nodded her approval, and then beckoned for him
to step into the small foyer. "I was never of Hyde Park,
you understand," she said. "It's only me work was there
for a short while."

Jack had his hat in hand and he was giving her his best
smile. He let just a little of the Irish cadence enter his
speech, a trick he'd often used when conducting police
investigations in certain neighborhoods. "Am I right in
thinking the Sheehans aren't at the moment home, Mrs.
O'Hare?"

"They've gone to the north, the both of 'em," she
said. "What's that state up there?"

"Vermont?" he said. "New Hampshire?"

"That's the one," she said. "They've taken a cottage
on a lake so the mister can fish. He's a fine gentleman,
Mr. Sheehan is."

"So I've heard," Jack said. "Do you think I could have a glass of water, Mrs. O'Hare, would that be too much trouble for you? I've only a few small questions, but it's hot as the very devil out there and my poor throat is dry as dust."

"Come out to the kitchen, then," she said.

Jack sat at the table. It was a new set of furniture, very modern, a square table with a shiny top, fancy metal trim, chromed legs, and matching chairs. A pink-curtained window overlooked a small, neatly groomed yard. It was just the sort of place Dottie would like one of these days.

Annie let the water run, holding an arthritic hand under the tap until she was satisfied. She then wiped the outside of the glass dry with a small rag, placed a doily on the kitchen table, and set the glass before him.

"Have you come from the priest, then?" she asked.

"Mrs. O'Hare, please have a seat and make yourself comfortable. This won't take a minute and then you can get back to your work here. It's an endless task, I suppose, keeping a house as spotless as this?"

"It is, yes," she said. "It wasn't the priest sent you?"

"No, it wasn't a priest. Your name was mentioned in the course of a routine investigation." Jack got out a notebook and uncapped his pen. The old woman sat opposite him, her posture rigid. She was obviously intimidated, possibly frightened, and although fear and intimidation were sometimes useful, he decided that in this case it would be better to put her at ease. "You're not in any trouble at all, Mrs. O'Hare, let's make that crystal clear from the start. You've only to answer a few small questions, which we'll keep in the strictest confidence."

"I've done nothing wrong," she said, staring down at her gnarled hands.

"Not a thing," Jack agreed. "There's not a blemish on your record. Now, just to be sure we have it down correctly, were you for a time employed as housekeeper with the McKanes of Hyde Park?"

"So it's him," she said, sighing heavily. "I might have known."

"Are you referring to Mr. McKane? Is that the man who employed you?"

"It was, yes," she said. "I'll not lie about it. It was him hired me through the parish, you see, all done proper with the blessing of the church."

Jack nodded to himself. Local parishes often placed immigrant Irish as maids and housekeepers with the better Catholic families. The system had been in place since the Famine, with the expressed intention of aiding the indigent and the less frequently expressed effect of providing back-stair access to wealthy parishioners who might not otherwise be so closely bound to the local church.

"We know it was all proper, Mrs. O'Hare, and we have it on the best authority that you're a devout woman, never miss a feast day, is that true?"

Mrs. O'Hare was nodding. "I've got me faith to sustain me, and that's a fact. Though it has been sorely tried, oh yes, indeed it has, by the likes of him. He's a demon, that man."

"You're referring to Mr. McKane?"

"Who else?" the old woman said sharply. There was a rosy color in her cheeks now, and her dander was up.

"Because the truth of it is, Mrs. O'Hare, what we're investigating—and I'm sorry to say we can't be more specific than that—but what we're investigating is a very serious matter indeed, and it touches upon events in the McKane household."

"Oh, I shouldn't wonder," said the old woman eagerly. "The truth will finally come out, even so terrible a truth as that we can't properly speak of."

"And what truth would that be, Mrs. O'Hare?"

Her small eyes, dark and cool, judged him from across the kitchen table. "Ah, but we can't speak of it," she said slyly. "That's what we said."

Jack smiled grimly, tapping his pen against the notebook. "Ah, but there must be a way, for if we can't have at the truth, the devil will never get his due, Mrs. O'Hare, and that's a fact."

"It is," she agreed. "It's a true fact and I can't dispute it."

"Let's see," Jack said, pretending to consult his notes. "Is it correct that you left the employ of Mr. McKane in April of this year?"

"That's true, yes. They took me in at the parish for a time, until this situation was found."

"Working for the Sheehans?" Jack said.

"Them, yes, and a nicer couple couldn't be found, though the truth of it is I prefer the mister. He's such a sensible man, and as clean as a cat. Which is not to say the missus isn't decent, because she is, quite decent."

She pronounced it *day*-cent, and Jack had to resist letting the lilt creep too much into his voice or she would see him for a fraud, and only half Irish at that. "And why was it, Mrs. O'Hare," he said, "that you left the employ of Mr. McKane without immediate prospect of another situation?"

The old woman shook her head. "Oh, but I couldn't stay. I couldn't stay in that house, not if it meant living on the street. It wasn't right. It wasn't *day*-cent. 'Twas blasphemy."

"Mr. McKane did something to offend you, is that what happened?"

Her head shook even more vigorously. "Not only meself, you see, he offended our Savior, the Lord Jesus Christ, on the very day He came back to life."

That took a moment to sink in. "You mean on Easter, Mrs. O'Hare? Whatever happened, happened on Easter, is that it?" Jack tried to contain his excitement, he didn't want to appear too eager.

"Easter Sunday, yes, the day our Lord rose again and walked from the tomb. If there's a holier day, I can't think of it."

Jack had in mind what Miriam had told him, that Deirdre been sent to Dr. Parkay's clinic on Easter. "Was the daughter at home?" he asked carefully. "Miss Deirdre McKane?"

The look on the old woman's face told him he'd struck gold. This unspeakable blasphemy, whatever it was, involved Deirdre. "Was there another person present in the home, Mrs. O'Hare?" he went on. "A young man named Roy Drake?"

To his surprise the old woman shook her head. " 'Twas just the two of them. Him and her."

"Mr. McKane and his daughter?"

"Dee Dee, yes, and she's the very devil, too, it wasn't only him."

"Can you tell me what they were doing, Mrs. O'Hare?"

"I can't say," said the old woman, "and I won't. But it was Satan's business, and on Easter, too, which made it all the worse. Of course, I should have known, what with all the creatures he kept in that room of his."

"Creatures?" Jack said, surprised again. "What creatures?"

"Gargoyles," Mrs. O'Hare said darkly. "Cut into the wood all 'round that room, so their eyes follow you. Creatures of the devil, up to devilish kinds of things. With horns and tails, you know, like Lucifer himself."

"What room was this?" Jack asked. "What room in the house was this?"

" 'Twas the room where he played his music."

She had to be talking about Sugar's study, where he kept his radio and his new high-fidelity record player and his collection of recordings. Jack wracked his brains but he couldn't remember any gargoyles carved into the woodwork of the study. Then again his visits to the Hyde Park residence had been rare—more recently than before—and never, as it happened, in those few months when Mrs. O'Hare had been employed as housekeeper.

"Mrs. O'Hare," he said, putting some no-nonsense authority into his tone of voice. "We have reason to believe a crime may have been committed. We really need to know what you witnessed that day."

"A terrible thing," the old woman said. "A terrible thing indeed."

"You'll have to be more specific," he said as sternly as he knew how.

"It was the devil's own business," she said, folding her arms across her bosom. "That's all I'll say."

And that, as it turned out, was all she would say, no matter how adroitly he posed the question, or how forcefully he badgered her for specifics. The old woman clammed up, as if proud of her inability to describe whatever evil act she had implied took place. She was playing the martyr, Jack finally decided, and her personal martyrdom involved a vow of silence. Rumors and inferences and dark references to devils were allowed, but when it came to actually speaking he words, she'd rather be nailed to a cross.

As he was getting up to leave, he thought, for a moment, that she had changed her mind.

"I've something to show you," she said.

Mrs. O'Hare got up from the table and went to the kitchen counter, where she'd left her purse. Jack waited, expected he knew not what to emerge from the bag. A note, a photograph, maybe even a gargoyle.

Not, certainly, a handgun.

"Put it down," he said when she turned to him with a derringer in hand.

Mrs. O'Hare, frightened by his tone, complied, setting the gun on the counter and drawing away her hand. "It's only to show them I mean business," she said, and he saw that there were tears in her eyes.

Jack went to the counter and examined the little handgun. An inexpensive, single-shot .22-caliber lady's derringer. Looked like a costume piece, but it was loaded with a real bullet. "This is dangerous," he said. "Where did you get it?"

Annie O'Hare used the corner of her frilly apron to wipe away her tears. "It's meant to be dangerous," she said, her voice trembling with defiance. "And never you mind where I got it. It cost all of five dollars and it was me own money, so where I got it doesn't matter."

Jack sighed. "Okay, fine. But what did you mean about showing them you meant business? Showing who?"

"Them that works for him," she said. "Them that brought me here."

She meant the Costello brothers. It was the Costellos who'd found this particular situation for the old woman, after she'd abruptly left the McKane house and taken refuge at the Hyde Park rectory. Which was how Jack had finally run her down, after prying the information from a very reluctant Liam Costello.

"I'll not go with them again," the old woman said, full of dread and fear. "They work for the devil himself, and that's the truth."

Four

When Salome Descends

Three nights later Jack Fitzroy was hiding in the devil's house and contemplating the pleasures of mortal sin. On assignment, as it were, working deep undercover to observe with his own eyes what forbidden things might happen between Boss McKane and his devil daughter.

"So here we are at last," Miriam said. "What are we going to do about it?"

It was Miriam, of course, who had let him up the back stairway and into her childhood bedroom. Now she was lying languidly on the canopied bed, surrounded by stuffed pillows and Raggedy Ann dolls, and her pale pleated skirt was well above her knees. Jack was perched uneasily in the window seat of a dormer that looked out on the tree-lined streets of this wealthy Hyde Park neighborhood. A canopy of oaks and elms out there, rustling in the hot wind. If he didn't look down at the streetlights, it was like being perched high up in a forest.

"What if your father comes up here?" Jack wanted to know. Sugar McKane was very much on his mind, so strong a presence in this house that Jack's desire for Miriam—slim legs bent slightly, her ankles crossed—was dampened somewhat. Not entirely, as she well knew. He couldn't be in a room with her and not get partially erect.

"Oh, he never does," Miriam said from her soft mound of pillows. "The last time Daddy tucked me in, I was about ten years old. I gave him a kiss—a real kiss—just to be wicked, and the poor man scampered away like a scared rabbit."

"That really happened, you kissing your own father?"

Miriam made a face. "Really, Jack, don't sound so shocked. I was ten, remember? It was the kiss of a ten-year-old girl. And Daddy ran away. So I know he's never done anything to Dee Dee. Not what you think, anyway, and not what that horrible old Mrs. O'Hare thinks, either. She had it all wrong, and now you have, too.''

Convinced that Sugar had committed unspeakable acts with his own daughter, and that this terrible secret had some mortal connection to the death of Roy Drake, Jack had gone directly to Miriam. Miriam who had claimed she was pregnant with his child, and who, this evening at least, was being mysterious and coy about it. Was she or wasn't she? It was maddening not to know. If she really was pregnant, then she had to leave Michael and he had to leave Dottie and together they had to turn the world upside down, for better or worse. Undoubtedly worse.

''We have to do the right thing,'' he said. ''We'll have to get married.''

Miriam had shifted and she was scratching lazily behind her knees, letting her bare toes wriggle. ''Really? That's doing the right thing? I make Mike miserable, you break Dottie's heart, and we both run away.''

Jack rubbed his forehead and concentrated on staying right where he was, on the virginal window seat. Summoning the courage to say the words he'd been thinking for the last week. ''Unless you want to get rid of it,'' he finally said. ''Unless you—''

Miriam interrupted. ''Jack, get it through your head. I want a baby. I've always wanted a baby.''

''So you *are* pregnant.''

''Quite possibly,'' she said. ''You never know.'' She patted the mattress. ''Come on over here, we can play doctor or something.''

''Miriam,'' he said. His heart was racing, he could feel his pulse in his ears.

''Come here,'' she insisted, and he did, he crept from the window seat to her bed, the bed of a ten-year-old girl, and when she spread her legs and moaned, it was much too late to continue the game of resistance. He was out of his mind, screwing the possibly pregnant wife of his own brother, in her father's house, while her crazy sister slept in a locked room nearby.

Jack knew. He knew he was choosing the pleasures of hell on earth. He didn't even have to believe in God to know that much. Hell had nothing to do with a God or a soul, as he had seen amply demonstrated in Germany.

Hell was a place you made for yourself and for those around you, a thought he managed to hold as Miriam bucked against him, knotting her fists and straining to muffle her cries of passion. She sighed sleepily after they were done, as they lay moist and disheveled and entwined atop the bed covers.

"I don't care," she said huskily. Her eyes were closed. "It feels so good I don't care about anything else. Not even you, Jack, do you understand?"

"How could I?" he said, propping himself up on his elbow. "You're not making sense."

Miriam said, "I'm making perfect sense," and when her eyes blinked open they were like green lamps. "If I really cared about you, really wanted the best for you, I wouldn't make you risk it all for just a fuck."

"It's not just a fuck," he insisted.

"That's my point," she said. "Whatever it is, it's bigger than both of us."

There was no arguing with Miriam. Try reasoning with her and he found his thoughts twisting around, knotting up. Jack pulled his trousers on, buttoned his shirt, and went to the window seat to retrieve his cigarettes. World of trees out there, Sherwood Forest. And then the leaves shifted and he thought he saw something move among the branches.

"You ever had a problem with Peeping Toms?" he asked.

Miriam was behind him, pressing her bare breasts up against his back, her breath hot on his neck. "You're imagining things."

"Maybe I am," he said.

Jack pulled the shade down and then his trousers were coming off again and Miriam wanted to do it right there on the window seat and he wanted it, too. For the next few minutes it didn't matter if she was pregnant, it didn't matter if Michael knew, or if Deirdre was crazy, or if Sugar had murdered a man. Nothing mattered but living inside her.

When the music started Miriam slipped across the hall and unlocked the door to Deirdre's room. Then she took Jack's hand and led him to a dark corner of the hallway, where they could remain unseen behind the banister spindles.

"How do you know she'll come out?" he whispered.

Miriam had crouched down beside him. "That's why we keep the door locked at night," she said. "You'll see."

Whispering wasn't really necessary because the music filled the lower floor of the big house and reverberated through the stairwell. It was, Miriam explained, a live radio broadcast of the opera *Salomé,* one of Sugar's favorites, and he always played opera at full volume, so as not to miss anything.

"I hate opera," Jack said. "It's stupid."

"Hating opera is stupid," Miriam said, patting his hand. "Now just relax and we'll see what happens. Maybe you're right. Maybe Daddy will dress up in red tights and a pitchfork and make Dee Dee ride a broom."

"This is serious, Miriam," he insisted.

"Nothing is serious enough to make Daddy hurt Dee Dee. You just hate him like you hate opera, because you don't know any better."

They crouched in the dark end of the hallway for more than thirty minutes as the great tide of Strauss swelled and waned, music that to Jack's ears seemed to circle endlessly, going nowhere. He wanted a cigarette, wanted desperately to ease his nerves, but he didn't dare because Sugar had a nose like a bloodhound. Jack was thinking about the cigarette he would have when he finally got out of this great, ghastly mausoleum of a house, into the clean night air, when Miriam squeezed his hand.

He looked up. Deirdre was floating out of her room. A slender, almost ephemeral creature clothed in a long gown. Not a gown, he realized, a nightdress that trailed over the carpet, so that she seemed to be gliding. Her eyelids were flickering and her head was rolling from side to side.

"What's she on?" he asked.

Miriam's eyes never left her sister. "We give her sleeping pills," she said. "They seem to help a little."

Deirdre raised her thin arms above her head and turned in place, an awkward kind of pirouette because she seemed to trip on the hem of her nightdress and almost lost her balance.

Jack reacted, intending to get up and help the girl, and Miriam gripped his arm with savage, unexpected ferocity. "Leave her alone," she hissed, and Jack settled down, transfixed by what happened next.

Deirdre was slipping out of the nightdress. She did not, as he might have expected, pull the gown off over her head in the conventional manner. Instead she seemed to undulate to the music, shrugging her shoulders in such a way that the neck of the gown opened and slipped down, exposing one small breast. Deirdre's head was lolling from side to side, more or less in sympathy with the music, and Jack knew that wherever she thought she was, it wasn't in this world. She was in some other, distant place of sound and light and shadows, where madness made sense. Jack was pretty sure he could stand up and wave his arms and Deirdre wouldn't see him. Those fluttering eyes were focused elsewhere.

Now the gown was down around her waist and he could count her ribs. She was little more than skin and bones, there was no real curve to her hips, just concave bones showing, and then the gown dropped away and she was naked. Naked and oddly sexless, the small tuft of pubic hair the only real proof of gender.

Jack realized that she was not actually moving to the music, at least not in a way he could understand. It was as if each pale, bone-thin limb responded separately, as if Deirdre was disconnected not only from the world, but from her own body. She was a pretty doll's head riding a frail machine of flesh, jerking inner wires and gyroscopes, causing feet to move, arms to writhe. It would be a miracle, he decided, if she managed to get down the stairs without falling. He wanted to help—this whole thing was simply too horrible to endure, he no longer cared what Sugar might do, or what he might have done— but Miriam's hand restrained him and he knew he could not rise from this dark place without her permission.

"Wait," she insisted. "You wanted this, now here it is."

Deirdre was descending the stairs. Her hands flapped, beating the air. Her head lolled, teetering from side to side, as if precariously balanced on the tip of her spine. Deirdre descending into the rising chorus of the opera, for Strauss was coming to a crescendo, Salomé was dropping her veils, and the sound of it resonated right through the carpet where Jack crouched, his bad leg going numb with pain.

"Come on," Miriam said, urging him to shift position. "You want to see what Daddy does to her, right?"

He scooted along the carpet until they had an angle on the whole stairwell, and beyond it the doorway that opened into the ground-floor music room. It was pretty dim in there, and all Jack could see of Sugar was a vague shape in an armchair. Deirdre's pale, skeletal body looked china white under the small chandelier that illuminated the stairwell. A ghost of a girl floating eerily down the curving steps. She kept looking up at the lights, that weird way she moved her head around, and Jack was convinced that she would inevitably trip and fall, shattered by madness and gravity.

"Stop her," he urged Miriam.

"Too late," she said. "Here comes Daddy."

It was true. The figure in the chair had moved, he was standing up, striding forward, out of the music room and into the relative brightness of the stairwell. Jack could see him clearly now, see his expression, or rather his lack of expression—it might have been crudely chiseled from knotted wood. What was the man thinking as he watched his mad naked daughter coming down the stairs? Did Jack detect a leer there, a hunger in those dark, unfathomable eyes? Was it lust for his own flesh that froze Sugar, hands at his sides, while Deirdre danced?

And then the old man let his shoulders sag and his head went down and he groaned. The big hands came up and covered his face. He seemed to shiver and then he pulled himself together, shook his head, and came forward purposefully.

"Poor Dee Dee," he said. "I thought I locked that door. You heard the music, did you?"

With that he picked his daughter up in his arms and carried her up the stairs. Jack and Miriam hurriedly shifted back to their hiding place. They needn't have bothered because Sugar was wholly absorbed in the task of transporting Deirdre, a handful not because of her negligible weight, but because her arms and legs were still undulating. As Sugar turned at the top of the stairs, her head lolled back and Jack had the distinct impression that Deirdre was looking into his patch of darkness, seeing him there, that he was for that moment part of her hallucinatory madness, and then the moment passed.

They lost sight of Sugar when he carried Deirdre into her room. A moment later he was outside again, pausing to slip the bolt. At the top of the stairway he stopped to pick up her nightdress. He folded it neatly, draped it over the banister, and as he turned to trudge down the stairs Jack saw that his cheeks were wet with tears.

Beside him, Miriam was crying, too. "You bastard," she whispered, punching his leg with a clenched fist. "Now you know. You saw what that old witch of a housekeeper saw. Are you satisfied?"

The punch hurt. He could feel the ache radiating from his bones. "Okay," he said. "Your father is not a monster, I'll grant him that. But I still don't know who killed Roy Drake, or why."

Miriam wiped her eyes on her sleeve and said, "Maybe nobody killed him, did you ever think of that? Maybe he just didn't try hard enough to stay alive."

Five

The Kid in a Bad Suit

Michael Fitzroy was going over the transcripts of a deposition when he heard the commotion in the outer office. The deposition related to testimony in a collision case and that's what it sounded like to Mike, a traffic accident right outside his door. Boom! His door shivered and the knob rattled.

"You can't stop me!" someone shouted in a high, frantic voice. "I'll kick it down!"

Mike opened the door and found himself looking at the bottom of a shoe. A boy dressed in an ill-fitting suit lost his balance in the act of kicking and fell into the office, groaning as he hit the floor.

Rosemary Phelan appeared. She had a yardstick in her hand and looked ready to use it—spots of red in her cheeks meant her temper was up. "Shall I call the police?" she asked. "He was threatening the girls."

Mike looked at the sprawled, miserable figure who was crawling to his knees. "Give me a few minutes," he said to Rosemary. "I think I know who this is."

Mike closed the door, walked carefully around the boy, and pulled out a comfortable chair, thumped it. "Have a seat, Mr. Drake. It is Mr. Drake, isn't it?"

Billy nodded and threw himself into the chair, which skidded under his weight. Michael settled behind his desk, thinking that he'd hit the kid with a paperweight if it came to that. Or give him a pop in the chin, that would slow him down.

"I don't have any booze in the office," Mike said. "Care for a cigarette?"

He was lying about the booze. He had a fifth of bourbon in a bottom drawer, but he wasn't about to share it with an underage boy, not even one who had attempted to kick the door down.

"I don't smoke," Bill Drake said. He tried to smooth down a cowlick and failed. "Guess the door wasn't locked, huh?"

"I'll have one if you don't mind," Mike said, lighting a cigarette with the Zippo his brother had sent him from Germany. He inhaled, basking in the malice the kid was radiating. "You regained control of yourself, Bill? Do you want to talk about it?"

Billy shrugged. The suit jacket was too short and his wrists showed. "I dunno, maybe I do, maybe I don't."

"Please try to make up your mind," Mike said. "Do you want to talk, or shall we have you arrested for assault and mayhem?"

Billy looked at the closed door. "I never assaulted no one," he said. "I cursed some, I never hit."

"Hitting is battery," Mike said. "Assault is making threats. They're both against the law."

"Are they calling the cops right now?"

Mike shook his head.

"Because I've got a gun and I'll use it," Billy said, sticking out his chin. "No cops, okay?"

Mike looked, didn't see a gun, but maybe the kid had it in his pocket, a concealed weapon. "No need for guns in here," Mike said, wishing he had one of his own. Reassured because although the kid looked angry and frightened, he didn't look like a killer. Not like, say, Richard Widmark pushing the old lady down the stairs in *Kiss of Death*, a movie he'd gone to see the night before, while Miriam was out in Hyde Park tending to her crazy sister. Double feature with *Lady from Shanghai*, Rita Hayworth and some guy with a phony Irish accent. Mike had fallen asleep before the last reel, awakened to find himself alone in the darkened theater.

"You're his brother, right?" the kid was saying. "The guy with the bum leg?"

"Why don't you tell me what you want? Maybe we can sort something out."

"The other one seen my gun. He knows."

"Jack?" Mike said. Jack hadn't mentioned that the Drake kid was armed.

"He knows," Billy said darkly.

"That was quite a stunt," Mike said in an admiring

tone. "Painting that billboard. How the hell did you get up there without a ladder?"

"Never mind the billboard," Billy said. "It didn't work, did it? They never put it in the paper. Nobody cares what that bastard does. He can steal land and see innocent people get killed, and nobody cares because he's a big name."

Mike looked at the kid—what was he, seventeen years old?—and it was hard to believe that one squeaky-voiced boy in a bad suit could be a danger to anyone. He didn't have a gun, that was bullshit. If he had a gun he'd show it. "You're not going to believe this," Mike told him, "but my brother Jack is on your side. He's actually investigating the possibility that foul play was involved in your brother's death. Which is, pardon me for saying this, but that is bullshit. It's some delusion you've got into your head. I'm sorry about your brother, I really am, but fishermen fall out of boats and drown every day in this part of the world, it's dangerous work."

Mike expected an outburst, but all Billy Drake said was "It doesn't matter now. All that matters is what happens to my mother. She needs help."

"What?"

Billy cleared his throat. Obviously it was a difficult subject for him. "Mother had what they call a breakdown," he said. "I want the money to put her in a hospital, that's why I come to you. You're a lawyer, you can get the money."

Mike sat back in the chair, pleased with this very interesting development. Wait until he told Jack about it, his successful negotiation with this supposedly unsolvable problem. "How much money are we talking, Mr. Drake?"

"I want ten thousand dollars."

"That's a lot of money. A hospital won't cost that much."

"I want ten thousand dollars," Billy insisted. His hands were fidgeting, touching his lumpy pockets. "That's what he should have paid for the island, so that's what I want. It ain't only the hospital."

Mike smiled, patted his own pockets. "Gee, Mr. Drake, I don't happen to have that much on me right at the moment."

"McKane has millions," Billy shot back. "Tell him if he gives me the money, I'll give him the pictures."

The mention of *pictures* made Mike sit up straight. He placed his cigarette in an ashtray. Made himself act calmly as he counted to three, then picked up the cigarette and took a nice calm puff. "Oh? What pictures might those be?" he said.

Six

Lady Macbeth

They looked like signal flags pinned to the clothesline. Doris in the heat of the second-floor porch, inhaling the asphalt smell of a three-decker neighborhood as she hung out the wash. The wooden taste of the pegs in her mouth, a tang of bleach. Jack's boxer shorts were the signal flags, she'd thought of them like that ever since the day an aircraft carrier had steamed into Boston Harbor in 1945, just after the war ended. Doris and her mother there on Castle Island with a few thousand patriotic residents of South Boston, waving futilely as the giant thing glided by, bound for the shipyard in Charlestown, and Mother had said, in her cranky, puzzled voice, "Look, Dot, they've got their laundry out, those dirty boys. It isn't decent."

Signal flags. Well, yes, in a manner of speaking. The full clothesline meant you had a husband, a family, a future.

The flags lied. Because Jack, her darling husband, father of her precious children, was screwing another woman. She had no proof of this, had never summoned up the courage to ask, but it was the only answer to a whole series of puzzling questions about his recent behavior. The strange distance he kept, even in bed, as if their lives were separated by a wall of glass. The furtive look in his eyes—it wasn't always there, but she'd seen it steal in like some small, frightened creature and she *knew*.

The bastard. The son of a bitch. The prick.

It was, she'd come to realize over the long summer, easy to hate and resent him when he wasn't there. The feeling was a lot more mixed up when he was around. You just had to see him playing with the boys and you began to doubt your senses. Could a man who loved his children really be screwing a woman who wasn't their mother? Would he take such a risk if he cared about the boys? Jack had to know that she would not, unlike some wives she knew right in this very neighborhood, she would not tolerate a cheating husband. The very thought of it made her breathless, not the cheating part so much as what she would have to do if it came out, if there was no doubt about the act of betrayal, if Jack told her.

Pack up the boys and leave, that's what she would do.

Where to go, that was a real problem. There wasn't room with her mother and father in that ugly little house in Dorchester. Small, dark rooms of her childhood reeking with the poison of *their* failed marriage, thirty years of simmering resentment, never missed a chance to inflict the pain of inexpressible disappointment on their own children, product of such an unpleasant union. They'd try to poison her boys—that was the reason she couldn't move back in with her parents, to protect the boys from a world of unspoken hatred.

No, she'd have to stay right here, make Jack pay for everything, the bastard, the son of a bitch, the prick. Jack who never raised his voice to her, who never started fights—well, almost never, that night in Rye Beach when he had come home so pitiful drunk he'd *wanted* to fight, but she'd made him leave before it could really get started—Jack who'd borne the pain of his withered leg without complaint. Her brave and handsome Jack of the black moods who always said, as he sat gloomy in his chair staring into some bleak corner she could not see, "It's not you, Dottie. It's me. I'll be okay."

Except he wasn't okay.

And it wasn't just with the family, she knew this for a fact, because even though Fitzroy Security was going, as Mike liked to say, "great guns," and the money was starting to be there like it had never been there before, the excitement of success, a success well beyond anything he might have experienced with the police department, none of it seemed to touch Jack.

He was aloof, lost in his thoughts, that small, frightened hiding in his eyes. Keeping himself apart from her. In love with someone else.

What could she do about it? After months of feeling sick about it, of hating him when he wasn't around and not hating him when he was there, being a good father to her sons, she had decided there was nothing she could do.

Nothing but wait and see.

Miriam was in a beauty parlor on Newbury Street, getting the whole treatment. Shampoo, cut and set, facial massage, manicure, and nail polish. The ritual was part of making herself feel clean and beautiful after a dirty, ugly week in Hyde Park. Finally she was returning to the Beacon Hill apartment, and what a relief. The expectation of normalcy—of Dee Dee returning cured—had been extinguished within minutes that first day. The big house scrubbed and polished, Dee Dee's old room newly decorated, her father's roses filling every vase, a charm to make things right. Except of course they would never be right. Ten minutes after Dr. Parkay had left his prize patient at the door, dressed up and clutching her little suitcase, ten minutes after that promising entrance Deirdre was curled up on the floor and weeping, terrified by something she could not describe.

Daytime was tolerable. Dee Dee more or less just sat in one place or another, sitting and staring at her hands, or making tentative forays into the garden with Daddy, where she seemed to be interested in watching him weed and cut and snip, but you couldn't be sure what she was really looking at with those bright and newly vacant eyes. At night, well, nights were a nightmare because if Deirdre wasn't locked in her room she would take off her clothes and wander around, seemed to think she was back in the hospital. Her father, crushed by the weight of disappointment, seemed to be entering a world of melancholy, growing ever more distant from Miriam.

He would love the idea of a grandchild, Daddy would. It would mean more to him than it meant to Jack or even to Michael. Of this she was convinced. Dee Dee was gone, she wasn't really there anymore, except as a helpless creature to care for . . . but a baby, that was hope.

"Excuse me, Mrs. Fitzroy?"

Miriam opened her eyes, picked her head up from the headrest. The manicurist, a round-faced thing with mouse brown hair, was looking at her. "Yes?" said Miriam, forcing a smile.

"What color, Mrs. Fitzroy? The nail polish."

"You choose."

"Oh, but I couldn't, Mrs. Fitzroy. What if you hated it?"

"If I hated it, I'd have you take it off, dear."

"I couldn't, really," said the girl. "All I can do is make suggestions."

Miriam sighed. "By all means, make a suggestion."

"I'll have to get the cart." The girl stood up, looking very vulnerable in her little blue smock. She seemed to be terribly worried about displeasing Miriam.

"Go get the cart," Miriam said, wanting to sound kind and patient, not feeling that way at all. "I'm not going anywhere."

The girl ran off and Miriam settled back in the chair, closed her eyes. What to do about Jack, sweet Jack, that was the next thing, now that Dee Dee was more or less settled. How big a mess to make, that was the question, and so far she had no answer. Preggers changed everything. Jack didn't get that part, you couldn't expect a man to understand, but it was different now. Not that she wanted him any less, but the clock was ticking. Ticking, ticking.

"Mrs. Fitzroy?"

The girl was back with a rolling cart, dozens of bottles of nail polish arranged by pigment. Blush Pink to Sable Red. Something called Earth Tone, sounded vaguely dirty to Miriam, she didn't want earth on her nails.

"What's this," she asked, pointing at a bottle. "Lady Macbeth?"

The girl was blushing. "Oh, that's sort of a joke."

"Explain it to me," Miriam said.

"It's from a play."

"I've heard of the play, dear."

"Well, in the play the woman gets blood on her nails, I guess. So that's the color."

"You mean it's supposed to be the color of blood?"

"I guess," said the girl with a shrug. She seemed embarrassed to admit it.

"What a clever idea," Miriam said, extending her hands to the table.

Seven

Pretty Pictures

The city of Boston, floating in a swarm of lights just across the harbor, looked close enough to touch. It was one of those clear early September nights with just a hint of autumn; the air was still warm, but you could feel where it might start getting crisp before long. Seen from the old Mill Street wharf in East Boston, where Jack leaned against the fender of his brother's Cadillac and smoked cigarette after cigarette, the heart of the city was like a luminous mirage. Clean and new and perfect, unlike the actual city reflected in the calm black water.

Is this going to be the end of it, Jack wondered, staring at the water and the lights, or is Billy boy playing another game?

"Gee, what an armpit, huh?" Mike said, looking around at the empty brick warehouses, the decayed pilings of the old wharf.

Mike was sitting behind the wheel with the radio on, listening to a Braves game. Jim Britt giving the play-by-play. Jack wasn't paying any attention because he didn't really care about baseball, certainly not the goddamn Boston Braves. Michael was the fan, he and the old man used to go together, bleacher seats. Supposed to be a big deal, but Jack couldn't get excited about it somehow. He was content to remain at the old man's grocery store, keep an eye on the canned goods. Sweep up that sawdust floor and eye the neighborhood girls coming in for chewing gum or whatever.

"You think he'll show?" Mike asked, not for the first time.

Jack shifted on the bumper, looked through the spotless windshield at his brother. "You're the one who talked to him, Mike. What do you think?"

"I think he's desperate to get his mother in the hospital, is what I think. Does that mean he'll show up here like he said he would? That I don't know.''

"Then we're even, Mike. I've got no idea what the little jerk has in mind.''

Silence for a while. Jack gazing at the dead calm waters of the harbor, aware of the game on the radio but not really listening. This was Mike's idea, meeting to pay off the kid. Except now they weren't actually going to pay him off because at the last minute Sugar had refused to come up with the ten grand. Just one reason the whole idea was, in Jack's opinion, half baked and bound to go wrong. Either ignore the threat or pay up. Having it both ways never worked.

As to the photographs, which supposedly proved that Royal Drake had been murdered, McKane swore they did not, could not exist. "He's bluffing," the old man had said. "He can't have any photographs because I never touched the man, can't you get that through your head? I had no need to threaten the young man, he had decided of his own volition to sell me the property, said he wanted to invest the money in some wretched little lobster boat. He left my house as alive as you or me, and he left it with a two-thousand-dollar check in his pocket, too. You want proof? I'll give you proof. The check was cashed by his mother the day after he died. So he not only left my house alive, he managed to get home and give the old lady the money before he fell out of his boat and drowned.''

Sugar went livid, actually bright red with rage when Mike gave him the boy's ultimatum. So mad he had trouble breathing, sounded like an asthmatic fighting for air. Pay him off? Never.

"You said fix it," Jack said. "Okay, ten grand might fix it. I think it's worth a try. Put the old lady away, at least half of the trouble stops.''

Sugar was adamant. "I won't reward a liar.''

"You'll bail out a gangster like Jimmy Keegan," Jack had pointed out, and Sugar had turned away, end of discussion.

So that was where things stood. Mike had told Billy Drake he would get the money in exchange for the photographs, and now they didn't have the money. Perfect, because Billy probably didn't have any photographs, Jack actually believed Sugar on that point: he was just too emphatic, too certain he could not be refuted.

"What do you think about square footage?" Mike asked out of the blue.

"What?" Jack had no idea what he was talking about.

"More square footage," Mike said. "I had a little discussion with the landlord today about the vacant office next door. We're going to need more space. Rosemary's new filing system is going to take up that back room where Snap keeps his gear. Danny Stearn is working out of a briefcase. I figure we could double the square footage and use every inch."

Jack ground a cigarette stub under his heel, reached for another. "Maybe we should hold off on that for a while," he said uneasily. "See how it goes."

"You need an office of your own, Jack."

"I'm mostly on the road now. You know that."

"Yeah, but you still need an office," Mike insisted. "A partner should have an office."

They were arguing about it halfheartedly when a black Cadillac limousine came around the block, fat tires thumping softly over the railroad track. It was a Costello Mortuary limo, and Sugar McKane was in the passenger seat.

The old man got out, stretched his legs. Dressed in a somber dark suit, as if he'd been assisting with a Costello funeral. He had a shoebox tucked under his arm and he looked pleased with himself. "Go on, Liam," he said, patting the limo fender. "Mike'll drop me off."

Jack eyed the shoebox as the limousine bumped back over the tracks and vanished into the night. "You're doing the right thing," he said to McKane.

"I very much doubt that," Sugar said. "But here I am."

Under the cone of light from the street lamp, McKane's massive head appeared silver tinted, and Jack saw how the old man would look if his thick black hair ever went white: a figure out of the Old Testament, the rock-jawed prophet with a honey tongue.

Mike was out of the car, and he nudged Jack on his way to greet his father-in-law. Jack knew what the nudge meant: be nice to the old man, he's brought us the money. As indeed he had. Ten-dollar bills bundled together with rubber bands, bills so soft and supple that Jack knew they hadn't come directly from a bank.

"What's this?" he said, lifting the shoebox up to his nose and sniffing. "I smell dirt, Sugar. Compost. You keep this buried in the garden? No wonder those roses win prizes, you're fertilizing them with money."

"Never you mind where it came from," Sugar said, but he was smiling ruefully and Jack knew he'd guessed right; the old man had money buried in his backyard, and this had been unearthed in the last few hours. "Ten grand won't break me, boys," he said. "Maybe it will do some good."

Jack closed the shoebox. He didn't bother counting the bundled money, it would all be there, right to the dollar. "You might get this back," he said to Sugar. "The kid hasn't shown."

Sugar nodded thoughtfully, studied the facade of the abandoned warehouse. "He pick this location, did he?"

"Yeah," Jack said. "Why do you ask?"

"Because I own the building," Sugar said. "We're going to take it down, put up a nice new steel structure. They tell me I can get a penny apiece for the bricks."

"If he doesn't show, we know where he lives," Mike pointed out.

It was Sugar who noticed the light in the warehouse window.

"There's somebody up there," he said, pointing.

Jack looked up and saw the silhouette of a figure leaning out from the second floor, waving a flashlight. "I don't like this," he said. "He never said inside the warehouse."

"Let me talk to him," Mike said, reaching for the shoebox.

Jack came very close to letting his brother have the box of money. Letting Mike enter the warehouse. A dark, shriveled part of his soul was thinking, *Billy has a gun, how much simpler if one of us dies,* and then his heart clenched and he pulled the box away from his brother and said, "You two stay here with the car, I'll handle Billy."

Mike didn't like the idea of his hotheaded brother entering the warehouse alone. "We'll all go in there together," he suggested. "Reason with him."

"You stay right here, the both of you, is that clear?" Jack said, making it an order. "Anything goes wrong, you call the cops."

There were pigeons cooing inside the warehouse, and the old, hard pine flooring was crusted inches thick with guano from the nesting birds. The cavernous interior smelled of bird droppings and the sewer stink of the harbor and the damp stench of huge wooden timbers slowly rotting. The windows on the wharf side of the building were gone, the lead casements torn out for scrap. All that remained was a row of huge, ragged holes blasted through the high brick walls, as if by a broadside of cannon shot. The only source of light was the city itself, unreal across the water, no more substantial than a swarm of fireflies. It made the deeply shadowed gloom twinkle here and there, in the wet spots of fresh bird droppings and where rainwater had gathered under the beams.

Jack picked his way cautiously around piles of fallen bricks and shipping dunnage. Here and there the thick pine flooring felt slick and dangerously soft underfoot—fall through and he'd be up to his neck in the shit-stink ooze beneath the wharf. What a terrible way to die, clotted in black mud. How much quicker the sudden, numbing shock of a .45-caliber bullet. Just a flash of hot light in the darkness and then eternity.

Not that he thought Billy would shoot him, or anyone. The boy had had his chance there at the YMCA, and he'd chosen not to kill. Small reassurance as Jack picked his way through the rubble to a wide, cast-iron stairway. Mounting the stairs, his bad leg began to twitch. Sparkles of heat in a foot that felt like a lead boot bumping the iron stairs. Thump, thump, here I am.

At the top of the stairs he stopped to catch his breath. Wheezing like an old man. The air up here was hotter and sharp with the ammoniated stench of the pigeons cooing gently in the rafters.

"You there, Bill?" Jack said, panting.

A thin voice drifted out from the darkness. "Over here."

Jack started toward the the voice. "Are you armed?"

The voice seemed to have changed location. "What if I am?" it said.

Jack held out his hands. "Because I'm carrying a shoe-box. See it? Money in the shoebox, Bill."

"This way," the voice said softly. Closer now, much closer. "Over here."

The flashlight clicked on and Jack's heart went bang, like that he was drenched with adrenaline. Bill Drake emerged from behind a pillar not six feet away, pointing the flashlight and maybe something else, it was hard to tell.

If he's going to do it, Jack thought, let him do it right now.

"You're limping pretty bad," Billy said. His voice was barely a whisper. "Have a seat."

The beam of the light settled on a crate. Jack hobbled over—the leg was starting to cramp up, stiffening at the knee—and lowered himself to the crate. This is what it's like to be an old man, he thought, afraid of dying and wanting it to happen, fear and pain and desire in a broken shell.

Billy clicked off the light. "Don't worry about the gun," he said. "I left it under my bed."

"Mind if I smoke? I'm just going to reach in my pocket, get my cigarettes."

Billy made a sniffing sound. "I didn't bring the gun, Mr. Fitzroy. Honest."

"And I believe you," Jack said. He tried to shake a cigarette out of the pack and was amazed at how much his hands were trembling. Just his hands. Inside he was calm, his heartbeat was back to normal. He inhaled deeply, let the smoke sear his lungs, and that seemed to help calm his hands. "Here," he said, holding out the shoebox, "for your mother."

Billy took the box gingerly, clicked the light on for just long enough to see that it did indeed contain money. Jack shifted over on the crate and made room for him to sit down.

"What a life, huh, kid?" Jack said. The pigeons were squabbling overhead, claws skittering on the beams.

"I didn't think you'd bring the money," Billy said. "I thought . . . well, I thought you might kill me and just take the pictures."

In the dark Jack grinned to himself. Mexican standoff

and not a gun between them. "But you came anyhow," he said, "thinking that?"

"I had to," the boy said.

"So what happens next?" Jack said. "With your mother, I mean."

"Never mind about Mother," he said sharply. "You want these pictures or don't you?"

"Sure," Jack said. "Let's see the pretty pictures."

The photographs were in a metal-clasp envelope. This is what Billy had been holding in his other hand, the shape Jack had mistaken for a weapon. Billy waited while he undid the clasp, fingered the scalloped edges of the snapshot-sized prints, detected the slippery, celluloid surface of a negative.

"The light," Jack said. "Let's have a look."

When the beam of light found the photographs and the images leaped out, Jack felt his heart quicken, his pulse hammering, as if he had suddenly been immersed in deep water. "Who took these, Bill?" he asked when he felt capable of speech again.

"I did. Roy wanted me to."

The images were, at a glance, quite innocent. A handsome young man with his arm around a pretty dark-haired girl. The couple was standing in the cockpit of a boat, looked to be the same boat Jack had boarded at the pier, and yes, there it was painted across the transom, *Irene*. Named for the mother, he hadn't noticed that before.

"What makes you think she killed your brother?" said Jack. The words were strange in his mouth, as if he was watching himself talk.

"Roy would never fall out of a boat and drown," Billy said, his voice barely audible. "He was always real careful. There's no way he'd let himself get killed accidental. I figure she must have pushed him."

"You saw her do it?"

"No," he said. "They wanted to be alone. I went on home. It was the next morning they found the boat adrift."

Out in the harbor a foghorn had started sounding. The pigeons had stopped making noise, as if responding to the mournful hoot of the foghorn. The tide had changed and the air felt different, cooler and redolent of salt and seaweed.

"Tell me something," Jack heard himself say. "These pictures, what do you think they prove?"

Billy sounded almost hurt. "They prove he loved her," he said earnestly. "That's what killed him, as much as anything."

Jack grunted and got to his feet. It was going to be a long way down the cast-iron stairway, carrying pictures that seared his heart.

"Maybe you should get a cane," Billy suggested.

Jack was about to tell him to go to hell when a woman screamed in the street below. A moment later there was a gunshot, and another scream.

"Mother!" Billy said.

They both ran for the stairs, into the darkness below.

Eight

Okay, He Said

That iron stairway. It was like leaping into a huge, dark mouth, giving himself up to an instinct he'd forgotten he had, the instinct for pure, unthinking action. Down he went, feet hardly touching the steps. It wasn't that his bad leg was functioning any better than it had on the way up, it was just that it didn't matter. It wasn't pretty, but he was running.

Behind him, Billy skittered and lost his balance.

"Ah, shit! Mother, wait! Wait!"

Irene Drake swayed drunkenly in the street. She was yelling incoherently and the old army-issue .45 was so heavy she had to use both hands to hold it. Slogging along in rubber boots. Jack noticed the boots almost before he saw the gun, black rubber boots with unsnapped fasteners, and her legs white and thick rising out of the boots, most of her squat, bulky body covered by a housedress. Ignore the gun and she looked like an elderly housewife who had hurriedly donned a robe to collect the milk on a rainy morning. Except that it was not raining and you could not ignore the gun because she squeezed of another round just as Jack stumbled out of the warehouse.

She was trying to shoot the Cadillac. Enraged by the gleam and the chrome and the insolent tonnage of Mike's pricy new convertible. Irene maybe ten yards away, struggling to hold the gun up, and the first two shots had missed, far wide of the mark. Jack heard—and later this would surprise him, that he remembered this particular detail—he heard the second cartridge being ejected, the bright ping of it being expelled from the chamber and tinkling onto the street.

"Jew bastards!" Irene screamed. "Killers!"

Jack picked up a brick. He was too far away to throw

it, and he was hobbling over the broken ground, trying to get in range, when Irene fell heavily to her knees, screamed as if in pain, and then emptied the gun at the big, glittering target of the Coupe DeVille. Jack saw the dark form of Sugar McKane struggling to pitch himself over the front seat, seeking shelter in the back, and he saw Mike open the door, one arm up to shield his head, as if he was about to get out and run.

By the time the brick was airborne, it was all over. The gun was empty, and Irene had thrown it away and lay facedown on the street, wailing and crying.

"Mother!" Billy shouted from somewhere behind him. "Mother, don't!"

Like the brick, which exploded into dust yards from its target, Billy's command came too late. The damage was done. The front windshield was gone and one of the tires was flat to the rim, so that the front end of the Caddy listed. When Jack got to the car Mike was still behind the wheel, shaking his head in amazement, his mouth open.

Sugar McKane's black head poked up from behind the seat. His eyes found Jack. "There's blood on my shoes," he said.

Mike had stopped shaking his head. He reached out and tried to touch where the windshield had been only moments before. Diamond points of the shattered safety glass all over the hood and dash and in Mike's lap. The radio was still working and Boston Braves announcer Jim Britt was talking about a stolen base, saying you wouldn't believe it, folks, that was grand larceny.

"Mike? Hey!" said Jack as his brother slumped from behind the wheel and fell backward to the curb.

The leather seat was slick with blood that looked oil-black under the street lamp. Mike's white shirt was drenched, sticking to him. His collar turned dark and wet while Jack was looking, that's how fast it was happening, and then Jack was down on the ground with his brother, heaving him away from the curbstone. He heard Sugar saying "Oh Lord, oh Lord," as the old man crouched beside him, Jack trying to rip open the soggy shirt and find the hole, stop the fountain of blood that was leaking out of Mike.

"He's dying," Sugar said. "Michael, can you say an act of contrition with me?"

Jack lifted his bloody fist and shoved the old man out of the way, and he slipped his hands through his brother's shirt and found the hole in his chest, pressed his hand flat, pressure on the wound, aware of something like a heartbeat under his palm. He heard his brother breathing, felt his chest rise and fall, and then he found the courage to look Mike in the face and into his eyes and see him alive in there, eyes looking right back at him; interested, curious eyes, what was Jack going to do about *this* little problem, huh? Did he have a plan? And Jack wanted the heart under his hands to stop beating, just for a while, until he had the situation under control, because every beat was pumping blood out the wound in his back, where the bullet had punched out a fist-sized hole of ragged flesh, a wound too large to be blocked, and there was only so much blood in any man, even a guy as big and full of it as Michael Fitzroy, leaking away in the street here, his eyes staring inquisitively at Jack's face, studying his young brother. He seemed very interested in everything Jack was trying to do, he'd always been interested in what Jack might do next, and he had the look he got when he was about to take out his steno pad, make a note of this.

Michael smiled and said, "Okay," and then he managed somehow to reach up and he squeezed Jack's hand where it lay against his heart. A reassuring squeeze. Mike took a deep shuddering breath, held it for a long moment, beat beat beat of his heart, and then the air went out of him and that was it, his eyes filmed over and he was gone.

"They ran away," said Sugar McKane, looming above him. "The kid and his mother, they ran away. Help me get a priest."

Nine

Rules of Behavior

On the T the other passengers slipped quietly away, avoiding him. Careful not to look Jack Fitzroy in the eye as if, he supposed, they instinctively understood that he was on a special quest. This was before he happened to glance at his hands, see the drying blood stains, and then he knew why the other riders were making room. They were frightened.

Let them be, he decided, let everyone be frightened. He was not like them, he was a stranger to himself, he was a small, unfeeling thing that traveled inside a limping, imperfect body. And he had not a clue as to what he was doing from moment to moment. Leaving his brother dead in the gutter, walking away from Sugar McKane as he whined for a priest, we must find a priest, and now here he was on the MTA as the train squealed to a halt in Park Street station, and he had still had no idea.

There was pain as he heaved himself up the flights of steps to street level, pain easily ignored, even welcomed because it kept him wide awake when what he really wanted to do was find a bench on the Common and sleep for a year or two. Instead he limped into the public lavatory building located behind the station, a notorious rendezvous for sodomites, and washed his hands in the iron sink. Avoided the mirror, he wasn't ready for a mirror. Had the place to himself, no lonesome queers in the loo tonight; they'd been rousted by sneering patrolmen, tormented by the townies who roamed the Common, looking for entertainment.

When his hands were clean, Jack limped up Park Street. The townies were lurking in the vicinity of the Civil War monument, flaunting their brown bottles of beer as they swilled and swore, and Jack expected to be

challenged, for he knew these brutal toughs did not con-
fine their efforts to humiliating queers, they preyed eagerly upon any perceived weakness. A beer bottle
exploded on the sidewalk a few yards away, but that was
all. No one followed it out from the shadows of the monument to taunt him, and then he was clear of Park Street,
walking west on Beacon with the State House over his
shoulder, the great bald dome rising like a gold-leaf moon
over Beacon Hill.

The apartment was on the first floor of an elegant
brownstone a few streets up from Beacon. The incline
was steep here, and he had to lean into it as he trudged
up the slope, dragging his foot, and he still had no idea
why he was going to this place, or what he would say
when he got there. Detective without a clue, cop without
a badge. Still, he was moving, doing something. Keep
moving for as long as he could because when he stopped,
well, he had no idea what would happen then and the
thought of not knowing frightened him. It meant anything was possible, anything at all.

The lights were on in the apartment. She was in there
and by all the rules of behavior he was supposed to stand
in the doorway with his hat in his hand and give her the
terrible gift, wrapped up with a ribbon of consoling
words. That was his duty as a brother and a lover and a
man of the law. But when she opened the door and saw
him, the inward expression on her face changed everything.

"Jack," she said. "What are you doing here?"

Words came to him. "It's about the pictures, Miriam.
Tell me about the pictures."

He walked into the room, closed the door, and locked
it. He'd never liked this apartment, with its white-painted
walls and the Picasso lithographs and the strangely modern furniture displayed like works of art. Hated the place
not because of how it was decorated, but because this
was where Miriam lived and slept with the man she had
married.

"Jack, what's wrong?" Miriam, slim-waisted in a
green silk dressing gown, smelled of lilac-scented bath
soap. "Where's Michael?"

"He's in East Boston," Jack said. Amazed at his ability to form sentences from thoughts that had never crossed

his mind. "With your father. They're waiting for a priest." More and more amazing, the way he could keep lying by telling the truth.

Miriam backed up until she bumped into a chair. She sat down, keeping her knees together, and her troubled eyes kept flicking to the door.

"Waiting for a priest?" Her husky voice was pitched higher and thinner than usual. "Did you kill someone, Jack, is that what happened?"

Jack found a chair, a chrome thing with black leather slings, and he placed it opposite Miriam and he sat down. Weight off his leg, the pain wasn't touching him, he was using the pain, but still it was a relief to be sitting down.

"The pictures, Miriam. The photographs." He reached into his breast pocket and withdrew the envelope Bill Drake had given him. He opened the clasp and something happened, his hand twitched, and the snapshots fell to the floor, fanned out like glossy playing cards with scalloped white edges.

Miriam picked up one of the small photographs, glanced at the image. "I don't remember this," she said, almost a casual tone. "Oh, wait, the kid brother, he had this little Brownie. I guess it must have been him."

"Billy Drake," Jack said. "Keepsake pictures of big brother and his girlfriend."

"I wasn't exactly a girlfriend," said Miriam. She put the photo down on the arm of her chair and did not look at it again.

"Snapshot taken on big brother's boat, the day big brother drowned."

Miriam shook her head, black hair full and soft on the green silk shoulders of her dressing gown. Was she glowing inside that gown, body heat radiating through the silk, or were his eyes playing tricks? "I wasn't there when it happened," she said. "It was an accident. He was drunk."

"You let me think it was Deirdre who was with Roy Drake that day."

"No," Miriam said emphatically. "I did no such thing. I told you Dee Dee couldn't have been involved."

"Because you were?"

She shrugged. "I knew it wasn't Dee Dee. And *I* didn't kill the poor fool. That's all that mattered. I can't help it if his pathetic, lunatic family invented a conspiracy. Roy was alive when I left him. Alive and drunk.''

Jack said, ''Tell me what happened that day.''

''I don't like your tone,'' she said. ''And what does it matter now, what happened?'' She studied him, made a little sound of impatience. ''Okay, you really want to know? It was nothing. Daddy had him over to the house a few times, on business. Roy was awfully good-looking, okay? Kind of a Robert Mitchum type, the way he was built, the way he walked. Except he was really sweet, you know?''

''I never saw the man alive,'' Jack said. ''How could I know?''

''Well, take my word. I just wanted a little fun, that's all. So I teased him for a while, just fooling around, and then the last time he was there I said I'd go back with him. To see this great island he was selling to Daddy. What a joke. Jesus Christ, a piece of rock with a shack on it, that's all it was.''

''You went out to Drake Island with him?'' Jack said.

''That's what I just said, Jack, aren't you paying attention? Anyhow, he had some booze out there and we drank it and we got pretty stoned. You want all the dirty little details, is that what you want? You want me to tell you what it was like screwing a guy named Royal Drake? Did I mention he smelled like lobster bait?''

''That's enough,'' he said. ''You're on the island. How'd you get back to shore?''

''On his boat, of course. I'd left my car at the wharf.''

''He stayed on the boat?''

Miriam nodded. ''Said he had work to do. Excuse me, traps to pull. I suppose that's how he drowned. They found him tangled up in a rope, I heard. Like maybe he lost his balance and was pulled over by the weight of a trap. I don't know about that. All I know is Daddy didn't have any reason to kill him, and I certainly didn't, so it was like the police said all along, an accident.''

''Billy found him,'' Jack said. ''Brother Billy. He said it was the crazy sister had been with him, I assumed Deirdre.''

''Dee Dee wasn't well enough to be chasing after handsome lobstermen from East Boston, Jack. It was right around then Daddy had to put her back in the clinic.''

"Because Mrs. O'Hare saw her dancing naked in the music room. Saw your father with his naked daughter and suspected the worst.''

Miriam made a sound of disgust. "That crazy old bitch. She never said a thing to us, no way to explain it to her, what Dee Dee was like, she just ran away to the priest. Daddy saw the old bat found another place to live, what else could he do?''

Jack picked up the photographs, returned them to the envelope and fastened the clasp, and left the envelope on the arm of her chair, to do with as she pleased. "Why did Roy Drake think you were crazy, Miriam?''

"Who says he did?''

"That's what he told his kid brother. That he'd met a crazy girl and he thought he could help her somehow.''

Miriam shrugged. "I'm a rich girl and I like my fun. The way some men see it, that makes me crazy. Any woman who enjoys sex must be insane, you know?''

"You could have told me,'' Jack said.

"You never asked,'' Miriam said. "If you asked was it me fooling around with Roy Drake, maybe I would have told you.''

"Maybe?'' he said.

"Maybe not,'' she conceded. "You get jealous of my husband, imagine how you'd feel about a guy I slept with on a whim.'' She paused, looked at her nails. "Are you going to tell me about it?'' she asked. "You can't have killed poor Roy because he's already dead. So who did you kill?''

"What makes you think I killed someone?''

Miriam pointed. Jack looked down, saw the brown blood spatters on his pant cuffs, his shoes, his trouser legs. If she wanted to think he had killed someone, then fine, maybe he would kill someone before the night was through. Anything was possible, since he never knew what he was going to do from moment to moment.

He stood up to leave, not really sure where he was going from here. Home to Doris and the boys? What was he supposed to do now? What were the rules of behavior for a death in the family? At the very least he was obliged to tell Miriam about her husband, dead in the street, and he hadn't done that, so obviously he wasn't all that concerned with obeying the rules.

"Has Michael seen those pictures?" she wanted to know. Trying to sound merely curious, but obviously quite concerned.

Jack shook his head. He had become aware of a vehicle in the street, right outside the apartment door, motor idling. He limped over to the window, looked out, and saw Sugar McKane exiting a Costello funeral limousine. Sugar with his face of stone. Sugar in his black suit, come to tell his daughter the terrible truth.

"It's your father," Jack said, turning from the window. "I'm leaving by the back."

"Daddy's here?" Miriam sounded suddenly on the verge of panic. "Is it about Dee Dee?"

Jack didn't bother answering. He left without touching her and limped to the corner of Charles Street, where he finally managed to hail a cab.

"Berkeley Street," he said. "Police Headquarters."

Ten

Two Men and a Bed

Later that night, much later, Jack Fitzroy found himself on the police boat *Argus,* cutting fast on a compass course through the harbor fog, heading for Drake Island.

"Pea soup," said Captain Delaney. "By God, you could cut it with a knife."

It was Delaney, of course, who'd taken charge of the Michael Fitzroy homicide investigation, and as the ranking officer in the prestigious unit he had every intention of being present when the suspect and her accomplice were arrested. Billy left the gun under his mattress, Jack had said, the old lady found it. That first eyewitness statement taken down by the squad's best stenographer, called out of bed to get it right, and the captain had coughed into his fist and said, the lad is an accomplice if he helped her to get away, Jack, surely you know that?

Surely he did, but his brain wasn't functioning very well, and he wasn't quite sure why Francis X. Delaney had decided to take him along, this fog-crazy boat ride. Or why he was being treated so special by everybody in the department—one of the new uniformed recruits had actually saluted, Jack didn't know him from a hole in the ground.

Delaney was on the marine radio for most of the trip, headgear and microphone, communicating with the police officers already staked out at the island, awaiting his arrival before they moved on the shack where, it was believed, Irene Drake, aided by her son William, had taken refuge. Jack wasn't paying attention to the radio reports, he was mesmerized by the fog, the shapes he saw roiling in the mist. A faint glow he noticed, that had to be the airport, shut down for lack of visibility. The steady thrum of the boat engine seemed to ease the pain in his leg, he was numb from the knee down. Aware that

he had done some damage to the already damaged muscles, maybe he'd take Billy's suggestion, get a cane. Ask
Hamish Higgins about that, the effete columnist had a
flair for canes.

Jack was staring into the mist and thinking about canes
and crutches when a ship took form, as if condensing
from invisible drops of moisture. A great gray thing lying
at anchor, streaked with blood. No, of course it wasn't
blood, it was rust, he saw that at once, it was scabs of
rust puckering the hull. A few lighted portholes indicated
there was life aboard, although none of it stirred, and no
one acknowledged the little *Argus* as it swerved under
the high stern. Jack saw chains as thick as a man's waist
drooping like watch fobs from the giant rudder, and for
a moment the smell of oxidizing steel was as strong as
the sewer stink of the harbor waters, as strong as the lilac
perfume of Miriam, all these smells mingling in his mind,
tastes on his tongue, and the taste of rust was very like
the taste of blood, that tang of iron and ozone.

The fog closed behind them and the ship was gone.
Maybe it had never been there at all, Jack thought. The
idea was appealing. A dream ship anchored in the mist,
cut off from the world.

The *Argus* steamed on. Jack had little sense of time,
was it minutes, an hour? All at once the cop at the helm
pulled back the throttle and threw the gear lever into
reverse. The stern of the *Argus* settled and the boat
slowed.

A small pier took form, extending from the wet shore
of an island. At the pier two other police patrol boats
were rafted together. The lobster boat *Irene* had been
shoved aside to make room, and the white hull was
bumping up against the kelp-encrusted rocks.

"All ashore that's going ashore," said the cop at the
helm, making a joke of it.

A swarm of uniformed men appeared, reaching for
lines, snugging the boat to the pier. Speaking in quiet
voices made hollow by the fog and the lapping water and
the hard, wet rock of the island.

"Oh, they're in there, all right, Captain," a sergeant
announced with an air of self-importance. "Didn't he
fire off a shot and make Officer Mahoney dance a jig?"

Jack didn't know the puffed-up sergeant, but he recognized Lou Moakley emerging from the dimness, a bolt-action rifle slung over his shoulder. "We'll get the buggers, Jack," he promised. "They've no place to run. Jesus, but it's terrible news about your brother. He was a helluva guy, Mike was."

Jack realized that virtually the entire Homicide Unit was on the island, called out in the middle of the night. God, even Corcoran was there, away from his desk at last. Accompanying the unit was a squad of rifle-toting patrolmen and a police sharpshooter named Eddy Briggs, who, it was rumored, had shot Japs by the dozen when they cleaned up Okinawa.

"You'd never guess it to look at him, but the guy can shoot out your eye at a hundred yards," said Corky. "Tough luck about your brother," he added, "but the bastards who did it, they're as good as dead."

Jack said, "It was an old woman, Corky. A crazy old woman."

"Well, she ain't gonna get much older."

Delaney was quietly exerting his authority, telling the eager patrolmen to keep down, make sure the flashlights and the lanterns were muted. Nobody knew what kind of armaments Billy Drake might have stored in that shack.

"Sounded like a carbine," Lou Moakley said. "You know the way a carbine whines? And we recovered the Colt at the scene, so we know he doesn't have that."

"The man actually fired at an officer," Delaney asked. "That's been established?"

"Somebody fired," Coakley said with a shrug. "I suppose it could be the old lady, we know she can fire a weapon."

Jack was just standing there on a patch of rock where the pier met the shore, couldn't quite make out the shack, not in the night fog. He was aware of the cop electricity starting to build and spark, the men getting charged up for a confrontation, possibly a gun battle, and he was thinking about what it was he intended to do, or if he really intended to do anything, when Corky thrust a rifle at him.

"Captain said it was okay, we'd make an exception for you."

"What?" Jack said. The rifle was slick and heavy in his hands, and so new the Cosmoline hadn't been properly wiped from the barrel.

"You being a civilian now," Corky explained. "We're to make an exception. You'll get a shot, he says, just like the rest of us."

He handed the rifle back to Corky and went over to Delaney, where the captain stood fiddling with a megaphone and the battery pack to power it. Delaney turned expectantly as Jack approached.

"Has anybody talked to the kid?" Jack asked. "Maybe he'll surrender."

"Mahoney tried and that was when the shot was fired, so they tell me. I won't risk another man, it wouldn't be smart." Delaney leaned closer, studying Jack's face, and then patted him reassuringly on the shoulder. "We'll try the hailer," he said, holding up the megaphone. "See what happens, if that's how you want it."

Delaney was as good as his word. He crept up the hardy, rocky path from the pier, skidding along planks laid over the rock, Jack following close behind. When Delaney switched on the hailer, his ragged breath was amplified into a blast of wind:

"This is Captain Delaney of the Boston Police Department. Surrender now or suffer the consequences."

He clicked off the hailer. Echoes resonated from rock to sea, distorted by the fog. The response was almost immediate. There was the crack and whine of a rifle shot—a carbine as Coakley had suggested—and then a man was shouting indignantly from the pier.

"He shot out a lantern, Captain! I heard the bullet go by!"

Delaney rolled over, looked back to where Jack crouched. "Well, we tried," he said. "He's making a stand, what choice do we have?"

Jack said, "Let me try," and he grabbed the hailer before Delaney could react. Hum of the megaphone in his hands as he found the switch.

"Billy, this is Jack Fitzroy. I want to come up there. I'm not armed."

Delaney snatched the hailer back. "You'll do no such thing," he said sternly. "You've gone a little soft in the noggin, lad, and it's no wonder, but there's no sense in you getting shot, too."

The next thing Jack found himself gimp-running up the path, evading the grasp of Delaney and the others who tried to stop him. It was slow and fast all at the same time, and he watched himself amazed, because he'd had no intention of doing this, charging cripple-quick up the path and waving his hands, not sure whether Billy Drake could see who it really was in the night fog. Shouting, ''It's me, Bill, don't shoot!''

There was a crack, a whine, but the carbine shot was aimed elsewhere, not at Jack, and somehow he knew this, knew that Billy Drake wasn't going to shoot him as he limped along the path, hands high in the air. Aware that Delaney's sharpshooter, the famous Jap killer, might be drawing a bead on his back just for practice.

''Billy! Can you see me?''

He was within a few yards of the little shack. The place wasn't any bigger than a garden shed, Sugar McKane kept his wheelbarrow in a building grander than this. He could make out a small window, black against dark, the shape of a shed door. The response, when it came, sounded like a voice whispering into his ear, as intimate as a kiss, but that was the fog doing strange things, had to be.

''What do you want?'' it said.

Jack lowered his voice, aware that a shout might set the sharpshooter off, make him squeeze that nervous Okinawa trigger finger. ''I don't know,'' Jack said. ''But you better let me in.''

''You don't know why you came?''

''No idea,'' Jack said. ''It seemed like a good idea. Now I'm not so sure.''

There was a faint creaking, and the shape of the shed door altered. When Jack got close enough a hand came out of the opening and pulled him roughly inside, into the enveloping darkness of the shack. Loose boards under his feet. Breath in his face, the sour pong of fear and adrenaline, and a strong hand shoving him down to the floor. He did not resist. ''She didn't mean to hurt your brother,'' Billy said hoarsely. ''Mother was shooting at the car.''

''At Sugar, I think it was,'' Jack said.

''Not your brother, though. That was an accident.''

The hand that had been grasping him by the collar let go, and Jack's eyes were starting to adjust, he could make out forms. "Where is she?" he asked. "Where's your mother?"

"Behind you," Billy said. "I had to tie her to the cot."

"They mean to kill you both," Jack said.

"What do you care?"

"I don't, not really."

"Then why'd you come up here?" Billy said. Faceless in the dark, he sounded about twelve years old. "For God's sake, what do you want from us?"

"Nothing," Jack said. "I don't want a thing."

"Mother will die in jail."

"You still got the ten grand?" Jack asked. "You can buy a good Irish lawyer for ten grand. Hell, you could buy three or four, really put on a show."

Billy sounded interested. "Irish lawyer?"

"You want to beat the system in this town, kid, you better get yourself an Irish lawyer."

Francis X. Delaney was lying prone, squinting through a pair of so-called night binoculars. The war-surplus gear made his eyes ache, made him think he was seeing things.

"Hey, Lou?"

"Yes, Frank."

"See anything there?"

Lou Moakley lifted his head and peered at the ridge. Was the fog a little thinner? Hard to tell. Nothing going on up there for almost thirty minutes now. Not a peep out of the Drakes or Jack Fitzroy, the damn fool. But like the captain, he thought he saw something, he couldn't say what, and maybe he'd been too long out here in the mist and fog, his mind was supplying images where none existed.

Then he heard Jack Fitzroy, top of his lungs, singing out, "Hold your fire, boys! We're coming out!"

Delaney swore and threw his binoculars aside. 'Can't see a damned thing," he said. "Which one is Jack? Jesus Christ, tell that crazy Briggs with the night scope to hold his fire."

The word was passed along, but no one needed to call off Patrolman Edwin G. Briggs, who had indeed shot Japs by the dozen, because he could see very well indeed through the night scope, and he had no intention of shooting an unarmed man, or possibly wounding a former police detective.

"Two men and a bed," Briggs said, and the word was passed back down the line.

"What?" Delaney roared. "Two men and a what?"

"Two men and a bed, sir. And it looks like they got the woman tied to the bed."

It was true, as Delaney finally saw with his own eyes. Jack Fitzroy and Billy Drake were coming down the path, carrying between them a cottage bed, and tied to the bed was Irene Drake, her eyes rolling wild and her mouth stopped with a handkerchief. Delaney didn't notice the eyes until he was close up and his men were snapping the cuffs on the unresisting accomplice, the kid just kneeling down with his head bowed, as if he expected to be executed.

"Should we cuff the woman, sir?"

"Damn right you'll cuff her," he said. "And leave the gag on, too, for the time being."

Jack Fitzroy had collapsed the moment he let go of the cot. Lying there on the wet ground in pain, that much was obvious.

"Are you hurt, son?" Delaney wanted to know. "Did he wound you with that carbine?"

Jack shook his head and said through gritted teeth, "Just a cramp. The old lady weighs a ton."

"You know you're a damn fool?"

"I do," said Jack.

He didn't fight it when Delaney helped him stand up, or when the captain and Lou Moakley linked hands behind his back and carried him down to the pier and the waiting boat.

Eleven

A Veil of Glass

Sugar McKane opened up his Hyde Park home for the wake, and it was Hamish Higgins in the *Transcript* who pointed out that the great house had been built for that purpose and never before put to use. Higgins mentioned the flowers, of course, for the flowers were indeed remarkable. Sugar had taken all of the roses from the garden, and had more brought down from the estate in Rye Beach. Roses pale red, roses pink, roses crimson, magenta, and carmine. Roses of every conceivable shade, including blood red, the luminous red that shows as full of life. Jack noticed this as intently as he noticed everything that evening of his brother's wake: he noticed that none of the roses were the color of rust, the color of death. For Sugar, too, had been splattered with Michael's fading blood, and although he never mentioned this to Jack, or to anyone, Jack knew what *he* knew. It was another thing they shared now.

The roses, displayed in vases of all sizes, in stem glasses, in fluted porcelain, were softly, blurrily reflected in the polished panels of walnut and mahogany in the grand foyer and the parlor. The roses were sharply, crisply doubled in the cut-glass mirrors of the connecting hallways, and the multitude and variety of the blossoms made such an impression on three-year-old David Fitzroy that more than forty years later he would distinctly recall the roses as he could not recall the sight of his Uncle Mike lying still and waxen in a velvet-lined box. On that evening, though, it had a profound effect on him, as he somehow caught a glimpse from the room that adjoined the parlor where Michael was being waked.

"Mommy, Mommy," he cried, pointing from her arms. "There he is, he's only sleeping!"

Robby Fitzroy, all of seven and wearing his stiff new

suit, fitted to him earlier in the day by two Brooks Brothers tailors, working softly over the solemn boy with pins held ready in their wet, chalky lips, young Robby was old enough to understand what had happened, even if he could not yet fathom grief. He, too, would recall certain images many years later, the most vivid of which was not, for him, the quantity and quality of the roses, but the sight of his Aunt Miriam dressed in mourning and wearing black sunglasses. Just like, he told his father proudly, a real movie star.

Miriam wore the dark glasses because the idea of a veil made her breathless, and because she did not want anyone to see that she hadn't been crying. Tears had not come at the death of her beloved mother, or indeed at any crisis, and they would not come for Michael, whose sudden departure from her life was as unreal as the notion that her father might transform her childhood home into an elegant, flower-infested funeral parlor. A dummy of her husband had been placed in a casket, she'd seen and accepted that, understood that he had died, but the man himself was in another room consorting with friends, and any moment now he would stroll in to greet her with his devoted eyes, wanting to be petted. Until that happened, until Michael made himself known, she was compelled to impersonate a widow.

I can't believe it, was her refrain that evening, and in some secret part of her she did *not* believe it. Dark glasses secure, handkerchief in hand to dab her dry cheeks, Miriam moved through the rooms as if she had been rendered weightless.

Jack Fitzroy saw her, of course, but for a long time hesitated to offer his condolences. What would he say to her, what would she say to him? What further pain, what promises of pleasure might they inflict on each other, even in these somber moments? He would speak to her before the evening was over, but for now he stayed close to the guest register, clasping hands, making herself greet the seemingly endless line of family friends, cousins, business acquaintances, and colleagues who eventually filled the McKane household.

Tony Grazi, looking slim and immaculate, an Old World gentleman in a dark blue suit, squeezed Jack's hands and said, "Anything we can do, just ask. Anything at all,'' and Dougie Donnelly was there with his damp-eyed wife, and Snap Edwards big as a black bear, and Danny Stearn in his quiet way keeping himself apart even as he silently acknowledged Jack with an expression that said: I understand this pain of yours and will not demean it with platitudes. Rosemary Phelan came with her husband, icily imperious, holding herself erect and proper with great dignity, until she entered the parlor and saw Michael Fitzroy in his coffin, and then Rosemary wailed, a cry so desolate and shrill that it put ice in the veins of even the most casual or distantly connected mourners, and she collapsed sobbing into her husband's arms and could not, would not be consoled.

Big Bob Cogan, head and massive shoulders above the crowd, avoided Jack's eye, nodding awkwardly as he glanced away, embarrassed by the spectacle, Jack supposed, and then he was distracted by Lawrence Corcoran pumping his hand and grinning, unaware that his jovial manner was out of place, unable to contain his excitement at the news he carried. ''They got him, Jack! Jimmy Torch! Jimmy Keegan! This guy up on assault charges ratted to a cell mate, see, about how Keegan had hired him to kill Stinky Doyle, and when the cell mate turned, the guy ratted back on Keegan! Beautiful, huh? We got a statement, Jack, it was only an hour ago, and they just picked up that bastard Jimmy, you should have seen his face!''

''That's great,'' Jack made himself say, ''that's wonderful. Glad you could make it, Corky, we appreciate it.''

Corcoran looked around at the crowd, understood that his enthusiasm was misplaced, and said, ''Oh yeah, and you know I'm sorry about your brother.''

''I do, Corky, yes,'' and so on to the next guest, and the next, a blur of familiar faces and faces not so familiar, one of them a Brahmin-looking creature whose eyes were set too far apart, whose flesh was so pale and mottled with freckles that Jack couldn't help but think he looked like a fish, a spotted flounder got up in a lawyer's costume, and talking with a prep school plum in his mouth. ''Emmett Dunning,'' this pale creature said. 'Of Dunning, Chase. I knew your brother briefly and I liked him well enough to sign up with Fitzroy Security. Liked him well enough that I see no reason to change our plans. Assuming you intend to carry on."

"I haven't thought about it," Jack said.

"Of course you haven't," Dunning said. "Plenty of time for that."

Doris Fitzroy had staked out an area in the room that adjoined the parlor, away from the slowly undulating line of mourners who wished to view the body, because she did not wish to view the body, did not want her boys to see it lying there on display. The whole idea of an open coffin, the notion of a wake, was so barbaric, in her strongly held opinion, that she felt like screaming. Screaming like Rosemary Phelan at this morbid celebration. Screaming—and this was the real reason for her anxiety—because her mother was sitting right beside her in a folding chair, weeping coyly and fingering a rosary. Her old mother who had openly despised the deceased for having ambition, for wanting to better himself beyond his station, and for marrying a wealthy and beautiful woman from the class above his own. Her jealous, spiteful mother weeping her satisfied tears. "You old hypocrite, knock it off," she finally said, little David sleepy on her hip. "Put those stupid beads away or I swear I'll slap your face," and her mother was so shocked by this command, so stunned, that she said not a word and complied, dropped the rosary into her purse and sat dry-eyed and bewildered, wondering when it was that her daughter had learned to read minds.

A while later Babs Marcotte came in to sit with Doris, and rest her baby-swollen belly. "My God, what if I go into labor right here?" she said, hands on the bump. "Wouldn't *that* be a scandal," managing to get a smile out of grim-faced Dottie. "Patsy Doulin would have come, but she and the baby are still in the hospital. Jaundice. They say it isn't serious."

"Patsy has jaundice?"

"No, the baby. It propped out looking like a bar of yellow soap."

That made Doris laugh and the laughing made her cry, and this was as Babs intended, because she wanted to share a good cry. What was the point of a wake if the women didn't weep together and seek comfort among themselves?

In the hallway outside the parlor Sugar McKane, who'd begun his career as a funeral director, moved through the crowd, making sure each guest knew he or she was welcome, and that their compassion and courtesy was appreciated. His eyes were dry and clear because he'd willed it so, and because it was fundamental to all he believed, that a man must show strength in times of tragedy, keep his sorrow to himself. At one point he carried out a cup of coffee from the kitchen, where food was being prepared by a caterer, and he insisted that Jack drink from the cup.

"You haven't slept a wink, I can see that," he said.

"I'm okay," Jack said.

"You're not at all okay, but you're doing your duty, son, and that counts for a lot."

"Where's Deirdre?" Jack asked, thinking of her on a stairway that was now mobbed with mourners.

"Dr. Parkay has her at the clinic for a night or two," Sugar said evasively. "Process of evaluation."

"But she's coming back home again?"

"Oh yes." Sugar seemed certain of this. "In the fullness of time."

Jack felt obliged to tell him about Jimmy Keegan's arrest, and was not surprised to learn that Sugar had already been informed, from sources of his own. "Not to worry," the old man said. "I'll not be bailing out Mr. Keegan, he'll have to fend for himself now, and let the chips fall where they may."

"He could tie you to the warehouses he torched," Jack warned.

"Let him try. I was purchasing the land *under* the buildings, and never saw a penny of the insurance money. That was Jimmy's doing, and so was poor Stinky Doyle. He's a hoodlum, Keegan is, and a man whose greed exceeds his intelligence, and I never should have done business with him. You were right about that."

"What happens now?" Jack asked, thinking of Emmett Dunning and all the others who had signed up with the company, expecting to be serviced.

"That's up to you," Sugar said. "Now, if you'll follow me into the parlor I intend to say a few words."

"You don't need me for that," Jack said, protesting.

"Oh, but I do." Sugar said, pulling Jack along in his wake. "It will help to have you near."

The parlor was full to bursting, not a seat empty and barely room to stand, but they parted eagerly for Sugar McKane, recognizing by his stride and demeanor that the grand old man was about to make a speech. The buzz and murmur subsided as he marched up to the casket, where he paused and made the sign of the cross. His shoulders broad and straight, he had, for those few moments, the posture of a much younger man. The young McKane who'd apprenticed in the wards, the still youthful McKane who'd ruled the Hendricks Club after Martin Lomasney passed on and who, like his mentor, spoke out on behalf of others, never directly for himself, from every stage and platform and truck bed that would have him, exhorting the citizens of the city to cast their votes not just for whatever candidate McKane was supporting, but for a larger purpose, for a future held in common by all those who strayed within range of his unamplified voice. And then his shoulders sagged slightly and once more he was an old man of sixty years and James Michael Curley had broken the ward bosses, siphoned off their power, and Sugar McKane like Curley himself was not the future so eloquently envisioned, but a past to be cherished or reviled as each citizen saw fit.

After gazing down at his dead son-in-law, Sugar turned with his head high and his eyes flashing. He began.

"My friends, a little while ago I heard a child say, 'Look, he's only sleeping' . . . and would that it were so. Would that it were so. Let me tell you a few things about Michael Fitzroy. He grew up among you. He was one of you. At the age of thirteen his mother died after a long illness, and young Michael pitched in and he worked without complaint in his father's South End grocery store, toiling there through the worst of the Great Depression, and when his father died he took it upon himself to make sure the debts were paid and the accounts settled honorably. He went on to college, the first of his family to do so, and he excelled there and kept working, nights and weekends and sometimes before dawn, at whatever job he might find, to put himself through law school and make a fine attorney of himself. All this you know. And all of you knew of his kind and generous nature. Many of you here were the recipients of that kindness and generosity and good-humored help that Michael Fitzroy bestowed without a thought to himself, except that he enjoyed being generous, and I'm certain there are none among us who would have denied him that pleasure.

"Let me speak in particular of Michael's generosity, for it brings me to a subject that pains me, a subject that must be raised because through no fault of his own it left a stain on an otherwise spotless record. A stain that I cannot in good conscience let be carried to the grave. I speak of Michael's disbarment from the practice of law. I see that some of you are shocked, distressed that I have raised such an unpleasant subject at this time of mourning. But raise it I must, for I want all of you here and the world beyond to know this: Michael Fitzroy never did the dishonest deed for which he was so sternly punished. It was I who forged that document, and when Michael learned that his father-in-law was about to be prosecuted, and thrown before the courts, he took it upon himself to see that I was spared. He said that it was *his* responsibility, the signing and dating of that wretched document, although surely he could not be faulted for something I had done, unbeknownst to him, and against his advice. And so he was disbarred and in the eyes of some disgraced, through no fault of his own, and because of his generous nature, and because of my weakness for having my way."

Sugar paused here and took a deep breath to fill his lungs, and there was not a sound in the room. It was as if they had all stopped breathing to spare him the air.

"Soon after this," he continued, raising his hand to make the point, a sweeping gesture that, much to Jack's surprise, included him in the orbit of Sugar's oration, "soon after this, misfortune also struck his own brother, and Michael responded in a way that was characteristic of his nature. His brother, whom he adored, a celebrated police detective with a bright future, was struck down by a disease that rendered him ineligible to continue in the department—unfairly ineligible, Michael believed, but he wasn't a man who was daunted by the unfairness of life. No indeed, he said to me that here was a great opportunity, he'd always wanted to work with his younger brother and now he had the chance. He looked on the bright side, Michael did, and if things weren't so bright, he shined his own light and made it so.

"It was typical of Michael Fitzroy, that facing misfortune he decided to turn it into a piece of good luck, with a little effort on his part." Sugar paused again and let his eyes settle on the open coffin for a moment, as if drawing inspiration from the one who lay there.

"Lastly," he said, turning back to face the living, "lastly let me speak of faith, for if ever there was a time that tries our faith, that time is now. We look at this man we loved, and we want to think, like the innocent child thinks, 'He's only sleeping.' And yet we know this cannot be so. Since my beloved wife passed on, I've somehow got out of the habit of attending mass each day, but my faith remains intact. My faith remains unshaken. I know that God exists, and that He has made a heaven of light for us. For all of us who have even the smallest shred of human decency. And I believe that Jesus Christ's great friend and disciple Saint Peter greets us as we seek to enter Heaven, and it is Saint Peter who demands that we give a true accounting of ourselves before we're let into the sight of the Almighty. Some of us may have great difficulty in making our cases to Saint Peter; in truth, we may need assistance when our souls are weighed in the balance. We may need, my friends, some of us, and I include myself when the time comes, some of us may need a good lawyer."

Jack, who imagined he had turned several shades of crimson, had actually grown pale, partly from anger and mostly from embarrassment at the contrived melodrama of Sugar's oration. He was able to see, however, that many of the mourners were smiling through their tears, tears that had begun to flow almost as soon as Sugar began speaking, as if in relief at the resonant noise of him filling the room. It was Sugar's final summation, his punch line, so to speak, that finally put laughter back into the house.

"I promise you, dear friends," he said, raising himself up on his toes so that his voice boomed out over the audience, for by now it was indubitably an audience, "have no fear, no, do not tremble at the sight of the great judge of souls, because two days ago a good man and an honest lawyer was made an angel of God, and if I know Michael Fitzroy he's looking for work!''

When Jack had recovered his composure he went to find Doris, who had taken the boys into the music room. Robby was sound asleep on a sofa, his small hands knotted in the fabric of a pillow, and David was sitting in his mother's lap, his head resting against her breast and his eyes wide open.

''The old coot,'' he said. ''Did you hear him in there? Quite a performance, the whole thing has been a performance.''

''You're raving, Jack,'' Doris said quietly, and immediately he lowered his voice.

''Did you hear him?''

Doris nodded. She was rocking David, trying to get him to close his eyes and sleep. ''I did, Jack, and I thought it was lovely, the things he said. You're just upset because he mentioned your polio.''

Jack shook his head. It wasn't that, at least he hoped it wasn't. ''Michael didn't believe in God,'' he said. ''You know that. He never went to church unless it was a wedding or a funeral. He *hated* religion, ever since we were kids. You know that, I know that, everybody who knew him, really knew him, they all know that about Mike.''

Doris stared at him and shook her head. ''That's not the point.''

''Then what is the point?''

''The point is that Sugar loved Michael and he wants to believe he's in Heaven. And you want to believe it, too. That's why you're so upset at Sugar for mentioning it.''

All at once he saw that she was right, absolutely right. He did want to believe it and he couldn't, and with that his anger at Sugar McKane melted away, and he felt his pulse return to something like normal.

Then in the hallway he came upon an unusual sight. A trolley of whiskey bottles, good Irish whiskey, and ice buckets being pushed along by one of the catering staff. Sugar, walking beside this contraption, winked at him. ''Come along, Jack, you're in for a surprise,'' he said, and Jack followed him into the room that adjoined the parlor. The crowd was less dense by now. More than a few had left after Sugar's oration, for tomorrow was a workday and many had to rise early.

The entrance of the liquor wagon produced the expected result. Shock and surprise. Sugar looked jubilant, very pleased with himself. "As most of you know, hard spirits have been forbidden in this house since the day I bought it. That has been my rule. But the rule is to be broken tonight, and for this night only, because our Michael liked to take a drink, which never seemed to do him any harm that I could see, and I know he'd want his friends to raise their glasses and drink a toast in his memory, to wake him as he saw proper."

"Sugar!" someone cried from the back. "Will you be joining us, then? Will you raise a glass with us?"

This was met with a roar of approval, but McKane shook his head and declined to participate. He could break the rule for the house, he could not break it for himself.

As for Jack, he had only one drink and did not finish it. Dutch courage for Miriam, but she was nowhere to be seen, off with the women somewhere and he hadn't the fortitude to seek her out. What would he say? What would *she* say?

Captain Delaney arrived late, after most of the whiskey had been drained from the bottles and the crowd had thinned further, leaving behind a core of intimates and hard drinkers, some of them drunk more on the novelty of imbibing in Sugar's house than on the whiskey itself, such was his reputation as a teetotaler.

Delaney had been supervising Keegan's arrest for the murder of Stinky Doyle, and then overseeing the necessary paperwork, but he did not want to talk about Jimmy the Torch. "Tell me something," he said, taking Jack aside, draping an arm over his shoulder in a conspiratorial manner. "What was it got into you? Risking your life after what they did to Michael?"

"No idea, Cap."

"None whatsoever?" Delaney seemed genuinely puzzled. "Because if I didn't know you better, lad, I'd say you were bucking for saint."

"Michael wasn't much for revenge," Jack explained.

"All his life he couldn't stay mad for more than ten minutes at a time."

"So that's why you saved her?" Delaney asked. He stroked his fist-flattened nose, thinking it over. "Well, never mind that now, what's done is done. Oh, and by the by, the mayor sends his condolences. He won't be attending, out of respect for his old rival Sugar McKane. This is the first important wake Curley has missed in years, since His Honor was in jail the last time down there in Connecticut."

"Curley knew Mike?" Jack said, surprised.

Delaney chuckled, looked around at those that remained, a fair sampling of the city from every level, all walks of life. "Everybody knew Michael Fitzroy," he said, "haven't you figured that out yet?"

A pat on the back and he was gone, absorbed by the crowd, and the next thing Jack knew he was facing Miriam, she'd emerged without warning. Black hair, black dress, black lenses to hide her green, green eyes, and there was so much to say, but he couldn't find a way to get it started. "We need to talk," he finally said. "Help me."

Her voice, when it came, was serene and distant. "Why should I, Jack? You're a guy who helps himself."

He caught her hand, steered her into a corner. "I should have told you," he said. "I wanted to, but I couldn't."

"The pictures were more important than Michael. Than me."

"You know it wasn't like that," he said. "I just couldn't find a way to tell you he was dead."

Miriam lifted the glasses for just a moment, let him see a flash of her eyes—how calm they looked, how untouched—and then the dark glasses were back in place, her veil of glass. "It doesn't matter now," she said.

"Of course it matters."

"No," she said. "Maybe it's the baby, or Michael dying, but I don't feel anything for you now. Whatever it was we had, we don't have it anymore. It's over."

Jack caught his breath, absorbed this as he had been absorbing everything that evening, and he asked, "What about the baby?"

Miriam tipped her head, touched her gloved hands to

her chin. "It's Michael's baby, of course. Would you say different, and insult the grieving widow?"

"You're not grieving," he pointed out.

Miriam shook her head and turned to leave. "How would you know?" she said. "You never knew a thing about me, Jack, not one thing."

Twelve

The Ghost in the Swivel Chair

He carried Robby, asleep in his arms, up two flights of stairs, and if every step came with a small white flash of pain, he did not show it. That old sciatic, yes, he'd have to stop pushing himself too hard. But not tonight.

"Jack, I can do that. Or you could wake him."

"I'm fine, Dottie."

David was finally asleep, his small mouth open and drooling on her shoulder. Two o'clock in the morning, the lights were out in Jamaica Plain and Jack was running on whiskey fumes, the sniff from the glass he hadn't finished. They walked through the darkened apartment—no need for light, they knew the way—and put their sons into their beds. Dottie helped him get Robby's suit off, the boy was so limp, so deep under, that his arms seemed like thin strips of rubber. David woke up just long enough to say, "Mommy, I smell flowers," and then his head burrowed into the pillow and he was asleep again.

In the kitchen Dottie offered to pour him a drink, a nightcap is how she put it. She needed one herself, she said.

"I'm going back out," he said, reaching in his pocket to check for his car keys.

Her head swiveled and for the first time in several hours she looked him right in the eye. It was not a friendly look. "You're what?"

"Back to the office, Dottie. It's something I need to do."

She nodded to herself, as if this confirmed something she'd long suspected, and said, "I'll bet you do."

"Give me a break, Dot."

"And when haven't I done that?"

He carried that with him out to the car, and all the way up Columbus Avenue. His seemed to be the only vehicle on the road at this hour, and Dottie's reply kept echoing because it was true: she'd always deferred to him, always given him the benefit of the doubt. It was more than that, it was the way she'd said it this time, her no-nonsense tone. The implication, and you couldn't get away from it, that some huge and insurmountable barrier had been erected between them, a wall he hadn't even bothered to notice until it was already built and capped with broken glass, curls of tricky barbed wire.

Jesus, she knew.

Parking for once was no problem, Park Square was deserted. The dog hours, that transition between dead of night and the earliest part of dawn when cops fell unwillingly asleep in their radio cars, and the phones stopped ringing at all the station houses, and a great silence enveloped the city. Didn't last, the peaceful, eerie silence. In another hour or so Bennie Bones would arrive to open up his newsstand. Armed with a knife big enough to gut a steer, old Bennie would cut the twine that bound the bundles of newspapers, the *Boston Transcript*, *Record American*, *Herald Traveler*, *Boston Globe*, and woe to any drunk who happened to stumble along at that hour, Benny was very nervous with that big knife. At about the time Benny had his papers out, the first trucks would be rolling along Tremont Street, heading for the Dock Square market with cabbages for kings—and for paupers, too, you could scoop produce out of the street for nothing minutes after the market emptied.

The main door to the lobby was locked. He'd never tried to get into the building at this hour, but of course it was locked. He went through his key ring, fairly certain that Rosemary Phelan had given him an extra key at some point. Much to his surprise he found it first try, and he was inside the lobby, the door locking shut behind him. Fingers crossed that the elevator was running, face another flight of stairs and he just might bawl like a baby.

The elevator door slid open as soon as he touched the call button. He closed the cage, set the lever on 2, heard the wire hoist whirr and hum as the car rose jerkily, bumping to a stop on the second floor. The hall lamps were out. Enough light came from the elevator car to let him find his way to the office suite. Someone had put up a wreath of black ribbons on the door, must have been

Rosemary, and a hand-lettered card stating that Fitzroy Security was temporarily closed.

Jack let himself in and reached for the light switch. Some secretive impulse made him hesitate. He didn't know what he wanted here, or why he'd come at this hour, but maybe it was better to endure the shadows rather than face the stark brightness of the overhead lights. There was at least one window in each room of the suite, he could see well enough to get around. It made him feel invisible and he liked that, it gave him courage.

The door to Michael's office was closed but not, as he discovered, locked. He stood just inside, confronting the dark mass of his brother's desk, the swiveling executive chair Mike had gleefully purchased at great expense, and then he lost courage—it was like air being let out of a balloon—and he hurried to the small bathroom in the reception area.

Just made it in time to cough up a little hot liquid into the sink. God, where had *that* come from, it tasted like battery acid, couldn't be the whiskey, that was hours ago. Jack ran cold water over his hands, rinsed his mouth, let the sink drain. The place wasn't much bigger than a closet, just room enough for a sink and a toilet, and he sat down on the closed lid with his head in his hands, trying to find a coherent way to enter his own thoughts. Not an easy thing, because his mind was racing with images imprinted in the last few days, snatches of conversation, faces looming at the wake and out of the past. Could he still smell the cloying stench of all those roses? No, impossible, had to be the perfumed switchboard girls who used this little toilet room.

Why had he come here? he wondered. Was he seeking torment? Did he want to punish himself, was that it? His brother's office had been so *empty,* that's what had turned his stomach, but what had he expected? Had he really thought that Michael would be there somehow, a wise and ghostly presence to ease his guilt? Had he really come here looking for *forgiveness*?

What a lot of nerve you've got! he thought. You pitiful, selfish bastard. Didn't know you needed a big brother until he wasn't there anymore, and now it was too late.

Some things could never be forgiven, not even by the dead.

An image came to him of Mike as a strapping lad of twelve, two very important years older than Jack. Mike has taken a boxer's stance, one foot forward, right fist extended, left curled under his chin, the classic John L. Sullivan pose. Not a pose, this image, because several townie toughs are there, bullies who've been chasing young Jackie Fitzroy for no reason other than the pleasures of brutality, and it's Mike who's heard him screaming, Mike in his grocer's apron, assuming that pose, and by God it works, the townies are backing off, spitting curses as they retreat to their own patch. Big Mike, defender of running boys. Only somehow it got reversed later on, and it was Mike standing back and cheering on the kid. Not knowing the kid secretly despised him for the weakness of loving a woman who did not, could not, love him in return. Seeing this, feeling it all over again, a body wave of revulsion made him gasp for breath, made him want to puke up whatever it was that had stuck in his craw, but there was nothing there. He had to endure the dry, shuddering heaves until his eyes were hot with tears.

Jack was still sitting there on the closed lid of the toilet, head in his heads, when he heard the whirr and hum of the elevator. Heard it being called down to the lobby. He waited, eyes squeezed shut because it seemed like his ears worked better if his eyes were shut, waited and then, yes, he heard the cage slam and the hoist was grinding away, the car was rising.

Sitting there in the dark and doing nothing as the elevator stopped on the second floor, the gate squealing as it opened, the pad of footsteps soft in the hallway. Key in the lock, click of the bolt, and whoever it was had entered the office. Heavy, deliberate steps—the intruder was male, that was certain, it wasn't Rosemary come on some early morning errand.

Jack realized he was holding his breath. There was a faint glimmer of light showing under the bathroom door, flickering quickly away. Flashlight. The muffled, slightly metallic click of a doorknob being turned, the intruder moving into another room.

Who was it, sneaking into the office of Fitzroy Security at this hour, when the Fitzroy who mattered was dead and not yet buried? Jack thought he knew. What he wasn't at all sure of was whether he had the guts to find out.

He was surprised at his own stealth when it came right down to it. Surprised that he was rising to his feet, manipulating the bathroom door in absolute silence, finding a way to move, limp and all, without making a sound.

The door to Michael's office was open. Jack positioned himself carefully against the wall, reached around the door jamb, and found the light switch. He came into the room just as the intruder's shadow hit the carpet.

"Hello, Bob," he said.

He watched Bob Cogan straighten up from the desk like he'd been shot through the back. Cogan, standing there with his hand over his heart, closed his eyes and sighed. "God damn," he said. "Whew! That just about canceled the ticket, that did."

Jack made no attempt to hide how badly he was limping. He took a seat, one of the comfortable upholstered chairs intended for clients, and eased himself down.

"There should be a bottle in the lower right-hand drawer," he said. "Would you pour me a drink? And help yourself, of course."

"Sure thing, boss."

Cogan located paper cups, poured out generous portions of good bourbon. Michael had preferred bourbon, but it hadn't seemed fair to mention that to Sugar, so proud of his Irish whiskey.

"What's in the desk, Bob, besides the booze, I mean?"

The drink in Cogan's hand hadn't made him any less uneasy. He squirmed where he perched on the edge of the desk. "Personal effects," he said. "A file of mine that your brother had."

Jack nodded, held out his empty cup. Cogan poured carefully, as if he didn't want to get a drop on the new carpet. "You find it?" Jack asked.

"Part of it," Cogan said, patting his breast pocket.

"Part of a file?"

"Well," said the big man, studying his nails, "there might have been two files."

"Ah," said Jack. "Two files."

"I wouldn't mention it, because it doesn't matter now, except that second file might cause some trouble."

"The second file you can't locate."

"It was a marital problem," he said. "Very sensitive."

"The file was about Miriam?"

Cogan nodded, it was almost a wince. "Mike had me tail her for a while. Wanted to be, uhm, apprised of her movement and activities."

"So you followed her," Jack said.

"I did, yes, for a few days. Mostly nights, that's when I could do it. Then I told Mike I was too busy, see, I had trouble of my own at home."

"Do you?" Jack asked. "Have trouble at home?"

"Hey, who doesn't? The point is, I told Mike his wife was being a good girl and he should drop it."

Jack drained the second cup of Mike's good bourbon and said, "Did he take your advice?"

Now Cogan was studying his knuckles, anything to avoid looking directly at Jack. "Nah," he said. "What he did was contact this other guy I happen to know."

"And that's the second file," Jack said. "Tell me, Bob, you happen to know what was in that file, this other guy who tailed Miriam because you decided she was being such a good girl?"

Cogan sighed. "Pictures. Photographic evidence."

"Photographic evidence of a sexual nature, is that the idea?"

"Graphic," the big man said. "In the act."

"And these were recent photographs?"

"Last week," Cogan said. "At the house in Hyde Park. This guy your brother hired, he climbed a tree outside a bedroom window."

Jack closed his eyes. The glint and movement in that tree, the night of the radio opera, Deirdre descending the stairs. He'd known what it was when it happened, tried to pretend it didn't matter.

"This guy called me when he heard what happened to Mike," Cogan was explaining, less inclined to reticence now that the ice had been broken. "Thought it might be a good idea if I destroyed the file, save everybody involved a lot of pain."

Jack concentrated. He wanted to get this right. It might

be his last chance to get anything right. "I want to know," he said, "exactly what happened. Did Mike see the pictures?"

"He was given the package," Cogan said. "An envelope, a brown clasp envelope. Mike paid him cash, this guy I know, and when he left, the envelope was on this desk."

Jack nodded. The bourbon was going to his head, making it a little easier to speak of the unspeakable. "Bob, could you do me a favor? Keep looking. Find it."

"Okay, boss. Anything you say."

Cogan was methodical. He removed the desk drawers, stacked them on the desktop, and went through them one by one. In the course of his search a golf ball got loose, dropped to the floor, and rolled to Jack's feet. Mike with his putter, bending over a ball and rolling his eyes, making fun of himself. The room was full of him now, not empty at all.

"Now here, Jack," Cogan said. "No, wait, what's this?"

He was bending over, peering into the metal waste can. He'd found something, too, from the look on his face. Passive satisfaction that his patience had paid off. Cogan reached into the waste can, gingerly removed the corner of a charred envelope.

Silently he picked up the can, brought it over to where Jack was sitting so that he could see it with his own eyes.

"Smell that?" Cogan said, sniffing the can. "Celluloid. You can see where some of it melted, too. That curled ash is photographic paper. He burned 'em, Jack. Prints and negatives."

Cogan was pleased. He seemed to think that was the end of it.

"You better get home and get some sleep, boss," he suggested. "Mind my asking when we can all get back to work?"

When Jack didn't respond, he said, "We *are* still in business, right? I mean, all of us guys who left a sure thing on the cops to come and work for you?"

"I'll have to think about it. It may not be possible with Mike gone."

Cogan leaned over the chair and Jack could smell the bourbon on his breath. "Hey, boss? Let me give you a little help, there. Think about this. You close up shop and I'll break your other leg.''

Jack looked up at him, couldn't read his face. ''Are you serious?'' he asked.

''I think I'm joking,'' Cogan replied after giving it some thought. ''But I ain't really sure. All I know, there's a lot of us depending on you. And most of us got wives to support, and kids. You fold up your tent, a lot of people get hurt. So think about *that* when you're thinking, and don't think too long, neither.''

When Cogan had gone, Jack got up from the chair and went to the desk and straightened things up. He put all the drawers back, neatened the files. Miriam was there in the photographs Michael kept on display, ranged along the edge of the desk. The wedding. Miriam on horseback. Miriam in her pleated tennis skirt. Take over this desk, he could put those pictures away, get them out of sight. That was the first thing he'd do, because he no longer loved Miriam. And then he thought no, you'll have to live with the pictures, all the pictures, the ones everybody can see and the one only you can see, and you'll have make it work somehow. Get down on your knees and beg Dottie, if that's what it takes, tear down the wall, make a life for your children.

Jack Fitzroy sat down in his brother's swivel chair—remarkably comfortable, worth every penny—and it came to him all at once as he leaned back and placed his head where Michael's had been, a sense of relief so complete and profound that he thought for a moment he'd fallen asleep in the chair. Michael, yes, before his big heart had stopped beating, Mike had squeezed his brother's hand and said it was okay. He was forgiven.